ISLAND BITE

RACHEL ARMSTRONG

Pink Paws Publishing

First published 2025
Print ISBN: 978-1-7638289-4-0
Ebook ISBN: 978-1-7638289-5-7

ISLAND BITE
© 2025 by Rachel Armstrong
Images sourced from Canva.

Published by
Pink Paws Publishing
Rachel Armstrong

For permissions, please contact:
Rachel Armstrong
PO Box 688, Aitkenvale QLD 4815
Australia
E-mail : rachelarmstrong_author@outlook.com

A catalogue record for this book is available from the National Library of Australia
www.librariesaustralia.nla.gov.au

For Deeanna West

Thank you for being my friend
May we always be book crazy together

Prologue

Unleashed fury hurdled Sly through the bush, up granite boulders, and into the air as he snapped at the slimy bat shifter. He missed, his gut lurching as he plummeted to the ground. Sly landed among the leaf litter and rolled down the hill, allowing gravity to take control until his back slammed into a hoop pine. An ordinary wolf might whimper or have broken his back. But Sly was no ordinary wolf.

Leaping to his feet, he snarled at the fucking pest. The shifter screeched, batted his leathery wings, and took flight through the bush.

Sly barked and gave chase, freedom rushing through his veins. He couldn't stop running, needing the outlet to work off the rage that would never die. Not until he used it to rip into the wolf who'd destroyed his life.

Tyrone Thorne.

Sly pumped his legs faster. The bat glided in and out of the trees, teasing him. Taunting him. Sly needed to catch the spying fucker before he left the island and reported back to his boss.

Tyrone Thorne.

But it was a worthless pursuit. He'd never catch the filthy creature. The Dark Alpha had been using the bats as spies for Moon knows how long, but the bat shifting vampires had no business on his island. The mountainous terrain, lush beaches, and quiet villages of Magnetic Island were *his* territory, and the bats were not welcome. No matter how broken he was or how much he couldn't bear to face the world, Sly would always protect the pack. His brother, the new Alpha, and the youthful scouts he'd welcomed and turned into daredevils.

He couldn't be there to lead them, to strategize his revenge and kill the bastard who'd ripped his heart out, but he could hunt the bats in the hope of sending a message to the vile creature who'd led his wife from his protection. Who'd compelled her, fed from her, then handed her to the rogue wolves. Only then, once she'd been free of the vampire's compulsion, had Sly sensed her in danger. She'd been beaten, raped, and fed from while he'd scrambled helplessly down Mount Cook, abandoning the tourists he'd been guiding. And he'd felt every ounce of her pain until Tyrone Thorne had practically eaten her alive and severed their bond forever.

Sly had been a savage animal ever since. Turning into the wolf was the only way he knew how to survive, and to take down the Pallarenda Pack. After all, the only way to kill an animal was to become an animal.

Or better yet, a monster.

So Sly would run himself ragged, to exhaustion, to his fucking death if he had to. But he wouldn't give up before he killed Tyrone. He wouldn't leave his brother in a world where that bastard lived. And he would protect him from the bats. The leeches could swoop onto the island undetected and wield their dark charisma on their victim, but Sly wouldn't allow it. The vampires had no business in a wolf's territory, which showed just how much Tyrone had turned his back on the Goddess given he'd recruited the vile creatures of Hell.

But Sly wouldn't let another innocent life to be coerced from Magnetic Island and into the hands of the rebels. Until last night, he'd been the Alpha, and every soul on the island had been his to protect. So, he'd trained. Learned. Hunted. The bats might have proven damn near impossible to catch, but he could smell the flighty fuckers from a mile away.

Not that it was any use when he'd failed to save the one soul he'd been bound to protect. His wife. His muse. His Shel—

Pain pierced through his heart, and Sly barely noticed as the trees gave way. He skidded, gravel sliding beneath his paws as he tried to latch onto the boulder, but it was too late. Gravity won as he flew over the edge of the cliff, dark waves beckoning as he fell and splashed into the ocean's welcoming embrace.

Closing his eyes, Sly let the current drag him down. The putrid scent of bat vanished, and his heartache floated to the surface as he sank into the quiet. Perhaps if he kept going, he would see her again. His beauty. His love. His Shel—

His ears perked, soul tugged, and Sly opened his eyes to the darkness as a force greater than the tide dragged him to the surface. He paddled his paws, kicked his legs, and his snout broke through the surface with a gasp as he welcomed oxygen into his lungs.

Not that Sly cared about breathing much, but he couldn't ignore the pull of the Goddess. She might have released him of his Alpha responsibilities, but she still wouldn't let him fucking go.

Then again, as much as Sly longed to spend eternity with Shelby, he knew his soul would never rest until he had his revenge.

As only when Tyrone Thorne was dead would he truly find freedom.

Chapter 1

Rain fell from the sky, tumbling through the air with a whoop of delight before releasing the drogue parachute and settling into the freefall. Wind flapped inside his cheeks as Magnetic Island loomed ten thousand feet below, his home a small patch of lush tropical bushland surrounded by the deep aqua and cerulean blues of the Coral Sea.

The young German tourist attached to his chest screamed with joy, reveling in the moment. Rain angled the camera towards her, recording a video that would tell only half the story as nothing could capture the thrill and terror of jumping out of an airplane and putting your life in gravity's hands. As a born daredevil, Rain had taken his first tandem dive the moment he'd been legally able to on his sixteenth birthday and had been living the dream ever since.

He glanced at the altitude meter attached to his wrist. The rush of falling towards earth at breakneck speed might be one aspect of skydiving that terrified most people—that and the fear the parachute wouldn't deploy—but Rain was meticulous and ran a well-trained team. One wrong move and the best experience in the world could end in death, one that even his supernatural healing abilities wouldn't save him from. Not that he wanted to test that theory. So, after a minute of freefall that was never long enough, they hit five-thousand feet, and he deployed the parachute. The nylon billowed behind him, catching the wind and slowing their speed as he and Maria swung into a seated position.

"That was amazing!" she cried with wonder he'd never tire of hearing.

"You liked that?"

"Yes!"

Chuckling, Rain took control of the chute as she continued to express her bewilderment. Sharing the experience with first time jumpers was a joy he lived for. Whether they were excited, nervous, or downright terrified, they signed up for the ultimate thrill and Rain loved nothing more than tossing a willing victim out of a plane.

He offered her the handles to steer and held the camera in place as he glanced around to check on his team. Dave, Johnno, and Hayden had deployed their chutes, all three tandem masters as experienced—or more—than himself. Chad had also deployed and was catapulting towards the beach beneath them, still in training for tandem but tallying many solo jumps as one of their camera crew. The kid was fearless and almost keener than Rain had been at his age, though that was no surprise. The wolf fed on adrenaline and Chad was a shifter desperate to work off a childhood filled with suppressed rage. Rain had been more than happy to take the seventeen-year-old runaway under his wing and offer him refuge and a job on the island earlier that year. Dave, Johnno, and Hayden, however, were human and decent men who Rain enjoyed working with. Though not as much as the one man missing from their team.

Heart sinking, Rain studied the mountainous island with its open eucalypt bush, boulderous granite headlands, and the tall hoop pines overlooking the glittering sandy bays. Reef surrounded most of the tropical paradise before fading into a deep blue to the east and hitting the mainland to the west. The city of Townsville spread from the base of the pink granite monolith, Castle Hill, and along the Ross River between two sentinel mountains, the land dry, yellow, and crisp since he was the only rain that fell around here. Hectares of scrub that made up the Town Common spread between the city and the rounded, steep landscape of Cape Pallarenda. But despite its glorious trails and deep-water lagoons, the mainland didn't hold a candle to the beauty of Magnetic Island and its lush national park—the perfect stomping ground for any wolf. And where Rain's brother Sly had prowled, nursing his shattered heart ever since Tyrone Thorne, Dark Alpha of the Pallarenda Pack, had slaughtered his wife.

Rain's wolf growled inside his chest as he glared daggers at the coast of Townsville. Somewhere along that stretch of beach, their enemy lingered, plotting and waiting for the opportunity to strike. And when he did, Rain and his pack would be ready. He hoped.

With a twist of his lips, he tore his gaze away and focused his attention on the job at hand.

"Pull down on your right," he instructed, and Maria turned them until they were spinning in a deep spiral. He let her marvel in wonder for a moment longer before taking control to line up their landing along the golden strip of beach in Nelly Bay where his five-star resort, Luna Views, stood glistening white beneath the morning sun.

Then his pulse spiked, and his wolf perked to attention. Rain scanned the crowd lining the beach and though it should be impossible at this distance, he spotted her. Eden. She was there, watching him. And likely a mess of anxiety until he landed safely and proved that, once again, he hadn't killed himself jumping out of his "stupid airplane."

"Legs up!"

Maria's legs shot out in front of her as Rain readied his, floating on the breeze before running onto the beach. Maria found her feet, saving them both from landing on their asses as he released her attachments and allowed her to cheer and revel in the thrill of the jump. He continued the video and asked all his standard questions until Hayden landed with Maria's boyfriend and she ran towards him, squealing with delight.

The rest of the team landed, wonder etching their customers faces and exhilaration springing their steps as they thanked the crew. Rain accepted everyone's gratitude humbly before they skipped up the beach to meet their friends.

"Nice conditions today, boss," Hayden said, slapping Rain on the shoulder. "Keen for the next jump. Not too windy, though it sure is heating up."

It might only be the middle of September, but the North Queensland sun showed no mercy as their scorching summer rapidly approached. Though the heat coursing through Rain's veins had nothing to do with the weather as the luscious scent of eucalypts mixed with cinnamon, mango, and antiseptic caught his breath.

"You're alive!"

Rain turned, his wolf pining as Eden's pretty lips quirked, her eyes undoubtedly dancing behind her oversized sunglasses. The ends of her dark ponytail lifted in the wind, assaulting his senses as her hip hitched, swishing the floaty skirt of her floral dress around her thighs. She was by no means tan, but her long pale legs appeared positively golden as the sunrise glistened off the beach, illuminating her in the pinkish glow of a beautiful morning.

Because every morning was beautiful when Eden was

there. But while his longing to forge their mating bond tugged at him like gravity in a freefall, he'd been destined to protect her. Even if that meant resisting their bond and living his life in abject torture.

What was a wolf to do?

"Yep," he said, reeling in his chute. "For the fifteenth thousandth time, I did not die. I'm racking up good odds."

"I still think you're mad, but ..."

"You get a thrill out of watching me jump." He flashed her a flirtatious grin, and his wolf snarled. It was such a dick move when he denied her any follow through, but when it came to Eden Starr, Rain was excessively flawed.

"More like a coronary," she huffed, her chest heaving beneath her pink cardigan.

"Then why do you watch?"

"To make sure you don't kill yourself."

"You run a greater chance of being killed driving to the beach than of me dying from the jump."

"So you keep telling me. Still doesn't take the fear away."

Rain hoisted the chute over his shoulder. "Does that mean you *won't* be joining me on a jump today?"

She stumbled back a step. "No! How many times—"

Rain laughed, and she swatted his arm. He might enjoy teasing her, but if he had one wish it'd be to strap her to his chest and fall through the sky with his beloved. To share in the rush and her joy. But the logical side of him knew that would never happen. Childhood trauma had left Eden scarred, and if she wouldn't ride the jet ski with him, like hell would she ever jump out of his King Air.

He tossed his arm around her shoulders, ignoring the shiver that coursed through him as her willowy body fit perfectly against his. "One day." He had nothing else if not hope.

"In your dreams."

The familiar, easy banter eased the tension that had gnawed at him these past few weeks. Since he'd sent out a Call for help and Finn Cassidy, lone wolf shifter and Warrior of the Moon Goddess, had sped in from the night on the back of his Sea-Doo. Then as Fate would have it, Finn had mated with Eden's best friend, Ava, and they'd defeated the Unfated wolves by killing Finn's half-brother, Blair.

Tyrone's son.

All to help Sly avenge Shelby and ease his heartbreak in the hope he'd shift back into a man, but that hadn't happened. Instead, Sly had relinquished leadership of the pack and the Goddess had blessed Finn as their Alpha. Sly had retreated to the bush and Finn had left Rain to wonder if resisting the mating bond was the right way to go. He'd always thought he'd need to defeat Tyrone and save Sly before he could live happily ever after with Eden. Keeping his distance had kept their bond a secret. Had kept her safe.

But Tyrone had known she was his mate all along thanks to the bat shifters he'd sent to spy on them. After discovering that, Rain and Finn had spun all kinds of lies to stop Eden and Ava from returning to Townsville. Ava had since learned the truth and had sealed her mating bond with Finn, but Eden remained under the impression that Rain was some kind of government agent since he'd declared that he had the means to end Tyrone's tyranny.

She'd been living at his house now for twelve days, and Rain had barely slept since.

"Yeah ..." He dropped his arm from Eden's shoulders and allowed her to precede him up the stairs from the beach. "I guess I'll just take the next person who has a death wish, then. Are you heading to the hospital now?"

"Yes, I have to check on Archie. He's so dehydrated, I'm not sure he'll make it."

Rain winced as they strode into the resort. Archie was the

newest patient at Eden's koala hospital and had been admitted yesterday after a local had found him lying at the base of a tree. "I hate it when you say that."

"Me, too. He perked up once I started treatment, so we might have got to him in time. Hopefully he's improved overnight. Then I have to research the cost of drones for my grant proposal." She grimaced. "They're going to be expensive."

Rain resisted an eye roll. Yes, the drones she wanted so she could search for koalas in the extensive national park and gain a better estimate of the population. So that she could write more grant proposals for funding that would allow her to expand and care for more koalas. Time and money she was wasting simply because she was too proud to let him write her a check and be done with it. Instead, he donated the measly amount she'd reluctantly agreed to each month to keep her happy, while also acting as three of her silent investors. His balls shriveled at the thought of Eden ever finding out, so lucky for him he was a master at keeping secrets.

"But worth it for your research." He forced himself to smile as they approached the Moon Dive shop. "Just let me know if you need anything. I'm happy to help."

"Thanks, Rain. You're a good friend."

Yes, he was. He'd made sure of it despite knowing she wanted more. Anytime he thought about how he treated her, Rain's wolf spat in disgust. He'd thought he'd done the right thing when he'd told her they could only be friends, but he never failed to notice her heart break a little more every time she took the ferry back to Townsville. Or how deeper the ache that consumed his mind, body, and soul grew.

Finn's words from the night of the full moon echoed inside his head. They'd played on a loop for the past two days.

Forget about Sly. Think about what you want.

That wasn't hard. He wanted Eden. Which would never happen unless he took a risk.

So as though some Alpha command had taken hold of him, Rain blew out his breath and said, "You know what we haven't done in a while?"

"What's that?"

"Have our usual Sunday lunch." It had been their routine, just like Friday night drinks at his place. After his morning jumps had wrapped up, he'd treat her to lunch before he headed back up for more and she left on the ferry.

But their routine had gone out the window since she'd moved in.

"I know it's Monday," he said, "but what do you say? Do you want to grab something later?"

He'd been certain she'd accept, so when the corners of Eden's pale pink mouth curved down and the spark inside her dimmed, shock slammed Rain still.

She shifted from foot to foot, her hair drifting over her shoulder as her teeth sank into her kissable lower lip. "Sounds lovely but ... not today. I think we've been living together for too long, so I actually wanted to ask if now that the Full Moon Party is over, if you had a room for me at Luna Views?"

Rain's hand tightened around his chute strings. She wanted to move out? Fuck, he should be gleefully tossing her into the Jeep to take her home, pack her bags, and set her up in the best suite available. Anything to get her out of his house and ease the tension that had tortured him since he'd shown her to Sly's old room, the master suite on the third floor. It was either that or the room next door to his and though he was well practiced in resisting Eden, even Rain knew he'd snap if only a mere wall separated them. Not that having her upstairs had been any easier as he'd spent the evenings slinking into the bush behind his house on Hawkings Point, keeping watch over the island from the lookout and napping in the trees bordering his backyard. Her scent had tainted everything inside his multi-story mansion and living there had been his own personal hell.

But it was also where she was safe and with the threat of Tyrone's revenge looming, Rain wouldn't dare keep Eden unguarded.

"It's okay if you don't," she said, and Rain realized he'd been silent for too long. "I could go back to Mum's house. She's still on her cruise. Although I don't know why I can't go home now that Blair's been arrested."

Rain cringed. He might be used to keeping her in the dark, but it didn't ease his guilt. He'd told her she had to stay on the island because she and Ava would be easy targets for the Townsville Underbelly to force him and Finn to bend to their will. Which, in a sense, was true. Tyrone had wormed his way into the position of Superintendent of the Townsville Police and was as crooked as they came, unleashing his rebel and Unfated wolves upon the town to wreak havoc with car theft, assaults, and high rates of violent murders.

That, Eden understood.

But Tyrone could also shift his body into the form of a wolf, and Rain couldn't exactly explain that to her. He also couldn't explain that Finn, in wolf form, had ripped Blair's throat out with his teeth, so they'd told Eden he'd been arrested. By the Federal Police considering Tyrone wouldn't have allowed his son to be arrested and charged. And she believed that because Blair was, apparently, Mafia.

Rain cleared his throat. "You can't go, Eden. And I'm sorry about that. Honestly. But Tyrone will be seeking revenge for Blair, and I can't risk your safety."

"I don't know why it matters," she muttered. "It's not like I'm—"

His wolf lunged as he grabbed her forearm. "You're my

friend. There is nothing I wouldn't do to save you, Eden. To protect you. I—"

He reined the wolf in before he could say anything foolish and loosened his hold on her. Stupid bloody animal. "Just give Finn and I a few more days."

Her shoulders slouched. "I don't *have* a few more days, Rain! I'm going to lose my job over this. Karen is *not* happy."

Good. Maybe Karen would fire Eden from her job in Townsville, where she worked four days a week as a small animal vet, and Eden could take some of the money he threw at her hospital to create a full-time role on the island like she'd always wanted. Like he'd always wanted.

"I'll explain everything to Karen, but I can't protect you if you're in Townsville, Eden. So, please." He forced his mouth to curve into a smile. "Trust me."

Exhaling, she crossed her arms over her chest. She wasn't happy, but fuck, what choice did he have? He hated that he was keeping her captive on the island. The first rule of forming the mating bond was ensuring free will. Making choices for Eden, forcing her against her will, or—Moon forbid— marking her with his teeth was a sure way to darken their relationship, claim her, and have her become beholden to him in a way only those who rebelled against the Goddess ever chose.

Not that he risked that. Eden stayed because even though she didn't understand why, she trusted him. She had no idea how deeply they were connected or that Fate had determined her to be the other half of his soul. The one person on this earth who could anchor him, humanize him, love him, and provide him with strong children.

And he'd foolishly kept her at a distance and entered a world of self-imposed torture.

"Fine," she muttered. "But ... you feel it, too, right?"

"Feel what?" He felt a lot of things, he couldn't put his paw on just one.

"The strain on our friendship? You've hardly been home since I moved in, so clearly, I make you uncomfortable."

"You—"

"Don't deny it." She lifted her hand, palm out. "Things have been awkward between us and I don't like it. We need to find our routine again. Weekends only, maybe? Because I'll never be able to move on if we live under the same roof, Rain. And I need to do that."

She continued to talk, but her words were white noise to Rain as his hand tightened around his jump harness. What? Had she just said ... *move on*?

His spine straightened, every muscle tensing as his wolf howled, echoing the pain that encased his heart while his chest squeezed as though locked in a medieval torture device.

Desperately, he reached through the bond—the mental and emotional connection he shared with Eden. It might be weak due to his years of resistance, but it was still there as he grabbed onto the threads and felt them tug, ping, and vibrate until he shattered.

Fuck. Oh, fuck.

"So, can I?"

Rain blinked, and Eden's face returned to focus. "Can you what?"

"Move into Luna Views like you promised?"

Move. Yes, he had promised. The resort had been fully booked in the lead up to the Full Moon Party on Friday and even though he could have made room for her, his reckless wolf had made selfish decisions for them both. Again.

But now, with the restless animal licking his wounds, the man emerged. And nodded. "Yeah. Sure. Look, I need to get to work." He glanced over to where the team were already preparing for the next jump outside the Moon Dive shop. "But I'll let reception know."

Rain turned and walked away.

"Thank you!"

He waved at her over his shoulder. "No worries!"

But as he wrenched open the door to the prep room, panic surged and clogged his throat until he could barely breathe. He'd taken it too far. He'd resisted his mate for too long and now she was pulling away.

And he was at risk of becoming a broken, rejected wolf.

Chapter 2

Two soy cappuccinos later, tension had eased from Eden's spine as she strode into the Koala Hospital. Why she continued to find herself standing on the beach scanning the sky when the red warning flags were out to mark the parachute landing, Eden didn't know. She hated watching Rain skydive. It twisted her up inside and made her heart race harder than HIIT training, spiking her pulse the moment he jumped. She didn't know *how*, but she always knew when he took the leap and his drogue chute deployed, despite being a tiny white dot in the sky and indistinguishable from the other jumpers until his black parachute with the crescent moon bloomed and she could breathe a partial breath of relief.

Then the bloody lunatic geared up to go again, and her heart didn't descend from her throat until hours after Moon Dive closed for the day.

Sighing, Eden strode towards the ICU. How could she love such a daredevil? It made no sense. She'd been terrified of people taking undue risks ever since her father had foolishly lost his life and didn't understand how she could be drawn to such a maniac.

But the moment Rain Blackwood had barged into her hospital with dirt in his long hair, his jeans unbuttoned, and a T-shirt pulled halfway down his fine, muscled torso with the sexiest happy trail she'd ever seen, she'd felt a tug of persistent longing. It hadn't helped that he'd been cradling a koala in his molded biceps. One he'd apparently found hiking near the Pinnacles, a six-hour trek he hadn't been dressed for. But that inconsistency and his bare feet hadn't crossed her mind until much later, after she'd saved the dehydrated koala in respiratory distress.

She'd fallen for Rain instantly and even though it'd broken her heart when he'd only wanted to be friends, her feelings had never diminished. She loved him. It was that simple. It wasn't mere attraction, curiosity, or the desire to see him naked. She burned for that man. Her heart had leapt from her chest the moment their eyes had connected over that cute bundle of gray fur and the stupid organ had stubbornly refused to come back, clinging to Rain like a joey did its mum.

No desire could be that strong or survive years of rejection. She'd had crushes and dated other men, but *nothing* compared to what she felt for Rain. She'd loved the way he'd cared for that koala—who she'd called Pixie—and how he'd checked in during the days that followed. They'd formed a friendship that had sent her hopes soaring.

Only to have them crash and burn two weeks later when they'd been sitting on the jetty in Picnic Bay and she'd misread his signals. Believing he'd wanted to kiss her—*feeling* it in her soul—she'd leaned towards him. But instead, Rain had taken her hands and told her that they shouldn't. She'd been shattered, but weekends on Magnetic Island had quickly become the highlight of Eden's life not only because she could dedicate her time to the Koala Hospital, but because she felt whole. Complete. At home. With Rain.

She was a bloody fool.

Stepping inside the ICU room, Eden knelt beside Archie, the young koala lying snug in a basket, and began her visual checks before hooking the stethoscope into her ears and listening to the little fella's heart. He still had a way to go, but was stable for now and, satisfied, she left Archie to sleep and headed to her office.

Sinking into her chair, Eden dropped her head into her hands as an ache speared from her belly and into her chest. Rain's scent of earth and ozone swirled inside her head until she wanted to throw up. Wanted to cry. She didn't know what she wanted except to move out of Rain's glorious house in Picnic Bay where she'd spent far too many nights curled up in his absent brother's bed aching with the urge to tiptoe downstairs and seek warmth in Rain's arms. The only place where she believed she'd be safe, secure, and would no longer care about his endless stream of fucking lies.

No, not lies. *Bullshit.*

"Morning!"

Eden spun around at the singsong voice of her best friend and forced a smile. Ava Hart lit up the doorway, her blonde ponytail swinging over the shoulder of her pink T-shirt and black yoga pants as she bounced into the office with all the joy of a woman newly in love. Eden understood as she'd be chipper too if she had Finn Cassidy warming her bed. She'd never seen her friend happier.

"I didn't expect to see you until later."

"Finn had a jet ski tour, so I thought I'd come help out."

"May as well since we're trapped on this bloody island," Eden muttered, unable to hide her resentment.

"We're not trapped, Eden. We just need to take precautions."

"But they arrested Blair!" Not that she knew how, nor did she believe the charges would stick. He might have been taken by the Federal Police, but his vindictive father would have a lawyer in his back pocket as twisted as him and his son for sure.

Ava's eyes shifted. "I know. But give Finn and Rain time, Eden. They'll sort Tyrone out."

Again, Eden sighed. At least one good thing had come out of this whole mess as when that bastard of a cop Blair had assaulted Ava, Eden had brought her to the island for refuge and the Mystery of Rain had been revealed. Sort of. She'd always known he'd been keeping a dark secret, but she'd never have thought the daredevil billionaire was working with a government organization to bring down the leader of the Townsville Underbelly. What exactly Rain's role was, she didn't know, but it made sense considering Tyrone had murdered Rain's sister-in-law and covered it up.

So, she couldn't blame him for being cautious and even though it frustrated her, she'd chosen to trust him and stay on Magnetic Island. And not only because she'd jump at every creak, crack, and thump if she returned to her unit in Townsville alone, fearing one of Blair's cronies had come to hold her for ransom to force Ava to go back to him. Eden liked her crime movies enough to understand how the Mafia worked, and she didn't want to become the best friend tied to a chair with tape around her mouth and tears in her eyes.

No, she might be in all kinds of trouble with her boss, but Eden had stayed because after two years of emotional torture, Rain had finally looked at her like *he'd* march into that dark room and rip Blair and his cronies apart with his bare hands to rescue her.

The thought had made her hot as hell, but once again, she'd found herself in a fantasy world because after she'd moved into his house, Rain had essentially moved out.

She couldn't take it anymore. She had to move on.

"I hope so. I still don't know what Finn and Rain's deal is

though, or how they think they'll stop Tyrone. And you haven't told me how Blair *really* got arrested."

"I did," Ava said, studying a poster on the wall. "He came after me the night of the Full Moon Party and ... well, Finn and Rain had plans in place, and now he won't be bothering us again."

God, Eden hoped so. She'd hated the fear in Ava's eyes and the hopelessness in her voice when she'd felt she'd never escape that monster.

Thankfully though, everything had worked out as Ava had met Finn, fallen in love, and Blair had gotten what he deserved. But Eden's life had only grown more complicated, especially now that Ava had adopted Finn and Rain's shifty ways and their tendency to spin the truth.

Eden leaned back in her chair. "At least now that the party's over, I can move out of Rain's."

Ava's mouth curved sadly. "You'll feel better once it's done, Eden. And even though I know it must hurt, I think you need to let him go."

Eden twisted her fingers in her lap, pain crushing her chest. "Yeah. I want to, but it's just been so long, you know? And I ... oh, dammit, Ava." She dropped her head into her hands, closing her eyes to stop the threatening tears.

Ava reached over and squeezed her forearm. "It'll be okay. I know how much you like him—"

"I fucking love him. Something chronic."

"I know you do."

Eden lifted her head to meet Ava's pale, compassionate gaze. "I feel like if I give up, I might die. Does that sound silly?"

Ava's eyebrows creased. "Well ... no, but—"

"He's *in* me, Ava. Anytime I go near him, I know we should be together. That we are meant to be. Sometimes, I think he knows it too. He acts like he'd slay dragons for me and looks like a kicked puppy every time I refuse to accept his handouts.”

“They’re not handouts, Eden. Rain’s a rich man and he just wants to help your charity.”

“Yeah, he can *help*. Not *fund* the whole damn hospital.”

“But he would if you let him.”

Eden rolled her eyes. “That’s the problem. You know he wanted to write me a check for the drones, right?”

“And what’s wrong with that?”

“It’s not a charity if he writes all the checks!”

“It’s a charity if it’s registered as a charity,” Ava reminded her with a laugh. “Besides, maybe it’s his way of showing he cares about you when he can’t do anything else about it?”

Eden’s mouth twisted. Yeah, she’d considered that as she knew Rain cared about her, even if it wasn’t in the way she wanted. “I know. Which is why I haven’t stopped him from being a regular donor. Although on that subject, I have news!” She sat up straighter. “I had a phone call yesterday from another businessman interested in supporting us.”

“Yeah? Who?”

“Someone who owns a club in Townsville. He said owning a club’s often construed as seedy, so he’d like to support local wildlife. His name is Lucas Capello, and I’m meeting with him tomorrow.”

“That *is* excellent news! What sort of club?”

Eden shrugged. “I didn’t ask for the name.” Clubbing wasn’t of interest to either Eden or Ava, though they’d certainly enjoyed screaming along to the rock band Jam on Friday night at the Full Moon Party in the gardens at Luna Views. “I just hope it goes well.” Her heart ached with longing as she studied her tiny office, the shelves stuffed with books, folders, and too many pictures of koalas—not that there was such a thing. “There’s so much I want to do here if I had the funds. More space and equipment. If only I could operate as a vet clinic and bring in the business to fund the hospital."

But it was a dream that had no legs as with cost of wages, drugs, and testing, let alone the expenses involved in accreditation and running a business, she'd never cover her operating cost, let alone make a profit to fund the hospital. Eden didn't remember when she'd fallen in love with koalas—she'd been way too young. Her mother had been friends with Vicky, the vet who'd opened the hospital, and as the manager of a popular backpacker retreat Eucalypts Grove, Eden's mum had helped open a sanctuary for the koalas who couldn't return to the wild. Having the opportunity to interact with koalas had boosted international tourism, and Eden had spent her weekends and holidays helping Doctor Vicky care for the koalas, cut their leaves, and clean their enclosures. She'd known from the age of ten that she wanted to take over the hospital, had studied veterinary science, and had spent a few years in Brisbane working at Lone Pine Sanctuary before returning to Townsville. But like Vicky, Eden had known she wouldn't be able to work at the hospital full time, so she'd taken a job in Townsville and worked on Magnetic Island during her days off. Sure, that meant she worked every day of the week, but Eden wouldn't have it any other way.

"I know." Ava smiled sadly. "But you've already done so much for this place in the two years you've been here. You've gained more local and financial support, improved the enclosures, and updated all the equipment. You've saved so many koalas and one day ... you never know? You might be able to work here full time."

"Maybe ..."

And that, she reminded herself, needed to remain her focus. She might have fallen for a daredevil who made her days on the island both beautiful and heartbreaking, but the koalas had been her priority long before she'd met Rain and no man would stop her from fulfilling her dream of saving the endangered marsupial from extinction.

Not that she could while the government deforested the country at an alarming rate, rotten arsonists deliberately lit bushfires in the forests where koalas thrived, and loggers felled trees while koalas clung to their branches bellowing as they crashed to their deaths. White hot rage flooded through her veins every time she thought about the injustice of the world and cruelty to animals just to make a dollar, and it drove her to keep fighting. Every little bit helped, but she was only one woman, and all she could do was focus on the koalas under her care. Magnetic Island had become a haven for koalas when they'd been introduced sixty years ago and now, it was home to the largest free-roaming colony in northern Australia with an estimated population of eight hundred to three thousand.

A figure that drove her insane, hence she wanted to conduct a census with drones using infra-red technology. Once she had a more precise number, she'd have a better chance of obtaining grants she'd previously missed out on due to weak population data and be able to expand her hospital to help more koalas.

"But I think it's still a pipe dream, Ava. The hospital will need multiple avenues of revenue before I can stay here full time. I mean, the sanctuary does well, but it only covers the cost of caring for the animals and upkeep. And I can't ask Rain if he'd like to be involved through Luna Views. Knowing him, he'd want to build me a koala theme park."

"Ooh, I wonder what that would look like!"

Eden narrowed her eyes. "I don't even want to contemplate it. Rain and his brother completely changed tourism on Maggie Island. Who knows what he'd come up with?"

"True. But you must admit, that man knows how to make money."

"He also knows how to give it away, and I won't accept

another cent from him. Not when I need to drag my heart back from his clutches."

"Yeah, that's true." Ava's eyes saddened as she stood. "And I'm sorry, Eden. But I might get started on Marco's rehab. Are you okay in here?"

"Yep." She wasn't okay, but she was well enough to get on with her work. "You go make that little man stronger. I have drones to research."

And hopefully she'd find one that not only did the job she wanted, but that also didn't cost the earth.

A girl could dream.

Though as much as she wanted the best for the hospital, she had little interest in living on Maggie if she couldn't build a life with Rain. The koalas might fill her heart, but he'd been her reason for breathing and now that she was letting him go—

Eden winced as everything inside her squeezed. Dammit, why did it have to be so hard?

Chapter 3

Rain stomped into his office on the fifth floor of Luna Views Resort Hotel and slumped behind his desk. Raking his hands down his prickly face, he swiveled in his high-backed chair and scowled out over the dream he and his brother had built. Their hotel overlooked lush tropical gardens on the edge of the beach with a lagoon-style pool and individual hut-shaped cabins creeping up the hill offering uninterrupted views of the deep blue Coral Sea. It was everything that Rain had ever wanted—to expand the billion-dollar empire his father and grandfather had built constructing the Moonrise Apartments with his own luxury resort, the skydiving company, and an array of activities and attractions on offer. And what did he have to show for it? Sly had turned his back on him and now Eden wanted to abandon him, too.

Rain's wolf growled inside his chest as a sneer twisted his lips. Even two more jumps hadn't settled the turmoil raging inside him. He'd known he'd been playing a risky game ever since he'd strode into the supermarket and had his world implode by the sight of a woman selecting vegetables. She'd been wearing a white sundress with bejeweled sandals, her long dark ponytail swishing down her back while her dark eyes assessed the produce with care. She'd have knocked any man off his feet.

Or in his case, trigger the mating bond and a possessiveness he hadn't been able to shake. A jolt of electricity had shot through his body while the world had flashed in a kaleidoscope of color. Rain had no idea how long he'd stood by the onions staring like a fucking idiot. Thankfully, Eden hadn't noticed him as she'd sashayed her hips towards the grocery aisles and left him to pick his jaw up off the floor.

He should have been the happiest wolf alive. Ever since he'd hit puberty, Rain had longed for the day he met his mate. He'd dated a little but had never particularly enjoyed it, as it'd never felt right to lead a lady on when he'd known he couldn't promise her forever. Every experience, though satisfying, had always made him feel cheap, which was why he and his brother had poured their focus into chasing thrills elsewhere. They'd ridden jet skis, secured their parachute licenses, and competed in various competitions for both to channel their wolfish energy. They'd later moved to the island to extend their father's company and fulfill their dreams.

Then Sly had mated. Rain hadn't been surprised considering he was the eldest and had assumed the role of Alpha. If possible, Sly had been even keener to mate than Rain—a closet romantic if there ever was one.

But then he'd lost Shelby, buried her in enemy territory due to fucking human laws, and had run into the bush, leaving Rain alone. He'd spent the first week chasing his brother to reason with him, but Sly had shut down and harbored only one emotion.

Rage.

Then Rain had seen Eden in that supermarket, and fear had taken root inside him. He'd just buried his brother's mate and had witnessed his gut-wrenching grief. The enemy lurked across the water waiting to destroy them, and Eden had been innocent. Forging their bond would have made her a target, and he hadn't been prepared to risk her life.

He'd made the choice then not to give into the pull and ignore the fact she existed. To never meet her and keep watch from afar. But Fate had had other ideas when he'd found that koala in respiratory distress. Unable to leave the little girl to struggle and die, he'd abandoned his hunt for Sly that night and gathered the courage to face his mate. And while resisting her might have been the most torturous thing he'd ever done, Rain treasured his friendship with Eden. He lived for the moment she arrived on the Friday ferry, where he'd show off on his jet ski and pull all kinds of stunts before sharing drinks on his balcony later in the afternoon. But he'd always made sure he was otherwise preoccupied on Sundays, unable to bear witness to her boarding the boat that took her back to enemy territory.

Now, a whole new fear had taken over Rain since he'd learned Tyrone knew who she was. The dark, twisted Alpha must have kept her alive for a reason, and wondering what Tyrone had planned kept Rain awake more than the fact that Eden had been sleeping under his roof.

Groaning, Rain spun around and slumped over the desk. Footsteps sounded in the hall and while his wolf stood to attention, Rain simply scowled, not bothered to look up as the man thundered into his office and the door clicked closed.

"What's the problem?"

"I didn't call you," Rain muttered, spearing his fingers into his hair.

"Yeah, but I'm the Alpha now. I know all."

Rain sat up. "Bullshit, you do."

Finn's thick arms crossed over his chest, his cheek twitching beneath the golden whiskers lining his jaw. Rain resisted a smirk himself. He liked Finn and was eternally grateful that the towering blond brickhouse had been the Warrior who'd come to his pack's aid a mere four weeks ago. So much had changed since Rain had climbed to the top of Mount Aurora, stood over that ledge, and gazed up at the full moon to howl his wish. Less than a week later, the Moon Goddess had answered his Call in the form of Finn when the crazy fucker had arrived close to midnight after riding his jet ski up the Australian coast with his pathetic excuse for a dog on the back. As a true believer in Fate, Rain had welcomed Finn and they'd formed a fast friendship. But since Finn had assumed the role of Alpha three days ago, the dynamic had shifted. And yes, the man did know everything, especially when one of his packmates was in trouble.

Sighing, Rain leaned back in his chair and changed the subject. He desperately wanted to fix his bond with Eden, but the lengths at which Tyrone would go to avenge Blair's death had him on high alert. "We need to prepare for Tyrone's retaliation."

"Yes, we should have a pack meeting. I took the jet ski for a spin around Cape Pallarenda this afternoon and tried to get a read on the situation without getting too close."

The rogues roamed the bush at Cape Pallaranda but also claimed the city of Townsville as there was no lore stopping them. Not that the rebel wolves cared about the lore. Pack lands were generally separated by water, meaning Tyrone had no claim to the south of the Ross River. Yet he'd abducted Shelby from where the barge docked in South Townsville and had left Rain with no access to the city. Not that he needed it with online shopping and his own private plane, which he took to Cairns when necessary. Air and water were unclaimable, hence why Finn could almost sneak up to Pallarenda's shore and get a sense of the Dark Alpha's motivations.

"What did you find out?" Rain asked.

"Nothing. All I could sense was impending doom. Blair wasn't the only son that was lost on Friday night, and the rebels are furious. But Tyrone would have sensed the shift in power, and the fact I've become Alpha will certainly have put his back up. And pissed him off."

Rain nodded, his lips quirking at the glitter in Finn's eye. Having spent his life trying to escape and then hide from his sire, Finn had every right to take pride in proving he wasn't as useless as Tyrone had always thought him. And for killing the one person Tyrone had loved most. Finn had avenged the greatest loss in his life—his mother—who, it turned out, Tyrone hadn't killed. Instead, he'd ordered Blair to do the dirty work and upon learning the truth, Finn hadn't hesitated in ripping his brother's throat out, also getting justice for the assault he'd committed against Ava.

Finn's jaw hardened. "He might not have been the one who ripped my mother to pieces, but he was still responsible for her death and he'll be lucky if I don't tear him limb from limb. But unfortunately, I think I'll leave that pleasure to Sly."

"But we need Sly to want to fight. And now that he's given the Alpha over to you, how can we be sure he hasn't given up entirely?"

Finn sank into the chair opposite Rain. "He hasn't given up. Trust me. And it's not that he didn't want to lead the pack anymore, it's just he didn't feel strong enough. He was letting you, Chad, Kai, and Nate down. And like he said, an Alpha needs his mate."

"And you have one." Rain tried, but failed, to keep the bitterness out of his tone. Not for the first time, he wondered what might have happened if he'd never resisted Eden. If he'd formed that bond, would the Goddess have bestowed on him the same blessing? Not that he wanted to be Alpha, but he couldn't shake the thought. Especially when Finn broke all seriousness with a shit-eating grin that Rain wanted to punch from his face.

"Yep. As I said, best thing ever."

"I know." Rain dropped his gaze as he recalled Finn's suggestion on Friday night. "And I think … you might be right about what we need to prove to Sly."

Finn's eyebrow quirked. "What part?"

"That we can protect our mates against Tyrone, and that Sly might get a second chance."

"I think he will. Like I said, it's cruel to think Sly's only chance to love and breed is gone. He's thirty-two. The Goddess should have a backup plan."

"Have you ever met a wolf who mated twice?" Rain hadn't, but he'd only ever known his family and the young scouts who worked for him at Luna Views, whereas Finn had worked with packs all over the country.

"No, but I've heard stories, so I have to believe it's true. Our mates are only human, and we can't protect them from cancer or viruses or dying in accidents. Maybe if Sly believed he could mate again, he'd be more willing to fight."

"I think he'd need to feel a bond trigger before that happened. He's so deep inside the wolf now I can barely sense the man he used to be."

Finn's lips thinned. "He certainly had an animalistic fight about him on Friday night."

Rain nodded. His brother had been downright impressive, but also terrifying in his urge to kill first, ask questions later. "It doesn't help that he's left the pack and has chosen a life of solitude. Can you even sense him?"

"Barely. He's broken the pack bond."

Rain's heart sank. "Will he ever be able to return?"

Finn slapped his hand to his chest. "I'll welcome him back in a heartbeat, but he has to *want* to come back before he pack bonds again."

"And how will he do that?"

Finn shrugged. "Not sure. It'll have to come from him. But trust me, Rain. The life of a lone wolf isn't pleasant as we're meant to run as a pack. We both know that. I spent fifteen years looking for my pack because I wanted a home. A family."

"And Sly feels he's lost his." Rain leaned back in his chair and released a long breath. "But we can't just cross our fingers and hope he mates. Who knows where this woman is or if she'll ever show up."

"And if she does, the bond will probably send him into an even deeper spiral while Tyrone's still at large."

"He'll be almost feral over protecting her. I understand that. It's exactly how I reacted to Eden. He might even resist it. Deny it."

"Pretty fucking hard to deny."

"Yes, but Sly's stubborn. More so than me. I've resisted Eden, but now ..." Pain speared through his chest, and he covered his wince with a scratch of his jaw. Fuck, he didn't want to say it, but with no one else to confide in, the words escaped him. "Eden's pulling away."

Finn straightened. "Shit."

"Yeah." Rain shot to his feet and began pacing, but it did nothing to lessen the humiliation of how big an idiot he'd been. "She asked me for a room in the hotel, said she wanted to 'move on', and I feel like I'm fucking dying."

Finn blew out a long breath and stood. Rain half expected him to say, "I fucking told you, you fool," but Finn was too kind for that.

"I'm sorry, man."

"It's my own bloody fault, I know. I shouldn't have resisted for so long. I mean, at first, I wasn't ready. I don't think we ever are."

"You know I wasn't ready for Ava."

"But you gave into the fear even though you knew Blair was hunting her."

"That's *why* I couldn't resist her. I had to protect her. And the best way to do that is to bond, Rain. No danger could come within miles of Ava without me knowing about it."

"I know." Rain could sense when Eden was in trouble too, but only when she was near. Completing their bond would strengthen that connection and he'd be able to sense her even if she was in Townsville. "I should have tried harder, but I was too worried about Sly when we met."

"And while I understand your devotion to your brother, you need to remember what's most important."

Rain glared at Finn over his shoulder. "I need to put myself first."

"Or at least consider what you want. Tyrone has already taken so much from you. Don't let him take Eden, too. Her life *or* your bond."

"I want Tyrone dead."

"We all do. But don't let Eden pull away because that will only hurt, man."

"You don't have to tell me." Exhaling, he turned his back on the view again and slumped against the window. "We need to strengthen the pack to be ready for Tyrone's retaliation. And I don't know about you, but I sense that he'll target Eden."

Finn's eyes darkened. "I'm not foolish enough to believe Ava's untouchable, but you're right. Eden is vulnerable, Rain. She's alone out there and remains ignorant of our world."

"I need to protect her," Rain breathed, determination cording his muscles. "And the best way to do that is to give into the fear and form the bond."

"Yep. So, listen here." Finn straightened to his full height, the Alpha oozing from him as he looked Rain dead in the eye. "Go and get your girl."

Chapter 4

Eden hoisted her veterinary bag over her shoulder as she strolled along the boardwalk through the bush at Eucalypts Grove. The retreat had always been a popular place to stay on Maggie with its quiet hospitality, access to nature, and her mother's dedicated management over the years. And now, it was officially the grandest backpackers retreat on the island since the Moonrise Corporation—a billion-dollar real-estate empire—had bought out their competition in Nelly Bay and built the majesty that was Luna Views.

Where Eden would curl up tonight in her mini suite without the intoxicating scent of Rain invading her senses and stoking the long sizzling heat between her thighs.

Heart sinking, she slipped inside the wildlife sanctuary and strode past the short neck turtles, the black cockatoo, and towards the koalas.

"Evening, Amaroo," she said, dropping her bag by the koala's enclosure and opening the gate. "How are you, girl?"

Amaroo had been at the retreat since she'd been found at the base of her tree some six years ago and was one of the few koalas on the island who'd ever contracted chlamydia, resulting in conjunctivitis and blindness. She'd received treatment and was disease free, but since she could only see shadows, she hadn't been able to return to the wild and had found a home at the sanctuary. As a wild koala, she didn't enjoy a lot of human interaction like Pebbles did and therefore didn't participate in the tourist interactions that the park provided, but she seemed to be happy.

Eden completed basic health checks on Amaroo, then moved to Thor, who was their oldest koala. He'd been born at Billabong Sanctuary in Townsville and had once liked people, until he one day decided he didn't and had started biting them. Eden listened to his heart and lungs before examining his teeth and claws. He was healthy for eleven years of age and hopefully would be with them for a while yet. After checking on their cuddly girl Pebbles, she pried Eddie the echidna from beneath his log, had a chat to Shadow, the black cockatoo who was currently learning to fly for the first time in his life, and cast her eyes over the freshwater crocodiles. The crocs always drew a crowd, though tourists would be better off skipping over to Billabong Sanctuary to see the massive estuarine crocs there if they wanted a show. They sure were something, though she wasn't as keen as Eucalypts Groves' rangers were to acquire an estuarine croc of their own. Their strength, power, and prehistoric nature might fascinate her, but those bastards were bloody scary.

Eden lifted Harry the wombat into her arms, sat, and cradled him against her chest as the light faded around her. Yet even the company of her animal friends couldn't shake the gloom that had settled over her since Jackie from reception had called to tell her they had a room prepared. Rain's eyes might have clouded with their usual shiftiness when she'd asked for the room, but while he might be a notorious liar, he was also a man of his word. And now she had her own mini suite waiting with a spa and king-sized bed that would welcome the dawn from her fourth-floor window. It might not be as opulent as the master suite at Rain's house that she'd already vacated, but it would offer privacy and reduce temptation.

So why didn't she look forward to it?

Eden dropped her head and touched her nose to Harry's, scratching his whiskery cheek. "You're so lucky you don't have to put up with this bullshit, Harry. I wish I could sleep all day like you do."

Though Eden was sure if she were to introduce Harry to a female wombat, he might perk up a little. Not that she'd do that to the poor guy. Love was cruel. There should be an off switch because she didn't want to feel this way about Rain. Not anymore. He might have the biggest heart of any man she'd met with his philanthropic contributions, and not just to the Koala Hospital. He sponsored the surf life-saving kids, the boy scouts, and probably other local groups she didn't know about. But it didn't help that he seemed to love koalas almost as much as she did. Ava might praise her for everything she'd done for the hospital since taking over, but Eden couldn't have achieved half of it without Rain. He'd helped her track koalas, plant eucalypts, and educate locals and tourists alike about protecting their endangered animals.

But that didn't mean she couldn't move on, date someone else, and treasure the friendship she and Rain shared. She didn't want to lose that and couldn't imagine *not* having him in her life when neither of them planned to leave Magnetic Island and their best friends were dating. In time, the pain of his rejection would ease. It had to because she couldn't imagine living the rest of her life with such heartache.

Eden adjusted Harry's heavy body against hers as a flying fox glided overhead and rainbow lorikeets made a ruckus in the palm trees. Rain might be the most sinfully sexiest man she'd ever met, but there were plenty of other men out there.

Sure, he'd featured in every one of her fantasies and while she didn't make a habit of entertaining herself, she'd spent many nights curled up in her cold bed dreaming about spearing her fingers into his long hair as he kissed every inch of her body. His piercing blue eyes would darken with lust as she ran her hands over his sinewy abs, pressed her breasts against his bulging pecs, and wrapped her legs around his waist as he plunged inside her and she cried out his name in ecstasy.

But sadly, that pleasure would remain only in her dreams. Rain lived in an entirely different world. One where endless streams of money allowed him to make all his dreams come true and made him think he could create hers, too. But how could Eden accept his help when she wanted so much more?

A girl needed to maintain her pride. She couldn't rely on him or take advantage of his fortune when she could barely pay rent in the current real-estate crisis. Hence another reason why she couldn't lose her job. She needed to remain independent and self-sufficient. So even though Jackie had said she'd been given complimentary room service, Eden would buy herself dinner, then move in. Rain could provide the room since he was the one who'd insisted she stay, but she could damn well feed herself.

Eden placed Harry back in his den, farewelled the animals, then quickly cast her eyes over the two pythons. They looked healthy, so with a shudder, Eden raced out of the sanctuary. She might love all animals, but she drew the line at handling snakes.

She returned to her ute, then drove to the Esplanade, where restaurants overlooked the fig trees lining Horseshoe Bay. Maybe tomorrow she'd enjoy dinner in her room— paying for it, of course—as Luna Views boasted the best menu on the island for people who didn't eat animals. But tonight, she wanted one of her old favorites as she parked in the lot at the end of the cul-de-sac and strode around the hedges onto the sidewalk.

Only to collide with a solid mass of black-clad muscle. Eden jumped back with a shriek, windmilling her arms as her heel caught the gutter. A hand shot towards her, but she fell out of reach, pain shooting through her hip and the hand that broke her fall as she collided with the pavement.

"I'm so sorry!" A hunk of butcher's paper landed at her feet, along with the greasy smell of fish and chips as a cold hand wrapped around her elbow. "Are you hurt?"

Wincing, she adjusted her weight through her hips. "No, I'll be—"

Then she glanced up at the man and words died on her tongue. His dark eyes bored into hers and everything faded around her—the crickets, the music, the chatter. Everything except the extraordinary face of the most beautiful man she'd ever seen. Black hair swished over his forehead, his eyes wide and cheekbones prominent by the gasp in his square jaw.

"Let me help you." With one hand around her arm, he pressed his other against her back and helped her to her feet. "Again, I'm so sorry. Are you sure you're okay?"

Eden nodded, blinking away her stupor as she examined her hands. "Ahuh. Not even bleeding."

"Good," he said, brushing his fingers over her palms with an odd gleam in his eyes. "You wouldn't want to see me around the sight of blood."

"Squeamish, are you?"

"If that's what you want to call it." His full, red lips quirked, and her toes curled inside her shoes. "I'm sorry I wasn't paying attention. I don't make a habit of knocking over beautiful women."

Eden blushed. "Don't worry about it. It's not every day I run into a man like you, either."

"Good." He tilted his head. "You're Eden Starr, aren't you?"

"Y-yes. Have we met?"

"No, but I'd recognize you anywhere. You're the vet who runs the Koala Hospital."

"Right! Yes, that's me."

His mouth widened as he flashed her a smile of pearly white teeth. "Well, this is a coincidence. I'm Lucas Capello. I have a meeting with you tomorrow."

Eden's eyebrows shot up, her heart skipping as her toes gave a little bounce. "Of course! It's nice to meet you."

"It wasn't the way I'd planned, but it's lovely to meet you, too." He released her wrists and extended his hand. Though rather than the usual handshake, Lucas wrapped his long, slender fingers around hers and lifted her knuckles to his lips. Eden's foolish mind turned to mush and barely registered that his kiss was cold.

"Are you heading out for dinner?" he asked.

"I was just grabbing something quick. It's been a long day."

He dropped her hand and scooped up the parcel at their feet. Eden drew in a sharp breath, blinking rapidly as the chatter and music from the pub rolled back into her conscience. God, this reaction wasn't normal. She'd never found herself flustered over a man, not since Rain had stormed into her life. It's not like she hadn't met handsome men since, it's just her heart had always been his. But now—

Lucas's gaze caught hers, and all thoughts of Rain vanished. "Would you like to share my fish and chips? I ordered too much and doubt I'll eat it all."

She smiled at the offer but shook her head. "I'd love to, but I don't eat animals."

"At all?" His eyebrows shot up, his silky voice pitching with surprise.

"Nope. But there's a great place down here that sells a vegan burger that I love."

"Then allow me." He placed his hand on his chest. "It's the least I can do after knocking you over."

Ordinarily, she'd decline such an offer, but by some force beyond her control, Eden found herself nodding. Lucas grinned and fell into step beside her as they started down the street. Though she couldn't take her eyes off his angular profile, pointed nose, and clean-shaven face. She'd never met anyone so stunning—

Her knee knocked into a chair outside the pub. Gasping, she tore her gaze from the exquisite man beside her and bent to rub her leg. Bloody hell, what was wrong with her? She wasn't usually clumsy or so besotted by a man. Unless that man was Rain.

Her heart clenched. *Rain*...

"I need to keep a closer eye on you, I think." Lucas chuckled as he led her around the table.

"Wasn't looking again," she muttered, blushing. "Must be hungry."

On cue, her belly rumbled, but not with hunger. Guilt churned inside her as she wrung her fingers. This wasn't right. What was she doing allowing a stranger to buy her dinner? After Ava's close call with Blair and the violence headlining every news article, a girl couldn't be too careful.

But as she stared up at Lucas, all rational thought melted away. He intrigued her, drew her in until there was nothing else surrounding her. She didn't question how or why, only that after the angst she'd experienced these past few weeks, it felt good to simply forget.

"Then I better feed you," he said as they arrived at Café Nourish. "And you can tell me more about the Koala Hospital."

If there was anything she could talk to death, it was her

hospital. But as Brenda the waitress greeted Eden and shifted her gaze between her and Lucas, doubt began to niggle. She'd only just decided to let go of Rain, which was proving ridiculously difficult when her heart refused to unlatch from the daredevil. This morning she'd declined his offer of lunch and now she was dining with another man?

It was wrong. Too soon. Made her sick.

"I take it you eat here often," Lucas said after paying for her burger and they moved aside to wait. It only took meeting his eyes again for her guilt to ease.

"They have good plant-based foods."

He nodded, though not disapprovingly. "How long have you not eaten meat?"

"Since I was a kid."

"And your parents didn't mind?"

"Mum stopped, too." It hadn't taken much considering she'd been the one who had found Eden bawling her eyes out after watching a documentary about the cruelty of animal farming and slaughter.

"Right ..." Lucas tapped his long fingers against his fish and chip parcel, his eyes flashing with either puzzlement or concern. Ordinarily, she'd be annoyed. But for some reason, Eden felt nothing.

Instead, she turned the focus on him. "How long are you on the island for?"

"I'm here for a two-day conference. I go back to Townsville after our meeting tomorrow."

"It's kind of you to take an interest in the hospital. We have a good team of volunteers and some regular funding, but we can always do with more sponsorship."

"And that's what I'd like to do. I'm *very* interested in you, Eden."

Her belly clenched. "In ... in the hospital?"

Lucas's lips quirked. "Sure. In the hospital and the work

you do. I like passionate women and the way you dedicate yourself to the koalas is something to be admired."

He looked at her with an intensity so deep it was like he was reaching into her soul. She couldn't stop staring at him, words failing her as a chill shivered up her spine.

"Here you go, Eden!"

She turned her head as though moving in slow motion, staring blankly at Brenda offering her the paper bag. Lucas shuffled his feet and Eden swallowed as her surroundings swirled back into focus.

"Thank you, Brenda."

Eden's cheeks flamed as she accepted her burger and strolled out into the night with Lucas beside her. She ordered herself to relax, but her belly was in knots. She'd been so hung up on Rain all these years she'd forgotten how to talk to another man.

Rain …

"Would you like to sit in the park?"

She nodded mutely, and they crossed the road, strolling beneath a large ficus to find a picnic table overlooking the beach. Eden sat opposite Lucas and they both unwrapped their dinner. She had to stop thinking. Even if she never saw Lucas again after tomorrow, she needed to give herself a chance. She didn't want to be alone and, if nothing else, she needed to feel comfortable around other men.

Though Lucas made her feel anything but comfortable. He was stunning. Captivating. Spellbinding.

"So, which club do you own?"

"Night Bite," he replied, and Eden's eyebrows shot up. "You ever been?"

"Sorry, I'm not the clubbing type and don't go out much at night. I'm a morning person."

"Not into nightlife," he muttered, though not unkindly. More like a statement as he bit into a chip.

"No, but I hear Night Bite's popular." Eden bit into her burger and resisted a moan as pumpkin and spices exploded over her tongue. Chewing softly, she watched Lucas's long pale fingers break apart his fish. "So ... why koalas?"

"Why not?"

"There are plenty of charities you could support, and mine isn't even a well-known one. You might do better at boosting your reputation by supporting a nationally recognized organization for disease or children or something."

A lock of hair flopped over his eyes as he grinned. "But it's not about that. I want to support something local, and I don't think you get enough recognition for your work. You're practically hiding on this island."

That was true. Eden's hospital remained private and she dedicated more time to work than shmoozing rich people. A few companies had come on board with regular donations, though most of them had remained anonymous and didn't have a big public profile. But Eden didn't mind as long as she could feed and care for the koalas. Only when she had a major project to fund did she host events or seek grants.

Which she'd need if she wanted to conduct her census, so caught in Lucas's riveting gaze, Eden spilled all her hopes and dreams for the koalas on Magnetic Island. Her ideas for the drones, extensions, and how she'd love to work full time and see local pets for veterinary care. Lucas nodded along, asking all the right questions as they spoke for what seemed like hours.

But it was only ten minutes by the time she'd finished her burger, and he'd barely touched his meal.

"I'll take it with me," he said, rewrapping the food as they stood. "I'm not very hungry, anyway."

Eden couldn't think of anything worse than reheated chips, but each to their own.

"Thank you for listening," she said as he walked her back to her ute. "I tend to get carried away."

His lips stretched to reveal sparkling white canines. "It was my pleasure."

"Do you still want to come to the hospital—"

"Absolutely. Our meeting still stands."

"All right." She turned to him at the door to her ute. "I'll see you then."

"You will." His gaze flickered to her lips, then her neck, and her stupid heart swooned. Then sank as Lucas stepped back. "You better go."

Eden nodded, her hand shaking as she reached for the door handle. Climbing behind the wheel, she tried to make sense of the strange sensations coursing through her as she lowered the automatic window and smiled softly at the stunning man backing away from the car. "Thanks again."

He lifted his hand in a wave, and she glanced over her shoulder to reverse out of the parking spot.

But when she turned back, Lucas was gone.

Chapter 5

Rain leaned his elbow on the door of his Lexus convertible, the wind whipping through his hair as he drove through Nelly Bay. It had taken every ounce of his self-control not to go see Eden last night. Finn's order as Alpha had taken hold and Rain wouldn't let anything stop him. Everything was on the line—his heart, his pack, his future, and her life. He was done resisting as no matter how afraid he'd been of mating and losing her, nothing had terrified him more than that crack he'd felt in their bond yesterday.

I need to move on.

Rain's fists clenched around the steering wheel. Bull-fucking-shit she did. Eden was his and hadn't deserved the pain she'd suffered for his stubborn refusal to mate. Once triggered, bonds rarely took more than a moon cycle or two to form, unless the man overpowered the wolf like Rain had.

Now, Rain wondered why the fuck he'd put this off for so long. Mating was what a wolf lived for. Finding that one person who complemented his soul, who strengthened him, who the Goddess had blessed to carry his children and continue the line of fierce warriors she'd bestowed upon the world. Eden was fucking special, and he'd been an idiot for ignoring the gift he'd been given.

Grinning, Rain surveyed the blue water, dull in the shade of the setting sun as he descended the hill into Arcadia. It'd been a perfect, cloudless day for skydiving, and with the adrenaline still pumping through his veins, nothing could dampen his spirits. He wasn't exactly sure *how* he would go about forging his bond with Eden. He'd done everything in his power to stop it for so long, it was hard to let go. Had the emotional connection even formed? Sometimes he thought it had, but he wasn't certain. They might be friends, but was that enough?

Rain sighed. He shouldn't overthink it. He'd watched both Finn and Sly successfully mate, and he had to do this right. But while mating looked easy, Rain didn't doubt it would be the hardest thing he ever had to do.

To complete a mating bond, he had to connect with Eden on three essential levels—emotionally, physically, and paranormally. She needed to love him, trust him, and respect him, and he her to form the emotional bond. Given their history and all the lies he'd told her, he'd have his work cut out for him there. She might be his friend, but she didn't believe half the words that came out of his mouth. He could see it in the subtle roll of her eyes, the twitch of her lips, and even though she seemed to have accepted his story about working with the government to take down Tyrone, he sure as hell didn't know why. He and Finn had come up with that off the cuff and while he'd thought they'd been convincing, it still sounded too far-fetched to be believable.

Yet he'd stuck with it. and Eden had never questioned him.

The next level was connecting physically, and that was self-explanatory. For years, he'd fantasized about exploring Eden's strong, willowy body, kissing her luscious lips, running his tongue around her glorious breasts, and making endless love with her deep into the night. Only by stubborn willpower had he managed to pull away from their almost-kiss on the jetty, and every Friday evening she'd spent in his home telling him about her week had ended with a long run through the bush and an ice-cold shower.

Then there was the paranormal level, and that was often the hardest of them all. A woman could fall for a wolf physically and emotionally, but to accept he was part animal who relished in hunting and killing? Rain wasn't sure Eden would accept the wolf. She dedicated her life towards the protection and welfare of animals, and his wolf was a predator who relied on meat for sustenance. The Goddess had sure had a good laugh the day she'd set him up with a vegan mate.

Rain shook his head as he left Arcadia. Some days, a relationship between him and Eden seemed impossible. But he had to try because even though by lore she had a choice whether she wanted to be his, he was hers. And even though he agreed with Finn's theory that a second mate was possible, he doubted they existed for rejected wolves. And after tasting that bite of rejection yesterday, Rain would do his damnedest to make sure that never happened.

He and Eden were meant to be together, and it was past time he told her that.

So, he cruised through the hills providing majestic views of the glittering ocean, and into Horseshoe Bay.

Arriving at the Koala Hospital, he stepped out onto the gravel parking lot and studied the dull, aging building. As always, thoughts of the improvements and changes he longed to make flashed through his mind, but he squashed them along with his wounded pride. He understood why Eden put the money towards the koalas' care rather than vanity features, but he wanted the best for her and to see her happy. Hence another reason to seal their mating bond because once complete, Eden would want him to be happy, too. And nothing would make Rain happier than to give Eden the best koala hospital in the country.

He pulled open the door, the scent of eucalypts greeting him as he stepped into the waiting room, as did the unique stench of koalas, the tang of bleach, and the garden that was Eden. He sensed her before he heard the wheels of her chair roll back and her pretty head poked out of her office. Eden smiled, and his wolf salivated with glee.

"Hey, Rain." She stood and strode out behind the reception desk. "What brings you by so late?"

He leaned his forearm on the counter, ensuring a full view of his flexed biceps. "Do I need a reason?"

"No." Pink flushed her cheeks, which was just so cute. "I guess ... I just ..."

"I missed you last night."

She stilled. "You ... you did?"

"Of course. It was too quiet in the house without you."

"But ... you've lived alone for years."

He flashed her a smile, trying to ease the confusion that flickered in her frown. "So? I enjoyed having you around. I know I didn't spend a lot of time keeping you company, as this thing with Tyrone and Blair kept me busy. But it felt wrong making pancakes for one this morning."

That, at least, was the truth. He might have spent the past few nights stomping around Hawkings Point and sleeping in the backyard, but he'd always been in the kitchen bright and early to make her breakfast.

Eden blinked, her teeth sinking into her lower lip as she fiddled with a pen she'd absently picked up. "I ... I'm sorry."

Rain straightened. "Don't be, Edes. I'm not trying to make you feel bad, just stating a fact. And I'd have brought you pancakes, but I'm afraid I ate them all."

She laughed. "I bet you did. I still don't know how you eat as much as you do and look like ... that."

"Unnatural metabolism, I keep telling you that. Besides, you taught me all about good, healthy foods." And he loved every bite of his whole wheat and oat milk pancakes, black bean barley stews, and kaleslaw tacos. If he were only a man, he'd adopt Eden's lifestyle in a heartbeat. But his wolf craved meat, and he couldn't help that.

"I did. And don't worry about the pancakes, I ordered my own from room service."

"Good. Order as much as you like. There's plenty on the menu that I know you can't resist."

He'd made sure of it. Luna Views had undergone a menu makeover about two months after Rain had met Eden to ensure it had options not just for herself, but for everyone with dietary requirements. He'd received rave reviews across the board and was damn proud of his restaurant. Sly might kill him when he discovered what had happened to his world-class steakhouse, but that's what his brother got for turning his back on their resort and pissing off into the bush.

"Yes, but I won't take advantage of your hospitality. I can pay—"

"I'm the one keeping you on the island, Eden. Take advantage all you want. I gave you the best room I had available, though if you want a hut, I can move you in there on Thursday. Or kick Finn out of his."

"Rain, please." Her hands shot up, palms out. "You've done enough. The room is lovely, even though I didn't need a suite."

Rain would have given her a house if he'd had the time, though there was no need when she'd just vacated the house she belonged in. "I want you to be comfortable."

"And I thank you for that. But you gave me what I asked for, so let's just move on, shall we?"

There were those words again. Move on? With their day or

in their lives? His snarling wolf chose the first option. "All right. What would you like me to do, then?"

Her eyebrows rose. "Don't you have work?"

"It's after five, Eden." Not as though that made a difference. He worked all hours, but he had a night manager, and he didn't jump again until tomorrow. Besides, nothing was more important than fixing what was breaking between him and Eden. "And like I said, I miss you. So, I'm here to help."

The subtle lift of her eyebrows had his fists clenching over the counter. She shouldn't be surprised as it wasn't the first time he'd volunteered. He often gave up part of the day to help at the hospital considering he loved her and the fluffy tree-huggers.

But it was the first time Eden looked uncertain about spending time with him as she lowered her gaze and rounded the reception desk.

"All right. Everyone's been fed and Caleb's outside cutting leaf, but I need everything cleaned by six o'clock."

"I can do that." He had no qualms about cleaning koala shit. "I'll start in the outdoor enclosures, hey? Check on Xena. How is she?"

Eden beamed. "Excellent. I told you we moved her out of the ICU last week, right?"

"You did." He'd been distracted with battle plans for the impending showdown with the rogues, but nothing Eden said ever went unheard.

"She's really bounced back these past few days," she continued as they meandered towards the outdoor enclosures. "We're going to see how she does independently for a few days, then hopefully reunite her with Cookie."

Rain smiled, glad to hear it. "I'm sure Xena and Cookie will love that."

Only two weeks ago, beneath the darkness of the new moon, Sly had alerted Rain of the bat attack on the koala.

Enraged, Rain and Finn had rescued Xena and her joey, Cookie, from the isolated bush near West Point and sped them across the island to Eden. She hadn't believed his tale about night fishing and taking a hike in the dark where he found the koala, but he couldn't tell her that a vampire had snacked on the local wildlife just to piss him off. Finn had named the joey, having bonded with the bub while she'd clung to his golden fur on the race back to the Jeep. Apparently, she'd been as cute as a cookie. But Eden had named Xena after the warrior princess once she'd made it through the night.

Rain unlatched the gate and studied the koala sitting on the Y-crossbeam, her mouth moving rapidly as she munched on the redgum. There'd been a moment when she'd been wrapped in a hessian sack swinging from his jaw as he'd raced through the bush as a wolf that he'd been afraid the poor koala wouldn't make it. But Eden was a miracle worker, and Rain was glad to see Xena thriving.

Though the mystery of what had bitten her still irked Eden.

Crossing the enclosure, he rubbed Xena's back. "Good to see you looking well, girl."

Xena's eyes met his. Fuck, she was adorable. He'd never taken an interest in koalas until Eden. Sure, he and Sly had searched for them when they'd visited Magnetic Island as kids, but it wasn't until he'd witnessed Eden's passion for the koala and learned of the threats that were killing their iconic Aussie marsupial that he'd fallen in love with the little creatures. And Moon help anyone who hurt a koala on his island.

So it wasn't *just* because of Eden that he wanted to fund the hospital. These animals were unique and they deserved to be protected. Sure, it was difficult to save those that got caught in the bushfires and images of koalas with burned hands and drinking water straight from the bottle all those years ago had melted his heart. He'd sent the hospitals down south thousands of dollars and sponsored many koalas. He had Tilly at Lone Pine, Ned in Adelaide, and Luna, who'd been released back into the wild outside Port Macquarie. He'd proudly display his adoption certificates at the resort, but he didn't want Eden to know about the extent of his contributions and risk her discovering his secret generosity towards her hospital.

Xena stretched up to reach for another branch, even though there were leaves close enough to avoid the effort.

"She's getting stronger every day," Eden said, moving to the other side of the branch and touching the surgical site from where she'd cleaned the wound left by the bat shifter. Thankfully, the pest hadn't sunk his teeth too deeply or hit a major artery. Koalas were delicate animals with thin, pliable skin, and they rarely survived any kind of attack. Dog bites were the worst and were a common problem for koalas living close to suburbia.

"She's healed nicely."

"And is much better at climbing." Eden beamed and scratched Xena behind her ear. "So, I've already cleaned the ICU, but these enclosures need hosing, and I need to finish some paperwork. Then I'll vacuum the halls. He'll be here before I know it." She dropped her head, muttering those last words as she crossed the enclosure.

Rain frowned. "Who will be?"

Eden stepped through the gate, facing him as she latched it closed. "I have an interested benefactor visiting. His name is Lucas."

Rain's eyebrows shot up. "Really?"

"Yeah. Coincidently, I bumped into him last night." She smiled and quickly averted her gaze, but Rain didn't miss the flash of pink in her cheeks. "He asked me all sorts of questions about the hospital over dinner, but he still wants to drop by and visit. So, I need to get those business proposals finished."

She tapped her fingers on the gate, then backed away. "I'll be in my office if you need me!"

Then she was gone, leaving Rain standing in the middle of the enclosure wondering what the fuck he was going to do first—hose down Xena's floor or shift and release a howl of rage.

Choosing the first option, he reached over the fence and dragged the hose in with more force than necessary. Eden had had dinner with another man? How on this fucking earth had he not sensed that? Was their bond that broken? He'd known when she'd returned to Luna Views last night as he'd stayed at his office pretending to work until she'd been safely locked up in her room. Yes, it'd been later than Eden normally returned home, but she often got caught up at the hospital or stopped by to check on a koala in homecare.

He'd never have thought she'd been out with another man!

His wolf howled in agony as Rain turned on the hose, anxiety ramping up his fear as he began cleaning the enclosure. Did Eden like this man? Was this her first step in moving on? It sure was quick if it was!

Who the fuck was this Lucas who wanted to fund *his* hospital? Rain wasn't leaving until he found out. So, he cleaned. And cleaned some more. Xena watched him with mild curiosity before curling up amongst her leaves and dozing off. After Caleb left, Rain paced the hall wondering what sort of creep would arrange a meeting so late when Eden swung out of the office.

"Everything looks good, right?"

The panic in her tone had Rain's fists clenching. Everything looked damn good, including Eden. She'd replaced her blue T-shirt with a lilac blouse and added pink gloss to her kissable lips.

Fucking hell.

"Yes, Eden. I'm sure you'll impress this benefactor. Does he even know the first thing about koalas?" He didn't bother hiding his bitterness. He had a right to it. Eden was his.

Except she wasn't.

"Are you okay?" Her brow furrowed and Rain blew out the longest breath imaginable.

"I'm fine."

"Riiiight." As usual, she didn't believe him. "Perhaps you should be going, anyway. The hotel can't run itself."

Rain blinked. Holy shit, now she was trying to get rid of him? His wolf whimpered as rejection hit him square in the chest. Over his dead body was he going anywhere.

"And leave you to meet this alleged koala lover after dark by yourself? I don't think so."

"I've already met—"

"Don't argue with me, Eden. I'll make myself scarce. But why would he want to meet you so late?"

"He was at a conference all day! And besides, I don't need a babysitter."

"But it pays to be careful. Besides, I have a vested interest in this place and if ..."

But words died on Rain's tongue as the scent of musty ammonia drifted through the doors. The hair on the back of his neck stood up as his wolf perked.

No ...

"Rain?" She frowned. "What is it?"

"Nothing," he growled, his fists clenching. "But you're right. I probably don't want to meet him." Because if he did, there would be a fight, and Rain didn't want to kill anyone today. At least not in front of Eden when he'd be forced to shift and reveal his wolf.

Eden's shoulders relaxed. "Maybe next time, then?"

"Maybe." But there wouldn't be a next time. Eden would

never see Lucas again. "Let me just say goodbye to Xena, and you might want to fix up your hair. It's out of place."

Her eyes widened as her hands flew towards her immaculate hair. He'd feel guilty about lying except ... he didn't.

"Thanks," she said, sweeping past him before hurrying down the hall.

Rain waited until the bathroom door closed, then clenched his jaw, straightened his shoulders, and marched into reception. Standing at the glass double doors, he spread his feet, folded his arms over his chest, and glared death at the bat shifter on the other side of the parking lot.

Predictably, the vampire stilled. Dark eyes bored into Rain's, but the slimy bastard didn't deter him. They were both supernatural creatures with strength beyond that of any man, but while wolves were blessed beings who loved and protected humans, vampires were undead creatures of Hell who lived to kill. They'd lived apart for centuries after endless wars that neither side had won as they were both notoriously difficult to kill.

But that didn't mean Rain wouldn't try. If that vile creature ever came near his mate again, Rain would have his head. Between his teeth. And Lucas knew it. So, Rain wasn't surprised when the bat turned, slipped into his car, and backed out of the parking lot.

But his pulse continued to hammer, his fists curling as he glared out into the night. Because now, he knew his enemy's next move.

Tyrone had sent a vampire after Eden.

Chapter 6

Eden's heart pounded in protest as she examined herself in the mirror. What the hell was wrong with Rain? Her hair looked fine! Not a strand out of place. Though doubt tugged on her self-confidence as she tightened her ponytail. She took a deep breath, then released it slowly, but the pressure inside her didn't ease. She felt like she was being ripped in two, her emotions in constant turmoil while her thoughts bounced incoherently inside her head. She couldn't forget the way she'd felt with Lucas. The depth of his dark eyes had transfixed her like no man's ever had, while his suave Mediterranean accent had made every word he uttered sound like a melody. Lucas Capello was beautiful, sophisticated, and exactly the type of man she'd always been attracted to with his clean-shaven face, neat hair, and impeccable dress sense. Whereas Rain with his dangerous eyes, close-cut beard, and shoulder-length hair often looked like he'd just walked off the set of a medieval fantasy film. He'd been sweaty, dirty, and positively wild the day they'd met, and he'd changed Eden's definition of drop-dead sexy forever.

Groaning, she pushed away from the basin. Why couldn't she stop thinking about Rain? Even last night, her conscience had called for him, tugging on her heartstrings until she thought she'd burst. And now Rain had the audacity to walk into her hospital and tell her he missed her? He'd barely paid her any attention the nights she *had* been in his home! Bar the breakfast times, he'd seemed uncomfortable having her there. It's why she'd needed to leave. Sure, he cared about her, but it wasn't in the way she wanted him to. And now he was concerned about her meeting Lucas after dark? The man was messing with her head! She couldn't take it, especially not when Lucas left her utterly spellbound. The last thing Eden needed was her feelings for Rain hindering the connection she could have with Lucas.

But her heart continued to ache until she could barely breathe. She loved Rain and he wouldn't be an easy man to get over. Especially if he continued to caress her hands, flex his biceps in tight T-shirts, and make every nerve ending inside her hum with the intensity of his blue-eyed gaze. If she wanted to make a good impression on Lucas, she needed Rain to leave. She couldn't let him jeopardize any donation Lucas was willing to give by getting all standoffish and protective as he crossed his bulging arms over his gorgeous chest and marked his territory. She'd found it sexy at times but now wasn't one of them. Rain might want to privately fund her hospital, but the moment she gave an inch, he'd jump ahead to make dreams she didn't know she had come true. And she'd become indebted to him. Beholden. Eden didn't want that. Especially not from the man who couldn't love her with his whole heart. This was not his hospital, and she was not his property, no matter how much she wished—

Eden spun towards the door. Bloody hell, she couldn't think like that. She was moving on and right now, her attention needed to be on Lucas.

She marched down the hallway, hoping she looked more confident than she felt as she strode into reception.

Only to find it empty.

"Rain?"

She opened the door to the enclosures where the cicadas serenaded the koalas with their buzzing, but Rain was nowhere to be seen.

Good. He'd said he'd make himself scarce, and so he should. Though as she sank into the chair behind reception, Eden had to admit knowing Rain lurked softened the unease in her spine. She'd been a little foolish to set up a meeting with a strange man alone after dark, even though she doubted the suave club owner had any intention of hurting her. She'd simply give him the tour and introduce him to Xena, Archie, and Marco, then discuss what he had to offer. Any donation would be gratefully appreciated, though she secretly hoped he wouldn't make an offer better than Rain's. She liked knowing that he was her second most generous benefactor. The largest was an anonymous donor who called himself the Cheeky Wolf, whose contributions had come out of nowhere a few days after she'd started seeking funds for a new X-ray machine. Again, Rain had offered to buy it for her, but she'd stalled him by insisting that something would come through. And she'd been right.

Eden glanced at the clock on the wall, and her heart sank. Lucas was five minutes late. Perhaps the conference had run overtime? She wouldn't be surprised. But nerves prevented her from sitting still, so she stood to tidy the desk, then wandered around the waiting room while keeping one eye on the door.

"He's late."

Eden jumped, turning to find Rain leaning against the hallway door, his arms and ankles crossed in a way that with anyone else would appear casual. But Rain made it look downright predatory.

Heat flooded through her vessels. "No, he's not. Maybe he's just ..."

"Fifteen minutes is late, Eden." He straightened and slipped his hands into his pockets.

But Eden wasn't prepared to give up. "It takes almost ten minutes to get here from Nelly Bay and ... and ... he's coming."

"Then let's sit and wait." Rain inclined his head towards the chairs.

"I thought you weren't going to meet him."

"I'll keep you company until he arrives," he said, sinking into a chair. Eden sighed and sat beside him.

"He shouldn't be so late. It's not like him."

"You don't know the man, Eden. He might not even be genuine."

"Of course he's genuine! He's kind and caring and I ..." She dropped her head, unable to finish that sentence. She didn't want Rain to know about her feelings for Lucas. Neither, apparently, did her heart as her ribs squeezed the stupid organ like a vise.

Her next breath escaped with a struggle, but before she could contemplate why she'd been so quick to defend a man she barely knew, Rain's hand fell to her knee and tingles shot along her bare skin.

"It's okay, Eden. Let's wait and talk about something else. I bet you're looking forward to the next Full Moon Party."

Eden grinned. He had that right. Eighteen months ago, not long after she'd met Rain, he'd begun hosting Full Moon Parties at Luna Views. They were tasteful yet high-energy events where popular artists rocked out by the beach while guests danced beneath the palm trees. It had only taken three full moons to put the event on the map and draw bigger names and crowds. And in less than thirty days, her and Ava's best friend Isla would take the spotlight in what was sure to be an amazing performance beneath the October supermoon.

"I can't believe Isla's coming home. I haven't seen her since she left for the States."

"She seems to be getting popular over there."

"I know. It's crazy how her career has taken off. She's always been a fantastic singer, but I'd never have imagined she'd be topping the Australian pop charts and opening for superstars in America."

Eden remembered the musicals she'd watched Isla star in during high school and the few times she'd attended a football game just to see Isla sing the national anthem. Her friend could belt out a tune that would make anyone shiver, and millions of fans around the world heartily agreed.

She, Ava, and Isla had been besties since the first day of high school, back when Isla had still been an introvert off-stage, Ava had recently arrived from a small rural town to board at a city school, and Eden had begun traveling to the mainland since Magnetic Island didn't have a high school. None of them had had any friends, but they'd shared a love of books and had met in the library when they'd been browsing the range of teen fantasy novels and bonded over their mutual Team Jacob-ness. Their friendship had bloomed and never been broken. Even with Isla's obsessive stage mum and endless traveling, Eden and Ava kept her with them by playing every new hit she recorded and stalking her social media.

"I should be lucky I managed to book her, then. She's sold more tickets than some other singers I've had."

"I'll admit, your Full Moon Party draws a crowd. Especially considering you sometimes host it on a weekday."

"Well, it's not called the 'Almost Full Moon Party.'"

"True. And it was lovely seeing the moon rise over the water as we danced. Isla's going to love it as she's obsessed with everything celestial." She'd taught Eden everything she knew about moonology and celestial events, most of which Eden had forgotten when she'd started studying real science. "When

I said the words 'Full Moon Party', she was sold. Though she loves Magnetic Island, too."

"How long has it been since she was here?"

"Not since I was still at uni. After that, I went to Lone Pine and then she only visited Ava and I in Townsville. But she says she needs a holiday and can't wait to hit the trails."

Rain's eyebrows quirked. "Isla hikes?"

"Hey, she might be a superstar who struts across stage in a leotard and six-inch heels, but she's an avid outdoors girl. She's always wanted to do the trek up Mount Cook and though I've talked her out of it before, I doubt I'll manage it this time."

"You've never been up Mount Cook?"

Eden shook her head. The trek up Mount Cook, the tallest peak on the island, was a full day return trip, so most people camped for the night. Knowing Isla, she'd revel in the thought of sleeping on the mountaintop with no running water.

Crazy woman.

Rain's hand firmed around her knee, jolting Eden out of her thoughts. "Don't fret. I can get Kai to take her."

"I'd appreciate that. But if she wants me to, I'll go with her. The views are supposed to be amazing."

"They are. Though not as great as the view from the sky."

Eden rolled her eyes. "So you keep telling me. And you know what? Isla will probably be insane enough to go skydiving, too."

Rain grinned. "She sounds like a daring woman. Pity she doesn't rub off on her friend."

"Keep dreaming."

"I shall," he said, his eyes glittering and, for a moment, Eden imagined catapulting towards the earth with the wind blowing in her face and Rain's strong body at her back as they—

"I don't think he's coming," Rain said, rubbing her knee again. "I'm sorry."

Eden turned towards the clock.

It was six-thirty.

Her shoulders slumped. What had she done wrong? Lucas had been so keen to see the hospital and meet the koalas last night, and now ...

"Yeah. You're probably right."

Yet she couldn't move. Couldn't look at him while her heart did stupid swooshy and squeezy things inside her chest, unable to determine whether she was relieved or disappointed.

"Eden?" Rain cleared his throat. "I'm sorry I didn't spend much time with you while you were staying at my place."

Her belly clenched, sharing his regret, though she kept her gaze on the floor. "It's okay. You were busy with that Tyrone stuff, and I've had koalas to look after."

"But it's no excuse." Rain lifted her hand and encased her fingers between his own, shooting shivers up her arm and down her spine. "You were a guest in my house, and I should have treated you better. Especially with the way it came about. It's just ... I wasn't used to having you so close."

Eden studied their hands, mesmerized by how hers seemed to disappear in his as he brushed his thumb over the back of her wrist. Her breath caught and heart kicked up another jig. What was going on? Her body shivered and sang, itching to leap from her chair and into his lap. To wrap her arms around his strong shoulders and never let him go. For years, she'd wanted Rain to show a little more affection than the conversation he offered, the smiles he shared, and the time he volunteered. Sure, he'd touched her every now and then, but not like this. Not like ...

Her breath caught. Oh no. After all this time, was Rain finally ...?

Eden slowly lifted her gaze to his. And froze. His blue eyes sparkled, but with what, she couldn't decipher. Kindness, definitely. Regret, maybe. Love?

"Rain ..."

His eyebrow quirked as he waited for her to speak, but Eden remained lost for words.

The prickly skin of his throat pulled taut as he swallowed. "You said you were afraid for our friendship. I just want you to know that will never change."

Her heart skidded ... then stopped. Never change?

"You'll always be important to me, Eden. It's why I need you here while we deal with Tyrone. And now we're one step closer to uncovering his plan."

She frowned. "His plan?"

"Yes. He won't be happy about what happened to Blair and will retaliate, so I need to keep you safe." He dipped his head, his eyes seeking hers. "You understand, don't you?"

She could barely breathe. "Ava tried to explain, but she's become as secretive as Finn." *And you.*

Rain turned her hand over in his and squeezed. "I'll tell you everything when the time is right, Eden. I promise you."

"And what *is* everything, Rain?"

"The truth. About Tyrone. Why Finn arrived out of the blue and what really happened to my brother after Tyrone killed his wife."

Dread hardened her spine as darkness flashed through his eyes. She'd always had questions about Rain and the secrets he kept, but for the first time Eden wondered if she actually wanted to know.

"And when will that be?"

"When you're ready." His impassive expression returned as he straightened. "But right now, I think we should give up on this guy and go home."

Her shoulders sank. "Yeah ... okay."

"I'm sorry." Rain eased out of his chair, lifting their joined hands to draw her to her feet. "Lucas doesn't know what he's missing, Eden."

"Yes, but I thought he ..." Eden glanced at her feet, not wanting to confess she'd hoped Lucas might want to see her again *away* from the hospital.

Rain placed his hands on her shoulders. "You deserve better, Eden."

Then he drew her into his arms, and Eden stupidly let him, wrapping hers around his waist as she sank against his chest. His broad, warm chest where she'd always found comfort. Where she wished she could stay forever. Her hands pressed into his hard lats as she breathed him in, the salt, bush, and ozone swirling and settling the doubt inside her. She loved how he always smelled of the sky. It felt so natural. So earthy. So Rain. Perhaps she could hold on to hope for a little longer?

His hands brushed up her spine, and she smiled against his pecs. "Thank you, Rain. For being here."

"Always, Edes. I wouldn't have it any other way. Now, let's go."

He stepped away, taking his warmth with him and leaving her tingling. Eden forced her feet to move, retrieving her bag from the office as Rain switched off the lights. They locked up in silence, then exited the hospital beneath the glowing sensor light.

"Thanks for keeping me company," she said as they strolled towards her ute.

"Anytime, Eden. I'll see you tomorrow."

Rain opened the door. It wasn't the first time he displayed such chivalry, so she smiled softly and climbed behind the wheel.

"Are you jumping tomorrow?"

"First thing, but I'll come see you afterwards so you know I didn't go splat." He flashed his cheeky grin, and she rolled her eyes.

"I thought I had more risk of being killed driving home right now than you diving tomorrow."

"Very true. Better follow you, then, to ensure you return home safely."

"But I was going to stop by the supermarket—"

"Do it tomorrow. In daylight." His eyes darkened again. "Trust me, Eden."

That intrinsic part of her soul did trust him. Absolutely. Which was why she found herself nodding. "Fine. But if I get hungry—"

"Abuse the room service. That's what it's there for."

Then he closed her door and tailgated her all the way back to Luna Views.

Chapter 7

Rain idled in the Lexus as Eden waved and strode inside the lobby. Only once he sensed she was in the elevator did the tension unravel around his spine.

Bloody hell, that had been close. Too close. Did he feel bad about disappointing Eden? A little. Did he care? No.

Fury he'd been suppressing since scaring the bat away scorched through his veins, and Rain slapped his hand on the steering wheel. How the fuck had he been so careless? Eden had dined with a *vampire*! She'd been in danger! And he hadn't sensed it because the charismatic, charming, undead slime who had no business touching his mate had compelled her and blocked his connection. Fuck! He was lucky she was still alive!

Rain gritted his teeth as his wolf paced hungrily, aching to escape and ensure the bastard had returned to whatever disgusting roost he'd flown out of. He should have known Tyrone would use the bats. He'd known they were coming and going, reporting back to Tyrone, but only because Sly had discovered them when he'd turned full-time wolf and waged war against the filthy creatures. The fact neither of them could sense the other's presence like they could their own kind was what made vampires the wolves' ultimate enemy.

And an even darker threat than the rebels.

Clenching his jaw, Rain shoved the Lexus into reverse and tore out of the parking lot. He sped up the hill towards Picnic Bay and barked at his hands-free voice activation system to call Finn. His Alpha answered after too many fucking rings.

"I need you at the house. Pronto."

"Aww, man. Ava's—"

"I know what Tyrone's plan is."

There was a pause. "I'm on my way."

Rain sped through the sleepy suburb and up the curved driveway to his illuminated three-story mansion clutching the side of the headland. He slipped his Lexus into the opening garage, took the elevator upstairs, flicked open the lock on the back door, and began pacing. His mind wouldn't stop reeling.

It wasn't normal for bats and wolves to live in close quarters and not want to kill one another, let alone actually work together. Vampires were cruel, devious creatures with no respect for human life. They feasted on fresh blood, compelled their victims into doing all sorts of heinous acts, and relished in the kill when their food expired. But Tyrone had turned his back on the Goddess and had a twisted set of morals, likely in line with the vampires. He must have conducted some sort of deal where they would do his bidding in return for wreaking havoc in the city. It'd been only a matter of time before he used the undead demons in his plans to destroy Rain's pack.

But Rain would be ready. He and Sly had trained in a variety of combat techniques since childhood, and Rain had meticulously prepared the scouts for battle. He would protect Eden and kill any fucking vampire who dared sniff her way again as the thought of what Lucas might do to her was one he did *not* want to contemplate.

The bushes rustled outside, then Finn strode in, bare

chested as he zipped up a pair of the spare shorts that the pack left on the back steps. "What do you know?"

"Bat shifter. He's targeted Eden."

Finn froze. "Fuck."

"Yep. I can't believe she's still alive."

Finn leaned against the counter. "What happened?"

Rain took a deep breath and released it slowly, but it did nothing to calm his frantic wolf. "Eden was contacted by some 'club owner' who was interested in donating to *my* hospital."

Finn snorted. "It's not ... well, I guess it is your hospital."

"Damn-fucking-straight it is with the amount of money I give. She was meant to meet the bastard tonight after a 'conference' he was attending. Lucky I was there because the moment he stepped foot in the parking lot, I caught a whiff of his odious scent, made my presence known, and the fucking coward couldn't get away fast enough."

"Thank fuck for that."

Rain hissed out a breath. "I know. But what's worse is she *likes* the fucker. She even changed her shirt and put on lip-gloss before he was supposed to arrive, and the disappoint-ment in her eyes when he didn't show ..." A burning vise squeezed his heart until he could barely breathe. "It fucking slayed me."

"I can imagine." Compassion laced Finn's voice as he gripped Rain's shoulder. "But I wouldn't panic, man. No matter how compelling these vampires are, they can't defeat the will of the Goddess."

Rain dropped his gaze to the floor. "You think?"

"Absolutely. Even if she is attracted to this creep, Eden won't be able to ignore the connection that draws her to you. So, it's even more important that you complete the bond."

Rain pushed away from the bench. "That's what I was hoping to start today. I don't want to resist anymore. It's been killing me. Except when I got to the hospital, I felt more rejected than ever." He ran his hand down his face but couldn't scrub the pain away. "Fuck. I don't know what to do. I can handle rogue wolves, but bats? I know the theory, but I've never had to kill one."

"Neither have I." Finn's mouth twisted as he scratched his jaw. "Our bite is fatal, so it's always been a mystery to me why the bats would work with Tyrone. Even if he is twisted, bats don't trust wolves more than we don't trust them. So, I wonder what their agenda is?"

"We know Tyrone's agenda. He wants to destroy our faith. To kill us for killing Blair. And to let the wolves run wild and free of obligation to the Moon Goddess."

"And we've already started to stop that by killing many of his Unfated wolves."

"Yes, that was a win for us. I just wish I was more prepared to face the bats. We'll have to start training. Get the scouts ready."

"Yep. And you know who else will be able to help us?"

"Sly. I know." Rain shot his hand through his hair with a grimace. "We need to find him."

"Yep. And I'll brush up on my lore as it's poor leadership for me not to know all I can about the bloody leeches."

"You've been in the job for four days."

"Which means I'm four days behind in my studies. But in the meantime"—Finn clapped Rain on the shoulder—"stick with your plan to form the bond and tomorrow night, we'll chase down Sly."

EDEN DUMPED her bag and collapsed onto the lounge. Everything inside her ached—her heart, her head, her stomach. The pain consumed her in ways she couldn't even begin to comprehend. But while she didn't want to deal with the riot going on inside her head or heart, she could settle her hunger pains. Though she'd barely reached for the room service menu when her phone rang.

Jumping up, she grabbed it, only to sigh in disappointment when she saw Ava's name on the screen and not a certain charismatic Italian man's. "Hey, Aves."

"I've been dumped. Finn took off and I need help. Want to have dinner?"

"Help with what? And why did Finn take off?"

"Work. Meet me in the restaurant?"

"Sure." It made no difference whether she abused Rain's hospitality in her room or the restaurant, and eating with Ava was certainly preferable to dining alone while contemplating the utter failure of her love life.

But as she waited for the elevator, her mind wandered back to Rain's farewell remarks.

There'd been something strange about him tonight. What was so dangerous about her pulling into the supermarket and grabbing some fruit? Was he afraid she'd be attacked in the parking lot? Sure, crime was out of control in Townsville, but this was Magnetic Island. People rarely locked their houses let alone worried about walking through the brightly lit car park by the ferry terminal of an evening.

Eden rolled her eyes and stepped inside the elevator. If staying on the island was meant to keep her safe, why the restrictions? And what did nighttime have to do with anything?

"Men," she muttered. They always needed to control everything and thought they could boss others around. But honestly ...

Heat rose in Eden's cheeks. She might complain about it, but she was the one who'd let Rain gain this control over her. *Trust me*, he'd said. And she did. No matter how unreasonable his request or unbelievable his story, she trusted that man irrevocably. Unequivocally. Her stupid, smitten heart took over at every opportunity, silencing her head that desperately wanted to descend from the clouds and take charge.

But why? What made Rain so special? Why did he have this hold on her incredibly foolish heart?

It needed to stop. And as she strode into the lobby, Eden vowed she would *not* think about Rain Blackwood for the rest of the evening.

"Eden!"

Ava arrived from the direction of the beachside huts where she currently lived with Finn. Her friend had moved in with him the same night Eden had moved in with Rain. But while Eden had spent that evening being ignored by the man she'd loved for years, Ava had been the lucky one who'd spent a sleepless night being ravished by the sexy jet ski instructor who worshipped the ground she walked on.

"How was your day?" she asked, hugging Ava.

"Good. Finn and I took Gracie to Huntingfield Bay for a picnic."

"Sounds lovely." Eden hadn't visited Huntingfield Bay in years since it was only accessible from the water, and she didn't trust boats smaller than the ferry.

"It was. And Gracie enjoyed getting out of the hut, too."

Gracie was Finn's Maltese-Shitzu and the most adorable dog who ever drew breath with her black, white, and gray patchwork coat, floppy ears, and quirky nature. Eden had met dogs with OCD, but none so much like Gracie.

"I bet she did, though I don't understand how she can enjoy traveling on the back of the jet ski."

"It's fun." Ava grinned and Eden suppressed a shudder. "I hope to get her to the beach a little more though as I think the sand will be good for her leg."

Eden nodded. Gracie had Leg-Calve-Perthes disease, a birth defect that caused hip degeneration and affected her mobility. But while she'd ultimately need surgery, Ava was determined to use her physiotherapy skills to build Gracie's hip strength and prevent the need for the operation for as long as possible.

"Wet sand to start, definitely," Eden agreed. "And swimming."

"She doesn't like water, but I will try."

A waitress showed them to a table on the edge of the deck overlooking the lush, illuminated gardens.

"What are you going to order?" Ava asked.

"Black bean stir-fry," she decided after a quick glance at the menu she knew by heart. "You?"

"Same." Ava pulled her phone from her pocket. "So, I need your help. Finn and I were looking at houses and I want to know what you think."

"Ooh." Eden leaned closer and ignored the swarm of bitterness in her belly. She was happy for her friend. Truly. Sure, Ava might have only known Finn for a month, but after her stalkerish interlude with Blair, she deserved a kind, loving man even if he was a touch overprotective. Finn was head over bare-feet in love with her, and Ava had chosen to spend her life with him, hence she'd altered her dream of buying a house in Townsville to purchase one on Maggie instead. "Where are you looking at?"

"Preferably Picnic or Nelly Bay so Finn's close to work. Arcadia maybe, but we want to avoid Horseshoe Bay. Check out this place."

Ava handed Eden her phone. "Nice street," she said, noting the address of the double-story wooden home surrounded by palm trees as she swiped. "Ooh, a pool!"

"I've always wanted a pool."

Eden continued to swipe through the photos, admiring the high wooden ceilings and sprawling undercover patio. "It's a beautiful house, Ava."

"Yeah, but I don't love it." Ava's nose wrinkled as Eden handed the phone back. "I know I can't be picky, but we'll keep an eye out. We *do* like this one."

Eden scrolled through the pictures of the gorgeous wooden home set among the treetops and boulders. With soaring cathedral ceilings, the split-level home filled with light from the tall windows overlooking the towering hoop pines and bushy gardens. "Wow. That is nice."

"Finn likes it because it has direct access to the national park."

"Yeah, but what about the stairs? Gracie won't be able to get out to the yard without help."

Ava's lips quirked. "Doesn't matter. Finn would carry her outside whether there were stairs or not."

"True." Eden wouldn't expect anything less as the brooding and tough Finn turned to marshmallow around that dog. "So, what did he dump you for?"

"Work stuff." Ava crossed her arms over the table, then her eyebrows shot up. "How'd it go with that new investor?"

Eden's stomach plummeted. "He didn't show."

Ava's jaw dropped. "Really? How rude!"

"Yeah. He wouldn't be the first person who changed his mind, even though I thought ..." Fiddling with the edge of the tablecloth, Eden couldn't put her thoughts into words, so she confessed, "I actually met him last night. On the Esplanade." She filled Ava in on her dinner with Lucas, the conversation, and how she'd found herself deeply entranced by his beautiful, dark eyes.

"So, I was keen to see him tonight to make sure I wasn't imagining things. But now ..." Groaning, Eden ran her hands down her face. "I feel like such a fool. And to make things worse, Rain was there."

"What? Where?"

"At the hospital."

Ava's eyebrows shot up. "Why?"

To screw with my head, drag me back into his orbit, and remind me that I will never get over him for as long as I live. "I don't know. He dropped by to see me, I guess. And to visit Xena."

"Finn used to use that excuse," Ava said as their dinner arrived. "But I can see how that would have been frustrating for you."

"I just want to move on! But I don't see how I'll ever be rid of him."

"No. It'd certainly be easier if you were Rain's ..." Ava averted her gaze and shoved food into her mouth.

Eden frowned. "If I was Rain's what?"

She shook her head. "Never mind. I just ... hate seeing you in this position as unrequited love hurts."

Eden sighed. "It sure is a bitch."

"Yeah. And I'm sorry." Ava reached across the table and interlocked her fingers with Eden's. "If there's anything I can do, please tell me. Okay?"

"You'll be the first person I call."

"Good. So, what are you doing tomorrow?"

"Well, Archie needs—" Eden jumped as her phone rang. Placing her fork down, she dug into her pocket and froze. "It's Lucas."

"Answer it! If he's anything like you say, he probably has a good reason for not showing up."

"You think?"

"He wouldn't call if he was trying to ghost you."

Realizing her friend was right, Eden accepted the call. "Hello?"

"Eden! It's Lucas. I'm so sorry about tonight."

The sincerity in his deep, Italian voice melted the tension in her shoulders. "It's okay ..."

"I should have called you earlier. I apologize."

"I figured something must have happened." She glanced at Ava, who nodded in encouragement. "Is everything all right?"

"I had an emergency at the club and needed to take the ferry back to Townsville."

Eden frowned, confused at the disappointment setting in her stomach while her heart sagged with relief. "Oh."

"But I feel terrible for standing you up, *bella*. I'd love to make it up to you. I'm tied up here for the next few days, but I can come back to Maggie next week. I'm hoping I could take you to dinner."

Eden's eyebrows lifted. "To dinner?"

Ava offered an enthusiastic thumbs up, and Eden wished she could share even half her friend's excitement.

"I hope that's not too forward," Lucas said, and Eden shook her head. To reassure herself? Maybe.

"No. Dinner sounds good."

Ava clapped her hands together.

"Excellent. I had a nice time last night, Eden. I look forward to doing it again. So, is Tuesday okay?"

"Tuesday's perfect."

"*Grazie*. I'll text you the details. Talk soon."

Then he was gone. Eden lowered her phone and blew out her breath as Ava grinned like an excited schoolgirl.

"I'm so happy for you, Eden."

"Yeah ..." She picked up her fork and forced herself to smile. "It'll be okay. You'd like him, Ava."

"If he's good to you, then I'll like him for sure." Ava squeezed Eden's hand again. "And it *will* be okay. I know it's hard, but one step at a time."

That was it. One step after another, one day at a time, and she'd have moved on before she knew it. Even if things didn't work out with Lucas, she had to at least try.

If only her heart would stop kicking and screaming in protest.

Chapter 8

Tyrone made the bat wait for the blood whore to finish sucking his dick, holding her head tight as he came down the back of her throat. His blood raged, wolf panting with orgasmic relief as he slowly withdrew himself. Then snapped her pathetic neck.

Snatching up his whiskey glass, Tyrone shoved the woman's body aside and stood, tucking his dick back in his pants as he downed the rich amber liquid. "You can enter."

Lucas slipped through the curtain into the private room in the basement of his club where the sun never shone, and women were kept compelled and dazed from the addictive vampire bite. It was a place usually reserved for vampires, but Tyrone and select wolves had been given privileges to the booze and whores.

The bat studied the hunk of flesh on the floor and blew out an unnecessary breath. "Why did you do that? She was a tasty one."

Tyrone growled. "I'm fucking angry."

"I know, but you can't keep killing my feedbags."

"You should have a permanent one soon, so don't complain."

Lucas's eyes flashed. "She is pretty, I'll admit. And smells fucking divine."

Smirking, Tyrone stepped over the whore and moved towards the bar. "I knew you'd be pleased. Pretty face and a body you'll never tire of fucking."

"She's got tits on her, that's for sure." Lucas ran his tongue over his top lip. "Though she's likely iron deficient."

Tyrone poured himself another whiskey. "What?"

"Bitch is a bloody vegan. And proud of it."

Tyrone spun around. "Blackwood's mated to a vegan? Bloody hell. Never thought I'd feel sorry for the bastard."

Lucas's eyes darkened. "It poses a problem."

Tyrone's mouth thinned as he tapped his finger against the crystal glass. "I don't see how. Have you—"

"If I had, I wouldn't be here."

"Then why are you?"

Lucas shuffled his feet. "I went to see her tonight and Blackwood was there."

Tyrone's lips twisted. "Fuck. Now he knows you're involved."

"Unfortunately. But I'll return and do my part—"

"You better." Tyrone was counting on it. He'd allowed the bats to live in Townsville with the out-of-control flying fox population to conduct their underworld deeds as long as he could participate in the fun and they helped him destroy the Fated wolves. They made the perfect spies with their ability to fly around Magnetic Island undetected, and since their compulsion blocked a wolf's bond, who else would Tyrone use in his mission to destroy Fated mates? Thanks to them, he'd killed the Alpha's bitch, discovered the koala vet was Rain Blackwood's mate, and that a Warrior had come to their aid. A Warrior who happened to be—

The crystal tumbler shattered in his hand. Shards pierced his skin, which healed quickly after a heaving breath or two.

But not even killing Lucas's whores could heal the agonizing pain constantly constricting Tyrone's chest.

Finlay. His Fated cunt of a pup who'd killed his true son. Blair. His beautiful boy, his heir, the son he'd raised to carry on his legacy and end their ties with Fate. Now dead and buried thanks to the whelp Fate had forced upon him when he'd met Cassidy.

He'd never wanted to mate, but Fate's pull was difficult to resist no matter how hard a wolf rebelled. So, he'd claimed the woman, marked her, and used her for his pleasure whenever it had pleased him. It hadn't taken long for the pup to come and though he'd done his damnedest to bash the fucker out of his mother, Tyrone hadn't been able to defeat the Goddess's will. So, he'd waited, hoping he could make good use of Finlay once he grew into his claws. He'd let Cassidy raise the tyke, and when Finlay had turned ten, Tyrone had taught him his first lesson about Fate's cruelty. He'd had Cassidy killed and had taken Finlay. But no matter how much Tyrone had flogged him in an attempt to show the pup he didn't need to be tied to Fate, the bloody Goddess had sunk her hooks into the kid, and he'd escaped at the age of fifteen. Tyrone had hunted him for years, but he'd never seen Finlay again.

Until he'd arrived on Magnetic Island last month and taken charge of the broken pack, mated with the whore Blair had tried to claim, and killed him for it.

That fucking Goddess had made Finlay Alpha, and Tyrone wouldn't rest until Finlay and Rain learned there were worse things to fear than the death of their precious mates.

Tyrone glared at the vampire. "I made you a deal, Capello, but you must strike now. Blackwood might have resisted his bond, but I sense a shift and you must make your move *before* he changes his mind and ruins our plan."

"I will." The vampire's mouth curved, flashing his fangs as

bloodlust darkened his eyes. "Sly's bitch might have been delicious, but this one ..." He drew in a breath and blew it out with relish. Hunger. Delight.

For Tyrone knew there was no tastier blood for a vampire than that of a Fated mate.

Chapter 9

Rain completed three jumps back-to-back on Wednesday morning, acting his cool, calm, and enthusiastic self as he strapped lives to his chest and relished the freedom of tumbling through the sky. But after he and Chad helped the team pack up, completed their safety checks, and waved a cheery goodbye, they slid into Rain's Lexus with their battle-hungry wolves prickling at their skin and drove to his house in silence. It still acted as the packhouse even though the Alpha didn't live there, but until Finn established his own, the kitchen and balcony overlooking Picnic Bay made a more comfortable meeting place than Finn's hut at Luna Views.

Rain strode out of the elevator with Chad at his heels and glared at the two young wolves lounging on the sofa. Kai and Nate, pack scouts and assets in their roles at Luna Views. Kai was the nature enthusiast who took guests for hikes and four-wheel-drive tours, while Nate was a sea-wolf and ran the scuba diving and snorkeling operations. They were both dedicated and trustworthy employees, but off the clock, they proved to be every bit the youthful twenty-two-year-old's they were.

"I thought I took away your keys," Rain said.

Kai snorted. "Like we need keys."

"We were hungry," Nate said around a mouthful of potato chips, his bare feet perched on Rain's ornate coffee table.

"Yet you didn't find those here." Rain snatched the packet out of Nate's hand. "Don't eat this junk. Real food is coming."

"Hey!" Nate blinked, salt glistening on his fingertips.

The crisps turned to dust in Rain's fists as he scrunched the packet and tossed it in the garbage without apology. "We have a war coming and I need you all in top form. Junk food is off the menu."

"You can't defeat Tyrone eating that shit," Chad agreed as he rummaged in the fridge.

"It's *po-ta-to*!" Nate cried.

"With all the nutrition of air." Rain slid open the balcony doors. "I'll chuck some real potatoes on the barbecue to go with your steak."

Nate scowled. "Better not be that crap you feed Sly."

"It's rib fillet. You know I only give Sly the cheap shit."

Kai clapped Nate on the shoulder. "He only gets the good stuff when he shifts back. Right, Rain?"

A lump formed in Rain's throat as he strode into the kitchen. "Right."

Which was *another* problem to add to Rain's growing list. Every night for the past two years, no matter how inconvenient, Rain had sought his brother out and left him meat from the fully stocked fridge he kept downstairs. Sly refused to come if Rain stayed, so he usually checked the next day to make sure his brother had eaten.

But since Sly had given up being Alpha, Rain could barely sense his brother, let alone his location or whether he was eating. And that worried him. If Sly wanted to assume the life of a lone wolf, then fine. He could sulk and live like an animal. But he still needed to eat and spare the wildlife.

Rain rounded the island counter and glared at the scouts. "But I *will* give you Sly's chuck steak if you don't get off your lazy asses and help."

Nate's face twisted. "Aww, man. You know I don't know how to cook."

"Slice the potatoes," Rain suggested.

"I'll cut my finger!"

"It'll heal."

Nate dropped his feet to the floor and blew out an exaggerated breath. "All right. As long as you don't mind a bit of blood with your chippies."

Kai shoved Nate in the shoulder as the elevator pinged. "You're disgusting."

"Get up and help," Chad said, dumping potatoes onto the bench. "Nate, you chop, and Kai can toss the salad."

"Toss it where?" Kai asked.

Nate snorted. "You sure are asking a lot. So, what's this meeting about, anyway? Where's the boss?"

"Here."

Nate and Kai leapt off the couch, their backs straightening as Finn strode into the kitchen. Rain smirked as their Alpha crossed his arms over his chest and narrowed his eyes at the young men.

"Why aren't you two helping with lunch?"

"On it!" Nate skidded past Finn while Kai scrambled over the back of the couch and snatched the bag of spinach Chad offered him.

Finn's mouth curved as he slipped his hands into his pockets. "Good to see you all here."

Kai chuckled. "Can't keep Nate away from the food, boss."

"I had food," Nate grumbled, his fingers fumbling as he

tried to hold the potato on the bench while poking it with the tip of the knife. "Food I didn't have to prepare. But Rain tossed it in the trash."

"Full moon is over, therefore so is the partying," Finn said. "No more junk food, gentlemen. We have a war to fight, and we need to keep our strength up."

"Dunno how I'll manage once I cut off my—"

"Fucking give it here." Rain snatched the knife off Nate, afraid the idiot really would cut off his finger with the way he was fumbling with the bloody thing. They might have super-natural healing abilities, but they couldn't regenerate severed body parts.

"Thanks, man." Nate smiled as Rain deftly sliced the potato. "This is why I buy them in a bag."

"And you'll die of a cholesterol problem."

"Do wolves even get cholesterol problems?" Kai asked, popping a cherry tomato into his mouth.

Rain rolled his eyes and reached for another potato. Fuck, now he sounded like Eden. "Forget it."

"Anyway," Chad said, strolling in from the balcony where he'd fired up the barbecue. "What's this meeting about, Finn? Any news on the Tyrone front?"

"Yeah." Nate sobered. "You've been doing a lot of recons along the coast. What do you know?"

Kai's eyes flashed. "If he's coming after Ava again, you know I'll do anything to—"

"It's not Ava," Finn growled, glaring at the flirtatious wolf before softening his gaze in Rain's direction. "And this isn't my fight."

Rain's wolf snarled as he slid the potatoes into a bowl. "Tyrone has sent a bat shifter after Eden."

All cutting and tossing of salad stopped, and guilt churned in Rain's gut as the scouts exchanged confused looks.

Kai frowned. "You mean the vet?"

"Yes."

"But why?" Nate asked. "I know we're scared of vets, but what's she done to Tyrone?"

Rain knew he'd dug himself into this hole. He'd kept his friendship with Eden private and while it wasn't a secret that he supported the koalas, he'd done all he could to hide his mating bond from the scouts. How he'd gotten away with it for the two weeks she'd been living there, he didn't know. It'd helped that they weren't the most observant of youngsters.

But he couldn't fight this battle alone, so he leveled his gaze with the scouts and said, "Eden is my mate."

"What?" Kai's auburn eyebrows shot up as the salad tongs dropped from his hands. Not that he'd been using them. "You're mated?"

"Since when?"

"Haven't you known Eden for years?"

Nate shook his head. "And you've resisted her all this time?"

"No wonder you've been such a surly bastard."

Rain bared his teeth. "Watch it, Kai."

"How did we not know about this?"

Chad snatched the bowl of potatoes from the counter. "Because you're too busy splashing around in the water to notice anything."

Rain blinked. "You knew?"

Chad shrugged. "Bit hard to miss when she's on the beach every weekend relieved you didn't plummet to your death."

"You never said anything," Rain said as they followed Chad onto the deck, where he proceeded to toss the potatoes onto the barbecue.

"Not my business. You mated before I arrived, so I didn't know what was holding you back."

Having only been with them for nine months, Chad had been the newest member of the pack before Finn had arrived.

"Honorable of you, Chad," Finn said, his lips quirking.

"Not like you to keep your mouth shut," Nate said, and Chad snapped his tongs at him.

Rain cleared his throat. "Anyway, it turns out she had dinner with a bat shifter named Lucas who claimed to be interested in donating to the hospital."

Nate snorted. "Sure, he is. Donating his services as a leech."

"He better not hurt the koalas," Kai snarled. He adored the iconic creatures and used to volunteer at the hospital until Eden had taken over.

"He won't if he knows what's good for him," Rain said. "But we can't sense the bats presence, so we need to figure out how to protect Eden and what Lucas's motive is. And why Tyrone is using the bats."

"We've been battling our own rebellious kind for so long that we've overlooked the vampires," Finn said. "But I believe Rain has tutored you in how to kill them in the past?"

"Be prepared to revisit those lessons." Rain had taken his role as battle master seriously under Sly and would continue to do so for Finn, so they'd start training tomorrow.

"Yes, Commander," Kai said with a cheeky salute. "Looking forward to it. Keen to kill some bats."

Rain resisted a smile, glad to see the young scout's confidence had boosted since their successful battle against the rogues.

"We'll get a bite on them." Nate snapped his teeth to demonstrate.

"Yes, but the bite only works in their vampire form," Rain reminded them. "They'll shift if they want to feed or fight us, but they're difficult to catch as bats since they can fucking fly."

"*So* unfair," Kai said, crossing his arms over his chest.

Chad slapped his hand on Kai's back. "Come fly with me anytime."

"Jumping out of planes is not the same thing."

"It can be."

"Gentlemen, focus," Finn said, not unkindly. "I know it's only been a few days since the full moon, but we knew Tyrone would retaliate quickly. And he has."

"I'm surprised he hasn't made a move on Ava," Kai said. "I mean, you're the one who killed Blair."

"Yes, and I'm keeping a close eye on Ava. None of us are safe until Tyrone is dead. But he's going after Eden because Rain's bond with her is weakening."

Rain growled. Fuck, he'd really screwed up. "And bats are even worse enemies than wolves. They're cunning and vicious and this creep can compel Eden to feel and do things that she ordinarily wouldn't." Rain's veins turned to ice at the possibilities. "I don't think he's staying on the island, but we need to be on guard and ready for when he returns. In the meantime, we must find Sly because if anyone knows about bats, it's him."

"But I haven't sensed Sly since he left us on Friday," Kai said, his brow furrowing. "I hiked Gustav Creek yesterday and didn't even catch a whiff."

"Yes, he's pulling away," Finn confirmed, his blond jaw hardening. "But I'm sure he's just taking a moment now that he's shed his responsibilities. We'll welcome him back when he's ready. Until then, we need to support Rain while he forges his bond with Eden. Once that's done, she'll be better protected, and we'll be stronger as a pack. Then we can face Tyrone head on and Sly might be inspired to join us."

"Sounds like a good plan," Chad muttered, turning the potatoes as the scouts nodded in agreement.

"I'll keep watch and see if I can track Sly," Kai said. "I have a hike to Mount Cook over the weekend and might pick up his trail."

Rain's throat tightened. "Thank you."

Kai shrugged. "I want him back as much as you do."

"We all want Sly back," Finn said. "The life of a lone wolf isn't kind, especially when you're as broken as Sly. But I think that with the right incentive, we can turn things around. Just stay on guard and let us know if you spot any bats. Flying fox *or* vampire."

"We will," Chad said. "But after we eat because I'm starving."

"I'll grab the beef!" Nate cried, already running towards the kitchen.

"Bottomless stomach, that one." Rain gripped the back of the outdoor dining chair and glanced around at his team. "But thank you, gentlemen. I know resisting Eden was an idiotic thing to do, but she's my best friend and means everything to me. When Lucas returns, I want him dead. And any vampires he brings with him."

Nate grinned, his blue eyes sparkling as he returned with the meat Rain had prepared earlier. "I'm looking forward to it. Haven't killed a vamp before."

"Me neither," Kai said, leaning against the railing and crossing his bare ankles. "Though I don't know what this vamp would get out of working for Tyrone. He might be a twisted old fucker, but why would he lower himself to working with vampires?"

"Because he *is* that low," Finn said. "The rebels and vampires both want the same thing—to kill us and seize power over the humans."

Chad nodded. "That's very true."

"What do you know?" Rain asked, staring at the young wolf. Shit, he should have thought about it before. Like Finn, Chad had grown up with a rebel father and had lived in Townsville after being dragged there against his will a year ago.

When he'd discovered there were Fated wolves on Magnetic Island, he'd swum eleven kilometers across the bay under the cloak of darkness to seek refuge, and Rain had taken him in with little questions asked. Sly had emerged from the bush to welcome Chad to the pack and he'd been their most solid source of information about rebel wolves since. "Have you interacted with the bats?"

Chad's lips twisted. "No, but you're right about the fact they want the same thing. Those rebel wolves just want to rut and eat and unleash their inner animal, and the bats are no better. I've heard of a club over there where they feed off humans and compel women to do the most horrific things."

Rain's fists tightened around the chair as, once again, he counted himself lucky that Eden was still alive. But if that slimy bastard came near his mate again, Rain would personally sink his teeth into every bloodsucker within a hundred-mile radius.

"We need to protect our mates," he said, glancing at Finn. "What have you told Ava?"

"Nothing yet. She had no issue with us wolves, but apparently vampires creep her out."

"Good. Don't give her all the details but ask her to keep Eden at Luna Views in the evenings. And we'll watch over them both."

If only he could insist that Eden move back into his house, but Rain knew it was too late for that. He'd already asserted enough of his authority by keeping her on Magnetic Island. He didn't want to make her feel any more trapped. Luna Views was just as safe as the packhouse, and even more so if he slept in his office directly above her room until they extinguished this threat.

Finn frowned, then nodded. "Yeah, I can work with that. I'll tell her we have a bat problem and she'll be scared enough to ensure they're inside before dark."

"Thank you. And we must stay sharp, too, gentlemen. The bats will fly in under the radar, but Sly's been hunting and monitoring them, so we need to find out what he knows."

And dammit, Rain would get his brother to talk to him, even if he had to sacrifice a piece of his eye fillet to lure him from the fucking bush.

Chapter 10

"Wow, Xena, look at you go!" Eden grinned as the koala grasped the branch on the makeshift jungle gym, pulled herself around, and reached up to grab her reward of gum leaves. "That's my big, strong girl."

Clenching her hands to her chest, she resisted the urge to reach out and hug the koala. She could cuddle and pamper all the cats and dogs she wanted, but while the koalas held a special place in her heart, she couldn't treat them like pets when her goal was to return them to the wild. That was the one drawback of working with the koalas, but the wild was where they belonged.

"Aww, I'm so proud of her," Ava said, stepping inside the enclosure.

"Yep. Who was on the phone?"

"What?" Ava blinked as though she didn't remember having just left to take a phone call, then shook her head. "Just a telemarketer. But look at this little one. She's come such a long way."

"Thanks to you," Eden said, nudging her friend with her

elbow. "Without you moving her little legs every day, she wouldn't have made such a quick recovery."

"Yes, but you're the one who saved her life. Although, I'll admit, I've loved being here these past few weeks. If I didn't have to go back to work, I wouldn't."

Eden's chest tightened. "Really?"

"Well ... no." Sighing, Ava slipped her hands into her pockets. "I miss work and helping people after heart surgery is just as rewarding. I need to go back."

"Me, too." Yet a week had passed since she'd moved out of Rain's house, no progress had been made on the Tyrone situation, and her boss was far from pleased with her thin excuses. "I can't afford to lose my job."

Ava wrapped her arm around Eden's shoulders. "I know. I'm so sorry I dragged you into this mess."

"It's not your fault. Blair had his own issues coming after you, and Tyrone ... I don't know how he's still on the police force."

"Because he has too much power."

"But there's a state police commissioner, isn't there? Can't he do something?"

"Yeah, but ... I ... I don't know how that works. We just need to leave it to those who do."

"Finn and Rain?"

Ava shrugged, unwrapping her arm as she extracted what Eden suspected was imaginary dirt from beneath her fingernails. Eden's heart sank. It wasn't like her friend to keep secrets.

"Are they really government spies?"

"They're as good as. Finn's been fighting the good fight for years and Rain ... well, he'll do anything to get his brother back."

Eden frowned, recalling what Rain had said last week. The

"truth" about his brother. "Do you know what happened to him?"

"He left to bury his pain after his wife was killed."

"And doesn't talk to Rain much. Which is strange because from what I understand, they were very close."

Rain rarely spoke about Sly, but Eden had always noticed his presence around the house. Family photos graced the downstairs living area and Rain hadn't touched the master bedroom until he'd let her stay there with a closet full of his dead sister-in-law's clothes.

"You know Rain better than I do," Ava said with a shrug, and the ache in Eden's chest deepened.

"Yet he never told me the police murdered Shelby. Not that I think we can call Tyrone and Blair police. What's the news on that, anyway? Has Blair avoided jail?"

Ava scrubbed her toe over the loose gravel. "No, he won't be going anywhere."

Eden's shoulders sank with relief. "That's good. Then you'd think Tyrone would step down for the shame of having his son charged with sexual assault."

"Yes, but it'll get swept under the rug like Shelby's murder. So, until the guys can figure things out, we just need to stay here on the island."

Eden nodded, though she couldn't stifle the panic that rose in her throat. She couldn't live like this. While she respected Ava's wish to keep her on Maggie, she was sick of Rain saying that she needed to stay because he cared about her, then blatantly ignoring her.

"Yeah ... but I still think I should tell Rain to shove it, pack up, and—"

"Are you ready for your date tonight?"

Eden blinked, startled by the change of subject. But she knew what Ava was doing, and Eden smiled as a shiver of warmth rose inside her. Tonight, she was going to dinner with Lucas Capello.

"I think so. I'm meeting him at seven at Amaroo on Mandalay."

"Ooh, nice." Ava blinked, frowned, then shook her head. "You love their beetroot gnocchi."

"I do. But … I'm nervous."

"Why? This is a *good* thing, Eden. It's been forever since you went on a date."

That's because she'd been in love with another man. Even now, her stupid heart felt like she was betraying Rain with the mere thought of Lucas. But she was determined to move on.

"That's true. Plus, I don't even know Lucas. He certainly seemed keen to support the hospital, but then again …"

"It's too soon, isn't it? You're not ready to move on from Rain."

Eden ran her hands down her face. "It sounds so stupid, Ava, but I can't stop thinking about him. Ever. It's like I'm drawn to him, but then I feel drawn to Lucas, too. In a different way. Rain makes me feel warm, safe, and protected. Like nothing could ever harm me. But when Lucas looks at me, my mind clouds and I get lost in his deep eyes and Italian accent."

Ava grinned. "He sounds dreamy."

"Yeah. He is."

"Then give him a chance, Eden. You'll never know unless you try. And if it doesn't work out, then no harm done."

"That's true." She only wished she felt as confident as she sounded.

"You'll be fine. Now, what's the plan with Xena?"

Eden contemplated the koala. "Do you think she's strong enough to handle Cookie?"

Ava laughed. "Even Finn isn't strong enough to handle Cookie. But yes, I think we should give it a shot."

"Then we'll add more branches to her tree, watch her for a few days, then reunite her with her baby."

Ava squealed and clapped her hands together. "Yes! Oh, I can't wait to tell Finn."

"I'm sure he'll be happy. And if all goes to plan, they can have another week here before we take them back to their home trees."

"Excellent!" Ava skipped over to Xena and scratched her between the ears. "Do you hear that, girl? You get to go home."

Eden smiled as tension eased from her shoulders. Releasing koalas and watching them thrive was one of her favorite parts of the job. She couldn't wait to set Xena and Cookie free, and to see for herself where Rain and Finn had rescued them from because she still wasn't buying their story about fishing and hiking in the dark.

But in the spirit of moving on, she would let that go, too. Rain could have his secrets. All she cared about was that Xena and Cookie returned home safely.

Which Eden continued to remind herself as she zipped up the little black dress later that evening. It might be a little too much for a first date with the straight neckline just hiding her boobs and the spaghetti straps leaving her throat bare, but while being held prisoner on the island, Eden had little choice in her wardrobe. So, she slipped on a pair of platform sandals, then strode out the door.

She drove into Nelly Bay as the last rays of sunlight disappeared beyond the horizon and cloaked the island in darkness.

THE PACK GATHERED around the large map of Magnetic Island after Finn and Nate wrapped up their last tours. For the past week, they'd scoured the bush for any trace of Sly while Nate watched over the ladies at Luna Views. It had gone against everything Rain believed in to leave his mate in the hands of his scout and go hunting, but if he had any hope of saving her, he needed to find his blasted brother.

Except the stubborn wolf didn't want to be found. With four thousand hectares of national park, there were countless places Sly liked to lurk. He enjoyed Gustav Creek and trekking up Mount Cook, but he preferred to roam the west coast where he could swim in Ned Lee Creek and play in Chinaman Gully while keeping watch over Townsville.

Yet, they'd found no trace of him. Sly had officially fallen off the grid, cutting himself off from the pack and sinking deeper into the wolf. Rain, Kai, and Chad had searched the whole western coast over the weekend, and Kai had continued tracking in human form during the day. But it was a struggle for the scouts to sense him, even Finn as he drove the perimeter of the national park. Therefore, they had to rely on the only bond that couldn't be broken—the blood bond—which was why Rain had spent his nights traipsing through the bush instead of watching over his mate.

"Tonight, we'll explore Retreat Creek," Rain said, jabbing his finger near West Point. "Else we're going to have to take boats over to the northern bays because I'm not climbing the bloody mountain every night just to get over there."

"It'd be easier if we had a chopper," Chad said, running his hand through his dark, spikey hair. "But I'm still a few months away from getting my license."

"Do you think we could get the pilot on board?" Kai asked.

Rain shook his head. "We can't bring him into this. We need to keep the resort business separate. Though, yeah ... I could do with a chopper."

Rain had always liked his toys, so it was a wonder he didn't already have a helicopter parked beside his King Air. He planned to buy one soon anyway so that Chad could begin running tours to the reef and Orpheus Island.

"I tried getting a read on him during the jumps," Chad said. "But nothing."

"Yeah, it's not easy."

The elevator doors opened, and the sweet scent of strawberry filled the room. Rain glanced up as Kai leapt away from the table with his arms outstretched.

"Ava!"

The scout didn't get far though as Finn's hand clamped over his shoulder and yanked him back.

"Don't you dare," he growled as Ava strolled towards them.

"Good evening, gentlemen."

Kai grinned and waved like a schoolboy with a crush, which wasn't too far from the truth. "Hello, Ava. You look lovely."

"Aww, thank you, Kai." Ava kissed Kai on the cheek, making the kid blush and Finn snarl. Wrapping his arms around her tiny waist, Finn lifted her off the ground and held her against his chest.

"Don't tease me, honey."

Ava giggled as Finn placed her down a good two meters from Kai and the rest of the pack. "Jealous, Finn?"

"Just protecting what's mine."

"From Kai? He's harmless."

"Hey!" Kai protested, his chest heaving before sinking beneath Finn's glare.

"All right." Rain held his hands up in a peace keeping gesture. "Gentlemen, you know the rules. No flirting with Finn's mate. What brings you—" Rain froze, his wolf perking in alarm as his senses shot into hyper-alert. If Ava was there, who was— "Where's Eden?"

Tension rippled through the pack bond as spines straightened around the table. Ava, however, stared at them as though in a daze.

"Eden? Why?"

"I thought Finn told you not to let her out after dark!"

Ava blinked, her forehead creasing as though she had no clue what they were talking about. "I ... I don't ..."

"Ava." Finn cleared his throat and placed his hands on her tiny shoulders. "Is Eden at the hotel?"

Her gaze darted from Finn to Rain and back again. "No. She has a date—"

"A date!" Rain stepped towards Ava, only for Finn's hand to slam into his heaving chest. "With who?"

"For fuck's sake, Rain!" Ava's glare punched Rain in the solar plexus. "I know why you can't love her back, but—"

"*AVA!*"

Any other time, Rain would have expected Finn to knock him dead for roaring at his mate, but Finn's face turned ashen as he shot his hands through his blond hair and swore beneath his breath.

Ava's eyes slowly widened. "Oh my God ... Eden's your mate?"

Rain risked his neck and grabbed Ava by the shoulders. It took all his control not to shake her as he leveled his gaze with hers. "Tell me where she is."

"Sh-she's on a date. W-with Lucas."

Rain's wolf released an almighty howl as his hands flew to his head. "*Fuck!*"

Ava stumbled into Finn's arms, blinking rapidly as Chad, Kai, and Nate swore, too.

"Where are they, Ava?" Finn asked.

"Amaroo on Mandalay. But Rain—"

"Rain!" Finn's shout carried through the house, but Rain was already out the back door as he sprinted across the yard, burst through his clothes, and lunged into the bush on all fours.

Chapter 11

Eden sat at the table on the cloistered balcony, sipping water as she watched the color-changing pool lights dance while diners chatted around her. Lucas was thirty minutes late and, once again, she'd been left playing the fool with not even a phone call or message to explain his tardiness.

Exhaling, Eden tossed back the rest of her water. Screw it. If this was the way Lucas treated his dates, then she wanted no part in it. He was disrespectful and just plain rude. He might be rich and used to having people bow to his every whim, but she would not be one of them.

Grabbing her purse, she stood and strolled out of the restaurant. But despite her straight spine and determination, disappointment filled her chest as she descended the stairs onto the poorly lit garden path and strolled towards the lobby.

So much for moving on. Dating wasn't worth the time, effort, or disappointment. No wonder she rarely bothered. She'd dated a couple of men during university and had been in a semi-serious relationship while living in Brisbane. At least she'd thought it'd been serious, until Jake had dumped her for a job in Adelaide and hadn't looked back.

Then she'd met Rain.

Wincing, Eden pressed her hand to her chest. Why was life so cruel? He might have only wanted to be friends, but a tiny part of her had always harbored hope as she hadn't imagined the affection he'd shown her over the years. He'd innocently caress her hand, shoulder, or hip and leave tingles on her skin while looking at her as though she was the most exquisite person on the planet.

But it must have all been in her head because if Rain had any ounce of romantic feelings for her, he wouldn't have held back. He might be the silent type, but he was an insane daredevil, a sturdy businessman, and he always got what he wanted.

Clearly, he didn't want her, and that ripped her apart as her heart continued to cling to his when she desperately wished to let him go.

Sighing, Eden slid into her ute and laid her head on the steering wheel. She couldn't take it anymore. She wanted to get on the ferry, sail away, and never look back. She'd find someone else to take over the hospital and use her contacts in Port Macquarie or Brisbane to find another position.

But anytime she thought about walking into that ferry terminal, she remembered the way Rain's eyes darkened the night he'd told her about Tyrone. The way he'd ordered her to stay on the island. And how she feared he'd sink the ferry by any means possible if she tried to escape.

She couldn't leave, but if he was going to act like an alpha, dominant jerk about it, then she needed to talk to him. Demand to know why she had to stay and what he was keeping from her. Sure, he'd been busy, but now she needed answers. He'd said he would tell her everything one day, but when would that day come? What was he hiding? Why couldn't he just be honest for once in his life and tell her the bloody truth?

Exhaling, Eden slipped the key into the ignition. Yep, she would talk to Rain and then—

The engine remained silent. Frowning, Eden turned the key again. Nothing.

"Fuck!" Slapping the wheel, she slumped in her seat. Now her car wouldn't start. This night was a bloody disaster.

Snatching up her purse, she climbed out and slammed the door closed. She didn't bother lifting the hood. She might be able to neuter an animal, perform a cesarean section, and do reconstructive surgery to remove tumors, but she wouldn't know a battery from an engine, so she stomped down the driveway sweep and started walking. Screw calling anyone, a pleasant walk along the beach was just what she needed to ease the horror that was this evening.

No streetlights illuminated Mandalay Avenue as she strode past the resort's tennis courts, but that wasn't unusual on Maggie. She didn't mind the dark and often walked at night to ease her mind and look for koalas. They weren't officially nocturnal animals, but koalas moved more at night, so it was—

A screech jolted her gaze skyward as a bat swooped overhead. That was interesting. Bats weren't uncommon on Magnetic Island, but they didn't usually—

Another bat screeched and swooped towards her. Squealing, Eden threw her hands over her face and hurried her stride. "What the—?"

Wings flapped and tiny claws scratched her arm. "Shit!"

Heart pounding, she clutched the wound, blood wetting her fingers. Another screech sounded, and Eden glanced up as a bat flew towards her. And another. Screaming, she tried to run, but they had her surrounded. Four? Five? Fuck, she didn't know. Terror clogged her throat as she lifted her bag and swung at the flapping wings.

"Go away! Leave me alone!"

But they continued to swoop, scratching her skin with sharper claws that seemed natural. Eden tried to move, but her feet rooted to the spot.

"Stupid bat! Someone, please—!"

Then talons latched onto her shoulder, fangs pierced her neck, and Eden's words turned to screams as white-hot pain set her veins on fire. She crumbled to her knees, tears blurring her vision as her hands clutched the dirt. Blood dripped onto her fingers and the world spun just as a roar thundered through the air. Her head hit the dirt, her eyelids fluttering as a massive black dog leapt out of the darkness.

Then she saw nothing at all.

RAIN BROKE every pack rule in his race to reach Eden. Taking the most direct route over Hawkings Point, he dashed through the trees along Nelly Bay Road and launched into suburbia. Sure, he could have taken the Lexus, but his wolf had taken over in his need to save his mate. A horn blasted as he narrowly avoided colliding with a bus, but his thumping heart contained no fear for his own life. Rain just ran, dashing through the trees and sending the domestic dogs into a frenzy of barking.

He didn't care.

Lurching into the bush, Rain sprinted over rock cairns and scrambled down ridges. It wasn't until his paws touched down on Kelly Street that he heard her scream.

His heart stopped beating. *"Eden!"*

It felt like miles but could only be a few hundred meters as he raced down the street. Turning left, he jumped over fences, onto a trampoline, and evaded a ferocious German Shepherd before launching into the darkness of Mandalay Avenue.

Where Eden, in a flurry of black cotton, fell to her knees with a bat attached to her neck.

Rain roared and leapt through the air. Lucas released her and Eden crumpled, but Rain's focus remained on the bats. He swiped at one, but the fucker flittered out of his reach. Rain growled and ran up a gum tree to spring back and snap at the fuckers. But he missed, landing on his shoulder in a cloud of dust.

Chest heaving, he jumped to his feet and glared death at the bats as all but one flew away. Lucas. He flashed his fangs, and Rain bared his teeth with a deep, menacing growl. Then the slimy cunt swooped off into the night.

It took all of Rain's self-control not to race after them. Heart in his throat, he spun around on all fours and fell to two knees beside Eden, his bare skin scraping the gravelly dirt. Fear pulsed through his veins as he observed the scratches on her delicate arms, the rips in her black dress, and the two small puncture wounds on the left side of her neck.

"Fuck ..." Rain hissed between his teeth before falling to his hands beside her. "Eden! Baby, wake up. Oh, shit ..."

He couldn't think. Couldn't breathe. What did he do? The bat had fucking bitten her, which meant—

"No!" Rain dragged her into his arms, dirt scratching his bare ass as he sat and held her close. Warm, sticky blood transferred from her skin to his, but he didn't care. "You stay with me. You hear? Eden, don't ... don't you ..."

Rain gritted his teeth as pain speared through his chest. He could make all the demands he wanted, but nothing would change what he knew was coming.

He lifted his head and roared up at the night sky. *"Fuuuuck!"*

Squeezing his eyes closed, he dropped his head to hers and slipped his fingers into her soft, flowing hair as he cradled her against his shaking body. This was all his fault. He should have forged their bond sooner. Should have protected her. Should never have let her out of his sight. He should have hovered over her until she felt smothered. But he'd been too busy searching for his fucking brother and now ...

The roar of an engine approached, headlights blinding him moments before tires screeched and sprayed dust into the air. Doors opened, slammed, and a pair of shorts hit him in the shoulder. Rain lifted his head and stared helplessly at Finn, his voice barely sounding like his own as he swallowed and said, "He bit her."

Chad's eyes widened. "Shit ..."

They knelt on either side of him, Finn's large hand brushing Eden's hair off her neck where the two ghastly wounds slowly clotted.

Finn cleared his throat. "Get in the car, Rain. Now."

The sound of another car approaching had reality hitting Rain like a brick. He was on the side of the road, naked, with an unconscious woman in his arms.

"Come on, man. I've got her."

Finn scooped his arms beneath Eden, lifted her pale body from Rain's hold, and carried her to the car. Rain leapt to his feet, dragged the shorts up his legs, and ran after them, slipping into the back seat just as the small truck drove past. Finn passed him his mate, closed the door, and jumped back behind the wheel of Rain's SUV.

He spun a U-turn, shoving Rain into the door since he hadn't bothered to put on a seatbelt. But Rain could do nothing but gaze upon Eden's beautiful face. Her long lashes fell over her delicate, creamy cheeks, her rosy lips parted softly as her head lolled against his chest. His wolf howled, echoing his breaking heart as pain he feared would never fade filled every cell in his body. He couldn't think. Couldn't breathe. He loved this woman so fucking much.

"What happened?" Finn asked once they were speeding towards Picnic Bay.

Rain shook his head. He didn't know what he'd been thinking by running across the island, but his mind had been on one thing, needing to get Eden away from the bat shifter. Whether that be by making his presence known with a subtle howl or by striding into the restaurant to toss her over his shoulder and cart her out of there, he would never know. But he'd have preferred to be the billionaire charged with indecent exposure than to have witnessed the scene he just had.

"I don't know. She should have been inside. Safe." Surrounded by people where the bats couldn't have attacked her. "There were five of them, and she fell with Lucas biting her neck."

Chad swore while Finn gunned it past Luna Views.

"We'll get her home," Finn said. "We'll keep her safe until she wakes up."

"She'll wake up?" Chad asked.

"Of course she'll wake up!" Rain cried.

Chad's eyes dulled as he turned from the passenger seat. "But ... won't she be ...?"

"It doesn't take one bite," Rain snapped. "I'll fucking save her."

But as he brushed his finger down her cool, delicate face, deep, undulating fear curdled inside him until he could barely move. He would not lose this woman. He would not let Lucas, let *Tyrone*, take Eden away from him. He might deserve to have his ass kicked for resisting her, but Eden shouldn't have to pay the price for his weakness. She was the one person who would bring him peace, balance him, compliment his soul, and love him for eternity, so he would protect her until his very last breath.

He would save her.

The vow ignited a fire inside Rain unlike any he'd felt

before. This was what he'd been born to do, and Rain would kill that slimy bastard and enjoy every bloody second of extinguishing his race from the region.

Rain's jaw hardened, arms tightening around Eden as Finn ascended the driveway and pulled the SUV into the garage. Ava rushed over, pulled open the door, and gasped in horror.

"What did he do to her?"

She stumbled aside as Rain shuffled out of the back seat and narrowed his eyes at Ava, barely able to control his anger. "What do you think vampires do to innocent women?" he spat.

Ava's hands flew to her mouth. "No ..."

Rain's lips twisted as he turned his back on her. He liked Ava, but right now, he couldn't witness the pain in her eyes when he could barely stomach his own. He wanted to blame Ava for the part she'd played in this. For letting Eden out of her sight when she'd been specifically told not to.

But he couldn't. It wasn't Ava's job to protect her. It was his, and he'd fucked up.

Rain strode inside, Kai and Nate jumping out of his way as he laid Eden on the sofa.

"Get some blankets." He issued the order to no one in particular, but Kai and Nate moved like lightning as he knelt by Eden and positioned her comfortably.

Ava fell to her knees beside him. "Oh, Eden. I'm so sorry," she said, her shoulders shaking as she stroked her friend's hair. Then she turned to Rain and shoved him. "Why didn't you tell me she was your mate? I thought you were sparing her feelings by not dating her!"

Rain swallowed, though it did nothing to dislodge his guilt. He had no excuse.

Finn moved towards them. "Ava, honey—"

"I encouraged her to let you go!" Ava shoved him again,

and Rain didn't stop her. "I told her to date that creep! That it'd be good for her! Why didn't you tell me?"

Those last words escaped in a hysterical sob as Ava broke into tears. Rain wished he could break down himself, but he needed to remain strong. Stay focused.

He glared at the bite positioned over Eden's left jugular. She wouldn't have lost much blood as that hadn't been Lucas's aim. Vampires drank blood, but bats did a lot worse. And the only way to save Eden from her new fate was to kill the bat who'd infected her.

Chapter 12

Eden winced as pain shot up her neck and she squinted against the harsh light. Her stomach rumbled. Damn, she could eat, and something around here smelled good. Rich and fragrant, exactly what she wanted to satisfy her cravings. She hadn't eaten in—

Her eyes flew open as the evening came flooding back—bats surrounding her as she screamed and they—

"Eden."

Warm fingers interlocked with hers as a large hand she'd recognize anywhere pressed into her shoulder, preventing her from sitting up. Her heart rate spiked, leaving her gasping for breath as her body sank into the lounge. But there was no need to panic. She was safe. Home. Hungry.

She turned her head until her gaze connected with Rain's, jolting at the hollowness in his red-rimmed eyes. His jaw hardened beneath his sexy scruff, but his touch was soft as he brushed his fingers down her cheek.

"Hey. What's ... the bats ...?"

"Don't worry about the bats. You're safe now."

His hand squeezed hers, leaving her with no doubt of her

safety as she glanced past him at his first floor living room. "How'd you find me?"

The corner of his mouth quirked. "I always know when you're in trouble, Edes. I'm just sorry I didn't get there fast enough."

The strange pull around her heart fluttered. "What do you mean? I'm—" Her hand flew to her neck where her fingers brushed two scabs at the base of her throat. "Oh my God, it bit me!"

Rain took her hand and pressed his mouth to her knuckles. "I'm so sorry."

"I need to get to the hospital." She kicked the blanket from her legs and sat up, blinking as the room spun. Her belly clenched. She really needed to eat.

Rain rose from his crouched position onto one knee. "Eden, you can't go anywhere."

"I've been bitten by a bat! I need to go to the hospital before ..." Her breath caught as abject fear flooded through her veins. Although untested, scientists assumed the entire Australian fruit bat population was infected with lyssavirus. She might have been vaccinated, but the disease could easily pass to humans through urine, scratches, and bites, presenting as normal flu-like symptoms before ultimately ending in death.

Eden pressed her hands to her mouth to stifle her scream. "What if it's infected me? I don't want to die!"

Rain sprung to his feet and dropped onto the lounge beside her, drawing her into his arms as she began to shake. Convulse?

"You are *not* going to die," he said sternly, his arms holding her in a vise. A sanctuary. "I promise."

"Then please! Take me to the hospital!"

"I can't."

"You can! We'll get on the ferry and—" Eden stilled,

blinked, then wrenched free from his grasp. "Oh my God! You're still worried about Tyrone?"

"No." Rain's eyes hardened. "I'll kill Tyrone before he ever has the chance to touch you. But Eden—"

She leapt to her feet. "Bats *attacked* me, Rain! Bats! I don't know why, but they surrounded me and ... and ..."

Extending her arms, she studied the scratches in disbelief. It made no sense. Bats didn't attack humans. Not like those ones had, anyway.

Rain stood and dropped his hands onto her shoulders. "Eden, calm down," he said, his touch easing the pressure in her spine that she didn't want to be eased. "Everything will make sense once I tell you—"

"Tell me what?" She narrowed her eyes, daring him to lie to her again while her traitorous heart clutched to his, her soul aching to hold him, touch him, and for him to tell her that everything would be okay. But the fire she'd found leaving the restaurant returned to roar inside her. "All the secrets you hold? The darkness you try to hide? Why you're scared of Tyrone? Or why you're so afraid to love me even though you clearly—"

His arm snatched her around her waist, knocking any other words from her throat as her body collided with the hot, hard contours of his. Eden's hands flattened over his heaving pectorals as her knees weakened beneath his touch. But her gaze remained locked to his as his lips curled, teeth flashed, and he growled. Actually growled.

"Yes. To all the above. But you need to trust me, Eden. Let me take care of it. The hospital won't help you."

His blue eyes smoldered, captivating her as he looked at her like ... like ... "That doesn't make sense."

"I know," he said, brushing his hand through her hair. "And I'm so sorry that it's come to this, but I will fix it. I promise."

Her panic eased as she ran her hands down his rock-hard biceps. She might not know why, but she trusted him. Always had. Except this time, she deserved some bloody answers. "Okay. But can you tell me while I eat? I'm starving."

That delicious scent wafted through the room, making her mouth water and stomach rumble as she stepped away from Rain. It smelled so rich. Bitter and strong. Delicious. She inhaled and moved towards the bar.

"Finn made dinner, so come upstairs and—"

"But something sure smells good in—"

She grasped the fridge door just as Rain shouted, "Eden, don't open—!"

The seals popped and Eden drew in a deep breath. That was it. Delicious. Exactly what she wanted—

Eden froze. Meat. The fridge was chock-a-block full of raw meat. Big hunks of red flesh rich with creamy fat and pearly sinew clung to shining bone and porous marrow. Filleted cow glutes sat fanned on a tray while hunks of diced beef oozed and an entire leg of lamb lay upon a sacrificial shelf, all of it dripping with the sweet nectar of rich red blood pooling in the base of the plastic trays.

A scream ripped from her throat as Eden stumbled back and slammed the door closed. Her stomach roiled as she pressed her hands to her mouth and turned to collide with Rain's broad chest.

"Why do you have so much meat?" she cried, revulsion shuddering through her. "And why do I want to eat it?"

Because she wanted to. She wanted to sink her teeth into that juicy beef and lap up every last drop of juice. She wanted to consume and ravish the blood to nourish her body with the life force of every one of those dead animals.

Or at least part of her did. Part of her that she didn't understand, that had taken hold to override her conscience's desire to vomit. Eden pressed her hand harder to her mouth, unable to tear her eyes from Rain's as he caressed her elbows.

Then he cleared his throat, his voice serious as he said, "Eden, it wasn't a flying fox that attacked you. It was a vampire. And now, you're turning into one."

Though he said it calmly, the words clawed at Rain's throat, stopping his breath as everything inside him ached. This was wrong. This wasn't how it was meant to happen. Not how Fate had planned it. But he was out of options. He couldn't hide what was happening to her. Tyrone had forced his hand, and Rain had to reveal the truth well before Eden was ready to accept it. And as he watched her stumble backwards, her eyes wide and mouth a perfect O of horror, Rain felt every remaining thread of their barely formed bond snap.

His wolf howled in agony.

"Wh-what?" she squeaked.

He drew in a staggered breath. "Eden, trust me—"

"Trust you?" she cried, her eyes popping. "Are you serious? Do you hear yourself? Vampires? Are you crazy?"

"No."

Eden backed into the fridge, glanced over her shoulder, and jumped away with a yelp. "Is that why you have all that meat?"

"No. And I know it must sound unbelievable—"

"Vampires don't exist, Rain!"

"Yes, they do," he said, struggling to remain calm as she scrambled along the bench. He needed to be careful as he couldn't tell her everything too fast. Accepting the paranormal world was the hardest level of the mating bond to achieve and the one a couple more often failed at. It wasn't hard to fall in love and like each other, nor was it difficult to physically mate.

But an ordinary woman accepting that the monsters in fairy tales were real? If the other two levels were done correctly, it could be easy, like Finn and Ava had achieved. But Rain was barely holding onto Eden and, as a woman of science, how would she ever believe that most of the flying foxes she lovingly defended in Townsville were actually bloodsucking demons?

"Eden, there's a whole world you know nothing about. One no one knows about except those part of it."

She shook her head rapidly from side to side. "But why me? I'm not part of this! I don't want to be!"

Another string around his heart snapped. "You're in it because of me."

Pressing herself against the wall, she froze. "Are you telling me you're a vampire?"

Rain's face twisted in disgust as his wolf growled. "No. Vampires are foul, devious creatures of the night who can't venture out in sunlight."

The horror in her eyes faded a fraction. "Oh. Right. Then how do you know about them? Who exactly are you? Because I don't believe for a second that you're a government agent, unless they have some spooky section that employs the Scooby Squad."

Rain stopped advancing and he drew in a breath. "You're right. I'm not a government agent. *Or* part of the Scooby Squad. I'm a wolf shifter."

Time froze, his heart pounding like a jackhammer while the hair on the back of his neck stood on end. His wolf paced, anxiously awaiting her response.

But all Eden did was stare. Her mouth opened, then closed. After what felt like an eternity, she blinked her big, dark eyes.

"A wolf shifter? Like a werewolf?"

His wolf hunched his shoulders and sneered while Rain's

lips curled in a similar fashion. "No. Even though I'm beholden to the Moon, I am not cursed, and I have complete control over my shift."

"So ... you're telling me you can turn into a wolf?"

"Do you need me to prove it?" Shifting was the last thing he wanted to do right now, but if that's what it took, then so be it.

"Yes. No." She shook her head. "I don't know. This is crazy, Rain. Wolf shifters, vampires ... none of it is real!"

"And you think an innocent little fruit bat swooping down and biting you makes more sense?"

She opened her mouth, then raked her fingers through her hair. "No."

"Eden, look at me." His voice cracked as he stepped towards her, and it took every ounce of self-control not to pull her against his body as her eyes filled with fear. "You've known me a long time, yes?"

"I thought I did."

He resisted a wince. "I'm still the same man. Nothing has changed except now I can tell you with reverence that you are everything to me. My anchor. The reason I breathe. It's why I've kept you on the island because Tyrone knows that. But it wasn't enough. I thought resisting you would keep you safe, but it only blinded me and now Tyrone is one step closer to ripping you away from me forever. I have failed you and for that, I will never forgive myself." He dropped his hands onto her shoulders. "I am to blame for everything that's happened tonight, but I won't let Tyrone succeed. Because I love you, Eden. You are my mate and I will protect you until the day I die."

Every word released a lock upon his heart, freeing his soul as he spilled everything he'd longed to tell her. Yet she continued to stare, her chest heaving as questions flashed through her terrified eyes.

"T-Tyrone did this?"

"His minion. The bat. Lucas."

Her eyes widened. "Lucas ..."

"He used Ava to get to you tonight. And I will kill him for what he's done."

"You can't—"

"I can, and I will. It's my only chance of saving you, Eden. Lucas is a dead bat."

A dark, primal need rose inside him, consuming his soul as Eden swallowed and curled her delicate fingers around his wrists.

"You can fix this?" she breathed, and his chest swelled with both determination and dread.

"Yes. I can."

Exhaling, she nodded and inched away. "All right. I'll believe that. I might not understand it after all the lies you've told me, but you are my friend, Rain, and I do trust you. I need your help, and I'll do anything you say. But after that ... I never want to see you again."

Then she tore from his hold and bolted across the room, shattering every inch of Rain's soul as the door slammed behind her.

Chapter 13

Eden's legs shook as the sloping driveway propelled her away from Rain's house. Fear clogged her throat and her pulse pounded in her ears. She could barely breathe.

That meat looked so good …

Shuddering, Eden reached the street and toppled forward, bracing her hands on her knees before she could nosedive onto the road. She didn't want to believe anything Rain had said. It was like something out of a horror film, and she avoided those for good reason. That feeling of terror …

Eden buried her face in her hands, but it didn't block the memory of her screams echoing through her head. Of begging her father to slow down. The crushing sounds of metal as the boat crashed and she tumbled into the water. It didn't block the memory of her ten-year-old self curling up in a ball on the beach as night closed in, shivering in fear until the police had found her.

She never wanted to feel that way again. Never wanted to feel out of control like she was racing towards death. Her father might have found his that day, but she'd survived. And now … she was turning into a vampire?

Eden screamed and fell to her knees. It couldn't be true. She'd been attacked by flying foxes. She needed to get to the hospital so that they could pump her full of medicine only for her to die anyway. No one had ever survived lyssavirus.

Except ... flying foxes didn't attack people. Not with the viciousness that those ones had. But vampires—

"Eden."

"Ava!" Eden scrambled to her feet. "Thank God you're here," she cried, flinging her arms around her friend. "You'll never believe what happened. Rain thinks—"

She stopped herself just in time. As crazy as it might seem, she couldn't tell Ava Rain's secrets. But as Eden drew away, she caught the truth in her friend's eyes and leapt back. "Oh my God! Finn's one, too!"

Ava took Eden's hand and interlocked their fingers with a soft smile. "Come on. Let's go back to Luna Views and talk."

Too shocked to object, Eden followed Ava back up the driveway. A strange pull drew her attention towards the house, and as her eyes locked onto Rain watching them from the first-floor window, a shudder coursed through her. The house she'd once thought beautiful was now filled with nothing but nightmares.

She tore her gaze away, her heart a lead weight inside her chest.

"What were you doing out here?" Eden asked as she climbed over the unnecessary doors into Ava's tiny pink Mini.

"Rain's a battle master, Eden. He prepares for every contingency. He considered you might run, but he couldn't let you go far with the bats lingering."

Eden's hands tightened around her seatbelt as she glanced up at the sky. "Really?"

"Don't worry, Finn and the scouts are watching."

"The scouts?"

"The young wolves."

"So, you've seen them? Turn into wolves?"

Ava nodded as she drove away from the house. "Yep."

"How long have you known?"

"About two weeks. Since Blair shot Finn, abducted me, and turned into a monster."

"Blair's one, too?" This just got crazier and crazier.

"Yes, but a bad one. I'll tell you what I can, Eden, but I think you should let Rain explain."

Eden sank into her seat, her heart aching. Belly churning. She was still hungry and craved a nice big juicy—

Carrot! A nice, big juicy carrot!

"This is unreal. I can't ..." Shaking her head, she couldn't articulate what she was thinking. Not with Rain's words echoing through her mind.

You are everything to me. My anchor. The reason I breathe.
I love you, Eden.

She choked back a sob as tears prickled her eyes. He'd said everything she'd always wanted to hear. He thought they were soulmates, and yet she couldn't ...

"Are you okay?" Ava asked as they descended the hill towards Luna Views.

Eden shook her head. She'd never be okay again. "Just get me home, let me eat, then you can help me make sense of this madness."

"All right. We'll order black bean stir-fry. You'll feel better then."

She'd feel better if it was beef. Raw. *Or fresh blood straight from the vein ...*

Eden's face twisted, her stomach retching as Ava parked the Mini. They took the elevator up to Eden's room and while Ava ordered room service, Eden cleaned herself up in the bathroom. Rain must have wiped any blood from her neck and the scratches over her arms and shoulders, but the wounds still stung as she cleaned them with alcohol wipes from her vet kit.

Not that any amount of antiseptic would prevent her from contracting lyssavirus.

Shuddering, she couldn't think about that as she covered her marred skin with her comfortable pajamas, then ran a brush through her hair before leaving the bathroom. Sinking onto the lounge beside Ava, she drew a cushion to her chest.

Ava's hand fell to Eden's knee, tears filling her eyes. "I'm so sorry, Eden. This is all my fault."

"No, it's—"

"It is! I wasn't supposed to let you out after dark! Finn told me the bats were lurking, but ... Lucas called me." Ava sniffed. "At the hospital. I didn't even remember until Rain had gone after you, so Finn thinks Lucas compelled me. Through the *phone!*"

Eden stared, recalling the blank look on Ava's face earlier before she'd brushed off that phone call as a telemarketer.

"Then again, Finn could have told me that *Lucas* was the vampire, then none of this would have happened. Rain was so worked up, Eden. He's usually so calm, but tonight ... He was bloody enraged."

Eden dropped her gaze. "He said I'm his mate," she muttered, her heart tug-a-warring inside her chest. She knew enough about werewolves—sorry, wolf shifters—to understand what that meant.

"Yes, which I *also* only discovered tonight. If I'd have known, I never would have encouraged you to move on from him. I thought I was doing the right thing. I thought *he* was doing the right thing by not leading you on when he had a mate out there. But I should have seen the signs. The way you feel about Rain is exactly how I feel about Finn."

Eden hugged the pillow tighter as everything she felt for Rain unleashed in an overwhelming flood of agony. "It's excruciating, Ava. I feel like I'll never be free of him."

"And you won't, unless you want to be. That's the power

of the mating bond, Eden. Rain has no choice and even though I don't know how he's resisted you all these years—"

"You mean he knew?"

"It would have hit him like a freight train the moment he laid eyes on you. And he's been a slave to you ever since."

Eden's heart twisted. Did that mean everything he'd done had been out of obligation? When he brought her koalas, volunteered his time, or donated money? Did he feel he needed to? Or did he do it because he cared?

"But *you* have a choice, Eden. The mating bond is special. Sacred. To Rain, you're the woman the Moon Goddess has chosen for him. You complete him. Balance him. Strengthen him. It's not a curse, but a gift."

My anchor. The reason I breathe.

"And once you give into that bond ... It's wonderful. Trust me." If the sparkle in Ava's eyes and joy in her smile were anything to go by, Eden had no choice but to believe her. She'd never seen her friend happier than she was with Finn.

Could she and Rain have even an ounce of that?

"So ... this 'bond.' How did it happen between you and Finn?"

"I'll let Rain explain the supernatural elements, but you remember how quickly I fell for Finn, right?" Eden nodded. "That was the pull. I felt it the moment our eyes connected when he was on the jet ski, and so did he. That's why he fell off."

Eden choked on a laugh. "Really?"

As usual, Rain had been showing off for the ferry except this time, he'd been accompanied by a new skier who was crazier than he was, and she'd had Ava by her side. Finn had suddenly lost control and belly flopped into the water, sending Ava into a panic over a man she hadn't even known.

"That was the trigger. And you know how attracted I was to him from the start."

"Who wouldn't be?" Even she'd appreciated Finn for all his hotness and would have gone there himself if she hadn't already been in love with Rain.

"Exactly. The Goddess knew what she was doing when she gave them bodies like that. But you know how Finn and I fell in love."

She did, and now she understood why it had happened so quickly. "But how did you accept he was a ... a ... wolf shifter?"

"It wasn't hard. Blair had shifted into an ugly, twisted monster—the Unfated don't look as glorious as Fated wolves like Rain and Finn—and he was about to kill me when a golden wolf came to my rescue. He had the same hair as Finn, and I just knew." Ava smiled softly. "It didn't scare me, Eden. It felt right."

Eden drew her knees up to her chest. "I don't know. I ... I just ..."

"Are you scared of Rain?"

Eden hugged herself tighter. Was she? He was *Rain*. He might be tough, badass, and mysterious, but he had a heart of gold and loved with an intensity she'd never seen in anyone else. The way he cared about the koalas and the look in his eyes tonight ...

I will kill him for what he's done. Lucas is a dead bat.

She shivered. "I don't know. What happened tonight—" Eden stilled. "Oh my God, Ava. Blair's not in jail, is he?"

Ava slowly shook her head. "He returned the night of the of the full moon with an army of Unfated. And Finn killed him."

Eden's eyebrows shot up, shock rendering her speechless.

"The pack fought for me, Eden. Finn was right in what he told us—Blair wanted to keep me as a sex slave and then kill me. He'd have forced me to produce his twisted heir, then he'd be done with me. So, Finn had no choice. It was terrifying and

Blair almost got to me, but Finn killed him and found some long sought-after personal revenge, too."

Eden blinked, something inside her softening as another riddle was solved. "It didn't make sense that he'd been arrested."

"I had to tell you something. And though we expected Tyrone to retaliate, we weren't sure how. But when I told them you were out with Lucas, Rain bolted out the back door so fast the shreds of his clothes are still clinging to the trees."

Eden's breath caught. The dog. Fangs had sunk into her neck when a roar had thundered through her ears, and that big black dog had leapt out of nowhere.

But it hadn't been a dog. It'd been a wolf. Rain.

"He rescued me."

"And he was a bloody mess that he hadn't gotten there seconds sooner."

Eden shook her head, dumbfounded. She couldn't shake the image of that moment when he'd lunged, his teeth bared with a growl that had shaken the earth. "But how? I was in the middle of the street. Someone could have seen."

"I don't think Rain cared. Finn's a little worried about exposure, but we'll deal with that if we have to. The important thing is that Rain found you." Ava squeezed Eden's hand. "Even if it wasn't in time to stop this ... complication."

"Is that what you're calling it?"

"It's just a setback. Don't worry, Eden. Rain will fix this."

"He did say that," she muttered, fiddling with the hem of her shirt. "But I ..."

Eden winced as she recalled the determination in his face and desperation in his beautiful blue eyes. He'd said all the right things, and she'd—

"Eden, why did you run from him tonight?"

Groaning, Eden dropped her head onto her knees. "It was too overwhelming. Everything was right and wrong all at once.

I couldn't comprehend what he was saying and I ... I was ..."
She took a deep breath and lifted her head. "I was scared, Ava."

Understanding flashed through Ava's eyes. "You run from things that terrify you."

Eden's breath hitched. Yes, it was her major flaw, though was it such a bad one to have? The things Rain had said tonight *did* terrify her. He wanted to kill the man she'd almost dated.

But she'd been terrified on Mandalay Avenue and had never been more relieved to wake and find herself safe inside Rain's house. Because he'd always been her shelter. Her safe haven. She'd even wanted Ava to stay at Luna Views when she'd come to hide from Blair because Eden trusted Rain. It's why she was risking her career by staying on Maggie, no questions asked. Because at heart, Rain was a protector. A badass daredevil.

And he loved her.

Eden's eyes fluttered closed as she drew in a breath. "It's all too much, Ava. I need some time to think."

"All right." A knock sounded on the door and Ava stood. "But please. Promise me you'll talk to Rain."

Eden nodded and swallowed a panic attack. "I will. In the morning." Because no matter how much she wanted answers, she couldn't face him tonight. Not after she'd run out on him. Her friend. The man she loved.

A wolf shifter.

"Fine. But I need to call him to tell him you're okay."

"All right." Eden couldn't argue with that. "Now, let's eat because I'm starving."

For black beans. And noodles. And broccoli and onion.

Not blood.

Chapter 14

Rain prowled atop the granite boulder that was Hawkings Point Lookout and surveyed the dark landscape below, wind ruffling his blond-streaked, midnight-black fur. Everything was silent in the surrounding bush as he watched, listened, and waited.

Somewhere down there, Lucas lurked. Rain was sure of it. He might not know what the bat's game was, but like any predator, Lucas wouldn't venture far from his prey. Not while the taste of Eden's blood lay fresh on his bat-fangs and his job remained unfinished.

Not that Lucas *would* finish it. Rain would kill him before he got within a hundred meters of Eden.

He glanced over at Luna Views. Rain couldn't blame Eden for running. He'd expected it because even though he longed to be the person she turned to, Rain knew he'd lost that right. He'd kept too many secrets from her, made too many mistakes, and now her life was hanging in the balance. No endless amount of groveling would make up for the fear he'd instilled in her eyes, but he would do it.

After he found Lucas and gnawed him to pieces.

Lowering his head, he reached out through the pack bond. "*Anyone find anything?*"

"*Not yet,*" Kai replied. "*Though I think bats have been lurking here for a while. The stench is unbelievable.*"

Rain snarled as he glared into the bush across the road from Luna Views where Kai hunted.

"*Negative,*" Chad confirmed. "*Though Kai is right. They've been here a few days at least.*"

"*Bloody foul, disgusting creatures,*" Kai spat. "*Fuck me, do they ever bathe?*"

"*They stink like rotten flying foxes,*" Chad agreed.

"*Are you sure you're not hunting flying foxes?*" Rain asked as he knew that's exactly what the bats smelled like, the stench of musty ammonia having haunted his senses since his stare-off with Lucas at the hospital. "*How can you tell the difference?*"

Kai snorted. "*It's not their smell, it's their presence. Flying foxes have a life force. A heartbeat. Vampires have neither.*"

Rain huffed out a breath, not surprised Kai had worked that out. It made perfect sense. More often than not, a wolf relied on his nose to hunt, but they could also hear a heartbeat from miles away, and that was just as vital to a wolf when tracking their prey.

Hence another reason vampires were difficult to kill.

Rain growled and continued to pace beneath the waning moon. He should have known this would happen. Tyrone wanted to destroy his belief in Fate, so what better way to end his mating bond by not only killing her, but by damning Eden to an eternal life of darkness where he'd have no choice but to kill her himself?

Not that it would come to that. Rain would save Eden. All he needed to do was find Lucas and kill him. The sooner the better.

"They seem to have been lurking in the national park more than around Hawkings Point," Finn said, prowling the bush below Rain. *"I don't smell them here at all."*

"Probably because they knew I'd have caught them." Hawkings Point was Rain's favorite stomping ground and where he'd spent most of his nights roaming while Eden and her sweet, intoxicating scent had slept soundly in his house.

But how long had the bats been watching him? Watching her? Obviously long enough to know he'd been venturing deeper into the bush these past few nights in search of his damn brother, leaving his territory open for the bats to swoop in and infect the human most precious to him.

"Nate, how's it going on your end?" Rain asked, glancing at the resort.

"No problems here. Ava stayed with Eden in her room. They're both safe."

Kai chuckled. *"Girl slumber party. Reckon they're hanging out in their underwear?"*

Rain growled at the same time Finn barked, *"Ava's underwear is none of your concern!"*

"Get your head out of the gutter, Kai. Eden's sick and Ava's staying because I asked her to."

"Jeez, guys! Neither of you can take a joke."

"Wait until you mate, then you'll understand," Finn said.

Kai moaned. *"Oh, that'll be the day. She's going to be tall, blonde, and none of you fuckers are going to be allowed within ten feet of—"*

"Found them." Chad's deep baritone shut Kai up and Rain stood to attention.

"Where?"

"Swinging from a hoop pine just below Good Juju's Lookout."

Without hesitation, Rain leapt over the lookout's fence. He skidded down the sloping rock and jumped onto a large boulder before scampering along the trail, eventually veering off the path and dashing through the scrub. His heart hammered, wolf salivating as he raced over cairns and scratched himself on stinging trees. Gravel shifted under his paws as he slid down the hill. Of course, the bats had to make things difficult by lurking in the open on the edge of the mountain between the road and rocky shores below, but nothing would stop Rain. Not when the bastard was keeping vigil in the trees only meters from Luna Views. And since the locals should be sleeping this late past midnight, it was the perfect time to slay some vampires.

"*Don't approach them, Chad,*" Finn said. "*Wait for us.*"

"*I won't. There are five of them.*"

"*Fuck me ...*" Kai breathed.

"*You need backup?*" Nate asked.

"*Don't you fucking dare leave Eden unattended!*" Rain roared.

"*Remain at your post,*" Finn replied in a kinder tone. "*This shouldn't get out of hand. Right, Rain?*"

He snarled. "*Depends. I've never had to kill a bat before. And don't forget, they have one distinct advantage over us.*" Which the bats used to position themselves in their favor. There was no possible way Rain could scale a hoop pine and take a bite, though the thought of leaping from the road to snatch the cunning bastard out of the tree was tempting. It'd be a long fall onto the rocks below and it would bloody hurt, but not as much as losing Eden would.

No, the Goddess might have given the wolves the power, strength, and endurance to kill the bastards, but if Rain were to have a chance of killing Lucas, he had to be in vampire form.

So, he scampered up the worn path from Rocky Bay Beach, reached Good Jujus Lookout, then ran down the boardwalk, risking exposure for the second time tonight. He was only a hundred meters from Luna Views when the foul, squalid stench of bat assaulted his nostrils.

No, not bat. *Vampire*.

"*Shit!*" Chad cried as Rain himself watched five sets of wings drop from the hoop pine and swoop onto the path. Shadows twisted as five tall, white bodies unfolded from the ground and Rain skidded to a halt, his claws digging into the plastic of the floating boardwalk.

The middle vampire drew to his full height and stepped forward, sneering as his dark eyes glistened with malicious victory.

"I can tell you one thing, wolfie. She tastes gooood."

Rage powered Rain's hind legs as he lunged at the vampire and opened his jaws.

Only to tumble through shadow and roll into his landing. Fuck! Springing back onto his paws, Rain glared up at the screeching bats as Chad's chestnut wolf jumped the fence from the road, and Finn and Kai thundered up the boardwalk.

Forming a line, the four of them lowered their shoulders and growled as the vampires shifted further up the path. Not that they needed the height advantage of the incline when the fuckers could fly. At least their fatal flaw of cockiness would work to Rain's advantage.

Lucas stepped forward. "Shift, little wolf. Then we'll talk."

"*Fuck me*," Finn muttered. "*Why do they always call us 'little?*'"

"*Inferiority complex*," Kai muttered as they shifted.

Rain stood tall on his two legs, rolling his shoulders back as he faced his enemy. "Tyrone has sent you to your death, vampire. That woman is my mate!"

The bastard cackled. "Which made it even more satisfying to sink my teeth into her neck and hear her scream."

Rain growled, ready to slay the bastard with his bare hands. But Finn's firm grip wrapped around his biceps and held him back. For which he was frustratingly grateful for as Rain wasn't equipped for such a battle. Not yet.

"You could have stayed in your roost and lived in peace, but you have fallen for the lies of a rebel wolf who promised you what?"

Lucas jutted his chin. "He promised me a bride. And since I have no wish to live near a pack of fucked up Fated wolves, who better to turn into one of my kind than your mate?"

Chad grabbed Rain's other arm as another growl resonated from his chest. "Eden will never be yours!"

Lucas scoffed. "She certainly wanted to be last week when she was gazing into my eyes and longing to accept *my* generous donation to her stupid hospital."

"Only because you compelled her!"

"I made her feel wanted. Special. *Heard.* All you ever did was break her heart by—"

"*Car!*" Finn shouted.

Rain hit the deck, falling to his belly with the rest of the pack while the bats vanished in a cloud of shadow. Seconds later, headlights passed over the boardwalk as some fucker took a post-midnight drive into Nelly Bay.

Once Finn deemed the coast clear, Rain followed him to his feet, glaring death at the bats as they cackled overhead.

"I was trying to protect her from the likes of you! From Tyrone!"

The bats swooped so quickly that Rain could do nothing other than throw his arms over his face, growling as he turned and watched them shift further down the boardwalk.

"And that was stupid of you, wolfie. A bonded mate is far safer than an unbonded one. Once she turns, you'll be left to die a lonely, rejected wolf as you'll never get a second chance while your original mate still walks this earth."

Fire scorched through Rain's blood. "She will not turn! I will kill you and save her!"

Lucas scoffed. "You'll have to find me first. And when you can't, you won't have the balls to save her the easy way."

Then he and his cronies shifted, screeched, and shot into the night sky. Rain's legs bulged as he longed to give chase. But Finn held him back.

"Not now, man. We need to strategize."

Rain gritted his teeth and drew a deep breath, but it did nothing to settle the rage coursing through his veins. Rage at the bats, at Tyrone, and at himself.

Because the undead fucker was right. He'd left Eden vulnerable and if he didn't find him—

Wait. "There's another way to save her?" he asked, turning to the pack.

Chad and Kai exchanged glances while Finn scratched his stubbly chin.

"I don't know ..." the Alpha said. "As far as the lore's concerned, you kill the vampire before his victim turns and you reverse the curse, saving them."

Chad nodded and ran his hand through his spikey hair. "That's my understanding too."

"But if there's another way ..." Rain's frown deepened as he stared up at the mountainous terrain where the bats had vanished. It was probably foolish to hope for something a vampire said was true. Lucas was surely baiting him. But if there was another way, would it be easier than killing the bat? That was the way Fate had intended it, and Rain wouldn't dream of completing the task by any means not depicted by his Goddess. Nothing was worth the consequences of acting against her will.

But Eden's life was at stake. The woman the Goddess had intended him to love, honor, and protect. He loved Eden. Worshipped her. Adored her. He wanted to lay the world at her feet and shower her with gerberas, bubble baths, and the most sophisticated high-tech koala hospital in the country.

Wouldn't he risk everything to save her?

Damn straight, he would. He'd prove that bat wrong. He'd promised Eden he would save her, and he'd already let her down too many times by not prioritizing her.

He would not do it again.

Chapter 15

Eden arrived at the hospital the next morning determined to find a sense of normal. Caleb would have started cleaning and restocking leaves, but she had morning rounds to do and a grant proposal to complete, which was more vital now that she no longer had a new benefactor to help buy her drones.

She placed her bag away and sank into her desk chair. Even after Ava's explanation about wolf shifters and vampires, Eden couldn't wrap her head around it. Yes, what happened last night wasn't normal. Bats did *not* attack people with such targeted ferocity, and it certainly sounded like something straight out of one of Ava's favored paranormal romance novels. Sure, Eden had once read that kind of thing, but then she'd grown up, become a scientist, and even though she still enjoyed a good book, she believed in facts. Vampires did *not* exist, and she would ignore the hunger in her belly because her breakfast of whole wheat pancakes had fulfilled her nutritional requirements, thank you very much.

Even if their usual fluffy sweetness had tasted like cardboard on her traitorous tongue.

Ava strode into the office, having stopped outside to take a phone call from Finn. "The scouts have looked at your car and there's nothing wrong with it. Just a disconnected battery."

Eden rolled her eyes, having suspected that would be the case. "And if I had half a brain about mechanics, I wouldn't be in this mess."

"It's not your fault. You did exactly what I would have done."

"No, you'd have called somebody."

"Maybe, maybe not. You were frustrated about being stood up and felt like a walk. I understand that."

But any other time she'd have called Rain, and he'd have come in a heartbeat. He always did. Except she'd been stubborn, determined not to rely on him when he didn't love her.

Moments later, he'd been saving her from the bats.

Guilt clawed in her belly as she grabbed the stethoscope off her desk. "I should have known better."

"Hey, if anyone should have known better, it's me. I should have recognized the mating bond between you and Rain, but instead, I encouraged you to give up on him and date that monster."

Eden shook her head. It still seemed so unreal. Lucas? A vampire? He'd been so ... charming. So nice. So attractive with depthless eyes that she'd found so incredibly ...

Soulless.

She shuddered. "I can't believe I fell for his charm. I should have known there was something ... I don't know. Fake about him?"

"Don't be so hard on yourself. How were you supposed to know he was a creature from Hell with an unnatural allure? That you were compelled to fall for his charm rather than the fact he was *actually* charming?"

"True," she muttered, understanding now why her heart had protested so much. She belonged to Rain. But even though she understood Ava's hesitancy to explain the lore of the paranormal world, the whole "bond" thing did Eden's head in.

Yet, she couldn't deny it. She'd been Rain's the moment he'd strode into this hospital, and it had nothing to do with how drop dead sexy he was.

Okay, maybe a little, but the tug inside her had been more than desire. More than lust. More than oh-my-God-he-looks-hot-with-a-koala. She'd always known they were meant to be.

But how could that connection between them be real if it'd been determined by a force she didn't believe in? Did Rain truly care about her? Or was he simply giving into the will of his goddess?

Sighing, Eden lifted her gaze to the ceiling. "Men aren't worth this shit."

"Maybe not, but don't forget, you were compelled by an undead creature of the night and I was targeted by an Unfated wolf shifter. That was unfortunate, but at least it led us to find the beautiful, protective men we were meant to be with. I have Finn and you have Rain."

"I don't have Rain," Eden muttered.

"You will once you talk to him."

"And say what? 'Hey, you love me because some spirit told you to?'"

"Not a spirit. The moon."

"Like that's any better."

Ava's eyes softened. "You didn't see him last night, Eden. The man was *wrecked*. You're the most precious person in the world to him. The mating bond is the strongest thing these guys ever feel. It's tough to forge and even tougher to resist. Finn didn't even last a week before giving into it. But Rain resisted for two years hoping to keep you safe, and Tyrone got to you anyway."

Eden felt a headache coming on. "I still don't understand how breaking my heart was meant to keep me safe. And I can't deal with this right now. I have koalas to check on and that proposal to finish, so can we just get to work?"

Ava sighed as she moved past Eden and into the hallway. "Fine. I'll start on Archie and since you're better at talking to animals than people, perhaps you can ask Xena about how it feels to be bitten by a bat."

Eden's eyebrows shot up as her friend marched down the hallway. "Wait. What?"

Ava pushed open the ICU door. "You wanted to know what bit Xena. Now, you do."

Eden blinked, clutching the stethoscope around her neck as Ava disappeared. A *bat* had bitten Xena? A vampire? But ... why?

Eden took two steps towards the ICU, then halted and ran her hands down her face, barely resisting the urge to claw her eyes out and scream in frustration. She had so many questions, yet she dreaded the answers. Ava might have accepted this crazy new world, but dammit, it'd been much simpler when she'd thought Rain was a government agent on a covert mission to bring down the Townsville Underbelly and avenge his sister-in-law. She hadn't liked the idea of him putting himself in danger, but it had made sense. It'd been plausible and noble and somehow very normal.

Not like this war between Fated and Unfated wolf shifters and the curse humming through her veins.

No, not a curse. Curses were a work of fiction. Poison, maybe, one that had affected her blood, heart, and darkened her sense of morality. But if it was poison, then there should be an antidote. So, was that what Rain had meant when he'd said he'd save her? Did he have the antidote?

Eden shook her head and strode outside. No, her pulse might be racing, but it couldn't be poison. Her affliction was more like a virus, which meant all she had to do was wait it out. Eden didn't know when the last time she'd been sick was as with her excellent diet and regular exercise regime she hadn't caught a cold in years, let alone a nasty airborne virus. This one might be in her blood, but she should be able to overcome it with plenty of fluids, rest, and good food.

Eden unlatched Xena's gate and smiled morosely at the bundle of gray fur curled among the gum leaves. "So ... a bat, was it?" she asked, examining the healing wound on the koala's shoulder. "Poor darling. Did it suck your blood or—"

Eden gasped as she recalled the night Xena had been attacked. Rain *had* mentioned flying foxes being in the area and after Eden had defended the misjudged mammals, Finn had suggested they were "vampire bats." Eden had laughed him off, saying that vampire bats only lived in South America and in the end, she'd settled her curiosity by deciding it'd been a strange sort of dog bite.

But ... why would the bats have attacked the innocent koala? Did they have something against the native wildlife? The poor animals already had enough factors threatening their extinction. They didn't need the villains of the paranormal world trying to kill them, too.

Sighing, she rubbed Xena's back and ignored the urge to scratch the scab hidden beneath her collared T-shirt. "Don't worry. I'll look after you. We won't let those nasty bats get either of us, will we?"

She hooked the stethoscope into her ears and pressed the bulb to the koala's fluffy white chest. Xena's heartbeat was strong and steady, her skin elasticity much improved, and her fur looked healthier, too. The young mum had certainly come a long way and hell, if the koala could survive a vampire attack, then Eden sure could.

Though by all appearances, Xena seemed to have only been a snack, whereas she, apparently, was turning into one.

"Ridiculous," she muttered, examining Xena's claws. "You need to die and rise again to become a vampire, right?" And unless there had been more to her blacking out last night, then she was still very much alive.

Yet she left Xena's enclosure with the koala's heartbeat echoing in her ears.

"Morning, Doctor Eden!"

She jumped and spun around, pressing her hand to her chest as Caleb entered through the back gate. "You scared me."

"Sorry," he said, his smile slipping. "How's Xena?"

"Good. We hope to reunite her with Cookie this week."

"That's excellent. She was having a great old climb when I was cleaning the enclosures this morning. I was about to fetch everyone fresh leaf."

"Good work." Caleb was certainly her most enthusiastic volunteer and she could always rely on him to be there cleaning and cutting leaves long before she arrived at a reasonable work hour. "I'll be checking on Archie if you need me."

"Righto. I've already ground up more leaf for his medicine."

"Thank you."

She smiled at the young man, then gathered what she needed from the treatment room before slipping inside the ICU. Ava had completed her mobilization and moved onto the koala kindergarten, so Eden sank to the ground beside his basket and pinched the skin behind his neck, grimacing as it softly deflated. Poor little guy was still dehydrated. He'd remained stable but had barely moved and slept far too much, even for a koala.

"It'll be okay, Archie," she said. "We'll get you feeling better in no time. But first, I need you to eat for me."

Picking up the syringe filled with ground gum leaf and a touch of soy milk, Eden slipped it between the koala's teeth. He jolted as she slowly pressed the plunger, then seemed to chew and took most of the food. Though he didn't lift his head, and his eyes remained closed.

She sat with Archie a little longer, ensuring he ate and offering him both care and comfort before checking in with Ava.

"I'll finish with Marco, then check in with Xena before Finn picks me up," Ava said. "He wants you to stay here, inside, and someone will be around later with your car."

Eden resisted an eye roll as she'd been told twice already this morning. "I know. I don't want to go anywhere anyway."

With all she had to do, the last thing she needed was to sneak off and find herself in trouble with the vampires.

Chapter 16

Ava left and Eden shut herself in the office away from the strange thumping of tiny hearts and the metallic smells as she started work on her grant proposal. Caleb stopped by when he'd finished adding branches to Xena's enclosure just as one of her wildlife carers, Paula, arrived with Cookie, but Eden let the young man set the joey up in her enclosure. She couldn't risk being around the koalas right now.

She worked steadily for another hour, determined not to think about the strange events of last night. She'd become efficient at writing grant proposals over the years, but it never got any easier to explain why you needed someone's money. When she was satisfied with her progress, she pushed to her feet and strode out to the enclosures to find Cookie happily nestled in her new tree. She'd thrived in home care and appeared healthy as Eden completed her checks. But now, it was time to get her back to her mum.

"How did you get away from the bat attack?" She had to wonder. Xena and Cookie would have been in the tree and, considering their injuries, Eden doubted they'd fallen. "Did Mama climb down the tree to help you get away?" It's usually what koalas did as, like any mammal, they were fiercely protective of their young. Xena would have tried to defend Cookie against their predator, and Finn had said he'd found her beneath a log.

"She's a good mama," Eden said as she reached for some leaves. "We'll put you back with her soon, I promise. But I'm glad the bats didn't get you. Mama barely survived and your skin is much more pliable. And thin." Smiling softly, Eden leaned closer to the little koala. She sure was cute with her big eyes, fluffy ears, and long nose. Of course, all baby animals were cute, but Cookie ...

Eden's nostrils flared, her chest expanding as she drew in a deep breath. "I bet you taste good ..."

Her hands tightened around the branch, hunger rising inside her and igniting her veins. Cookie blinked her big black eyes, munching on leaves as Eden leaned closer and—

Jumping away from the tree, Eden pressed her hands to her mouth and shook her head in horror. No. No, no, no ...

"I'm sorry, Cookie! Oh my God, I didn't mean it! You know I'd never eat you." *Or suck your blood dry.*

Shuddering, Eden wrapped her arms around herself and squeezed. Hard. Bile burned in her throat as she backed away from the koala.

This wasn't happening. It was just an aftereffect of the attack. Her mind playing tricks on her after the stories Rain and Ava had told. She ... she wasn't ...

Turning, Eden ran out of the enclosure and locked herself inside her office. Pressing her back against the door, she took a deep breath. In ... and out. In ... and out. She needed to relax. Calm down.

But Cookie's pulse continued to hammer inside her head.

Whimpering, Eden slipped down the door into a squat and clenched her knuckles to her lips. Her heart raced. Belly groaned. She was hungry. So hungry. She had a chickpea curry and pasta napolitana in the freezer, apples in the fridge, and three fresh salads to choose from for lunch, but while her tastebuds craved them, her body wanted something else. Something dark. Sinister. Evil.

Tears filled her eyes. This was crazy. Wrong. Her legs wobbled, and she sat, hugging her knees to her chest. Her shoulders shook. Belly clenched.

But she couldn't deny that a cursed virus was plaguing her bloodstream all because she'd fallen for the wrong man. And not just Lucas. *Rain*. He'd lied to her, broken her heart, and because the fucking moon had determined her to be his soul-mate, a vampire had targeted her to be his next meal. Or lover. Or whatever it was a vampire wanted when he turned a human into a member of the undead.

But why? What had Rain ever done to Lucas? Or Tyrone?

Eden groaned as her heart tugged in that unique way it always did when she thought about Rain. She knew she couldn't avoid him forever. He was the man with the answers and, apparently, the means to save her. If she wanted to fix this and understand, then she needed to gather her courage, steel her spine, and talk to him. She'd been in too much shock to accept what he'd been saying last night, but perhaps after he answered her questions, everything would make sense.

Though the thought of Rain shifting into a wolf ...

Eden shuddered as she pushed to her shaky feet. Yeah, she'd need to see that to believe it.

Poking her head out of the office, she checked the coast was clear, then stole away into the tearoom. It was too early for lunch, so she grabbed an apple in the hope it would satisfy her cravings. Eden sank her teeth into its juicy flesh, delighting in the crunch and sweetness on her tongue.

Then her lips twisted with the urge to spit it out.

"Deal with it," she muttered. "That's all you're going to get."

She sat and ate slowly, employing mind over matter. She loved apples. They and mango were her favorite fruits, but mango season remained a few months away and her freezer full of frozen mango was unfortunately being neglected at home in Townsville.

She was halfway through her apple when the front doors opened. "Hello!"

Eden shot to her feet at the desperate shout. Leaving the tearoom, she found a young couple inside reception, the woman peering over the desk while the man held a koala wrapped in a beach towel.

His shoulders sank. "Thank God. This guy's been hurt. Badly."

Eden gestured them towards the treatment room. "Come this way. Where did you find him?"

"On the walk to Balding Bay," the woman said. "He was sitting at the base of a tree about five minutes up the hill. We know we should have called, but he was easy to wrap up and bring in."

"It's all right." Eden preferred that her trained volunteers retrieved the koalas, but if they were within easy reach or on the ground, people often brought them in. They seemed to be carrying him rather appropriately, but she'd still check the little fella for bruising around his ribs. "Place him down here."

The man laid the koala on the exam table and as the towel fell away, the scent of blood filled the air. Eden's shoulders hitched. Inhaling, she drew the delicious, bitter aroma into her lungs as she stared at the gray lump on the table. The koala was still conscious, though tiring quickly thanks to the gash on the back of his head and the scratches on his nose and shoulders.

His big, dark eyes met Eden's, and her mouth salivated.

"We're not sure what happened to him."

Eden swallowed. And again. She silently counted to three, then took a breath ... and shuddered.

"Are you okay?" the man asked. "You are the vet, right?"

Eden tore her attention from the scratches and glanced at the man. "Yes. Sorry. Um ... you didn't see what hurt him?"

The couple shook their heads as Eden snapped on a pair of gloves, ignoring her strange cravings. "It could have been anything. A dog, maybe." Though the scratches appeared too shallow to be a dog. "Koalas also get into fights with other koalas, especially the boys."

She tapped the koala's nose as the couple exchanged glances.

"So ... he'll be okay?"

"I think so. He's upright, which is a good sign. I'll check him out and clean him up. Then I'll keep him here until he's strong enough to go home."

Relief flooded the woman's face. "Thank you."

Eden rubbed the koala's ears. "It's what I do. Thank you for bringing him in. If you leave your name at reception, you can drop by to check on him later."

"Okay." The man took the woman's hand and backed towards the door. "Thank you. Good luck, big guy."

Once the couple left, she examined the koala more closely. "Your claws look a little scratched. Did you try to fight them off, buddy?"

She traced her finger along the scratch over his forehead, and he twitched. He'd certainly been clawed at, but she doubted it'd been a dog. Dogs mauled and their attacks were far more brutal. Koalas were unlikely to survive a dog unless they managed to escape where the dog couldn't follow, so it seemed more likely that another koala had hurt this fella.

Though the markings weren't consistent with that scenario either.

The little man tried to move, and Eden tightened her grip. "Just a minute, buddy. You need to let me look."

But as she parted the fur to examine the gash on his shoulder, Eden froze. Thick, red blood oozed over pink flesh and trickled down to mat in the soft, gray fur. She stared, mesmerized. A steady thumping filled her ears as her tongue darted out to wet her parched lips.

Blood. Deep red blood. So fresh. So warm. Her thumb traced the laceration and the koala kicked, but she didn't care. The wound shouldn't require surgery. A stitch or two and this little man would be fine. She'd fix him soon. But right now ...

Eden released the koala and stared at the dark smears on her gloved fingers. A clot clutched to her thumb—round, sticky, and oozing with delicious goodness. It looked like a cherry. A thick, plump, gooey cherry.

She fucking loved cherries.

A tingle shot through her as her lips parted. Her breath quickened. One little taste. Just a drop. She was hungry. So damn hungry. Her mouth watered. Hand lifted. Power unlike any she'd ever felt surged through her body as she opened her mouth—

"*Rrrrragh!*"

Eden jumped out of her skin as the koala released a painful bellow. Gasping, she held her hands out in front of her and blinked in horror. Shit, what was wrong with her? Chest heaving, she glanced around the room, then at the koala. Blood. So much blood. And ... if she tasted it ...

Eden screamed. She lifted her hands to her face, paused, and screamed again. Scrambling backwards, she hit the wall and rummaged in her pocket for her phone. Blood smeared the screen as she swiped, tapped, and pressed the phone to her ear. She couldn't breathe. Couldn't think. What the fuck was—

"Ede—"

"Rain, help me! I want to eat the koala!"

Tears filled her eyes as she pressed her bare arm over her

nose and mouth, but it did nothing to block the stench of blood.

So much blood.

"Don't, baby. I'm coming."

Hiccupping, she squeezed her eyes closed and focused on his voice. Deep. Determined. Comforting. She exhaled. "I'm scared."

"I know you are," he said gently, and a sob strangled from her throat. Blood filled her senses and the room spun. She wailed. "Eden?"

"There's blood on my phone. My hands. It's everywhere!"

Shaking, she stared at the juicy, clotted blood-cherry. Hungry. So hungry—

"Get out of there, Eden."

She didn't need to be told twice. Dropping the phone, she ripped off the gloves and ran out of the room.

She collided with Caleb in the hall.

"Watch the koala and call Dee!" Her nurse could take care of his scratches. "I ... I need ... give me a minute!"

She ran down the hall, skidding into reception as the doors flew open with a bang.

And there was Rain—tall, broad, and sinfully sexy with his dark hair curtaining his face and eyes wide in alarm. Eden gasped, her breath catching in her throat seconds before he crossed the room and caught her crumbling body in his arms.

"I've got you, baby. You're safe."

The dam broke. Tears spilled from her eyes and the strength to fight them vanished as she clutched at his T-shirt, the air warming around her as her breath burst from her lungs in great, heaving sobs. "I-I'm sorry!"

"You have nothing to be sorry about," he breathed, brushing his lips over her hair. "Just let me take care of you. Okay?"

She nodded, and as he lifted her into his arms, her earlier

determination for independence shattered. She couldn't deny what was happening to her. She was hungry. The thirst for blood consumed her. Filled her mouth with longing and her heart with desire unlike a bowl of berry porridge ever had.

And that terrified her. She couldn't fight it alone. She needed Rain. He was the only person who could help.

Eden snaked her arms around his neck and buried her head against his warm, hard chest. "Take me home. Please."

His stubbly mouth brushed her forehead. "Yes, baby," he whispered, before turning around and clearing his throat. "Caleb. Doctor Eden is on leave until further notice."

Then he carried her outside into the sunshine.

Chapter 17

"**I**'m really turning into a vampire, aren't I?"

Rain's eyes softened as he settled onto the lounge beside her. "Yes, baby. You are."

Eden shivered beneath the blanket draped over her curled legs and clutched her mug of tea. She wasn't surprised Rain had been lurking outside the hospital keeping watch over her. He'd been scouting the surrounding bush for bats when he'd received her call, hence the seconds it'd taken him to arrive. Once Rain had settled her into his Lexus away from the smell of blood and incessant drumming of tiny koala hearts, she'd stopped crying, and they'd driven across the island in silence. His hand had rested comfortably on her knee as though it was the most natural thing in the world, and her terror had eased, leaving only an echo of fear humming through her veins.

And lust, though that was nothing new. Just perhaps reborn into something far stronger and out of her control as she glanced at the man she'd loved for two years and saw him for who he truly was. Not just her friend, but a warrior. A protector. A man of legend who'd swept her to safety, tucked her up on his lounge, and made her a cup of tea in the hope it would stop her from shivering.

All while pulsing with the power to kill the creature who'd cursed her.

Acknowledging that—believing in the impossible—settled the turmoil raging inside her head and intensified the pull in her belly.

"But ... don't you need to die to become a vampire?"

"There are two processes," Rain explained, caressing her ankle over the blanket. "A vampire can drain you and force feed you blood to complete the change, or their bat can infect you and let you complete it yourself. I suspect he chose option two as it's more effective at torturing us both."

She nodded and gazed into her tea. "I never thanked you—"

His hand tightened around her foot. "You don't need to thank me. I should never have let this happen in the first place."

"It's not your fault. I'm the one who wandered alone in the dark."

"Yes, but—"

"Let's not do this." She was too scared to play the blame game. "Just tell me how we stop it."

Rain shot his hand through his wild hair. "I need to kill the bat who did this to you. The vile creature is working with Tyrone, who you should know is—"

"Ava told me about Tyrone. And that Blair's dead, and Tyrone's seeking revenge."

"Right." Rain's thumb brushed the inner arch of her foot, and her skin tingled. "I should have known he'd use the bats."

Eden's heart clenched at the fury in his eyes. "Is it hard to kill Lucas?"

"I won't say it'll be easy. Battles between wolves and vampires seem to never end. We're both strong, fast, and powerful. One bite from us will debilitate a vampire, but we need a second in its throat to kill it. And they're just as capable of killing us with their super strength and breaking our necks."

"Not to mention they can turn into bats."

"Exactly. It's why centuries ago, bats and wolves agreed to stop trying to dominate the other and live apart. Vampires settled in the cities and we wolves generally remained in rural locations. We still hate how they treat humans, but no one can stop all the evils in this world. They enjoy feeding off humans but rarely turn them, which is why you were vulnerable." Rain's beautiful face twisted. "I didn't expect it. Feed from you, yes. Try to kill you, yes. But turn you? That bastard is going to fucking pay."

Rain's eyes flashed as he pressed his thumb into her foot. She didn't doubt he'd kill Lucas. In fact, he'd take great pleasure in it. And she would let him.

Eden ignored the thrill that thought created in her belly. "What will happen to me in the meantime?"

"The power will slowly take over your body until you give into the hunger, consume blood, and are reborn as a member of the undead."

She shuddered. "So, like a virus?"

"Don't try to explain this with science, Eden. This is a dark power that works against Fate and everything I believe in."

So, it was more like a curse, then. She'd rather it be a virus since she understood viruses, but she could work with a curse. Curses could be broken. "So, all I need to do is resist the taste of blood?"

Rain nodded. "Though your hunger will grow stronger, and you'll feel sick, tired, and maybe even feverish."

Wincing, she leaned over to place her tea on the coffee table. "Great. But ... I can do it."

"You can."

"Just not forever as I'll need to do surgery again, so I hope you can kill him quickly."

"I will. Because ..." He paused, pain filling his ice-blue eyes. "Eden, you only have seven days."

She blinked. "Seven days until ... it consumes me?"

It took him a moment, but Rain's gaze remained on hers as he said, "Seven days until you die."

Eden's hand flew to her mouth, but Rain caught it before she could cry out, leaving her breath to catch in her throat as her chest began to heave. She was dying. Actually dying. It was like she was back in that speedboat racing towards death unable to save herself except this time, death would be slower as she grew sicker and—

"Eden. Baby, breathe."

She blinked, her memories fading as Rain inched closer, his hands caressing her face as his thumbs brushed tears from her cheeks. She drew in a shuddering breath and choked it out.

"Slowly," he coached. "Come on, baby. Don't be afraid."

She saw the promise in his eyes, his determination, but it did little to ease her fear. "I ... I don't want to die."

His hands hardened around her face. "You *won't*. I promise. You die, I will die, and that sure as fuck isn't happening. Trust me, Eden. This fucker will make a game out of me hunting him and drive me insane, but I will get him."

She believed him. How could she not when his mouth twisted, teeth flashed, and fury darkened his face? Yet still ... "I hate not having control, Rain. I've rushed towards death. I can't do it again!"

She squeezed her eyes closed against the onslaught of tears, and found herself pressed to Rain's chest, his strong arms holding her tight.

"I know. And it's okay to not fuel fear. To not chase it. I understand." She'd told him about that day in the boat, her reckless father, and her fear the third time she'd refused to ride on his jet ski. "But I need you to trust me. I will hunt Lucas and kill him long before the seven days are up. He won't have gone far. He'll be watching you. Craving you. He admitted—"

Eden pulled out of his hold. "You've spoken to him? When—?"

"We hunted him last night, and the bastard gloated his intentions. I'd have gone for the bite if I could have, but going into battle without a strategy is a death sentence. So tonight, the pack and I will devise a plan."

Rain seemed so certain that Eden didn't question him as she focused on normalizing her breathing. "So, what does he get out of this? Why would he risk his life for Tyrone?"

"We've established a few possible reasons," Rain said, easing back now that her tears had stopped. "We know Tyrone wants to destroy our belief in Fate, which basically means killing our Fated mates."

"Like why he went after Ava? And what happened to Shelby?"

Rain nodded. "I tried to hide our bond so that you wouldn't become a target. But apparently, Tyrone knew about you and sent the bats not only to take you from me forever, but to make you walk this earth undead until I had to destroy you myself."

Ice chilled Eden's blood. "He wants you to kill me?"

"It would give him great pleasure," Rain muttered through clenched teeth. "It would be the only way I could move on because I'd never get a second chance to mate while you still walked this earth. Undead or alive. Though I doubt *I* could do it as we can't kill our Fated mates."

Eden shuddered. Fuck, this Tyrone was a cruel, twisted bastard.

"But like I said ..." Rain clasped her hand. "I promise I won't let Lucas or Tyrone take you from me. My purpose in life is to protect you."

Rain's jaw hardened, passion filling his eyes. His hand squeezed hers, and Eden's heart fluttered.

"Because we're Fated mates ..."

"We are."

"And you've known that since the day we met? When you brought me Pixie?"

"No. I knew the moment I saw you in the supermarket a week earlier."

Eden's eyebrows shot up. "What?"

"I walked in and bam, there you were. You wore a white cotton dress and knocked me right off my hinges. The bond triggered and having just buried my sister-in-law days earlier, it scared me to death."

Eden's stomach sank as she struggled to recall that day. It must have been the weekend she'd returned to the island as it'd only been a week later when she'd met Rain and Pixie.

And he'd loved her all this time. Just like she had him. He'd been suffering the same torture and yet ... "I guess I understand why you were scared. Ava said mating is frightening for you wolves."

"It's thrilling and terrifying in equal measure. We never know if we will like our mates or fall in love with them, which is why I tried avoiding you. But when I found Pixie, I took it as a sign that we should meet. I watched you examine her, saw your devotion to the koalas, how big your heart was, and I knew that the Goddess had been kind to us." He grinned. "I'm one lucky wolf, Eden."

Everything inside her softened as Rain's hand snaked around her waist and he inched closer. She'd waited for this moment for so long, to hear him say these words and see her feelings mirrored in his eyes. But he *had* resisted her, and that had hurt worse than this insatiable hunger.

"Yet when I asked for more ..."

"I couldn't take the risk, no matter how much my wolf

and I wanted you. Now, I see I was wrong. I'm not perfect. I make mistakes. But you lived in enemy territory and your safety was my priority. As you know, I tried many times to keep you on the island." Rain lifted her chin and forced her gaze to meet his, his eyes dark and cheeky. "I've encouraged you to work here full time. I've offered to sponsor your hospital to make it happen. But you wouldn't accept more than a measly amount to keep the koalas fed."

Eden couldn't suppress the guilt that rose inside her. "It just seemed wrong. Especially when you wouldn't love me like I wanted you to."

"I know. But my offer always stands. I'll give you anything you want. Nothing is too big or too small."

She smiled weakly. "Your bank balance isn't endless. Besides, I have enough sponsors to keep me going. You're one of the biggest, but this other guy—" Eden gasped, her spine straightening in equal parts shock and outrage as she shoved Rain's hand away. "You—you *cheeky wolf!*"

It was *him!* Her anonymous donor, the Cheeky Wolf, who gave a shitload of money every month and was one of the main reasons her doors remained open.

Rain lifted his hands in defense. "I'm not sorry. You wouldn't accept the money directly from me, and I'll do anything to keep you on Maggie Island." His arm wrapped around her waist again and, unable to fight him, she let her legs fall from the couch as he pulled her against his warm, muscular body. "I want you to have everything, Eden. Including the best koala hospital in the country."

She sank against him and inhaled his woodsy, salty scent. "But I'd have stayed on the island if I'd known I could have you, too."

Rain's lips dropped to her brow. "You have me, Eden. I am yours and nothing will change that. I am bound to you, connected to you, and at the mercy of your every whim. Resisting you has been fucking torture."

The small, evil part inside her thought it served him right, but she couldn't bring herself to relish that. Turning her head, she pressed her face to his chest and embraced the comfort of his hold as his warmth was the only thing keeping her uncontrollable shivering at bay.

She was so cold. So hungry. "And now?"

Rain lifted her chin. "I'm done fighting it. After watching Finn mate and become Alpha, I realized that I've been a fool and that neglecting my happiness only harms the pack. It weakens me, hurts you, and I don't want to do it anymore."

Tears prickled in her eyes as he took both of her hands in his, intertwined their fingers, and pressed them to his wide, warm chest.

"Eden, you are my mate. My best friend. I want to forge our bond and solidify our connection not because it's what Fate intended or because it'll strengthen my pack, but because I love you. With everything I am, I am yours. Everything I have is yours. And it's about time I stopped playing the victim to Tyrone, the martyr to my brother, and seize what I truly want. Which is you."

Tears rolled down her cheeks. "You love me."

He nodded vehemently. "I do."

"Because the Moon told you to?"

"No, because I love *you*. My friend. You're smart, caring, and your passion for animals is inspiring. You're also stubborn, strong, and aren't afraid to fight for what you believe in. You changed me, Eden, and gave me something to hope for when it felt like I'd lost everything that ever mattered to me. The reason I long to help Sly and kill Tyrone is for you. So that you and I can be together. Because Eden ... life without you isn't worth living. And I don't want to experience it any longer."

Eden melted against him. "I don't want to live without you either, Rain. Because I love you. I always have."

He lifted their clenched hands and brushed his thumb over her chin. "I know, baby."

It was the moment she'd longed for, the words she'd always wanted to hear. She hungered for his touch. His kiss. But not even desire could break through her insatiable thirst for blood, and she turned her head away.

"So, how do we form a mating bond? Don't you bite me or something?"

"No." The word snapped from his mouth and her eyebrows lifted at the horror in his tone. "I mean, I could, but that's not the way the Goddess intended it. You see, the bond needs to form on three levels." He drew her against his chest again, where she nestled comfortably. "And you might be surprised to learn we've already completed two of them. The first we formed years ago. It's the emotional level, where we accept we care about each other."

"I'm not surprised about that," she whispered, and Rain chuckled.

"No. I thought we lost it last night, but it's still there. The second level you completed today when you accepted you were turning into a vampire and called me. You acknowledged the paranormal world existed and welcomed my wolf into your heart. It's usually the hardest level and therefore the last to complete."

"I still can't wrap my head around the whole vampire and wolf thing. But considering how much I wanted to drink that koala's blood ..." Eden shuddered. "I can't deny that I'm turning into a monster. And I need to believe that you can save me."

Rain's arms tightened around her. "I will save you. Mark my words."

"And I trust you, but it still seems a lot easier to just bite your mate and be done with it."

"That's how the rebels do it," he said, his voice darkening. "Even though they don't believe in Fate, they still meet their mate and they don't care to do the hard work. So they bite them and take away their mate's free will. To seal the bond properly, you, Eden, need to choose to be with me on all three levels. And that means you can leave whenever you like."

Eden's spine softened. "I'll never leave you."

"I hope not. It would rip me to shreds and doom me to live alone and rejected. When you asked to move out, I felt you pulling away and had never been more terrified in my life. Until I saw Lucas sink his fangs into your neck."

Eden cringed. She couldn't believe she'd even fallen for Lucas with his slick hairdo and clean-shaven face when Rain was so much … *more*. Wilder. Exciting. And far sexier with his long hair, bearded jaw, and a smile that never failed to weaken her knees. He loved her, wanted to spend his life with her, and they would forge a bond so strong that—

"Wait!" She lifted her head. "What's the third level?"

Rain quirked his eyebrow. "What do you think the third level of a 'mating bond' is?"

His hand hardened on her back, and Eden's skin heated. "Oh."

"Yes." His throat worked as his gaze darkened. "But while I've dreamed of sealing our bond and loving you, Eden, I won't. Not until you're one hundred percent human again."

Oh, how she'd dreamed of it, too. But she wouldn't allow herself to ponder such pleasures as with great pangs, she agreed with him. She wanted to feel present and strong when she first made love with Rain. Wanted to feel alive. And that wasn't possible when she wanted nothing more than to give into her fatigue, sleep, and not wake until Lucas had been killed so that she could escape this gnawing hunger.

So she nodded, her breath catching as Rain pressed his forehead to hers. Her eyes fluttered closed and their noses brushed, his stubbly jaw scraping her cheek as their breaths mingled. Then she cupped his face to feel those prickles against her palm before spearing her fingers into his long, luscious hair.

He held her silent, unmoving, breaths apart and hearts thumping in almost synchronized beats. She longed to stay in that moment forever.

But then his nose rubbed hers once more, and he lifted his lips to her forehead. "Will you move back in, Eden?"

"I'm not going anywhere, Rain." She ran her hand down his tan throat to rest on his large, strong shoulder. "I'm where I've always wanted to be."

"Thank you. I'll have Ava bring your things over from Luna Views, but I want you in the room next to mine. Upstairs is too far away in case ..."

"The bats get me?"

"Yes."

"Okay. Or I could just stay with you."

She didn't know where the suggestion had come from, though she meant it without hesitation. But Rain's eyes simply glittered as his mouth stretched into that wolfish grin she loved so much.

"Oh, Eden. I might have resisted you for two years, but even I don't have that much self-control. Don't forget, you know the man. But deep down, I'm a fucking animal."

A thrill shot through her as he kissed her once again on the forehead, then drew away. But she didn't move, captivated by his piercing blue eyes. She watched his jaw tick beneath his stubble. Watched his lips part. And as his heart beat against hers, she surrendered as her own heart wept with the joy of coming home.

Then her stomach growled, vision blurred, and she jolted away as hunger clawed up her throat.

Rain shot to his feet. "Can I get you something to eat?"

"Sure. Whatever's in the fridge downstairs would be nice."

She meant it as a joke, but Rain's eyes flashed with anything but humor. "That fridge has been emptied. You'll find no meat in this house and the scouts are having a feast."

"I'll have to meet these scouts."

"You will. They'll be here tonight to prepare for the hunt. One of them will stay with you and Ava. Now, I'll make you some porridge."

Eden frowned. "It's lunchtime."

"Yes, but I haven't become a chef overnight. I have no pasta, and porridge is what I know how to make."

Shrugging, she lay down and nestled her hands beneath her head. "All right. Thank you, Rain." After all, porridge was good at any time of the day.

"No worries. With apple and cinnamon?"

"You know me so well."

"Of course. You're my mate." And with a smile, he squeezed her shoulder and strode towards the kitchen.

Chapter 18

Rain returned to the lounge with a steaming bowl of porridge only to find Eden curled up asleep. Blowing out his breath, his shoulders relaxed as he placed the bowl on the coffee table and sat down beside it. Eden might be sick, shivering, and terrified out of her mind, but with their bond strengthening, his wolf couldn't help but howl with pride. She was so beautiful with her hands tucked beneath her creamy cheek, her dark hair cascading over her shoulders and plump lips gently parted. He'd barely slept last night and had been in constant turmoil until she'd phoned earlier. He'd sensed her unraveling and the fear in her voice had slain him. Yet the moment she'd skidded out of that hallway, the air had pulsed, and he'd sprung into action. Their connection was growing in ways Rain had never expected and telling Eden the truth about his feelings, saying those three little words and hearing her say them back had eased the tension inside him. She'd accepted him for who he was and she wanted to stay, both of which fueled his urge to kill Lucas, face Tyrone, and end this war. Because after sending Lucas after Eden, Rain wanted Tyrone's head on a spike. And he meant that. Literally.

But he couldn't get ahead of himself. Right now, he had to care for Eden like he would if she'd been thwarted by any other virus.

Placing the back of his hand on her forehead, he winced. She was like ice. He ensured the blanket was tucked around her, then raced to the cupboard to fetch another. Draping the thick quilt over her, he pressed his lips to her forehead and his heart burst from his chest. He loved that he could do that. That he could touch her, hold her, and watch her while she slept.

Yet at the same time, a soul-deep ache consumed him. He couldn't imagine what she was going through. He knew what terrified her and even though his jet ski, jet boat, and even skydiving was perfectly safe, all she saw was the speed and adrenaline ending in fear and death. She'd been ten years old when her reckless father had lost control of his speedboat going way too fast and crashed into rocks. Thankfully, Fate had saved his beloved that day, but her father had died, and she'd sat on the tiny beach for seven hours before police had recovered her.

She'd never been on a speedboat again. And while he often teased her about skydiving, he'd never asked her to join him on the water since she'd shared her story that day on the jetty, moments before she'd tried to kiss him. She was afraid of taking a risk, of facing danger. And now, she faced a slow, painful death. Hunger she couldn't control. Urges that scared her. What she felt wasn't normal, and if there was anything he could do to stop it, he would.

So, what was the easy way to save her that Lucas had taunted him with?

Exhaling, Rain twisted off the coffee table, slid to the floor, and leaned back against the lounge. His wolf was restless, reeling from last night's events and the questions that gnawed at him. The urge to escape to the bush and hunt overpowered every one of his senses. He needed to find Sly and learn what he knew about the bats. His brother had spent two years with a vendetta against the slimy creatures and knew more about the lore than he'd ever let on. Rain knew how killing vampires was done in theory and teamwork was vital, but Lucas's threat continued to haunt him, echoing inside his head.

You'll have to find me first.

Rain's breath hissed between his teeth. Vampires were stealthy at the best of times, and the older they were, the more powerful. And Rain had a feeling that Lucas was very, very old.

But it was his other remark that taunted him even deeper.

You won't have the balls to save her the easy way.

Swallowing a cry of frustration, Rain shot his hands through his hair. Sure, killing a powerful vampire who didn't want to be killed couldn't be easy, but how else was he supposed to save Eden?

Maybe his brother might have an answer, but to find him, Rain needed to hand over the responsibility of hunting Lucas to the pack, and he couldn't do that. Not tonight. Eden was *his* to protect. He had to put her first no matter how desperate he was to seek his brother out and beg him to rejoin their fight.

Considering options for tonight's hunt, Rain sat and listened to Eden's steady breathing for a while, then stood to slip her porridge into the fridge. He kept himself busy completing trivial work tasks until the sun dipped towards the horizon and he started dinner. The scouts would have to deal with vegetables tonight or go hungry as he filled a pot with water to boil chickpeas.

A few minutes later, Finn arrived after wrapping up the day's jet boat tours with Eden's bags tossed over his shoulders while Ava trailed behind with Gracie tucked under her arm.

She placed the pathetic excuse for a dog on the ground, then rushed to Eden's side. "How is she?"

"She's slept all afternoon. Shivering on and off, but I've been keeping her warm."

Ava touched Eden's forehead and flinched. "She's like ice! Is that normal?"

"I expect so," Finn said. "We're not sure, but it makes sense."

"Vampires are cold-blooded and undead," Ava muttered, pulling Gracie into her lap as the little dog trotted over. "I'm glad she called you, though. Did you guys talk? She had so many questions, but I didn't want to overstep."

"She knows everything she needs to know," Rain said, taking potatoes from the fridge and glancing at Finn. "You can put her things in the room next to mine."

Finn nodded and strode down the hall. Rain actively avoided Ava's gaze as he grabbed the peeler and unleashed his anger on an undeserving potato.

"Rain?"

"Hmm?"

"I'm sorry I yelled at you last night. And for what I said."

Potato skins went flying as his hand clenched around the pathetic piece of plastic. "It's okay. I understand. And I'm sorry, too. I can't believe that bat *compelled* you over the phone." It was simply unheard of, and another reason Rain suspected Lucas was old and very, very powerful. And that terrified him.

Ava remained silent for a moment, then asked, "Do you want some help?"

"No, keep Eden company. It's hard for me to leave her, Ava, but I need to hunt with the pack tonight. I want to be the one who kills the fucker." He threw another peeled potato into the bowl. "So, I need you here to know she's not alone."

Finn's footsteps padded in from the hall. "I also need you

here to keep you both safe. While we're hunting, one of the scouts will stay with you."

"You still think Lucas will try to turn me, too?"

"Tyrone wouldn't object. Until that bastard's dead, I'm not leaving either of you unguarded, day or night."

Ava's gaze dropped back to Eden. "Okay ..."

Finn's shoulders relaxed a fraction as he turned to the fridge and grabbed a bag of carrots. Then he leaned towards Rain and whispered, "What are we cooking?"

"Sweet and sour chickpea curry. It's Eden's favorite."

Finn frowned as he extracted a handful of carrots. "And how do you make it?"

"Winging it." Rain slapped the peeler into Finn's outstretched hand. "Though I doubt it's any different to sweet and sour chicken."

"And how do you make that?"

"No idea."

But Rain wasn't worried as he prepared the vegetables and set brown rice to cook. He heard the scouts arrive downstairs, then the elevator pinged, and heavy footsteps skipped into the living space.

"All right! Bat killing time!" Nate cried, before huffing out a breath when Rain smacked his hand to the kid's chest.

"Quiet. Eden's sleeping."

"She's here?" Kai rounded the lounge to stand beside Ava. "Shit. Has she always been that pale?"

Chad threw his hands in the air. "Dude! She's been bitten by—"

"I know, but I didn't think the infection would progress so quickly!"

"She *is* paler than most people," Ava said gently. "Though, no. She's not usually this white."

"Fuck." Kai shot his hand through his long, auburn hair. "She sure is pretty, though. Lucky you, man."

Rain glared at the young wolf. "Stop ogling my mate and get your ass over here."

Kai rolled his eyes and turned his smile to Ava. "He's just as bad as your mate."

Finn cleared his throat. "Kai. Pack meeting. Now."

"Man, can't we eat first?" Nate groaned, rubbing his belly as he sank onto a stool at the island counter. "What's cooking, anyway?"

"Chickpea curry."

He frowned. "Chicken curry?"

"No. Chick*pea*."

"What the fuck is a chickpea?" Kai asked.

Rain grabbed a tiny pea from the bag and flicked it at the wolf, hitting him square in the forehead. "A far superior food to chicken. And I gave you all my meat, so don't complain."

"Oh, we're not," Nate chuckled as Kai leaned his elbows on the bench.

"Fine. Beats fighting over the last slice of pizza, anyway."

Rain drew in a sharp breath. "I specifically told you, no junk food!"

Kai and Nate exchanged confused glances.

"Pizza doesn't come out of a packet," Nate said.

"It's carbs. And protein."

Rain gritted his teeth and flicked another chickpea at the scouts. "Don't pull that crap with me. You know better."

Finn crossed his arms over his chest. "Rain's right. Do you want to be warriors?"

Nate's shoulders squared. "Yes."

"Sorry, boss." Kai had the decency to look guilty as he straightened. "Won't happen again. We have a fridge full of fine meat now, which we appreciate. And we will eat our vegetables."

"Good. Now, set the table. We'll eat, strategize, and then it's time to hunt."

"Whoohoo!" Nate fist pumped the air and sprung off the stool.

Minutes later, Rain was contemplating whether he should consult Google on how to make the curry when Ava's soft voice whispered, "Hey. How are you feeling?"

Rain dropped his phone onto the counter and crossed to the lounge, resisting the urge to nudge Ava aside as he knelt beside her and met Eden's sleepy eyes.

"Hey. You okay?"

"I ... I don't know," she said, sitting up. "How long was I asleep?"

Rain settled beside her and wrapped his arm around her shoulders. Outside, the sun had truly set, leaving the jetty illuminated in glowing pink lights as Townsville sparkled in the distance. Was it a coincidence that she'd woken as darkness fell? He didn't know, but it wasn't a good sign. Nor did he like that she was cold. So cold.

"You've been asleep all afternoon," he said, rubbing his hand up and down her arm, though it didn't seem to generate any heat. Shit, Kai was right. He might never have witnessed the turning of a vampire, but he hadn't expected these symptoms to present so quickly. "We're just making dinner. Your favorite. Sweet and sour curry."

Her eyes glittered with their usual mirth, and the fear in his spine eased. "I thought you said you hadn't become a chef."

"I haven't, which is why you woke just in time. I have no idea what I'm doing."

"You never know what you're doing in the kitchen."

"Not when it comes to the culinary masterpieces you create, I don't." Though he could roast a leg of lamb better than any of them.

"I'll help you."

She stood before he could stop her and stumbled a step.

Rain leapt to his feet and grabbed her around the waist as she fisted the front of his T-shirt. "I'm so hungry."

"I know," he whispered, pressing his brow to her temple and holding her tight. "But you can fight this. We're all here to help you."

"We?" She glanced towards the kitchen. "Oh. Hi."

Nate and Kai leaned against the island bench, both grinning as Nate waved and Kai wriggled his eyebrows. Chad stood with his arms crossed and shook his head before sparing Eden a polite smile.

"Hel-*lo*, Eden," Kai said. "Welcome to our world."

"K-Kai? You're a ... shifter, too?"

"Damn straight. You didn't think all these muscles came from hiking, did you?"

Rain's jaw clenched. "Yes, you know Kai." His wolf growled as he shot daggers at the young man. "And Chad, too. This is Nate, and he runs the watersports with Finn. One of them will be staying with you and Ava tonight while we hunt."

Her eyes widened as her hand flattened over his chest. "Do you know where Lucas is?"

"He won't be far."

"We'll find him," Finn said, sounding more confident than Rain felt. "But first, let's eat and make a plan."

Rain nodded. "Eden, how do you make your sauce?"

"Sweet and sour? The main ingredients are sugar, vinegar, and pineapple."

"Damn." Rain's shoulders sank. "I don't have a pineapple."

"I do!" Kai shot his hand in the air like an overeager preschooler. "How many do you need? One? Two?"

Rain frowned. "You have a bloody pineapple, yet you've been eating pizza?"

"Ahh, yeah, bro." Kai looked at Rain like he was demented. "What the fuck is pizza without pineapple?"

Chad groaned. "Oh, man—"

"Pineapple doesn't go on pizza!" Nate cried, slamming his fist on the counter.

"Yes, it does! Ham and pineapple, bro. What else?"

"Meatlovers!"

"But we're supposed to be eating *healthily*." Kai winked at Rain. "And see? You thought we were eating junk."

"Pizza *is* junk," Finn said. "Putting fruit or vegetables on it doesn't negate the cheese and processed meats. Now, stop bickering and go get the pineapple."

"One should be enough," Eden supplied, her eyes sparkling.

"Oh man ..." Nate shook his head. "I don't get it. Pineapple in a curry?"

"Pineapple's the bomb!" Kai said. "And you like sweet and sour shit."

"Yeah, sweet and sour *pork!*"

"What did you think sweet and sour was made from?" Eden asked with a laugh. "That pork is covered in pineapple juice."

Nate groaned and Kai roared with laughter as he ran out of the kitchen. "We're eating healthy tonight, Nate! Gotta be big and strong to kill the bats!"

Eden giggled, and Rain slapped his hand over his eyes. One day, the scouts would grow up.

Chapter 19

Fed and energized, Rain stood with his pack around the dining table and consulted their map of Magnetic Island while Ava helped Eden settle into her new room. He wasn't sure how he'd get any sleep with her mango and eucalypts scent torturing his neglected libido through the thin wall, but he would exercise restraint. His wolf could go fuck himself.

"Two bats spent the day hanging from a fig tree outside the pub," Chad said with a sneer. "But I doubt either of them was Lucas. Right at sunset, they took off towards the golf course."

"He must be close though," Finn said. "Lurking. So, let's get a bite on any vampire we find and interrogate them. Understood?"

The scouts nodded.

"They should be in vampire form while they hunt, and that's when we'll catch them," Rain said.

"And they'll hunt animals," Chad told them, confidently. "They keep their humans on a tight leash in Townsville, so they won't risk exposure by feeding off some random person. Not when they don't have the local cops to hide the body."

"Then, they should stick to the bush," Finn said, before jamming his finger on the map. "Kai and I will search near the golf course. Chad, look in the bush near Cockle Bay." Finn turned to Rain. "Do you want to stay close and check out Hawkings Point?"

"Yeah, because I don't think he's gone far."

"So, I'm on guard duty?" Nate asked.

"Yep. Just don't eat the rest of that curry," Rain said, as it hadn't escaped his notice that Nate had gone back for not only seconds, but for a third helping of dinner. "That's for Eden. Don't forget, she's hungry."

"But she craves blood. Will food even satisfy her?"

"She's still human," Rain snapped.

"But what if—"

"No." Rain thumped his fist on the table. "I don't want to hear any other options. We will kill the winged bastard before he forces her to change. I will *not* have her turn into a vampire."

Finn clamped his hand over Rain's heaving shoulder. "We've got this, man. We don't want to lose her either. Or you." He glanced at the scouts. "So, let's go kill some bats."

RAIN VEERED off the tourist trail as he scoured the headland, sniffing every familiar tree, shrub, and rock. But all that greeted him was the scent of moss, pine, and wallaby. No bats. No stench of death. Finn and Kai located a pair of slimy shifters, and Rain had to restrain himself from tearing across Picnic Bay to join them. Instead, he tuned into the wolves' side of the interrogation. Finn was a straight shooter, and his Alpha tried and went for a bite, but the insidious vampires got away.

By the wee hours of the morning, Rain's frustrations

reached a whole new level of violent as they called it a night. Scampering through the trees, he leapt into his backyard and shifted, shoving his fingers through his hair and pulling as he padded across the cool grass to where Nate waited on the veranda.

"This bastard is going to drive me feral," Rain growled.

"I'm sorry, man."

Shaking his head, Rain glared out into the darkness and wrangled with his control. He couldn't risk losing his shit when Lucas was likely watching, lurking in the darkness and cackling to himself.

Blowing his breath between his teeth, he turned to Nate. "How are things here?"

"Eden and I had a good night. She's cool to talk to. But I'm glad she's yours as I don't understand how anyone can hate the ocean."

Rain resisted a snort. "Of course you wouldn't."

"But I'm happy for you, man. She's special, and it's my honor to help you save her."

"Thanks, Nate." Rain clapped the scout's shoulder. "Head on home and get some sleep. See you tomorrow."

Nate nodded, stepping off the veranda as Rain strolled into the house towards the kitchen. He'd hydrate, shower, then check on his mate before he—

A gasp pierced the silence, and Rain's gaze lifted to connect with Eden's wide eyes. Shit, she was awake.

And he was naked.

Heart lurching, he turned his back to her, his hands falling to cover his crotch as he glanced over his shoulder. Eden stood by the lounge with his bedspread cocooned around her. "I thought you'd be asleep."

"I ... I just ..." Her voice pitched. "I'm nocturnal."

He hissed out a breath. "You're not a vampire, Eden. Nor will you be."

She nodded, pressing her lips together as her gaze trailed down his back. Heat shot up his spine, and his cock stiffened beneath his hands. Fucking hell, that was the last thing he needed. He had no problem with nudity and if it was any other night, he might be tempted to shed his modesty in the hope of making her blush. But no matter how much he ached for her, Rain gritted his teeth and wrestled the animal inside him back into its cage.

Now was not the time to act on his primal desires.

"Give me a minute," he muttered as he shuffled sideways into the hall. Out of sight, he exhaled, dashed into his bedroom, and pulled his boxers up his legs. Thankfully, he wasn't too dirty as a shower would have to wait. But fucking hell, he'd better save her humanity soon because the way she'd stared at his bare ass ...

Rain took a moment to smirk, then forced his libido back into hibernation as he returned to the lounge. Eden sat curled up in the armchair, looking so small with her dark hair tumbling over the blue stripes of his bedspread that she'd wrapped around her shoulders.

His ribs squeezed. "Sorry about that. I thought you'd be asleep."

Her eyes lifted and roamed down his bare chest. "I don't think I can sleep."

Fear filled her dark eyes as Rain crouched before her and gripped her knees through the blanket. "You can, Edes. You're still human. Are you feeling any better?"

"The same. Hungry. Fatigued. Feverish."

"Did you eat?"

"I had soup. And bread. And managed to spare Gracie."

Rain smiled softly. "That's good. So ... why'd you steal the blanket off my bed?"

"I'm so cold," she whispered, burying her face in the blue folds. "I had another hot shower, but I couldn't stay in there all night. Nate grabbed the blanket and found me some socks, but I've just been drinking tea and curling up to stay warm."

"Doesn't help that the temperature's dropped either. But I know what might warm you up."

Knowing he'd regret this, Rain stood, scooped his arms beneath her back and legs, and lifted her out of the armchair.

Eden gasped. "What are you doing?"

"You know wolves run hotter than the average man, right?"

She blinked. "I read that in *Twilight*."

Rain rolled his eyes, refusing to comment as he carried her down the hall and elbowed open the door to his room. It wasn't how he'd imagined it'd be the first time he invited her into his bed, but his chest swelled as Eden took in her surroundings. His suite wasn't as open as the one upstairs, but it didn't disappoint with the impressive view over the balcony, generous ensuite, and the large wooden sleigh bed that dominated the space.

Her gaze lingered over the mattress, the blue sheets rumpled and pillows askew after Nate had taken the bedspread, then lifted to his, her eyes brimming with lust and her breath shallow. "I thought you were an animal."

"I can be," he breathed, his jaw clenching and arms tightening around her as he suppressed his wolf. "But I'm also a gentleman, and my only intention tonight is to keep you warm."

Even though he was certain it'd kill him.

Rain laid her down on the bed, the mattress dipping as he knelt beside her. Rolling Eden to her side, he made quick work of untangling the blanket and scooted in behind her before tossing it over them both. He spread his fingers over the flannel covering her belly and drew her against his chest, tucking her head beneath his chin before trapping her legs under his thigh.

"Is that better?"

"Ahuh," she whispered. "Never felt warmer."

Neither had he as desire waged war with the turmoil raging inside him. Eden intertwined her fingers with his, and his every fantasy came to life as she wriggled in his arms and nestled their hands by her head. With her boobs squished between his biceps, Rain closed his eyes and subtly shifted his pelvis away from her gorgeous ass. If only she wasn't dressed in layers, he could run his hands over her soft skin and feel—

"Any luck on the hunt?"

Exhaling, Rain welcomed the conversation. "Finn and Kai found two bats. They tried to get a bite, but they kept shifting, throwing taunts, and then took off. I searched Hawkings Point for Lucas, but nothing."

"I thought you said he wouldn't go far."

Gritting his teeth, Rain stared out the window where the crescent moon continued to wane. "He shouldn't have. He'll hunger for you, Eden, and crave you until you turn. But I couldn't find him."

"You said he'll be hard to find ..."

Yes, but that didn't ease his guilt at letting her down. "Vampires are stealthy, but I won't stop. Besides, come the sixth of seventh day, he'll come for you to complete the change, and I'll get him then."

She shuddered. "Please get him sooner."

Rain's chest squeezed as he dropped his lips to her hair. "I will, baby. Trust me." It was a promise. "But if I don't get him by Friday, I'll have to leave the hunt to go find my brother. He might be able to help."

Eden's forehead crinkled, her toes rubbing over his calf and shooting heat straight to his groin. Rain drew in a breath and wriggled back.

"Your brother? I thought he'd left?"

"He didn't go far. He's been roaming the bush ever since we buried Shelby."

"You mean ... as a wolf?"

Rain exhaled. "Yep."

"Wow." She twisted her neck to glance up at him. "I thought he was just away, traveling while he grieved."

"I wish it was that simple. But nope, he's taken to the wolf full time."

She frowned. "How does that work?"

"It's not natural," Rain admitted. "We're supposed to be men in control of the wolf. We're not meant to let it take over. But Sly has been a wolf for two years now and I'm afraid he might never come back."

Concern etched her pale face as she rolled onto her back. Rain didn't fight it, dropping his thigh from hers as she brought their clasped hands to her chest. "I'm sorry, Rain. That's awful."

"Yeah, it hasn't been easy. Helping Sly has been my sole focus as I need to bring him back to the man he once was. It's part of why I resisted you, so that I wouldn't flaunt my mate in front of him. And why I started the Full Moon Party, to cover his tortured cries that echoed across the island every month."

Her eyes widened. "I remember that. There were all sorts of rumors circulating about something dark lurking in the national park."

Rain untangled one of their hands and stroked her arm. "I needed to put an end to those rumors. Sly hasn't made life easy for me. I would leave meat every night, but it took months before he'd come near me. We spent a few full moons together, but then he stopped coming. It's why I called Finn, to help bring down Tyrone. He's a Warrior of the Moon Goddess who has helped many packs in the past. But after we killed Blair, Finn assumed the role of Alpha, and Sly sank deeper into the bush."

Eden's mouth twisted. "So, how do you think he can help?"

"Sly's been waging war against the bats since we learned they were spying on us, so I wonder if he has ideas about how to defeat them. And how to save you. I searched for him before you were bitten, but he wasn't in any of his usual hang-outs, and it's a big fucking island."

"And most of the national park's inaccessible."

"For you, maybe. But even for a wolf, those boulders and mountains can be hard to climb. Besides ... I fear Sly's too far gone."

Only with Eden in his arms could he confess what scared him most.

"I'm sorry, Rain."

"Don't be sorry." He tightened his arms around her as she turned onto her side to face him, drawing her close until her breasts squashed against his chest. Her nipples pebbled beneath the flannel and breath caught as she stared into his eyes. Rain swallowed a groan and hooked his foot around her calf, moving her legs until he had her slender thighs wedged between his again. His cock stiffened and belly burned, but he kept inches separating their hips and used conversation as a distraction. "I'm the one who should be sorry. If I hadn't been so focused on Sly, I wouldn't have fought our bond. If we'd mated, you'd have been safe. You'd have been strong. *We'd* be strong. I might have become Alpha, taken on Tyrone, and saved my brother. But I was a coward."

Her eyes flashed as she pressed her hand to his chest. "You are *not* a coward, Rain. You are the bravest person I know. But we all make mistakes." Her cool fingers spread through his chest hair, and his pulse spiked. "Mine was not fighting for you when I loved you so much."

He pressed his hands into her back, shifting his hardening

body again. "I love you more than life itself, Eden. And I promise, I'll always do right by you."

"I know you will," she whispered, her eyes softening as she ran her fingers over his jaw, his beard bristling beneath her touch. Rain's breath caught as his gaze dropped to her plump, pale lips. He longed to kiss her, to ravish her mouth with his and every other inch of her slender, delectable body. But he knew that if he did, he wouldn't be able to stop.

"The bats aren't as easy to fight as I'd hoped," he confessed. "In theory, yes. They'll be out as vampires at night to feed, but they're tricky bastards and take flight at the drop of a hat."

"Yeah, and they're quick. I know a little about bats. *Real* ones, that is. Flying foxes roost during the day and feed at night, so it makes sense that vampires—" Her eyes widened. "Wait! Are they *all* vampires?"

"No, trust me. There are plenty of flying foxes in Townsville, Eden. The bats just use them as cover. And they might be flighty little fuckers, but they'll fight as vampires. They're stronger that way, but we're quick and can take the brunt of their attack as we heal fast."

"But you can't get hurt, right? You said you were invincible."

"Broken bones still bloody hurt, and I can't survive everything. With the right weapons or attack, a wolf can be killed as easily as any man."

Eden bit down on her lower lip. "Now you're scaring me."

Rain took her hand and brushed a kiss over her knuckles. "Don't be scared, baby. The pack and I have trained for this, and we have each other's backs. Vampires are only out for themselves, and with one of our bites, they lose their shift. With another, they're dead."

Eden nodded. "Was Lucas the one who hurt Xena?"

Rain's eyebrows quirked. "You know about that?"

"Ava told me. And I think a bat attacked that koala today, too. So, do you think they're feeding on my koalas? Because—"

He pressed his finger to her lips. "No, Eden. The koalas are safe. I make sure of it."

Her gaze searched his as he slid his finger down her lip and away. "You really care about them, don't you?"

"Yes."

"Because of me? Or—"

"I started caring because you cared, but I've honestly developed a great love for the little guys. Which is why Sly called me when the bat attacked Xena. And no, it wasn't Lucas. It was another vampire."

"But why would it have bitten Xena? Considering their poor diet, koalas don't taste good. Even dingoes spit them out in the wild. Although the blood today ... Oh, God."

Eden shuddered, and Rain hugged her closer. "Don't think about it. You won't eat them. You're safe."

Eden buried her face against his chest. "I could hear their pulses ..."

"You can't now."

She curled into herself, her legs twisting tighter with his as she whispered, "I can hear yours. What if I—"

"You hear mine as not only is your head pressed against my heart, but because my heart is yours, and you'd be able to hear it beat even without this infection coursing through you. You are my mate, Eden, and we're connected. My pulse is your pulse."

Her body softened. "Is that true?"

"Yes, baby," he murmured, brushing his lips over her creamy forehead. "The mating bond is so powerful that once fully formed, we'll practically be one. And do you know what else?"

"What?" she breathed.

"You can't eat me."

She stilled. "Really?"

"Really. A vampire's teeth can't penetrate a wolf's skin, let alone your measly human canines."

Eden uncurled her fist, spreading her fingers over his pecs before slowly lifting her head. "That makes me feel so much better because, Rain ... you look delicious."

He smiled as his hands hardened on her back. "I bet I do taste good, Eden. And when I kill that flying fucker, I'll let you taste, lick, and suck any part of me you want. But you won't get my blood."

Eden's toes curled as her fingers brushed down the hard ridges of his quivering belly. Fire ignited in her eyes and dammit, he longed to let her feast on him. His wolf hungered for her kiss, to feel her tongue trace his abs and her mouth around his cock as she drove him to madness. He wanted to kiss every inch of her body and bury himself between her legs to feast on her until her knees buckled and she forgot her own name.

Fuck, what was holding them back? She lay in his bed, in his arms, and in seconds, he could have her buttons undone and—

A shiver coursed through her and she curled in on herself.

"Fuck, baby," he growled, scolding himself for his indecent thoughts as he tightened his arms around her. "You're cold again."

"And tired," she whispered, burying her face back into his shoulder. "I hate this."

"I know. Me, too." He pressed his lips to her hair, unable to express just how much. All he could do was hold her, protect her, and help her through this the best he could. "Let's just go to sleep. We'll work out a plan in the morning."

DESPITE FEELING as unsexy as humanly possible in her flannels with a deadly virus coursing through her body, nothing could have eased Eden's fears like the warmth and safety of Rain's arms. He'd certainly achieved his goal as she'd never felt hotter. Rain's body was like a furnace, one she never wanted to escape. And right now, she didn't have to as she breathed him in and relished the pounding of his heart in the palm of her hand.

Rain's eyes fluttered closed as their conversation ceased and her gaze wandered down his throat, pectorals, and the ripped ridges of his belly. She couldn't see any lower thanks to the blanket, but if she wasn't on death's door, she wouldn't hesitate to explore the hard contours of his body and satisfy her aching desire to make love deep into the morning.

I'll let you taste, lick, and suck any part of me you want.

Heat ignited inside her, quickly suppressed by a deep shiver that shook her joints and constricted her muscles. Rain's biceps were like steel as he tugged her even closer and locked her legs between his heavy thighs.

"I've got you, Eden," he mumbled, his voice thick with sleep. "Don't be afraid. Just close your eyes."

"You won't leave me?"

"No, baby. I'm not going anywhere."

She snuggled beneath his chin, and, within minutes, Rain's breathing softened in slumber. But Eden remained wide awake, fearing her symptoms were worsening by the hour as the vampire curse took hold of her body.

Whimpering, she curled her toes into the thick, fluffy socks Nate had found in Rain's closet. All night, she'd been struggling to remain calm as she'd sat at the window staring out into the darkness, shuddering with anticipation for the moment Lucas's dark eyes appeared and captivated her again. Compelled her and stole her free will. She knew what was at stake. It was a fight to the death. Rain would kill Lucas or Lucas would kill her, whether she be dead-dead or undead.

But the moment Rain had strode into the room, stark naked and rendering her speechless with a glimpse of his cock and the perfect view of his taut, bare ass, most of her fear had slipped away. And as she peeked up at his gorgeous slumbering face, a whole new hunger threatened to break through her insatiable thirst for blood.

She longed to kiss him, to feel his mouth against hers, her skin, and to experience his lips working their magic in her most intimate places. One more fantasy she couldn't wait to explore once he killed the vampire and she wasn't so tired. So hungry.

Closing her eyes, she pressed her face back into his chest, inhaling his woodsy and eucalypt scent that had never failed to calm her while she considered everything she'd learned about vampires since yesterday. She'd mulled it over all night as the facts didn't differ much from what she'd read in books, though fiction always gave a unique twist to the truth. For instance, the only vampire she knew of who could shift into a bat had been Dracula. Had he been real? If so, it hadn't been a wolf who'd killed him. Decapitation and a stake through the heart had ended Count Dracula, and the same rules had applied to the Undead and Unwed series, books she'd loved in high school.

Though Betsy, despite her many extraordinary abilities, hadn't been able to shift into a bat either.

After Ava had gone to bed, Eden had asked Nate if staking Lucas was an option, and he'd merely shrugged as he'd dug into another bowl of sweet and sour curry.

"If humans are good enough, they can fight vamps that way. The medieval vampire hunters were real, Eden. But we wolves are more efficient at killing them with stealth."

"What about garlic?" she'd asked.

"Yeah, I believe they hate that."

"And holy water?"

"The church is a no-go zone."

"And sunlight?"

"Why do you think Lucas arranged a tour of the Koala Hospital after hours?"

She'd shivered. "Is that why I woke at dusk?"

"I don't think so. But let's just say that everything you believe about vampires is true."

"So, they do sparkle?"

Nate's forehead had crinkled. "Who the fuck said that?"

"Never mind," she'd muttered, then Nate had returned to the kitchen, complaining about the lack of chocolate and cookies in the cupboard before eating all of Rain's cashews.

She liked the young wolves. Their carefree and rambunctious nature had eased her fear over dinner earlier as they'd joked, laughed, and complained heartily about the vegan food while helping themselves to multiple servings. She hadn't been surprised to learn Chad was a shifter as the young man was as daring as Rain, but the rest of the Moon Dive crew were apparently ordinary human thrill seekers who enjoyed jumping out of planes. Mad men, the lot of them. Though, Eden considered she might be reckless, too, if she were invincible. And now that she knew that about Rain, the thought of him falling from the sky didn't terrify her nearly as much. Sure, he could still get hurt, but he could tumble through a rough landing and probably walk away scot-free.

Though she doubted even he would survive if the parachute didn't open.

Kai, however, surprised her. As an avid nature enthusiast, he'd been one of her best hospital volunteers when she'd returned to Maggie and she'd missed him when he'd left shortly after. At the time, she'd understood the difficulties of volunteering while working full-time, but now, Eden wondered if Rain had anything to do with his departure.

As for Nate, he was like a dog with a bone as she hadn't been able to escape his watch all night. But he'd been pleasant company, their conversation keeping her at ease while he'd kept communications open with the pack. She'd been shocked to learn that the wolves were telepathic in their shifted form, possessing the ability to talk wolf to wolf or human to wolf, though apparently not human to human despite the long looks she recalled Finn and Rain often sharing when trying to get their stories straight.

Smiling, Eden settled against the pillow of Rain's pectorals, basking in his warmth. He might be disappointed about the hunt tonight, but she had every faith in him. As animals, wolves were exceptional predators, and Eden had no reason to doubt the shifters would be any different. They would hunt Lucas, use the natural elements to trap him, then strike to end her curse.

Then Rain could deliver his promise from earlier today to complete their mating bond by loving her in ways she'd often dreamed about. Of feeling his hard body over hers, his prickly face kissing every inch of her skin while she pulled at his hair as he made her come with that wicked mouth of his. Of how she'd wrap her legs around his strong hips and dig her heels into his fine ass as he plunged deep inside her. Oh, how she wanted that. More than anything. And as she snuggled into his embrace, Eden's body ignited like a furnace as her eyes drifted closed into deep, peaceful sleep.

Chapter 20

Rain awoke with the dawn, welcoming the shards of light casting sunshine over the most solid sleep he'd had in weeks. It might not have been long, but it'd been restful because the object of his worry had lain safely in his arms. Warm, protected, and moaning as she—

"Eden?" Rain jolted to his elbow. "Fuck, Eden!"

She squirmed, her whimpers shooting fear through his soul as her face contorted with pain. Rain untangled his legs from hers and scrambled onto his knees, grasping her shoulder as his breath caught in his throat. Her pale body shook violently in a pool of sweat, her damp hair clinging to her ashen face. Rain touched his hand to her forehead. She was on fire.

"Shit!" Leaping to his feet, he tore the blanket away. "Eden, wake up!"

She groaned, but her eyes didn't open. Fuck. She was only two days into the change. She couldn't be this far gone. It wasn't possible.

Rain ran around the bed, knelt on the mattress beside her, and slipped the socks off her feet. Had he overheated her? Or was this just the fever? Fuck, if he didn't get a grip on how this cursed virus worked soon, he'd bloody kill her!

He fumbled for the buttons on her shirt, then paused. "Fuck it," he muttered, growling at himself as he consciously threw her dignity out the window. Her life was on the line.

Yet he sighed in relief at the sight of her camisole. She'd been cold, so of course she'd worn layers. And he'd stupidly enveloped her in his intense body heat.

Fucking idiot.

Rain lifted Eden's arms out of the shirt before tossing the flannel over his shoulder.

"R-Rain?"

"I'm here, Edes. I've got you."

She groaned and curled onto her side, her legs wriggling. "Fever."

"Yes, you have a fever. I need to get you up."

"Hungry. So hungry."

"I know—"

A knock sounded on the door. "Rain?" Ava called out. "Is everything—"

"Come in!"

The door opened and Ava stumbled inside with Finn on her heels.

"She's burning up."

"Shit ..." Finn breathed as Ava rushed to Rain's side.

"What can I do?"

"Help me get her into the shower. Cool her down." He lifted the waistband of Eden's pants and thanked the Moon she wore underwear as he stripped the flannel from her legs. Eden arched her back, her whimpers wrenching at his heart as his wolf howled in agony.

"Her pulse is racing," Ava said, clutching her friend's wrist. "Finn, grab the paracetamol!"

"You think that'll work?" Rain asked as Finn left without question.

"She's still human! She had some last night, and it helped."

Eden slapped her hand to her forehead, her eyes squeezing tight. "Rain!"

He scooped his arms beneath her and lifted her from the saturated sheets. "I'm here."

She sobbed. "My head ..."

"I know." He took Eden into the bathroom while Ava hurried to turn on the shower.

"You said she had seven days!"

"She does! It's just a fever!"

Eden groaned, her hand clawing at his chest as her head lolled onto his shoulder. "*Hungry. So hungry.*"

"That doesn't sound like a fever!" Ava cried, her voice pitching as Rain stepped beneath the tepid water. "Last night she was cold and hungry, and now—"

"We don't know how this works, honey," Finn said, striding into the bathroom with two pills and a glass of water. "But I suspect it's like any virus where she'll experience fever and chills."

Rain slid down the shower wall, afraid to let Eden go as he cradled her against his body and brushed hair from her flushed face. "You're all right, baby. I've got you. Let's cool you down."

Her chest continued to heave with sharp, shallow breaths, water rushing down her face as her eyes fluttered open. "Rain?"

"I'm here."

"I ... I can't do this."

"Yes, you can. We'll cool you down and you'll feel better. Can you swallow these tablets?"

She groaned and lifted her head. Rain took the tablets from Finn and placed them between her lips before offering her the glass of water. Eden swallowed, then coughed, spluttered, and groaned.

"We'll leave you to it," Finn said, backing away. "Ava, grab Eden some clothes. We'll be back, man."

Rain barely noticed as they left, his attention solely on Eden. Cradling her warm, limp body in his arms, he sensed her pain through their forming bond and his heart shattered. Her anguish and fear tore his soul to pieces and ignited fear unlike he'd ever felt before as he rocked her gently.

He couldn't lose her. Wouldn't. But fuck, for the first time, Rain finally understood why Sly had run away to the bush.

Life without Eden would be absolute agony.

"I promise, baby," he whispered, pressing his lips to her hair. "I'll kill Lucas, and the pain will go away."

"I know ..." Her hand lifted to rest over his heart, though it did nothing to ease the guilt fueling his rapid pulse. Rain tightened his arms around her. He would do anything, *anything*, to save her. To ensure she was safe. And if there was an easier way ...

Rain gritted his teeth and squeezed his eyes closed. They sat there for what felt like hours, but it was only a few minutes until Eden's breathing normalized. Once her skin cooled, he helped her stand and switched off the taps before passing her into Ava's care.

"Dry her and help her change," he said, grabbing a towel and striding back into his room. The bed had been stripped and fresh linen placed on the mattress, bless Ava's heart. Not that it mattered. Rain didn't plan on sleeping again until he had Lucas's neck between his teeth.

He kicked off his wet boxers, dried, then pulled on jeans and a T-shirt.

"You good?" he called out to Ava.

"You can come in."

He returned to the ensuite to find Eden wrapped in a fluffy dressing gown with a red towel tied around her head, fatigue filling her eyes.

"I want to go back to sleep."

"Food first," Ava said. "Then I'll brush your hair."

Eden groaned. "I don't want food."

"Well, you're not getting blood! Just have some Weet-Bix to keep your energy up. Please!"

"I'm with Ava," Rain said, wrapping his arms around Eden's shoulders to help her stand. "Weet-Bix or dry toast, then back to bed."

She leaned on him, her tiny fist clutching his T-shirt. "I don't know how people resist this shit."

"They don't." He scooped Eden into his arms and carried her down the hall. "But you will because you're strong."

"And you have a wolf protecting you," Ava added.

But even though Eden managed to eat two Weet-Bix and a few strawberries, Rain wasn't sure that *he* would be strong enough to handle this as she shuddered through another round of chills, then sweated through her dressing gown before midmorning. He'd already canceled his jumps this week and fucked up the Moon Dive schedule, but he couldn't bear to leave her side, let alone put someone's life in his hands. All day, Eden cycled through the illness, the virus taking hold of her body as her cheeks heated and she panted and groaned. Her chest heaved and pulse thudded in his ears. Rain showered her three more times, then lay with her on his bed, promising he wouldn't leave. She gazed up at him with her tired, chocolate-colored eyes, then slept, easing the tightness in his chest a fraction.

Then she started shivering again.

Ava couldn't bring herself to leave either as she helped Eden wash, dress, and administered more paracetamol, which strangely seemed to help.

After activities at the resort were over, the pack arrived to plan this evening's hunt. Rain didn't want to go, but his wolf paced, restless and ready to be unleashed. To run. To hunt.

To kill.

Because he'd kill that fucking bat. He'd rip Lucas to shreds, then take pleasure in sinking his teeth into the bastard's pulsating carotid.

If blood was to be spilled, it would be Lucas's.

Chapter 21

Rain raced up the track through the rainforest that bordered Gustav Creek, the path undulating over the rough mountainous terrain. He leapt across rocky creek beds and scampered up leaf littered steps in thrice the time he could as a human, slipping and sliding over the soft, unstable ground. But nothing would deter him from his task. Finn had smelled two vampires up this way and the wolves were in hot pursuit. Rain knew this trail as well as he did the others on the island, and he wouldn't let the bats outsmart him in his own territory. His relentless wolf could hunt all night. He *would* hunt all night. The vampires—known for their greed, speed, and impulsiveness—would give in long before he grew agitated.

Though agitated was all his human side felt, along with anger, fear, and desperation as they closed in on the vampires.

Growling, he leapt across the creek. His back legs slid sideways on the loose dirt, and he struggled to maintain a good grip. But he managed to pull himself up and powered on.

Behind him, Nate swore. *"Bloody hell. Why'd they have to hunt on top of the fucking mountain?"*

"Thinks it'll give them the advantage of an easier escape."

They reached the saddle of the mountain and continued along the ridge, the scattered lights of Horseshoe Bay shimmering in the distance three hundred meters below as Rain put his nose to the ground and followed the trail of cold death.

"*Fuck, do you think they're compensating for something?*" Nate breathed. "*Or will they try to push us off the cliff?*"

Kai's chuckle sounded through the pack bond. "*They need to make up for their small dicks.*"

Nate snorted. "*Man, you reckon if I became a vamp—*"

"*Wolves can't become vamps,*" Kai interrupted.

"*I know. But if I did, would my dick shrivel, too?*"

"*Since your blood wouldn't circulate, probably,*" Kai replied. "*Hey, how do vampires get it up?*"

"*Gentlemen.*" Finn's commanding voice contained a warning. "*Concentrate. You can contemplate philosophy after the hunt.*"

"*Yes, boss. But if I catch a vamp—*"

The rev of what sounded like a motorbike cut through the air and Rain's head snapped up. Nate swore while Kai's low growl echoed through his head.

Rain's hind legs sprang into action as he raced down the trail.

"*Remember the plan!*" Finn shouted. "*Don't—*"

"*They have a koala!*" Rain's heart pounded harder as the little guy's bellow ricochetted through the trees.

"*I know, but we can't go in teeth bared. Control yourself!*"

Rain skidded to a halt, his chest heaving. Bloody Alpha and his orders. But Finn was right. He needed to keep a clear head and control his impulses if he wanted to save Eden. He needed a vampire to interrogate. Only once he got his answers could he rip them apart.

So, with a deep breath, he approached the rock that created Horseshoe Bay Lookout, where a bat flew around a koala, snapping and swiping in an attempt to scare the little guy down the tree and into the hands of the vampire waiting below. The bloodthirsty fucker who would tell Rain where his boss lurked before his time ended on this earth.

Gritting his teeth, Rain shifted. Nate did the same as they squared their shoulders and strode into the clearing.

"Don't you know? Koalas taste like shit."

The vampire turned, a wicked gleam in his eyes as his mouth stretched into a wide, toothy smile. "We're under orders from our lord."

The other vampire swooped down and shifted out of shadows. "We will kill as many koalas as possible until you give up his bride."

Rain's fists clenched. "She is *not* his bride."

The first vampire—blondie—smirked. "She will be."

"Over my dead body."

The second vampire cackled. "Happy to oblige."

"Don't fuck with me. This is my territory and you're not welcome. Tell me where your lord is, and we'll let you go free."

"You'll never find him," the second vampire sneered. "Our lord is a stealth master. He's only seen when he wants to be seen."

Rain's stomach twisted. Stealth master? That didn't sound good.

"And he won't come until his queen is ready to rise."

Every muscle in Rain's body bulged. "She will never be his queen."

"Oh, yes she will." The vampires cackled harder. "Listen, little wolf. The Lord Lucas always gets what he wants, and he's waited decades for a new bride."

"Why Eden?" Rain growled, wondering if there was more to Lucas's actions than he knew.

Blondie cackled like a loon escaped from the asylum. "Fated mates have the richest blood of them all, and she has rare AB negative coursing through her veins. She's as delectable as she is fuckable, and my lord wants her."

"*Control yourself*," Finn said before Rain could do something stupid like lunge at the slimy vampire in human form and get himself killed.

The second vampire sneered. "I'm sure you can relate. You want to fuck her yourself."

Rain gritted his teeth. "She. Is. My. *Mate*."

"Not for long." The darker one lifted his chin. "Your mate will feed, little wolf. No human has ever resisted the urge. The hunger is insatiable. She won't last much longer. They never do."

"She will ache for death. For never-ending life. A life where she can be free from the pain currently searing through her veins."

Rain's toes dug into the earth, his wolf longing to spring free and attack. But he needed to stick to the plan. Practice patience.

"Eden is strong. She will fight it. Now, tell me where Lucas is, or I'll kill you."

They both laughed, white chests heaving with enough mirth to make Rain's jaw twitch. Nate growled.

"Kill us? Just the two of you?"

Now it was Rain's turn to smirk. "Nope."

On cue, Finn and Kai lunged from the bush behind the vampires, the Alpha ripping the blond fucker off his feet and flinging him into a boulder. The sickening crunch of bone breaking snapped through the air while Kai tore into the flank of the other. Blood-curdling screams tore from their previously cocky throats as Rain and Nate shifted and leapt into battle.

Blondie vanished in a swirl of smoke, his bat flopping on the ground like a fish out of water before twisting back into his vampire form. Rain pinned him to the rock and sank his claws into the creature's pale, heaving chest.

"Tell him!" Finn commanded, rising to his two feet beside Rain. "Where is Lucas?"

The vampire coughed, winced, then glared at Rain with loathing. "You can't kill him. He's the most powerful vampire you'll ever encounter."

Unimpressed, Rain sank his teeth into the vampire and ripped flesh from his arm. Blondie's screams tore through the night as his bone met fresh air. Rain spat the undead flesh in the creature's face.

Finn growled. "Try again."

"Let the bitch turn!" the other vampire cried. "Kill her! Maybe your next mate will have a decent rack."

Rain's claws dug into his vampire's chest. "*Nate.*"

And the young wolf became the first of them to make a kill as he ripped into the vampire's neck and ceased the bastard's cries with the wet tearing of flesh.

Blondie cried out as he reached for his companion, and Rain dug his claws in harder.

Kai chuckled. "Fucking sick. And deluded. I don't know what he considers a decent rack is when Eden—"

Rain growled and Kai clamped his mouth shut.

Finn crouched beside the snarling vampire. "We're not fucking around here. Tell us how to find your lord or join your friend in Hell."

Blondie bared his teeth, then spat at Rain's snout. "Why bother? Save her the easy way and be done with it."

Rain's claws tore flesh, but Finn had his back.

"What do you mean by that?" the Alpha demanded. "How do we save her without killing Lucas?"

The vampire's eyebrows shot up. Rain thought he would have laughed if not for the holes in his chest. "You don't know? Some Alpha you are."

Rain ripped into the vampire's other arm. He kicked and screamed, but Rain showed no mercy.

Finn cocked his head. "Ready to talk now?"

"You'll never find Lucas. He'll lie in wait until his bride is ready. Close to turning. And if you Fated pussies don't grow the balls to do what needs to be done, you'll never save her."

"Good to know." Then Finn stood, his eyes connecting with Rain's, who took the order and ripped into the vampire's neck. His stomach roiled at the rotten taste of centuries old flesh, but his wolf relished the kill as the creature stilled, then crumbled into dust.

Shifting, Rain stood and turned to Finn. "What was that? We could have—"

"No use dragging it out. The bastard told us enough."

"No, he didn't, but he might have—"

Finn grasped Rain's shoulder. "He did. An Alpha should know. So tomorrow, I need you to find Sly."

Rain gritted his teeth, his fist clenching by his side. He didn't want to abandon the hunt, but fuck, Finn was right. An Alpha *should* know, but Finn was too new to his role to possess all knowledge. So, that left Sly. And this time, his brother better come the fuck out of hiding because Rain had never needed that bastard more.

EDEN SAT with Ava in the jacuzzi on the first-floor balcony, enjoying her iced tea and the warmth bubbling around her.

"Finn and I will need a hot tub in our new house," Ava moaned, her eyes drifting closed as she tilted her head back and exposed her long, lean throat. "If we buy that one in Nelly Bay, we could put one out the back overlooking the national park."

"I do like that house." Eden's heart pounded as she slid

along the bench seat. "And it's perfect as it allows Finn to come and go as a wolf."

"Exactly. So, what do you think?" Ava peeked her eyes open. "Should I ask for an inspection?"

Eden shrugged, her stomach rumbling. "Honestly? Don't bother."

"Why? What do—"

Ava never finished that sentence as Eden grabbed her shoulders and bit down on her friend's neck. She screamed, kicking water over the side of the tub as warm, fresh blood seeped onto Eden's tongue, and a moan rose inside her.

"Stop! Eden!"

Her vessels heated as her teeth elongated and she sank her new fangs deeper into Ava's throat. Blood gushed over her lips and down her chin as, with a surge of power, Eden drew breath through her nose and drank deeply.

Gasping, Eden's eyes flew open. Darkness surrounded her as she clutched the bed covers to her chest, her heart thumping while her dry throat ached for moisture. Hydration. *Blood*.

It had tasted so good ...

Pressing her knuckles to her mouth, Eden screamed. Then, like an echo on the wind, a soft voice whispered, "*Yes, bella. Rich, warm blood* ..."

Eden flung herself face down into the mattress and covered her head with a pillow. It wasn't real. The voice. It wasn't real.

Hunger curdled inside her, and Eden groaned. She couldn't take much more of this. She couldn't settle her hunger and though she longed to get up and eat *something*, she'd more likely find herself bypassing the kitchen and prowling upstairs to where her friend slept to make that dream a reality.

Eden squeezed her eyes shut. "Don't think about it. You're not hungry. *Not* hungry ..."

She didn't know how long she lay there for, but when she awoke again, she no longer hid beneath the pillow and soft footsteps padded towards her. The clench in her chest told her it was Rain, but like the coward she was, she couldn't face him without breaking down in tears.

"Eden?" The mattress dipped as he lowered his weight onto the edge. Rain stroked his fingers down her cheek, and it took all her strength to keep her eyes closed. She longed to roll over and ask to be held, but instead, she welcomed the kiss he placed on her forehead. His growing-longer-by-the-day beard brushed through her hair and warm breath tickled her ear as he whispered, "I'm going to the hospital to check on the koalas for you. Dee said everything's under control, but I want to stop by and be sure."

She melted.

"Then this afternoon, I'm going to hunt down Sly. I won't be back until late but if you need me, ask the scouts and I'll come straight away." He kissed her again, and her heart stumbled inside her chest. "I love you, baby."

Then the mattress sprang as his weight lifted, and he was gone, the door closing softly behind him.

Eden curled into herself as tears slipped down her cheeks. It wasn't fair. She finally had everything she'd ever wanted and was dying alone in the dark while the man she loved tried desperately to save her.

Chapter 22

Rain arrived at West Point, his body thrumming as he slammed the Jeep door, tore off his shirt, and raced into the bush. Shifting, he reached inside the blood bond to release a deep, desperate call. *"Sly!"*

He stood, legs spread, as he strained his ears for any sound of his brother. A footstep. A heartbeat. The swish of his tail.

But nothing.

Grunting with frustration, Rain tried calling again but received no reply. Fucking hell. Leaping up the creek, he put his nose to the ground and ran. Sly couldn't hide forever. And though Rain had failed to find him last week, he wouldn't give up. He'd held onto faith for this long believing that Sly would return, and though he wasn't the Alpha anymore, surely part of the man he'd once been lived on. The brother Rain had known and loved. The brother who'd do anything to protect him. To guide and educate him. The brother who'd followed him to skydiving school to make sure he didn't kill himself, who had jumped at Rain's idea to expand the family business and take up extreme sports for a living while also upholding the Blackwood name and making the old man proud.

Rain missed that brother like a wolf missed his tail, and

over his dead body would he let Sly leave the pack. Sly couldn't do that to him and, more importantly, he couldn't do it to himself. Rain would run over hot coals to stop him from giving up on life, love, family, and everything they'd ever worked for.

And if Sly knew of a way to save Eden—

Rain leapt onto a rock, lifted his head, and howled. *"Sly! If you can hear me, brother, I can't do this anymore! Please! Talk to me!"*

Wind whistled through the trees. Birds chirped. Rain's ears quirked, his senses attuning until he could even hear the slither of a death adder's tongue. The rustle of eucalypts as a koala fed. And then, faintly, the slow and steady thump of a beating heart and the padding of paws far larger than any animal that should live in this bush.

Rain darted to his left and ran. Adrenaline coursed through him as he traversed hills, ducked beneath low trees, and jumped over fallen branches, barely caring to avoid the stinging trees as he clawed at the dirt. Rain had him now. Sly couldn't escape. Not this time.

Though it seemed the bastard was going to try as his footsteps quickened. Rain growled, his heart pounding as he ran faster. Harder. Realizing they were nearing the beach, he banked right. Rain raced up the slope, around a boulder, and drew in a breath. He was gaining on Sly. Just a little closer ...

Rain leapt off the cliff and slammed his shoulder into Sly's flank, knocking his brother off his feet as they barrel-rolled into the scrub. Rain's neck cricked as his hip hit a tree, but he quickly scrambled to his feet as Sly jumped to his and shot Rain a glare that used to make him cower as a kid. The one he'd always looked up to. Sly had been his leader, his big brother, his Alpha. But Rain was done with that shit. If either of them was in any position of power here, it was him.

"Sly—"

"Fucking hell, you're a persistent bastard, aren't you?"

"When it comes to those I love? Always. I've been hunting you since full moon!"

"Yet you gave up these past few nights. Thought you'd finally taken the fucking hint. I don't want to talk."

"You stopped eating."

"I don't need you to take care of me. I'm no longer your concern. I did what I needed to do for the pack. I gave you a new Alpha. Now fuck off and leave me alone."

"No!" Rain jumped in front of Sly as he turned to run. *"I'll never leave you. I'll never stop trying to bring you back. You're my brother and I miss you."*

Sly growled and shouldered past Rain. But since he made no move to flee, Rain took the hit and turned after him. *"Come on, man. We need you. Do you have any idea what's going on out there?"*

"Not my concern. The Goddess can kiss my hairy ass."

Rain's heart sank. *"You could have a second chance, you know? Finn and I believe there's hope. You can find another mate. Fall in love."*

"I'd rather fuck a green ant's nest," Sly growled. *"I had my mate and now she's gone. After I kill Tyrone and the vampire who took her, there's nothing worth fighting for."*

Rain's ears perked. *"Vampire?"*

Sly snarled, then lunged up the hill.

"Wait!" Rain raced after him. *"What do you mean a vampire took her?"* It was first he'd heard about this. Shelby had gone to Townsville for an appointment and shopping south of the river in territory Tyrone technically couldn't claim. At least, that's what Sly had told him. So how had the vampires been involved?

"Drop it, Rain. I'm not talking about it." Sly leapt over a fallen tree. Rain gritted his teeth and followed. His brother had always been a moody bastard, but right now, Rain would

take what he could get as this was the longest conversation they'd had in almost two years.

"I know it hurts to talk about Shelby—"

Sly spun around so fast Rain had to dig his claws into the ground to avoid colliding with his brother's bared teeth. *"Hurts? It fucking kills me! I couldn't fucking protect her because that sadistic cunt sent the one creature who could block my senses! Those bats are fucking dangerous, brother! Some fucker compelled her off the island and I had no fucking clue until she was in Tyrone's claws!"*

Blinking, Rain shuffled back and leveled his gaze with his brother's violent eyes. *"That's why you've been hunting the bats all this time. Why didn't you tell me?"*

"The bats aren't your problem. They're mine to kill."

Sly turned his back and continued through the bush, but at a slower pace.

Rain resisted a growl and followed. *"Not anymore, brother. You might be pissed with Fate, but you know more about the lore than any of us, and I need your help. There's a vampire who's lurking out of sight. Lucas. They call him a stealth master."*

Sly's ears twitched. *"A stealth master?"*

Rain's breath caught at the interest in his brother's tone. *"Yeah. Why?"*

Sly remained silent as they weaved through the bush, then released a low growl. *"Forget it, brother. You'll never find him. He'll only come out when he's ready to fight and you won't beat him."*

Rain blinked, affronted. *"We killed two vampires last night."*

"That's because you have the pack. It takes teamwork to kill the vampires, as you know. I only managed to get that one measly bat because your new Alpha distracted him, but then he let the bastard get away."

"*And that's why we need you! The stronger we are as a pack, the better chance we have of killing the bats.*"

Sly scoffed. "*Don't bother yourself with the bats. Focus on Tyrone and leave the undead scum to me.*"

Rage surged through Rain's vessels as he jumped onto a boulder and rose to his full height. "*A bat attacked Eden! He bit her and I need to kill the fucker to save her before she dies!*"

Sly stilled, his dark shoulders bunching. Rain's heart hammered as his brother lowered his tail. "*A bat bit your mate?*"

"*Yes. And she's terrified. She's dying and I can't deal with this alone. I cannot lose her. Not if it means turning into a brooding, moody piece of shit like you. So, I'm begging you.*" Rain took a tentative step forward. "*I need your help. You have all the wisdom of an Alpha and the strength of two of us. I need you to fight beside me to kill the bats. Then, I promise, we will kill Tyrone. You can kill Tyrone. But we are on the clock because Eden only has four days left and the cunning bat said there might be another way to save her. But as far as I'm aware, you kill the vampire, you save the human. So ...*"

Rain trailed off, time slowing as Sly's ears twitched, his tail swishing slowly from side to side.

"*How much do you love her?*"

"*What sort of question is that?*"

"*One you need to answer before I tell you.*"

Shock rendered Rain still. "*So, there is another way?*"

"*There's always another way,*" Sly muttered, his eyes flashing as he turned to face Rain. "*But that doesn't mean you'll like it.*"

Rain swallowed. "*I don't care. Every day she gets worse, and I feel her slipping away.*"

"*And she'll continue to until the end, unless you take it upon yourself to ease her pain.*"

"*What do you mean?*"

Sly's shoulders drooped as he sat. "*It's very simple, brother. She's infected by the venom of a vampire, and you carry the antidote. So, you can kill what's inside her the way you can kill a vampire.*"

Rain sank onto his haunches as a weight equal to a boulder rammed into his chest. "*But ... to do that I'd have to—*"

"*Bite her. Yes.*"

"*But I can't!*" he cried, his ears perking in horror.

"*Then kill the bat. But if you can't get to him in time, mark Eden and she will live. She will be safe.*"

Bile rose in Rain's throat until he thought he'd be sick. He couldn't believe what he was hearing. No wonder Lucas had been so cocky. The easy way? More like the darkest way imaginable!

"*But if I bite her, it'll seal our bond against the terms of Fate! I'll claim her as mine and take away her free will. She'll be beholden to me and trapped.*" Rain shook his head. "*I won't do that to her.*"

He couldn't. It went against everything he believed in, everything he'd been taught about bonds, love, and his purpose on Earth. Eden would be unable to leave him, forever in his hold, and his ties with the Goddess would be severed. Forever.

Which was exactly what Tyrone wanted.

Rage surged through Rain on a low snarl. When he got his claws into that bastard ... "*Eden deserves her freedom, and I won't forcibly take it away from her.*"

Sly cocked his head. "*Oh, brother. You really are obtuse.*" He had the audacity to heave a sigh. "*Biting your mate isn't the end of the world. But if you want to waste time trying to kill the bat, then go ahead. He's obsessed and waits for her, so he'll give up the stealth in the end and force her to turn. But if you want to do what's best for you and Eden, then bite her, seal the bond, and save her fucking life."*

Rain cringed as every one of his nerves quaked with pain. *"But ... Finn will oust me if I cut ties with the Goddess. I'll have to leave the island. The pack. Luna Views ..."* The mere thought of it broke his heart. There had to be a better solution. *"I'll just have to catch the bloody bat."*

"Then hopefully he'll reveal himself within the next twenty-four hours."

"Hopefully, because I'm fucking sick of—wait!" Rain shot to his feet. *"What do you mean twenty-four hours? Eden has four more days."*

"She does, but you don't. Luck is on your side, brother, as there is a way to make things right with the Goddess."

Rain's breath caught. *"Tell me."*

Sly smirked in the cocky way only a wolf could. *"It's quite simple, little brother. Bite her when the Moon isn't looking."*

THE PACK MET in darkness atop Hawkings Point, soft clouds obscuring any natural light from the time bomb in the sky—the tiniest sliver of a crescent moon. Finn stood tall and proud on a higher curve of the rock floor, his golden fur blowing in the heavy wind while Kai and Chad sat on their haunches. Nate tuned in from the house below where he remained guarding Eden and Ava while Rain filled them in on his conversation with Sly.

"Fuck," Kai interrupted before Rain had even gotten part way through the story. *"Do you think Sly's going to rebel?"*

Rain's hackles rose. *"No. He's hurting and pissed off with the world. As long as he doesn't do anything drastic to cut his ties with the Goddess, he'll remain in her good graces."*

Unlike Rain would if he gave into the darkness and claimed Eden as his mate. He shuddered at the mere thought.

"*Do you think Sly might join us in this fight?*" Finn asked, and Rain's shoulders slouched.

"*He wants to be left alone, though I wouldn't doubt him. He showed up last time we went into battle.*"

"*Yeah, but he was still our Alpha then,*" Nate said. "*He didn't turn his back on his duties. But now, I wouldn't put the same faith in him.*"

"*He's keen to take down the bats, though.*" Despite Sly's attitude tonight, Rain didn't have it in him to give up on his brother. "*He seeks vengeance on them as much as he does Tyrone as he told me tonight it was a vampire who had compelled Shelby off the island. So, no matter how much he hurts or falls into the lone wolf, he won't let us have all the fun when we face the vampires or rip Tyrone's head from his shoulders.*"

Chad snorted. "*I bet Sly will, too. Literally.*"

"*And I'll help,*" Finn growled. "*But let's focus on one fight at a time. Did Sly have any idea about the 'easy way' to save Eden?*"

Rain flicked his gaze from the scouts, towards the tiny moon, then back to Finn. He cleared his throat. "*There's nothing easy about it. And I tell you now—*"

A screech sounded, and all four of them ducked as two bats swooped over the railing, their claws extended and fangs glistening. Rain growled and sprang into the air but missed them by a mile. Clawing at the rock, he glared murder at the bats as they flew into the trees by the entrance to the lookout. A wisp of shadow blew, and a skinny bat's torso rose from the leaves.

"My lord was right. That woman has you by the balls."

Rain sank between his shoulders, growling at the vile bastard as Finn shifted and rose to his full height.

"Watch it, bat. We have more balls than your lord, hiding like a fucking coward. Now, tell us. Where is he?"

The bat cackled. "He watches over his bride. Speaks to her. Continues to encourage her to give in and feed."

"*Nate! He's by the house,*" Rain called through their bond.

"*I'll circle the perimeter,*" Nate replied.

"*Keep an eye on Eden.*"

"*I won't go far.*"

"She won't feed," Finn said. "And unless you give Lucas up, you won't live to feed another night, either."

The bat's laughter grated along Rain's last nerve. Bunching down on his hind legs, he sprung at the vampire, snatched him around the shoulder, and tore him from the tree. The creature screamed and Rain spat him out onto the path below before he collided with the boulder. Pain shot through his shoulder, and he hissed, but he rolled back to his feet as Finn killed the undead scum. Another scream cut through the air as Chad took out his own vampire, then silenced him.

"*Fuck, they taste like shit,*" Chad snarled.

"*Sure do,*" Finn agreed as he, Kai, and Chad joined Rain on the path. "*Now, what did Sly say about saving Eden?*"

Rain's shoulders hunched as he stared miserably at the dark, rocky ground. "*I can kill the vampire inside her the same way I'd kill them.*"

His pack stilled, shock chilling the air around them. Heads turned, ears quirked, and tails dropped sadly.

Finn soon broke the silence. "*Fuck.*"

"*Yep.*"

"*You can't mark her!*" Kai cried.

"*I know!*"

"*What if you trigger the bond before—*"

"*It won't matter.*" Finn shook his golden head. "*Before or after, the bite still denies her free will. Eden would be subject to Rain's every whim."*

Kai exhaled. *"Shit, really?"*

Chad nodded, his chestnut ears twitching. *"My father marked all his women. It was sickening to watch."*

"I didn't understand it growing up," Finn said, *"but I know now it's why my mother never left. Why we stayed on Flinders Island at the bequest of my father. She was independent and free because he didn't live with us, but he had her under his thumb."*

"I won't do that to Eden." Rain squared his shoulders. *"I couldn't live with myself."*

"And Sly actually suggested this?" Finn tilted his head. *"That you cut your ties with the Goddess?"*

"No, he—"

"I knew he was rebelling," Kai growled.

"He's not! He said if I were to bite her beneath the new moon, I might escape the Goddess's wrath."

Snouts turned left and right as the wolves exchanged glances.

"Well ... that is when humanity is at its strongest," Kai said.

"It's the time of rebirth. A reset."

"And she can't see," Finn said. *"Which makes it the perfect time to get away with doing dark deeds."*

Rain peeled his gums back. *"But it's tomorrow fucking night! We have twenty-four hours before the window closes. Nate!"* He reached out to the other wolf. *"Any sign of Lucas?"*

"It's so dark out here, man. I can't see any bats."

Typical. *Stealth master.* It would be easy to hide on such a dark night. But despite what he'd learned, Rain needed to find the fucking bastard because the thought of biting Eden, of claiming her and marking his beautiful mate in such a barbaric way shot agony through his body unlike any he'd ever felt.

But more than the thought of losing her? Of the virus ending her life or Lucas forcing the change?

Rain's claws dug into the rock. *"He's lurking. Somewhere. So, come on, men. Let's hunt."*

Rain ran down the path with the pack at his heels. He'd search all night if he had to. He would get the fucker. Then he'd claim Eden the *right* way. Out of light and love. Before marching over to Townsville to rip Tyrone's balls from his body, shove them down his throat, and tear them out again along with his jugular.

Neither Finn nor Sly would be able to stop him.

Chapter 23

Eden moaned, arching her back as she pressed her hands into the hot, wet flesh laid out before her. Blood. Rich, juicy, delicious blood seeped down her throat, quenched her thirst, and sparked new life through her body as heat ignited in her cold, dead core. She scraped her nails over the chest of her victim with relish.

He tasted *so good*.

If only the sleeping bitch in her mind would stop thrashing about. Eden knew she was dreaming, but she couldn't get out. Couldn't wake up. Not this time. In fact, it probably wasn't a dream at all but an act of a far greater power as she swallowed the last of the coppery blood and gazed into Lucas's dark, sinister eyes.

His fangs flashed with pride. "That's it, *bella*," he whispered, cupping her cheek and tracing her blood-soaked lips with his equally wet thumb. "Drink for me. You love it."

The bitch screamed. No, she hated it. Wanted to wake up.

But the blood tasted like the sweetest maple syrup as she sucked it from Lucas's long, cold finger. His grin widened. Then he lunged over the body of their victim and sank his fangs into her neck.

Eden gasped, pleasure snaking through her as blood gushed down her shoulder. Lucas groped her naked ass, no doubt leaving bloodied handprints as he pulled her flush against his body. Her legs widened across his lap as his hands roamed, caking her skin in the thick, sticky liquid before dropping his mouth to her breast and pulling her down onto—

Eden screamed as she flew upright in bed, tears burning in her eyes. Her chest heaved. Heart pounded. Pressing the covers to her mouth, she screamed again.

"*Yes, bella. Blood. The rich, warm taste of blood sliding down your throat like the smoothest cocoa ...*"

She squeezed her eyes closed, muting her screams as she kicked her heels on the mattress and buried her head in her hands. That voice. Talking to her. *Lucas.*

"Go away!"

"*Never. I am in you. You'll become me. Feed and join me. You crave it. Be my bride, my partner, and I can give you everything you've ever desired.*"

"No ..." Eden rocked back and forth, pressing her hands to her temples. "You're not there. I can't hear you."

"*Telepathy is natural with mates. It's why you can't hear the wolf. He's not meant for you.*"

"We're not mated." She wasn't mated to Rain—yet—and certainly not to Lucas. "This is still a dream." A terrifying fucked up dream she wished she could escape.

"*Your dream can come true. Feel the power. It is time, my sweet. Take it. Relish it. Be brave.*"

"Eden!"

She gasped and kicked the blankets away at the sound of her friend's shout through the door. The handle jiggled, and Eden scurried back to huddle against the timber bedhead.

"You can't go in there!" Chad cried.

"I heard her scream!" Ava replied.

"I know, but—"

"No! Don't come in!" Eden curled into herself, hugging her cold thighs to her heaving chest. Fuck, if Ava came in here, she'd kill her for sure. "I ... I'm *hungry*."

She dropped her head onto her knees with a wail. Hungry. So hungry. If only Rain hadn't removed all the meat from the house as she could certainly do with a big, juicy steak. Taste flesh, blood, and feed—

Gagging, Eden pressed her fist to her mouth. No, she couldn't do it. She wouldn't!

Shouted whispers filtered through the door, but she paid no attention until Chad called out, "Are you okay? Can I help?"

Tears filled her eyes as she pressed her head to her knees. "Where's Nate?"

"We switched. We're hunting Hawkings Point as we think Lucas is lurking nearby."

He lurked all right. In her head. In her nightmares. Tugging at her soul that ached for Rain.

Her heart broke. *Rain*. She wanted Rain. His comfort, his strength, his warmth.

"I made dinner," Ava said gently. "Lentil loaf and vegetables. Including zucchini and broccoli."

The human part of her groaned, aching for sustenance. Fuck, she loved those vegetables. But the vampire inside her almost hurled. Lentil loaf? Try beef! Or black pudding.

Hmm ... black pudding ...

Wincing, Eden curled up tighter. She wouldn't let the darkness win. She had to fight it. "Can you leave it by the door?"

"Chad will fix you a plate," Ava said, and after a few heated whispers, footsteps stomped down the hall. "Eden, are you sure there isn't anything I can do?"

She squeezed her eyes closed as Ava's pulse thumped hard and low, fear shivering through Eden with every beat. Then the rapid thud of a smaller heart joined Ava, accompanied by the sweet scent of cute canine.

Eden choked on a sob. "Please go."

"What?"

"Go away!" she screamed, tears blurring her vision. "Please! I'm hungry, Ava! And I don't want to hurt you. Or Gracie."

Footsteps signaled Chad's return. "Eden, I understand this is difficult, but I'm heating up food for you so please try to think about that."

Ava's voice hitched. "Do you think she'll—"

"Take her away, Chad!" Eden clawed at her shins as fear undulated through her body. "Please!"

"She can't leave the packhouse, Eden. I need to keep you both here."

"I'm reaching out to Finn ..." Ava whispered.

"He says not to take any chances—"

"No!" Eden cried. "Don't take *any* chances!"

Their conversation softened and Eden tried desperately to block them out as she rocked herself back and forth. Footsteps faded, then a single set returned. Chad's.

"I can leave your dinner here or bring it in."

Exhaling, Eden lowered her knees and welcomed company she couldn't kill. "You can come in."

A sliver of light filled the room as Chad entered and placed the plate on the bed beside her. Oregano and basil filled her senses while her mouth watered at the sight of the lentil loaf. And though her stomach repulsed at the thought, she would force down the side of steamed vegetables even if it killed her.

It probably will ...

"Is Ava safe?"

"I sent her upstairs. Are you staying in here?"

Eden nodded. "I don't trust myself."

"All right. Just call out if you need me. The pack aren't far away tonight."

"Thank you."

Chad nodded, then left Eden alone. And though it looked delicious, she left her dinner untouched, her appetite not cooperating as she sank into the pillows.

She was turning into a monster. Everything inside her burned and ached until she wanted to tear her hair out and scream. She could hear voices and wanted to kill her friend. If fiction had taught her anything, it was that young vampires rarely had control over their thirst. She'd probably taste that first drop of blood and be unable to stop herself from drinking the dam dry.

Shuddering, Eden pulled at her hair, then reached blindly for the plate and shoved a piece of broccoli in her mouth. Broccoli. Soft, spongey, delicious broccoli.

"*Disgusting.*"

Wailing, she reached for another. "It's not. It's delicious and I won't give in."

"*You will. Humans always do. Eternal life is better than death, and your boyfriend will never find me.*"

"Because you're a coward!" she cried, flipping onto her back. "Face him! I dare you!"

Eden slammed her leg against the mattress. After minutes passed with no snide reply from that Mediterranean voice, her body softened, and she curled around her dinner plate.

"That's right. You grow some balls or shut the fuck up."

She ate in silence. The food tasted like ash, but she forced down her vegetables and most of the loaf. At least she'd keep up some of her nutrients for when Rain saved her. And once he did, she would eat the biggest bowl of apple and strawberry porridge she could, followed by Thai chili lime rice or savory beans.

Food. Real, delicious food.

Time dragged, the hour unknown. Lucas seemed to have gotten over his hissy fit at being called a coward as he tried to claw his way back inside her head, but he'd only ever managed to infiltrate through her dreams, and she stubbornly refused to fall asleep. The bastard *was* a coward and if Rain couldn't save her, it wouldn't be for a lack of trying. Her man, her *mate*, was a strong, powerful creature, a true hunter, and she didn't doubt for a second that he would try everything he could to keep her with him. Alive.

But how could he defeat a monster who hid in the shadows, who wouldn't face his foe and fight?

Nate returned and paced restlessly outside, then was replaced once again by Chad and his heavier footfalls. But she wished just for a moment that Rain would give up the hunt and hold her. She couldn't do this without him and longed for his touch. His scent.

She needed him.

But he also needed to kill Lucas so she could feel normal again, have the curse lifted, and touch Rain like she'd longed to all these years. Because oh, how she longed to touch him. To run her fingers through his hair and down his body, taking in the hardness of his pecs and the ripple of his abs before dipping her hand further down to—

Eden groaned and shook the fantasy away. She couldn't think about that. Not now.

But the moment Lucas was dust, she would be human again. Instantly? Fuck, she hoped so. She'd never known terror like this. The unknown. Clinging to hope. Even that day she'd been stranded on the beach waiting to be rescued while her father lay motionless and broken on the rocks, she hadn't been as terrified. Not even when she waited for Rain's parachute to open. None of those things mattered anymore, not when her life literally hung in the balance. The lives of her friends.

Hell, if she survived this, she hoped to never feel fear again.

She might even do something reckless. Maybe she *would* ride the jet ski or—

The back door slammed. Eden bolted upright, then winced at the unmistakable sound of a fist plowing through the wall. Rain's. She knew it by the tug around her heart. The heat in her thighs. Her mate was home.

"The sadistic bastard's tormenting me. He's out there, Chad. Lurking. Watching. He's just ..."

Eden clutched the pillow to her chest as she waited for Rain to continue speaking, but the silence dragged until he huffed out a breath, and she could picture his strong shoulders sag.

"I can't lose her, Chad. I have one more chance tomorrow night and then ..."

Eden's breath caught. What? Tomorrow? But she had four days left!

"Maybe it won't be as bad as you think."

Rain hissed and put his fist through another wall. Eden jumped.

"How can you say that? You've seen it. It goes against everything we believe in. Even if it saves her life, I can't ... I won't ..."

Eden's heart raced as she clutched her knees and pillow tighter.

"But it's an option," Chad said. "I know it's awful, but dude—"

"I can't think about it right now. I need to de-stress. Strategize. Tackle the hunt with a clear head tomorrow."

"We'll get him, man. We'll form a battle plan and won't stop until—"

"Two thirty-nine," Rain huffed. "We need to have him before then. Else ..."

"The opportunity's gone. I know."

Eden placed the pillow aside. What were they talking

about? Was there another way to save her? If so, then she needed to know about it, even if it did cause Rain to put his fist through the wall. Because Chad was right. How could it be worse than her death or eternal damnation?

But if Lucas continued to hide and Rain failed ... then Eden would give in. Not to the monster, oh no. She would not stalk this earth for the rest of time, killing and ripping people apart. Images of such an existence played on a continuous loop inside her head, terrorizing her, making her scream even harder and igniting the extreme thirst that clawed at her throat and curdled in her stomach. Were the vampires that lurked like the creatures in the folktales? Did they *only* drink blood?

Eden shuddered. She'd never find out.

Taking a deep breath, she stretched out her tired, shaking legs and eased off the bed. Her head swam and vision blurred as her hands curled over the edge of the mattress. She'd never felt so weak. Hunger that dinner had failed to satisfy leeched all the energy from her system. But she could beat it. She was still human. For now.

Eden pushed to her feet, took two steps, then crumbled against the door and turned the handle.

"So tomorrow, I'm going to—Eden!" Darkness faded from Rain's blue eyes as he strode past Chad towards her.

Eden's lips parted as she stared at his tall, mud-smeared body, dirt caking his torso, arms, and thighs, but not the shorts he'd zipped and failed to button. His toes squelched on the hardwood floors, leaving a trail of footprints. Where had he been hunting, the creeks? He smelled of gum leaves, moss, and wet ... dog. She'd never seen him so filthy, yet she wanted nothing more than to throw her arms around him and spear her fingers through his damp, dark hair.

"How are you feeling?" He pressed the back of his surprisingly clean hand to her forehead, then stroked his fingers through her hair to cradle her cheek. "Are you okay? Did you eat? Food?"

Eden's pulse quickened at the hasty addition to his question. "I ate dinner, but it didn't help. I'm still so hungry."

"I know." His lips pressed together beneath his wild, overgrown beard. "But you need to keep your strength up."

"I had to send Ava away."

"I heard." His thumb brushed over her cheekbone. "And I'm sorry. But you won't hurt—"

She clutched his forearm and squeezed. Hard. Rain's eyebrows shot up. "That's the thing! I'm scared I will! I dreamed of biting her. Of killing her. I dream of feeding, and I can't take it! He's in my head, Rain! Lucas. He speaks to me—"

"He does?" Rain's eyes turned stormy. "When? For how long?"

"L-last night. It started—"

"Fuck!"

"I know! And I'm fucking terrified, so please!" She pressed her hand to his hot, dirty, hairy chest. "Do what you need to do and save me!"

"Eden, I am—"

"No!" She shook her head and dug her nails into his pec. "Do whatever you and Chad were talking about. Before the opportunity passes."

Rain's jaw hardened. "You don't know what you're talking about—"

"I don't care!" Tears sprung to her eyes as she grabbed his shoulders and shook him. "Tell me! Do it! Please!"

Her knees crumpled as all the strength drained from her body. Rain's arms came beneath hers, catching her before she collapsed onto the floor. Though he offered her no comfort.

"Take her, Chad. I need to shower."

Eden's shoulders shook, sobs raking from her throat as she

found herself moved into Chad's clean arms. Clutching the other wolf, she peeked over her shoulder at Rain. "Please! If ... if you love me ..."

"I do love you. Which is why I can't ..." His voice cracked, pain etching his face as he shook his head and stumbled backwards. Then he escaped into his bedroom, slamming the door behind him and shattering her heart.

Eden pressed her face into Chad's chest in a fresh wave of sobs.

Chapter 24

Rain leaned his forearms on the shower wall and squeezed his eyes shut, but no amount of deep breathing could ease the shame and guilt that pulsed through his body as Eden's hysterical cries wailed from the hall.

His fists curled beneath the scalding water. This wasn't how he'd planned to introduce her to his world. It wasn't how he'd wanted her to learn the truth about him. He'd wanted more for her. More for himself. For their future as a couple and Fated mates. So, so much more.

But that future had been squashed and his chance to get it back grew slimmer and slimmer.

He'd never felt so helpless.

Rain watched the filthy water swirl down the drain, wishing it could take his pain with it as the dead bat's words continued to haunt him. *"He watches over her. Speaks to her. Continues to encourage her to give in and feed."*

He knew vampires were connected to their prey. It was a power stronger than compulsion, a lustful mind control that could almost make their puppet bend to their will.

And Eden had heard Lucas.

Fuck!

Rain banged his head against the wall, and once again for good measure. Eden wasn't coping. She might be tough in mind, body, and soul as a human, but she wasn't strong enough to fight the deadly evils of his world. The virus inside her continued to fester, and Lucas had managed to make a connection. His bite had seeped deeper into her system and if she didn't give in and make a kill, she would die.

Unless he bit her first. He could save her life and damn his. Whether the Goddess saw, whether he gained forgiveness or not, it would make no difference. He and Eden might have already formed two levels of their bond, but if he bit her, nothing would erase the darkness of their newly sealed connection. He couldn't do it.

But wouldn't he sacrifice himself for Eden in a heartbeat?

If you loved me ...

He did love her. To the moon and back. Which was why he couldn't do it. Sure, marking his mate wouldn't stop them from completing the task the Goddess had set out for them, but they couldn't possibly maintain the light of their bond if he sealed their Fate in darkness and stole Eden's free will.

Rain pushed away from the wall and scrubbed his hands down his face. What had he done to deserve this? What the fuck was Fate doing to him? Was he being punished? Fucking hell, why did it have to be so complicated?

"It's not. You're overthinking it. Just bite her, brother. Fate might be cruel, but the Goddess can be forgiving."

Rain froze. *"How the fuck does this help, Sly? It's an impossible choice."*

"No, it's fucking not. I told you what to do and how to get away with it. Don't hesitate. Take the hours you have left to get used to the idea, but you need to bite her before the turn of the new moon. Not a minute after. Don't miss this chance. She's your mate. Fucking save her!"

Rain dropped his hands, drawing on the comfort that Sly's presence had always brought him. The comfort that, despite the turmoil and anger clawing at his throat, allowed Rain to admit, *"I'm scared."*

"You should be! Mating is fucking terrifying, and this vampire is one sadistic fucker. But there is no one more important than your mate, little brother. Remember that. You fucking die protecting her!*"*

Sly's words contained such venom that Rain's heart plunged like a lead weight. Pain might consume his brother, but a small part of Rain had died the day Shelby had, too, when he, Nate, and Kai had restrained Sly on the beach at Cockle Bay. When his brother had roared in agony, feeling his wife's terror, pain, and their connection sever the moment Tyrone had slaughtered her.

Sly hadn't died protecting his mate.

"I know. But, Sly ... I'm so sorry—"

"Don't be fucking sorry! You have a chance here. Don't blow it. Don't be like me. This isn't the life I want for you, brother. I should have kicked your ass the moment I realized you mated months ago! You're a wolf. So fucking kill the vampire inside your mate and be done with it!"

Rain blew out his breath. *"Do you think Lucas was the vampire who took Shelby?"*

Sly's low growl rumbled through Rain's head. *"Maybe. He's a slick fucker and if you have a chance, ask him before you rip his throat out. Just fucking* do it *already! Eden is fucking dying and you were born to protect her! Don't be like me, Rain. Forget about me. Be like Finn. Mate and be happy."*

Warmth spread through Rain's chest. He could be happy. With Eden, he'd be the happiest man and wolf alive.

But would she be happy when she was no longer free?

"How can I be happy when our love is tainted?"

"How can you be happy when she's dead?" Sly cried, and

Rain cringed. *"It doesn't get much worse than death, brother. So, take the other option. You'll be fine. I promise."*

The warmth in his chest dared to turn to hope. Was the old Sly still inside the angry wolf after all?

"I'll think about it."

"Don't take too long," Sly snapped, and the connection cut.

Rain dropped his chin to his chest. "Fuck."

RAIN STOOD on the balcony and glared out over Picnic Bay, anticipation and fear warring inside him as the tide rolled in and sank the wreck of the *George Rennie* offshore. He curled his hands around the banister, the pink and golden rays of the sunset torturing him as stars emerged in the inky sky. His teeth refused to unclench as he surveyed his surroundings. He could *feel* Lucas watching him. Waiting him out. Rain had never felt such anger. Such hate. And he only had eight hours left to find the malicious bastard.

Footsteps approached and Rain glanced over his shoulder to find Finn, his jaw tense beneath his blond beard.

"How you doing, man?"

Rain turned his glare back to the jetty. "I don't know what I'm going to do."

Finn stepped up beside him. "I understand your hesitation, but—"

"What's it like? The marking?"

Finn paused. "Why? Because my mother was marked?"

"She's the only person either of us has ever ... never mind. I shouldn't have asked."

Rain unclenched his hands and straightened, blowing out a long breath. But his turmoil didn't ease.

After a moment, Finn cleared his throat. "The marking is

everything we hear about, but Eden will be fine. Devoted to you, but fine. And you will be, too."

Rain's heart thudded as he turned to his Alpha. "Would you do it?"

"In a heartbeat." Finn's eyes softened, his words sincere. "Given no other choice. You're not biting Eden to be cruel, Rain. You're not biting her out of hate like the rebels do. You're not trying to defy Fate. You're saving her life and in turn, you will mark her as yours. It might not be what any of us intend, but the Goddess will understand that. And no matter what, you'll always be welcome in my pack." Finn clamped his hand over Rain's shoulder. "I owe everything to you, Rain. You know that. I'll never turn my back on you."

Rain managed a small smile. "Thanks, man."

"Don't mention it. Now, come inside. The scouts have arrived, and we need to organize tonight's hunt."

Chapter 25

They gathered in the dining room, Finn standing at the head of the table with his hair tied back, legs spread, and arms crossed while his elegant mate sat beside him with Gracie cradled in her lap. Rain tried to remain focused, determined not to let anything distract him from his task, but he couldn't ignore the pang inside his chest as he studied the couple. Finn and Ava were strong, capable, and so ridiculously in love it was hard not to feel a touch of envy at the way they interacted. The small touches, the lingering gazes. Rain wanted nothing more than to have that intimacy with Eden. To have her support. Her love.

But she wouldn't give herself willingly unless he killed that vampire, and he needed her to choose to stand beside him. To choose to be with him because of the love in her heart, not because he'd marked her.

"We have every advantage," Finn said. "Four against one, with one of you guarding the ladies. Lucas hasn't shifted from bat form for three days, but he will need to feed. He can't hold off for much longer."

"How often do vamps feed?" Nate asked.

"I'd have thought every night," Kai said, and Finn nodded in confirmation.

"I thought so, too, but since he's so old and powerful, the rules may not apply. But he must be growing impatient, and this is our best chance to lure him out so that Rain can save Eden under the Goddess's terms."

Rain's chest tightened. "Sly said the more she resists, the more he'll try to turn her."

"Then why doesn't he come for her?" Kai asked. "What's he waiting for?"

"Do you think what the bat said last night is true?" Nate surveyed the pack. "Is he getting inside her head?"

"Yes," Rain and Chad confirmed, and the scouts' eyebrows shot up.

"She told me last night," Rain continued, terror cording his forearms. "I didn't have a chance to ask her about it, but she said he's been speaking to her."

"Then there's our answer." Kai clapped his hands together. "Eden's connected to the prick, so why don't we lure him to us?"

Rain's hands clenched. "You want to use Eden as bait?"

"Hey, I'm just saying. We've spent all this time looking for a bastard who doesn't want to be found. But if he wants Eden, he'll come for her."

"You can't be serious!" Rain advanced on the young wolf. "If you think I'm going to put her in danger—"

"She's already in danger!" Kai cried. "What's going to happen if—"

"You used *me* as bait." Ava's soft voice halted Rain in his tracks. "Blair wanted me, so you brought me to Cockle Creek. He came, and you killed him."

Rain gritted his teeth. "But you were never in danger. We protected you."

"Exactly!" she cried, and Rain groaned. He'd walked

straight into that one. "And Eden won't be either. But if he can reach her, maybe she can reach him? We just need to be ready for when he comes. Because I think he will."

"She has a point," Finn said, and Rain's lips twisted. "Eden's the only chance we have. We can spend another night mindlessly trying to sniff out his scent, or we can see if she can call for him—"

"And make her embrace the vampire inside her? Because that's what you're asking! That connection isn't natural. It's formed by the virus he infected her with. How can I ask her to use that when she's already terrified of him? I won't do it!"

"You won't have to."

Rain spun around, his breath catching as his gaze locked with Eden's. She stood at the end of the hall, her pale fingers clutching the wall and face almost translucent beneath the bright downlights. Yet determination darkened her eyes as she stepped forward.

"They're right, Rain. I want to help you so maybe—" Her legs wobbled, and she stumbled into the lounge.

Rain bolted across the room and caught her before she could fall. "I've got you." He helped her into a dining chair, then leaned back against the table, indecision ricochetting through him as he caressed her cold hand in his.

"I can try, Rain. If he can reach into my mind, maybe I can reach into his."

"But you're sick. Tired and weak."

"And I can't go on like this. It's exhausting." Even her speech was slow she was that tired, but Rain remained patient and heard her out. "I don't want to go down without a fight. So, let me help you defeat Lucas."

She set her jaw and shot him a pleading yet decided look that would slay any man.

"Are you going to argue with that?" Kai asked, and Rain's lips curled.

Finn cleared his throat. "Come on, man. It's her life."

"Exactly! I won't die like this, Rain. And you can't protect me from everything."

"I can try," he growled.

"No." She squeezed his hand. "You can't. He doesn't want you to find him. I told him to face you. Dared him."

Rain blinked. "You did?"

"Yes, and he didn't like it. I called him a coward and he went silent."

"He *is* a coward," Kai muttered, and Rain nodded in agreement. Lucas had certainly taken the coward's route. He'd hidden before attacking Eden and they hadn't laid eyes on him since he'd issued his challenge. And yet, Rain continued to fight, which clearly proved wolves were the stronger of the two creatures. He was a hunter. A fighter. He never gave up. And though he might not like it, Rain knew what he had to do. He'd searched to no avail, but Eden could lure Lucas out of the shadows. She could tell him she was ready. After all, that's what Lucas wanted, wasn't it?

Rain glanced around at his pack, then back to Eden. "He said he wants you to be his bride."

She shivered. "Yes. He wants a partner. Someone to feed with and ... and ..."

"He's not going to get it." Rain turned to Finn. "You don't think Tyrone actually wants more vampires, right? He only asked this of Lucas to hurt us?"

Finn nodded. "To break our ties with Fate." By killing Eden or forcing Rain to bite her. "But Lucas will fight for her. He's a coward, but he won't leave a job unfinished."

Rain took a deep breath. Then, before he could change his mind, he locked eyes with his mate. "Tell him. Tell him to face us and claim you as his own otherwise ... I'll mark you."

Rain's wolf growled as fear rose up to choke him, but nothing made more sense. Lucas didn't think Rain had the guts to bite Eden. Hell, Rain wasn't sure he had the guts either, but right now, Lucas had the advantage. And if Rain threatened that, then the bat would rise to the challenge.

Eden's mouth fell open. "Wh-what?"

"You can't!" Ava cried, her chair scraping back. "If you mark her—"

"I'm not going to mark her!" Rain glared at Ava as Finn drew her into his arms. "But if Lucas thinks I might, he will come to stop me."

Eden opened her mouth, closed it, then shook her head. "I thought ... is that how you can save me? By biting me?"

Bile filled his throat, but he was determined to remain strong. He wouldn't have to *actually* do it. "Like I can kill a vampire, I can kill the virus inside you. But in doing so, I'll trigger our bond and claim you as mine against the Goddess's wishes. I'll darken our connection, take away your free will, and bind you to me forever."

"Which you said was barbaric ..."

"It is." Four nodding heads backed him up. "I won't lie to you. I love you, Eden, and I don't want to lose you. But to take away your choice ..." He shot his fingers through his hair and tugged. "It goes against everything I believe in."

"And you don't want to do that."

"No. But Lucas won't know that. So, if you want to help, tell him to face me. Then I can kill him and won't need to doom us forever."

"And if he doesn't come?" Kai asked softly.

"He'll come." Rain didn't want to contemplate any other possibility. "He grows impatient and won't risk losing her."

"He does," Eden breathed. "He wants me to turn. Wants me to join him so that we can feed together and—" She shuddered violently and clutched her elbows. "Oh God, his thoughts are beyond evil."

Rain's hands tightened over her knees. "Is he with you now?"

Her limp hair swished as she shook her head. "No, but what he wants to do … I-I can't think about it. Blood and sex and …" Cringing, she snatched his forearm and dug her nails into his skin with more strength than Rain feared was natural. "If he doesn't come, you will bite me, right?"

The room stilled, and Rain's pulse skyrocketed. He couldn't … didn't want to think …

"Lucas will come." He shot to his feet and glanced at the scouts. "Open the doors. Once Eden makes contact, be ready to fight."

EDEN BREATHED in fresh air for the first time in days as Rain and Finn opened the French concertina doors to welcome the night. Everything lay still, the ocean barely rippling beneath the dark sky shining with a thousand stars. Part of her longed to go outside and search for the few constellations Isla had shown her years ago, if she could remember them. Isla had always believed Eden should take an interest in astronomy considering her surname and had loved sharing her passion for the stars. But Eden doubted she was strong enough to stroll onto the balcony, never mind the fact Rain would stop her before she even put a toe over the threshold. The ferocity in his eyes, in his movements, reminded her of the man she'd fallen in love with. The dangerous, sexy daredevil who would slay dragons for her.

Or in this case, vampires.

And while her belly twisted in all kinds of knots at the thought of Rain biting her, the image of Lucas licking blood from her breasts rendered Eden motionless with terror. She would not take that risk. She didn't even want to communicate with Lucas, but she couldn't spend another night curled up in fear either. She wanted to help, wanted to fight, but she had to choose her battles, and calling Lucas to face Rain was something she could do.

Rain latched the door, then strode towards her, his dark hair lifting in the breeze and curtaining his bearded face like the untamed knight of her dreams. No shining armor for her man, though. No, give her dirt and rage-steeled muscles any day.

Eden swooned as he extended his hand. She longed for this plan to succeed, for this fight to be over so she could love Rain the way she'd always wanted. So they could complete the bond she was beginning to understand. But if things went wrong ...

"You will sit here by the door and not step a foot outside," Rain said, his eyes lethal. "Nate will fetch you a blanket."

The young wolf moved like lightning while Kai swooped in to push the armchair across the room. Though she was strong enough to take the few steps, Eden welcomed Rain's arm around her waist as he helped her towards the doors.

She sat, and Nate draped a blanket around her shoulders.

Rain knelt in front of her. "Do you know how the connection works?"

"No. He's only come to me. Usually in a dream. Dark, horrible dreams." She shuddered. "Why do vampires need to be so crude?"

"Sex and blood is what they live for," Rain said, his hands caressing her knees and shooting inconvenient heat to her thighs. "And when it's all they eat ... it's like we might do with certain foods."

Eden imagined Rain lathered in maple syrup and bit down on a smile. "I guess. But you guys are telepathic, so how do you do it?"

"It's kind of like a thread. We're connected, and we reach through that thread to the other wolf."

"I focus on the person in the pack and the bond pulls," Finn said. "So, think about Lucas—"

"Oh God." She shuddered and pulled the blanket tighter.

"Eden—"

"No, I've got this." She drew in a breath, gathering strength as she sank into Rain's touch. His eyes. The determination in his face. "I'll just ... well, last night I spoke out loud."

"That could work."

She nodded, but she couldn't do this while looking at Rain. "Can you give me space?"

He pushed to his feet and moved to stand behind her, his fingers brushing through her hair before settling on the back of the armchair. That was better. He was far enough away for her to concentrate, but close enough to keep her balanced as she focused on the man she did *not* want to think about.

"Lucas?" she whispered, gazing out into the dark, starry night. "Lucas? I'm ... I'm hungry." Not a lie. "So hungry ..."

A bird called. Leaves rustled. The kettle boiled in the kitchen. Otherwise, everything remained silent.

Eden swallowed and straightened her spine. "I'm ready to feed."

The armchair creaked as Rain's hands clenched. One of the scouts shuffled his feet. The kettle clicked.

Blowing out her breath, Eden reached for Lucas with her mind. "*Lucas, I can't take this anymore! I'm hungry. I don't want to die. I want everlasting life. With you. I want to feed and hunt and play with you.*"

She waited. But seconds ticked by with no response, and Eden's shoulders slumped. "It's not working."

Rain's hand dropped to her shoulder. "Give it time."

"He probably doesn't believe me," she muttered, dropping her chin to her chest. "I wouldn't believe me."

"Don't give up just yet," Ava suggested, handing Eden a

steaming mug of tea. "He'll come. But perhaps you should all go eat and leave Eden alone so she can concentrate."

"Yes. Please," Eden said.

Rain growled at the suggestion, but dropped his head beside Eden's, his beard brushing her cheek as he whispered, "Be brave, baby. You can do this."

He pressed his lips to her jaw, then swept away, his heavy footfalls stomping into the kitchen.

Eden's knuckles whitened around the mug. She stared at the glowing pink jetty, her heart pounding as her breath escaped in short, sharp bursts.

She could be brave. She had to be if she wanted to destroy this evil inside her and start her life with Rain. Because if she didn't, she believed with all her heart that Rain would succumb to his fear. Risk his soul.

And mark her.

Chapter 26

Rain couldn't wait any longer. For two hours, he'd paced, eaten, and was practically clawing at the floorboards while Eden had sat muttering quietly, communicating in silence, or shouting out into the night. But nothing had worked. Lucas was one stubborn fuck, and Rain could no longer ignore the itch between his shoulder blades.

He turned to Finn. "We need to go." The inky sky tormented him. Time was of the essence. Five hours and counting until the next moon phase began and he wouldn't have a second past that flash of darkness to save Eden.

He had to kill that bat. Now.

Finn nodded. "Let's hunt. Nate, stay here." He grabbed the young wolf by the collar and leaned in close, his gaze stuck on Ava curled up on the lounge behind Eden. "Guard them with your fucking life."

Nate squared his shoulders. "Will do, boss."

Rain shoved his hand through his hair and dropped to his knee beside Eden. "I'm going to find him. Keep trying, okay?"

She nodded, determination peeking through the exhaustion clouding her eyes. "I will."

"You can do this." He cupped the back of her neck and

pressed his lips to her cold forehead. Drawing a soft breath, Rain didn't fail to notice her natural garden scent, usually so floral and woodsy, was slowly fading to one of decay. Heart pounding, he lowered his gaze to hers. "I'll be back soon."

Before two thirty-nine and the moon started waxing again.

Rain tore himself away from his beloved and followed Finn into the backyard.

"We'll let you know when he responds," Nate said.

"Thanks." Rain stripped off his shirt. "And if he comes, kill him. Don't hesitate. That goes for you all! See, bite, kill. I don't need to be the one to do it. I just need the fucker dead."

Then he kicked off his shorts and shifted as he leapt into the bush. The pack ran after him, claws scratching at the dirt and kicking up leaves as they raced east towards the ocean.

"*He has to be around here,*" Kai said. "*There's no better place to roost.*"

"*Unless he's lurking along the Esplanade,*" Chad said. "*Do we dare look?*"

But Rain had already veered right and was scampering down the hill back towards the house.

"*Rain!*" Finn called. "*You need to shift back!*"

"*And put clothes on!*" Kai reminded him, which was a fair call when Rain certainly wasn't thinking straight. His mind focused on one thing. *Find Lucas. Kill Lucas.* Because of course that bastard was roosting along the Esplanade, taking up residence in one of the glorious fig trees outside houses and bustling restaurants. Or in someone's backyard. Anywhere that would make it difficult for Rain—as a wolf—to sink his teeth into what appeared to be a man and risk exposing their paranormal world.

But that wasn't going to stop him as he ducked beneath the first-floor balcony of his home and plunged into the gardens. Shifting, he ran onto the driveway barefooted and reached into the mailbox for a convenient pair of board shorts. It wasn't much, but at least he was half decent as he scampered through the scrub, cut his foot on a rock, and leapt off a boulder onto the beach. Waves lapped softly in the gentle wind as the tide rolled in. The dry sand made his ankles weep as Rain raced towards the fore-shore, slowing only once he hit the pathway weaving past houses. Chest heaving, he lifted his nose and inspected the trees as he walked. His supernatural senses might not be as strong when he was a man, but they were heightened beyond a human's capability and by the fucking Moon, he would find that cunt of a bat.

"How is he so fucking good at hiding?" he asked, reaching out to his pack as he circled a tree.

"Well, as a stealth master—"

"He manipulates shadows."

Rain froze as Sly's voice interrupted Finn's. *"They what?"*

"What?" Finn asked.

"Sly. He said Lucas manipulates shadows."

"Sly's there?"

"Fucking hell, brother, listen to me! You'll never find the bat. Unless everything goes dark. And don't even think about cutting power to the island. Just save! Your! Mate!"

Rain grunted, craning his neck as he ran to the next tree. "I'm trying! But I—"

"Are you okay, mate?"

He turned and almost tripped over a border collie's leash. The dog scampered back, panting happily while his owner studied Rain with a frown.

"Yeah. Just … looking for something."

He dashed away before more questions could be asked. Fuck, he must look a sight, the barefooted billionaire running down the Esplanade talking to himself like he'd lost his bloody mind.

"Fuck, man," Finn said. *"Play it cool."*

"How hard can it be to find one measly bat?" Rain

muttered, striving for a more non-conspicuous demure as he approached the restaurants where diners enjoyed an evening meal. Rambunctious chatter filtered down from the pub while people strolled along the illuminated jetty. It wasn't the ideal place to hunt a vampire and, therefore, was the perfect place for Lucas to hide.

"*Very,*" Sly growled. "*You're wasting your time as they can't be caught!*"

"*Bullshit! We've killed four so far.*"

"*Yes, but not the vampire you want! Come on, Rain. Give it up!*"

Rain gritted his teeth and peered into another fig tree. "*Like you've given up? I won't lose faith in Fate like you have, brother. I'm sorry for what happened. You know I am. But I still have something to fight for. You said it yourself, you* die *for your mate. And I'm not giving up. Not now, not ever.*"

And with the fear of biting Eden surging through his veins, Rain continued to run.

By MIDNIGHT, Eden feared she'd faint from starvation. She'd tried an apple earlier and after one bite, had thrown it over the balcony. She feared what the lack of nutrition was doing to her body and longed for sustenance. For porridge. Pancakes. She wanted Thai chili lime rice and chia pudding.

But all she could think about was blood. She yearned to feed. To kill. Her eyes drifted closed and she imagined sinking her teeth into Dee's soft neck. Blood pooled on her tongue and dripped down her chin as she drank ravenously, relishing the warm coppery taste of the thickest juice she'd ever had the pleasure of savoring while her nurse screamed.

Gasping, Eden sat upright and stared into the dark night.

But the pink lights of the jetty refused to focus as the edges of her vision blurred.

"*Yes, bella. It is time. You will come to me.*"

Eden's lips parted, her breath escaping in sharp bursts as she dug her fingers into the arms of her chair.

Nate knelt at her side. "Lucas?"

She nodded, clinging to the connection. After hours of trying, she'd thought it was a lost cause. But he'd come.

"Yes," she said aloud. "I ... I can't take this anymore. I don't want to die and Rain ... he said if you don't face him, he'll destroy your plans and bite me."

Lucas's low chuckle grated on her last nerve. "*Bite you, will he? As if. A Fated pussy like Blackwood would never bite his mate. Do you know what it will do to him? To you?*"

Eden risked a glance at Nate. "No, I don't know what Rain biting me will do to him. But it'll kill the vampire inside me and stop you from claiming me as yours."

Lucas snarled. "*And sacrifice his connection with his goddess. He'll be ousted. It'll destroy his soul and everything that he is. He'll have nothing left, only you. You to control and order and have submit to his every carnal desire.*"

Eden shuddered. She didn't want to die. She wanted her life with Rain. To love Rain. But could she live with herself if saving her life cost him everything that he was? Would he choose her, *love* her, if it meant giving up his pack, his brother, and all he'd ever worked for?

"Is that true?" she asked Lucas while staring into Nate's pale eyes. "Rain will cut his ties to the Moon Goddess?"

Lucas cackled mercilessly, but Nate vigorously shook his head and saved her heart from plummeting.

"Not if he bites you before two thirty-nine," Nate whispered, indicating the night sky with his chin. "Beneath the new moon."

Eden's breath caught as her gaze shot to the sky. *One night left*, Rain had said. That's what he'd meant? The new moon?

"*Why do you think he's still hunting me?*" Lucas crowed. "*You might be the stupid wolf's mate, but you aren't the most important thing to him. That bloody moon bitch in the sky will win every time. He's not beholden to you, he submits to her. Your life isn't worth giving up all that he believes in. He's a bloody* coward!"

The blanket tumbled from Eden's shoulders as she shot to her feet. "Don't call him a coward! You're the one hiding from the fight! Waiting in the shadows! So, if I'm really the woman you want to spend eternity with, then come and get me! Face Rain and prove that you're worth me giving up my life for. Fucking fight for me!"

She shouted those final words, her fists curling as her heart pounded with newfound strength. Because Lucas didn't know about the new moon. He couldn't. Which meant finally, Rain had the advantage.

"*Why do I need to fight when I can just sit back and watch the little doggies chase their tails? When I know that you'll submit and be mine anyway?*"

"I'll never be yours. The Goddess created me for Rain. I'll always be his and nothing you do will ever change that."

Lucas snorted. "*I think I've proven you wrong there. You're turning, bella. You crave the taste of blood. You long for death.*"

That was true. She might have. But that was before she'd realized that killing Lucas wasn't the only way to save her. "No, I don't. I long to be released from this hell you've inflicted upon me. To feel normal and strong and loved again."

"See if you can find out where he is," Nate whispered beside her, his eyes searching and biceps bulging as he preened for the fight.

Eden blinked, remembering she had a task to do, and that Nate must be communicating with Rain.

"You can feel stronger than you ever have before, Eden. And I can end this torment. You're conflicted with your human soul, so let it go. Give into the hunger. I promise, it'll be worth it."

An image of herself flashed before her eyes, her skin pale but bright, strength vibrating from her as she bit into human flesh and satisfied her hunger. "Then tell me ... how do I find you? How do I do it? Because yes, I am hungry." *So hungry ...*

"You don't need to find me, bella. I've been here the whole time."

Eden froze. "You're here?"

Nate's eyes widened as he exchanged glances with Ava and stepped towards the open doors. "Get back to the packhouse!"

"I've been watching you," the suave, compelling Mediterranean voice continued. *"Waiting. Hoping. But I'm no fool. I won't throw myself to the wolves. But if you're ready ...?"*

Eden swooned at the sweetness in his words, the temptation. "I am. I'm exhausted, Lucas. And food ..." She shuddered at the thought of the apple she'd tasted earlier. "I can't stand it. I need to feed."

Her mouth salivated. *Hungry. So hungry.*

"Then I shall come for you. If that's what you want."

Eden drew in a deep breath and embraced the cold shivering through her body. The soft, beating pulse of fresh blood racing through arteries echoed in her ears.

"Yes ..." Eden said, her voice deepening. "That's what I want."

Drawing in a hungry breath, she spun towards Ava. Eden's lips parted as she stepped forward, and her friend's eyes widened with a gasp.

Nate leapt in front of Ava and pushed her back. "Dude, I don't think she's pretending anymore!"

Chapter 27

A howl echoed through the night and Eden's gaze shot across the bay, blinking away the darkness as her heart lurched at the anguished cry. *Rain* ...

But the screech in reply to the wolf's howl had Eden turning as wings descended from the sky, dropped to the balcony, and shadows coiled upwards. Lucas unfolded his tall, pale form and swept his hands through his dark hair. His pecs and biceps bulged, rendering Eden breathless as she studied the dark hair trailing down his belly towards his—

Ava's high-pitched scream tore through the night, and Eden stumbled backwards, gasping as she pressed her hand to her heaving chest. She'd done it. She'd drawn Lucas out and now the wolves could—

His soulless gaze locked onto hers and the edges of her vision blurred, words dying on her tongue. He was so beautiful. Slender and cut like a marble statue. He could end her pain and bring her peace.

Lucas smirked. "Come to me, *bella*."

He extended his hand, and Eden stepped forward.

Only for Nate's arm to shoot out and knock the wind from her chest. "Don't! Eden, look at me!"

He grabbed her shoulders, turned her away from Lucas, and the fog cleared from her head. Eden's eyes widened as her hands shot to her mouth. Her heart pounded. Stomach roiled as she sank against the lounge. Her hunger burned. Soul wept.

She couldn't take this any longer.

Then Nate's body contorted, his shoulders and back bulging as hairy thighs burst through his shorts. Eden blinked as seconds later, a large sand-colored wolf separated her and Lucas, baring his teeth as he released a low, menacing growl.

Lucas scoffed. "You think one wolf can protect you?"

"No, but I—" Her eyes caught his and words vanished. Why fight it? This could all be over in a second. She could satisfy her hunger. All she had to do was reach out and take it.

"Don't resist it, my love. You can't. I'm inside you. You're drawn to me."

She nodded. Yes, she was. He was a beautiful man, charismatic, and radiated power as he stepped forward once. Twice. Eden longed to reach out and find sanctuary in his arms and—

"*Eden!*"

She gasped, her step faltering as Rain's voice cut through the night and Nate lunged at the vampire. Eden jumped back, her hands covering her mouth as she watched Lucas shift in a whirl of shadow. Wings flapped by the ceiling, accompanied by a gleeful screech as glass shattered at the railing—

And Nate tumbled off the balcony.

Eden screamed. "Nate!"

Running after him, Eden grasped the steel banister and leaned over the edge, gasping as she watched the water ripple and Nate, all man, surfaced.

"Are you okay?" she shouted.

His head snapped up from twenty meters below. "Eden! Go back—"

"*Eden!*" Her name shrilled from across the bay, the fear in

Rain's voice stabbing through her chest and knocking her breathless as she realized her mistake.

Eden spun around and pressed her back into the banister as the bat dropped to the ground and shifted.

"Eden, don't look at him!" Ava cried, but it was too late. Lucas was inside her head and as he stood before her, Eden's traitorous body curved towards him, aching and wanting nothing more than to fall into his hold. Embrace him. Allow him to bite her, suck the life out of her, and let her rise again as a vampire.

His bride.

"It is time, my sweet. Let's feed."

His icy hands fell to her shoulders as he lowered his head and pierced his fangs into her neck. Eden screamed, pain setting every nerve ending on fire as she crumbled against the railing. Lucas pressed his tongue to her flesh and sucked, moaning in delight as—

A door crashed open, wood smashed, and the pain subsided as Lucas vanished in a swirl of shadow. A fierce growl followed the pounding of paws, and Eden cried out as a golden wolf launched onto the outdoor table. Hackles raised, he bared his teeth at the screeching bat flapping meters off the balcony.

Eden slumped against the banister, gasping as she pressed her hand to her left shoulder. The clouds in her mind dissipated and unadulterated panic flooded through her as she drew her fingers away and stared, horrified, at the blood dripping from her fingers.

Blood. Sweet, nourishing, delicious—

"*Eden!*"

Hair whipped in her face as she glanced over her shoulder. Rain sprinted along the beach, his name escaping her lips in a whisper as her heart lodged in her throat.

Rain. She needed Rain.

The bat screeched and swooped. The wolf—Finn—lunged after Lucas and shattered a sunlounge into a million pieces. Two more wolves raced into the house. Furniture broke. Eden heard her name again and tore her gaze from the fight. Her eyes locked onto the man on the beach, and everything around her faded.

Rain. He would save her. She didn't want him to lose his ties to the Moon Goddess, to darken his soul and give up everything he believed in. But as she surveyed the dark sky, she had to believe that the power of the new moon would protect him. New moon was the time for rebirth. To start again. Isla had taught her that. And while Rain might think she'd lose her free will if he bit her, the curse he inflicted couldn't be worse than the monster who currently manipulated her mind.

Besides, it wouldn't be a curse. Eden loved Rain. She'd chosen him the day he'd brought her Pixie, and she hadn't wanted another man since. He wanted her to keep her free-will and make a choice? Well, she was making it.

Resisting the temptation to lick the blood from her fingers, she wiped them on her tank top and used the balcony to pull herself upright. She didn't need to ponder the depths of her heart. It was now or never. So, with all the strength she could muster in her tired body, Eden dashed past the raging wolves and ran out into the night.

SHELLS CRUNCHED beneath Rain's feet as he sprinted along the beach. He hadn't dared shift and risk exposure, though anyone looking up at his illuminated house right now might wonder when he'd adopted three vicious dogs. Finn, Chad, and Kai scrambled over the second-floor balcony in their attempt to bite Lucas despite him being in bat form.

"*He had her, guys,*" Nate said, panting as he swam to shore. "*I never thought compulsion could be so strong.*"

Rain snarled as he pounded along the sand. "*He bit her!*"

"*He didn't have her long enough. He hasn't forced the change,*" Finn said.

Thank fuck for that. Her scream had ripped his heart in two when the fucking bat had sunk his fangs into her.

"*She's covered in blood,*" Kai said. "*She's losing control.*"

"*Told you,*" Sly sneered, who'd remained Rain's unwelcome companion all evening. "*He's in control of this game. There's only one way for you to win.*"

Rain gritted his teeth as fear had him shouting her name again. Their bond had pinged back and forth like a guitar string while Eden had battled with her wills and fought the compulsion. Now, she was slipping away, weak, broken, and with temptation at her fingertips. How could she resist—

"Rain!"

His head snapped up as Eden leapt out of the bush and onto the beach. She landed on her hands and knees, flicked her hair back, and locked her gaze with his. Rain's wolf howled, and he powered his legs harder. "Eden!"

She pushed to her feet, reeking of desperation, desire, and fear as she stumbled, tripped, then ran towards him while calling his name.

"*This is your chance,*" Sly growled. "*Your only chance. Save her, brother.*"

Rain gritted his teeth. A shell pierced his foot, but didn't slow him down. Fifty meters ...

"Rain! Help me!"

Their bond tugged. His wolf whimpered. Blood oozed from her left shoulder. Oh fuck ...

Lucas swooped. She screamed and threw her arms over her head. Rain roared. Thirty meters ...

"Get away, you fucker!"

"Rain!" Her cry would have shattered any man as she stumbled forward. "Please! I know you don't—"

She screamed again, covering her face as Lucas slashed his claws at her back, and the animal inside Rain broke free. Tossing his head back to the night sky, his wolf unleashed a mighty roar. That was his fucking mate and by the Moon, he would do what he'd been born to do.

Save her.

Sand flew as he skidded to a halt and grabbed Eden by her shaking arms. Then, without hesitation, he dropped his mouth to her neck like any captivated lover and bit down on the soft, cold skin of her right shoulder. A blood-curdling scream ripped from her throat as he broke through her flesh, and his wolf howled. But Rain didn't let go as he drew Eden's stiff body into his arms and held her tight as tainted blood dripped down her creamy skin. Her scream turned into a whimper, and the world around him stilled.

Then a shuddering pulse emanated from their chests, stirring the air, lifting the sand, and rippling the water as the mating bond solidified. Rain softened his hold, turned his bite into a kiss, then pulled away, his lip curling in disgust at the wounds on Eden's skin as he cupped her pale, icy cheek. Her breath escaped in shallow bursts. Her eyes remained closed.

Rain froze. "Eden ..."

"Nooo!" Lucas's wail rang across the beach, but Rain didn't dare turn his gaze from his beloved. "You stupid wolf! You'll fucking regret that!"

He already did, but Rain couldn't dwell on that. Lucas screeched and Rain ducked his head to protect Eden's as the bat scraped his talons over the back of Rain's neck. Not that the bastard could ever draw blood.

He vanished into the night.

"He's gone."

Rain didn't acknowledge Finn's whisper as he stared at

Eden's pained, pale face. She didn't move. Barely breathed. Fuck, no. No, no, no ...

Then her body softened, her lips parted with a gasp, and warmth flooded color back into her cheeks. Eden brushed her delicate fingers up his chest as her lashes fluttered open to reveal life sparkling in her chocolate brown eyes.

"Rain—"

"Are you—"

Her mouth collided with his on a gasp as Eden threw her arms around his shoulders. Rain didn't hesitate to pull her close. Lifting her onto her toes, a primal hunger surged through him as he urgently swept his tongue over hers. His wolf howled, chest expanded, and hands hardened on her back as he relished her sweet, vibrant taste. One he'd yearned for. His Eden. His mate. Safe, warm, alive.

Marked.

Anguish battled with raging desire as she lifted her knee and brushed his hip with her thigh. Rain hoisted her up and pressed his hands into her back as she wrapped her taut legs around his waist. Her budded nipples brushed his bare chest through her cotton singlet, sending heat surging through his vessels to his hardening cock. The primitive urge to take her, claim her, and to ride her tiny body into the early morning took hold like a vise. He wanted her. Needed her.

Eden drew on his lower lip, then cupped his face to press kisses over his dirty, sweaty jaw.

"Thank you. Thank you, thank you, thank you ..."

Rain winced. "Don't thank me."

"You saved me."

"I *destroyed* you."

"No." She drew back and caressed his cheek, tears glistening in her eyes. "Don't say that. This was my choice."

"You didn't *have* a choice," he snapped, digging his fingers into her back as rage took hold. "Now you're mine."

"But I've always been yours."

Growling, he dropped his forehead to hers. "You don't understand."

Her hands fell to his shoulders and rubbed gently. "Maybe not. I might not know everything about Fate, but I do know there was no other way. Lucas had a hold of me, Rain, and the moment he bit me ..." She shuddered violently and flung her arms around him. "I couldn't take it anymore. Not when I love you. I choose you. I choose life."

"You're all I've ever wanted, too, baby. The woman I've waited for. The bane of my existence since we met and I knew I couldn't have you. I fucking love you, and it's time I showed it."

"Then love me, Rain. Seal our mating bond the way we were meant to and take me to bed."

Chapter 28

Heat pooled between Eden's legs as she teased his erection with the damp seam of her flannel pants. Rain's breath hissed between his teeth, his eyes darkening as his fingers dug into her ass.

"Eden, you've been—"

She silenced any pointless rejection by kissing him hard, relishing his salty taste as she surrendered to her unquenched desires. "I've been dying," she whispered, enjoying the sensation of his beard rubbing against her skin as she dug her nails into his strong back. "Now, I'm alive and I want to feel everything. I want you, Rain, and I know you want me, too."

He drew on her lower lip, then dropped his head to her marked shoulder and inhaled deeply. "Fuck me. Yes. I do."

The bite had been a surreal experience. Only a force greater than herself could have propelled Eden's exhausted, energy-depleted body through the house, down the hill, and onto the beach while her knees trembled and feet stumbled in the sand. The scent of blood had taunted her with every step, but nothing could have stopped her from reaching Rain. Her love. Her mate. Her savior.

Though the moment Rain's teeth had bitten her flesh,

scorching pain had rendered her heart still. For a moment, she'd feared he might have killed her. But then the cold had vanished, her hunger had ceased, and all fear had slipped away. Her freed heart had latched to his and rejoiced. She was no longer cursed, poisoned, or sick. She was alive. Unleashed. Fearless.

She was Rain's mate.

And though he might have mixed feelings about biting her, Eden would do anything to convince him they would be okay. And the first step was to complete the final level of their mating bond.

Eden brushed her hand down his hard pecs. "Don't resist it, Rain. Give in."

His head lifted and control snapped in his fierce blue eyes. "Those wolves better be out of my fucking house. Because, baby, I'm going to ravish you."

She grinned, then yelped as Rain pushed her legs from around his waist, tossed her over his shoulder, and ran along the beach. She held on for dear life, her toes curling as she pressed her nose to his spine and a whole new hunger took over. Inhaling his sweaty scent, she wanted to devour him, feel every inch of him over her. Inside her. Damn, how could he even sprint with that hard rod between his legs? But desire only seemed to fuel him as Rain climbed through the scrub, his bare feet crunching over sticks and dry gum leaves on the journey to the base of his driveway.

"I can walk from here."

"Fuck no," he said, barely out of breath as he started up the steep drive, his calves bulging with every step. "You're tired. I should feed you first."

She would have agreed, but her cravings for him were more urgent than those of her stomach. "We'll eat later. I need you first. This ... this bond makes me feel like I'll combust."

Rain growled. "Let's not talk about that."

"Rain—"

"No. You might be marked, but we're not bonded, not mated, not until I've buried myself inside you and heard my name rip from your throat in ecstasy."

Eden shivered, delighted to hear it as she pressed a kiss to his spine. "Then hurry. Get me to the bedroom. Or door. I don't fucking care, just—"

"Shower," he grunted, punching in the code before kicking the door open. "You're covered in blood, and I've spent the night hunting through the scrub and climbing trees to find that fucking bat. So, shower first."

The door slammed closed, and Rain bent to place her feet on the floor. Eden had barely straightened and regained her equilibrium when his mouth was back on hers, his rough hands spearing into her hair with all the heat and angst of a man starved. She gasped into his kiss, stumbling backwards as their lips worked, tongues dueled, and he hoisted her off her feet to cross the room and slam her back against the elevator doors.

"Should have fucking stairs," he muttered, as he nipped her chin, her throat, then pressed his lips to the throbbing pulse point in her neck near his mark. It still burned, but so did the rest of her body as the elevator pinged and Rain moved them inside. His hands speared up the back of her singlet and clutched her shoulders as he grazed his teeth over her collarbone.

Eden threw her head back and tugged at his silky hair. "Rain ..."

"You're so soft. So creamy. Can I ...?"

"Anything," she breathed, fearing nothing he could do to her as he placed his mouth over the thick cotton of her supported singlet and sucked at her pointed nipple. Eden moaned and arched her back to encourage him. "I'll do anything—"

"That's what I'm afraid of," he growled, his teeth nipping as he traced kisses over her cleavage. "You have no choice."

But Eden didn't care. She'd longed for this moment. To see Rain's body, feel him, touch him, play, and make love late into the night. But sensing that the anger, guilt, and bitterness rising inside her weren't her own emotions, she had to help him squash such negative thoughts. Quickly.

"No bondage," she said as the elevator doors opened. "I'm not fond of toys and though I haven't tried it, I don't like the idea of anal. So don't ask."

Rain lifted his head and quirked his eyebrow. "Anything else?" he asked as he carried her from the elevator and down the hall.

"I don't think so."

"Then what *do* you like, Edes?"

The brush of his lips over hers left her shivering. "I like to be close. To be held. I like to have fun, to be sweet and sexy. Hard, fast, or slow. I like to make love, and I like to play."

"Play?"

She grinned. "If I had sexy lingerie, I'd strip for you. But it's all in Townsville."

Rain bared his teeth and spun her into his ensuite. "I would kill Tyrone and Lucas just to rescue your sexy knickers, baby."

Eden giggled as she dropped her head to his shoulder and kissed his hot, salty skin. "You still might get lucky. But right now, I'm in no mood for teasing."

"Neither am I." He plopped her on her feet. "But even though it might kill me, I'm going to make this last, Eden." He speared his hands into her hair and tipped her head back. "I want to make it long. Pleasurable. And absolute torture for us both to solidify our bond."

Eden trembled. "I'd like that ..." The pleasure, the torture, she was down for it all, especially if it would help ease Rain's conscience over what he'd done.

"Good. Don't move."

She couldn't, anticipation flooding her as he grabbed a hand towel and wet it in the sink. Then he brushed the hair from her left shoulder, his eyes dark but touch gentle as he cleaned away the blood left by Lucas's painful bite. She dipped her head but couldn't see the damage as Rain dropped the towel onto the floor.

The anger in his eyes softened, then he brushed his lips over hers. "Speaking of stripping ... take off your shirt."

Eden's hands fell to the hem of her singlet, his body brushing hers as he reached past her to turn on the shower. But she waited until their eyes locked again before quirking her lips and lifting her tight cotton singlet up until it bunched at the shelf-bra supporting her breasts. Rain's jaw twitched as he shot his hand through his hair, biceps and obliques bulging. Eden shivered, then crossed her arms over her chest and yanked her singlet over her head.

Her breasts bounced free and into Rain's eager hands, her breath catching as his thumbs flicked her budding nipples. Once, twice, a billion times. Eden gripped his arms and held on tight as his mouth swooped down to swallow her moans. His thumbs were like magic.

Then his head dropped, and he sucked her tight, sensitive nipple between his lips.

Eden clawed at his granite biceps. "Rain ..."

"Fuck, you're beautiful." His hands and mouth worked in unison as he switched breasts, his overgrown beard igniting the fire coursing through her body.

Then he abandoned her chest all too soon and sank lower, dropping to the floor as he pressed his lips down her belly one inch at a time, his fingers trailing over the grooves of her ribs before tightening around her flannel-covered hips. Holding her in place, Rain pressed his nose to her hot, aching core and inhaled.

Her knees buckled.

"You smell divine. Sweet. Tasty." He ran his finger along the damp seam of her unsexy flannels. "Wet."

She tugged at his hair. "Yes. I ... I am ..."

Rain cupped her ass and rested his chin on her pubic bone. Eden's belly clenched as she met his wild gaze, a wicked smirk twisting his delectable mouth. "Shall I take these off?"

"You better!"

He didn't hesitate. Rain hooked his fingers through the waistband of her pants and bared her to him in one quick tug. Then he pressed his mouth to her hot, aching clit, and Eden hit the roof. His name screamed from her throat, her legs trembling as his tongue darted along her warm, slick flesh.

"Ra-ain!"

"I've gotcha," he whispered, his hands tightening around her ass as he pressed his tongue back to her sensitive bundle of nerves. He licked and sucked, his beard doing crazy things to her quivering thighs. Eden was afraid she'd tear his hair out as she stumbled in his hold. Then he eased her torture and began the slow, sensual journey back up her body, racing his tongue along the groove of her rib cage and to the base of her sternum.

Straightening, he brushed her hair behind her ear. "Sorry, baby. Had to taste. But I'm not ready to let you come."

Eden hissed between her teeth. "Evil."

"Yes, but I want you sated. Warm and relaxed. And clean." His jaw hardened as he glared at her right shoulder. He'd cleaned her left, but as she glanced in the mirror behind him, she noticed a crust of blood still outlined his own larger bite. Regret filled in his eyes, and her heart ached as she shared his pain.

But she would help him through it because she did not regret a thing.

Eden pressed her hands to his hard, quivering belly. "Then let's get in this shower so we can both be satisfied," she breathed, wasting no time as she flicked open his shorts and reached inside to wrap her hand around his hot, thick erection. Rain shuddered, his eyes drooping as his breath hissed between his teeth. "You can wash me, and I'll wash you."

"Fuck, Eden ..." Tendons strained in his neck as she stroked her thumb over the head of his throbbing cock, brushing away the budding moisture at the tip. "You're going to—"

She stroked again and unleashed a growl from his chest as he shoved his shorts down his legs. Then he grabbed her thighs, hoisted her legs around his waist, and spun them into the shower. Her back hit the tiles, and he took her mouth with an animalistic snarl, shooting a thrill through her from head to toe as the water soaked them in seconds. Her thighs tightened around him as his tongue toyed with hers, brushing, sucking, and raging a war with her desire. Eden held on tight, pressing one hand to his back while reaching between their bodies with her other for his cock. He hissed and kissed her harder. She wanted him. Needed him. He was huge, just like the rest of him, especially his generous heart as he relinquished the assault on her mouth and trailed his lips down her throat.

Then he eased back, brushed her hair off her shoulder, and glared at his mark.

"I'm so sorry, Eden."

Her heart broke for him. "Don't be. Please. Don't torture yourself, Rain. You saved me, and I thank you for it."

"Still ..." His face twisted as he reached for a gray loofah and pumped the bodywash that smelled of sea salt. "I just ..."

He circled the loofah around her breasts, the coarse sponge tantalizing her sensitive nipples before he washed up her chest and over her shoulders. Then he dropped his head to place a butterfly kiss over his bite. Eden closed her eyes as he sucked, lathed, and caressed the wound as though he could somehow make it disappear.

But it never would. He'd claimed her like she'd claimed him. She was his. Wanted to be his. And would show him in every way possible that nothing had changed.

Eden cupped his hairy chin and forced his head up. It killed her to see the pain in his eyes. "Don't think about it. Remember? We're completing the bond the *right* way."

"That's not—"

"Rain!" She thrust her breasts against his chest and grabbed his cock. "Please!"

She stroked her hand up his long shaft, and his eyes glazed over. "Fuck," he moaned, pressing the loofah between her breasts. "Okay, baby. I promise. Let's do this fucking right."

Taking the loofah from his hand, she took control and lathed his sculpted shoulder with bubbles.

"I love you, Rain." She kissed his deltoid. "Always have. Always will. I love you now the same way I did yesterday, and every day for the past two years. I will love you the same way tomorrow." She washed his pecs, bubbles catching in his chest hair. "Remember that, okay?"

Rain tilted his head back. "I know."

"Then hurry up and wash as you're killing me here."

Eden tossed the loofah at him as she loosened her legs from around his hips. Helping her back to her feet, Rain flashed his wolfish grin, then proceeded to wash what dirt remained from his limbs, carelessly managing to put on a show as his muscles bulged and stretched, his cock standing to attention in the center of his glorious form while bubbles dripped from his tanned skin to swirl around the drain at his feet.

Eden didn't move, hardly dared to breathe until he set the loofah down, switched off the taps, and led her from the shower. Rain grabbed a towel and cupped the terrycloth around her breasts as he massaged gently and swooped in for a kiss. "Dry quickly."

She ran the towel over her limbs, body, and squeezed water from her hair while Rain did the same. But fuck, she'd forgotten how good he looked wet with his hair dripping over his shoulders. Desire shot to a whole new level. This was really happening. She was naked with Rain Blackwood, and he was going to claim her as his.

Finally.

Rain snatched the towel from her limp hand, dumped it on the floor, then dragged her towards him. "You like to be held," he whispered, one hand on her back while he interlocked his fingers with hers and backed her out of the bathroom. "I can work with that. I want to hold you close. To worship you. Taste you. Never let you go."

She shivered. "I want to feel you everywhere."

"I'm reaching the end of my tether. I hunger for you. I need to feast."

His throbbing cock against her belly told her no different. The back of her legs hit the edge of the bed, and he cupped her bum, lifting her as he crawled to position her across the mattress.

"Yes, Rain. Please."

He kissed her, parting her lips and seeking her tongue, for which she happily obliged. His beard was longer than normal, and probably softer than the prickles he usually sported, but fuck, it was thrilling, nonetheless.

Eden moaned as his mouth released hers and trailed kisses down her body. After nipping the top of her pubic bone, he looped his arms beneath her thighs, hoisted them over his shoulders, and slipped his fingers through her slick center.

Eden gasped, clutching his long, damp hair as his mouth

opened, lowered, and sucked her hard. Her hips bucked off the bed. "Rain!"

He chuckled, running his tongue around her clit as his hands lifted to cup her breasts, caressing and squeezing in sync with his lips. Closing her eyes, she tried to remember how to breathe. But that escaped her too as he tweaked her nipples and darted his tongue inside her.

Eden screamed as she came, heat flooding through her body as her hands flew up to clutch her head, certain it had blown off. The tug in her belly intensified, her heart pounding in harmony with Rain's as he rubbed her nipple between his thumb and forefinger, grazed her thigh with his hairy cheek, then circled his tongue and dove again.

"Oh, fuck!" She clutched at the covers, the upside-down view outside the window blurring as she arched her back and rasped for breath. Rain was exactly what she'd always thought he'd be. Dangerous. Wicked. A fucking sex-god designed to make her scream. And he did a bloody good job of it too, downright torturing and pleasuring her all at once as he abandoned one of her breasts and slipped his finger inside her.

"Rain!"

"Fuck, I'd forgotten how small you are. You're so tight. Perfect. I don't—"

"Stop talking! We're Fated. Meant to be. You might be fucking big, but I was made for you."

Rain hissed out a breath as a growl rumbled from his chest. "Too fucking right, you were." He flicked her clit, slipped a second finger inside her and wriggled until Eden saw stars. "I can't wait much longer ..."

"Then don't! Get up here already!"

He obliged, kissing up her body while his fingers continued their tantalizing massage. Eden dropped her legs open as she reached between them and took his cock in her hand. Her fingers barely touched around his girth.

Rain's head fell to her marked shoulder. "Fuck. There's got to be ... I don't know if ... Shit. I might not have condoms."

Eden rolled her eyes. "If you can heal broken bones, I doubt you can catch an infection. Right?"

"Yeah, but—"

"So, stop fucking around and—"

Rain reared, slipped his fingers from her and spun her upright on the bed. Eden's head hit the pillows just as his chest crushed hers and she welcomed his kiss. His beard was wet from his long visit between her legs, but Eden didn't care. He lifted her hips, and she planted her feet on the mattress, her knees shaking in anticipation as she dug her nails into Rain's quivering back. His cock nudged at her entrance, then inched inside her.

Air clogged inside her lungs, his growl reverberating through her as he moved out, then back in. His lips pressed to hers as he did it again. And again. It was slow. So fucking torturous. Then his mouth lifted from hers, their breaths panting as they locked gazes, and Rain slid in deeper.

"Yes!" she gasped as she stretched beyond belief. "Keep ... there!" Eden lifted her hips, her toes curling over the covers as he slid on home.

"Oh, Eden ..." He brushed his fingers down her thigh before gripping behind her knee. "I need to—"

"Move." She flung her arms around him, locked her ankles tight, and held him in a vise as he withdrew, then she moved with him to meet his thrust.

Shockwaves ricochetted through her body. Again and again as she clawed at his traps while reaching with her other hand to grab his ass. Rain held her tight, his nose inches from hers as his eyes darkened. Breath panted. Heat scorched through her as she built and built. He grew thicker. Everything tightened. She longed for it to last forever, this moment everything she'd dreamed it would be and more as a powerful force pulsated through the air.

She'd experienced a similar moment on the beach, when Rain had claimed her and her body and soul had become his. But this time, it was different. Their world righted, and Eden believed with the very essence of her being that nothing could break them. Their strength, their unity, their love. Together, they could conquer anything.

"Eden ..." His jaw hardened, lips parting as he continued to rock into her.

"Don't stop."

"Never." His head dipped back to her throat, his ass clenching as he gathered speed, her breasts burning from the friction his chest hair created on her delicate skin. His control began to unravel and then, with one nip of her right shoulder, she jolted and cried out his name as tension unleashed and she came in a wave of mind-blowing pleasure. Rain squeezed her breast as he found his own, riding through his orgasm until they both collapsed in a sweaty, panting, and thoroughly sated heap.

Chapter 29

Rain nuzzled his face into Eden's soft hair, her scent of mango, eucalypts, and sea salt scorching heat through his primitive vessels. She reeked of him, always had, but sharing shower gel and body sweat was a whole new level of erotic pleasure that soothed his soul as her heart beat in time with his.

Fuck, that had been an experience. He'd always known sex with his mate would blow any other encounter he'd had out of this world. He craved Eden in a way that almost felt unnatural. Deeper than he ever had. He thirsted for her. Hungered. He didn't want to let her out of his reach, let alone his sight.

And that terrified him. It wasn't how the bond was supposed to work, but he'd darkened their connection and now, his animalistic nature was taking over.

He had to fight it.

Growling, he scraped his teeth over Eden's prominent collarbone and kissed her breasts, his wolf salivating as he ran his tongue over her peaked pink nipple. His cock hardened, and her hands tightened in his hair. He couldn't get enough. He'd always been a boob man, and Eden's were glorious. Round, sensitive, and big enough that they bounced and sat perfectly in his large hands. The thought of seeing them displayed in blue silk, pink lace, or red leather as she stripped for him sent his mind reeling with endless fantasies he couldn't wait to explore.

Not that he didn't already have enough of those. But while kissing her glorious breasts soothed him deep inside, his soul remained torn. His heart warmed, yet his mind was lost. Tormented. Because that should have been their moment. When he'd lost himself inside her, he should have solidified them as mates. As lovers.

But he'd tied her to him in a way he'd never imagined, and he had no idea what that would do to the bright, loving future he'd envisioned.

Exhaling, Rain nestled his head against the pillow of her heaving chest, keeping one hand on her boob while snaking his other beneath her. "Are you okay?"

She huffed out a laugh. "More than okay. We sure forged that mating bond."

"Yes, but it doesn't negate what I did, Eden. The Goddess will never forgive me."

"But Nate said ... the new moon ..."

"I might not have severed my ties, but I marked you. And that's unforgivable."

"Then why'd you do it?"

"I lost control. The wolf took over—"

"Because you love me." Her hands lifted to grip his shoulders. Hard. "You didn't want to lose me. You did what you promised, Rain. You saved me."

"Not the way I wanted to. Not the way the Goddess intended."

"I don't think she'll mind. And while you might say I didn't have a choice, I did. I am yours, Rain, and that's all I've ever wanted. Besides, shouldn't the fact that we have a solid bond count for something? You could say we're double bonded."

Rain hissed out his breath and lifted his head. "Don't, Eden. You can't make me feel better."

Her smile dropped. "But I want to."

"You won't," he whispered, as he brushed a kiss over her lips. Part of what she said made sense, but Rain couldn't accept it. No matter the circumstances, biting her had been forbidden, and sooner or later, he'd have to face the consequences. But he didn't want to make her feel bad. It wasn't her fault. She'd done her best. He was the one who hadn't killed the fucking bat. "And though I'm not sure if I'll ever forgive myself, I don't want you worrying. Okay? Just let me love you."

"But I want you to be happy!" She clutched his shoulders. "Please, Rain. Don't blame yourself. I'm okay."

"You think you are. But the truth is, we don't know. We don't know any couples who are bonded *and* marked, so I don't know if we'll keep the blessings the Goddess should bestow on us or not."

"What blessings?"

"Doesn't matter." He didn't want to tell her and have her face disappointment when they didn't possess the powers of a mated couple like Finn and Ava. "But I promise you one thing, Eden. I will stay true to my word. I'll stay true to you. I love you something fierce, and I'll never let any predator harm you again."

His gaze dropped to her left shoulder, and Eden's followed, though he doubted she could see where the vampire's fangs had pierced her throat. It was small in comparison to his bite and would thankfully fade by morning. Vampires enjoyed hiding in the shadows and therefore didn't leave evidence behind.

But Rain's mark would scar Eden forever.

"Finn could have arrived sooner," he muttered.

"It's okay," she whispered, squeezing his deltoids. "He bit me for only a second."

"A second too long. And now ..."

Eden's breath caught. "Lucas is going to come back, isn't he?"

Rain growled. "Don't say his name in this bed. But yes, baby. And when he does, I'll fucking kill him."

He didn't know what the bat and Tyrone would have in store or what their next move would be, but Lucas would be back. Now that he'd drunk from Eden as a vampire, he'd crave her and wouldn't stop hunting her until she was his.

Rain dropped his face to her chest, hiding his snarl as he kissed down her sternum and dragged his teeth along the edge of her ribcage. Let the bastard fucking try. Their bond might be dark, but it was real and no way in hell would Rain let anyone touch his mate again, let alone that undead filth.

Her belly rumbled beneath his lips, and Rain jolted onto his elbows. "Fuck, you need to eat." Flying off the bed, he reached for her hands and pulled her upright. "You haven't had a decent meal in days. So, let's clean up and find you some food."

Eden groaned but didn't protest as he led her into the bathroom. "Now I wish I hadn't let Nate eat all that sweet and sour curry."

"Wolves sure can eat," Rain agreed, still mad at Nate for helping himself to her food. "Though the scouts certainly enjoyed dinner these past few nights, didn't they?"

Eden laughed. "The scouts are funny. How did they not know what a chickpea is?"

"Because we're half carnivore," he muttered, running warm water over a washcloth.

"That was the hardest part," she muttered, her mouth twisting. "Smelling that meat and wanting to eat it. Suck on it." Her whole body shuddered in revulsion. "It was disgusting. And wanting to eat Cookie—" She whimpered and dropped her head to his shoulder.

"It's okay, baby," he whispered as he washed her thighs. "You've been through a horrific ordeal, and I know how awful it must have been for you to crave blood. Flesh. To want to hurt an animal."

"It was awful." Sighing, she leaned against the counter and lifted her foot to rub the back of his calf. "But I wouldn't give in, Rain. Not for a moment."

"I never doubted it." He kissed her nose, stroked her one more time, then tossed the cloth away, stepping back before he surrendered to temptation and made a mess of her again. "Come on."

Back in his bedroom, Rain handed Eden a T-shirt, and she slipped it over her damp hair. His wolf preened at the sight of the hem scraping her thighs as he pulled on his boxers, then led her into the kitchen.

He froze. "Fuck me! What the ...?"

"Yeah ..." Eden bit down on her lower lip. "The wolves broke some furniture. Nate—shit!" She spun to face him. "Is Nate okay?"

"Nate's fine. And I know what happened, but Finn didn't say it was as bad as this."

The lounge lay on its side with rips in the cushions. Claws had scratched the wooden floors, and two sun lounges lay shattered on the balcony while his outdoor table had been snapped in half. Not to mention the missing glass panel where Nate had fallen through the railing.

But the damage didn't matter. Eden was alive.

"I'll clean it up later," he said, moving her to the breakfast bar. "Now sit and let me make you dinner."

She grinned. "It's three a.m."

"Breakfast, then?" He quirked his eyebrow. "What would you like?"

"What do you think? Porridge."

"I should have known," he whispered, kissing her forehead before pulling the French doors closed and moving to the pantry. "Strawberry, apple, and cinnamon?"

"Yes. With an apple to start, please."

He took a pink lady and granny smith from the fridge, tossing her the red while keeping the green. Eden's eyes glazed over as she stroked the apple, then bit into the juicy flesh with a crunch.

She moaned. "Oh God, that is so good."

She continued to eat as Rain diced the granny smith. Slipping the pieces into a bowl, he added oats, water, a touch of sugar, and placed it in the microwave. Taking the strawberries from the fridge, he cut the greenery away, popped one into his mouth, and sliced them, too.

"So, what do we do now?" Eden asked around her mouthful of apple. "How have you been, anyway? We've hardly seen each other these past few days. Did you find your brother?"

"Yeah. Last night. He's the one who told me how to save you and to bite you beneath the new moon."

"That was fortunate timing."

Rain blew out his breath as he opened the beeping microwave and mixed the strawberries into the porridge. "Yep. Though he could have been more supportive. Sly seemed to think I'd never catch the fucking bat, and even though I wish I had—"

"Lucas didn't want you to," Eden said. Rain reset the microwave and turned to her. "He thought I'd give in, that I wouldn't be able to resist the hunger. When he came tonight, the compulsion was so strong, and he didn't hesitate to bite me. He would have turned me if Finn hadn't come, and I was terrified by how easily he could control me. Which is why I ran to you."

Rain's shoulders slumped. "I was fucking terrified, too. You were getting worse, and time wasn't on my side. And when I saw you running towards me ..."

"You did what you had to do, and I'll always be grateful for that."

"Of course you will be." She had no other choice. "But while there's no going back, I'll need some time to come to terms with marking you, Eden."

"I know." Her eyes dulled. "Lucas said that marking me would destroy your soul, but I don't think he knew about the new moon thing. Do you think that was his plan?"

"No, Lucas bit you hoping you would turn or die. Tyrone might have hoped I'd mark you, but Lucas wanted you for himself, and didn't count on me saving you. So, I don't think either of them knew about the new moon loophole else they'd have timed your attack differently, for sure."

"Lucky they didn't, because I don't think your soul's been destroyed, Rain. You'd have been ousted from the pack if you had been, right?"

"Yes, but it doesn't change the fact that you're marked. And it will change you. We're not sure how as the only person we know who was marked was Finn's mum, and she lived on the island Tyrone imprisoned her on as a victim of his abuse until the day she'd tried to run. But being claimed, there was no escaping him."

"He killed her."

"He did. But you don't have to worry about me trying to control you, Eden. I don't want to. What scares me is I might do it anyway, and you'll do something you don't want to do."

"Like what? Skydiving?"

"Don't even joke about that," he said, blood rushing

through his body in both anxiety and delight. "You'd be petrified."

Yet if he had her consent, he'd have her strapped to his chest in a heartbeat.

"Very true," she said as the microwave beeped and he stirred her porridge. "Have you been up there since—"

"Not since Tuesday." And even though he wouldn't have done anything but fight for her these past few days, Rain longed to take to the clouds and jump. To feel the rush and the good kind of adrenaline pumping through him rather than rage and terror. But even with their mating bond, he held no hope that he'd ever get Eden in the sky with him.

So instead, he'd just have to live his other fantasies, those in which she was naked. And he had enough of those to keep them thoroughly occupied.

Rain added cinnamon to Eden's porridge, then walked around the bench, placed it in front of her, and dropped a kiss to her hair. "Eat up, baby, then we'll go to bed. Tomorrow, we need to meet with the pack. I don't know when Lucas will return, but we need to be ready. Tyrone will send him back before the full moon, I'm sure."

"Well, I hope it's over by then because Isla will be here and —wait! You're not going to keep me locked up until he comes back, are you? Because the koalas—"

"No." Rain chuckled lightly and dropped another kiss to her forehead. "You can return to your koalas tomorrow. But first, please eat so we can go to bed. I'm bloody exhausted."

Eden scooped up her porridge and moaned in delight. "Oh my God. Food. Real, fairdinkum food."

Chapter 30

Tyrone stormed into Queens Gardens, pissed to have received the call from Detective Kamar, his new right-hand man, to deal with the enraged vampire. Lucas had been on the island for almost a week, his spy, Eric, having reported he'd bitten Blackwood's mate and initiated the change. Tyrone had known it would only be a matter of days before Lucas returned with Eden and the Magnetic Island pack weakened further with Rain's heartbreak. But by what Kamar had reported, things had not gone to plan.

Tyrone found Lucas on the path beneath the fig trees as the vampire ripped his fangs from his dinner with a roar. Blood dripped down his chin and onto his naked chest, his dark eyes blazing as he dropped the pale, lifeless corpse of Constable Jenny Nell at his feet. If Tyrone wasn't annoyed, he'd be impressed with Kamar for sacrificing the naïve recruit to the vampire.

"What the fuck happened?" Tyrone demanded. "Where's the vet bitch?"

"Slut got away," Lucas spat, his lips twisting. "I finally got a real taste of her, and your fucking pup barged in. I shifted, and she ran. Then Blackwood bit her."

Tyrone froze. "He did?"

"Yep." Lucas spat blood over Jenny's body. "I honestly didn't think he'd have the balls."

But Tyrone had hoped. Chest swelling, he threw his head back and laughed up at the flying fox infested trees. Rain Blackwood had succumbed to the darkness. He'd followed his dick over his faith and turned his back on the fucking moon bitch.

"This is a glorious night!" he cried, throwing his arms out in victory. "The Blackwoods are history. Sly's given up, and Rain rebelled!"

His plans were falling into place. Finlay may have been sent to stop him, and the fucking tyke would pay for killing his beloved Blair, but Tyrone had finally brought down the all-powerful Blackwoods.

"But what about our deal?" Snarling, Lucas kicked Jenny's body before stepping over it. "I need a bride, and I want *her!*"

Tyrone's laughter eased into a smirk as he observed the vampire—the desperate hunger in the way he licked his fangs, the obsession in his cold, dark eyes.

"Our deal stands. You will return to the island. Fight for the bitch. Drink her dry and force her to turn. Then fuck her every day for the rest of your existence while Blackwood lives out his life alone. Broken. Just like his brother."

Though Blackwood's days were numbered considering Finlay and his broken pack would be dead within weeks. Now that Tyrone had Kamar by his side, he wouldn't hesitate to storm the island and kill that fucking kid.

After Lucas eradicated the vet.

"Yes." The vampire practically drooled. "And this time, I won't have to fight the whole pack. A few bats and I can take Blackwood."

Tyrone's mouth twisted. "Don't count on that. Knowing Finlay, he won't oust Blackwood straight away. The pup's loyal to a fucking fault and will probably still support him, like he supports Sly. But the pack bond will be broken."

"Then I will gather the bats and take back what is mine." Lucas thumped a fist to his chest. "She tasted just like the other bitch, boss. Sweet, divine, and *powerful*."

Tyrone sneered. "I'm sure she did. Now, go gather your colony and call for reinforcements. I'll clean up this mess."

The bat sneered, nodded, then shifted and shot up into the trees the native flying foxes had all but destroyed.

Blowing out a frustrated breath, Tyrone shook his head and extracted the bottle of gasoline from his pocket. It wasn't much, but enough to start the job as he set fire to the bloodless body of the young cop, then strode out of the park, leaving her for someone else to find and bother her colleagues with in the morning.

Just another night of crime in Townsville.

Chapter 31

Eden woke with a smile as midmorning light streamed through the open windows. One of Rain's heavy thighs pinned her hips down while his large arms trapped her against his body, deeming the covers redundant as she snuggled into his warmth. Dropping her chin, she breathed him in and relished the heat pulsing through her as his morning erection teased her hip. And though she desperately wanted to check on the koalas, she needed to satisfy her more primal needs first. That for Rain, and then food, as once again, she was starving.

But it was a hunger she welcomed, and Eden would be forever grateful to him for that as she brushed her hand up his rough, hairy thigh. Rain pressed his face into her hair and groaned.

"Morning, my precious one."

"You're happy to see me." She moved her hand down, brushing her fingers over his balls before stroking the underside of his magnificent cock, grinning at his hiss of breath. "You like that?"

"Best morning of my life."

"I can make it better."

His thigh dropped from her hip, and she turned to face him in his still-too-tight arms. But Eden didn't mind being squished. There was no safer place in the world than Rain's embrace. She met his hooded eyes, then reached up to kiss him. Rain pulled her close, his hard biceps digging into her shoulder as he brushed his tongue against hers in long, tantalizing strokes. Tossing her leg over his, she grabbed his ass and moaned into their kiss as his erection slipped against her throbbing clit. If every morning was like this for the rest of her life, she'd die a happy woman.

Rain rolled onto his back and draped her body over his. Eden's knees fell to either side of his hips while gravity sank her nipples into his coarse chest hair, sending shivers shooting through her to fuel the desire pooling in her core. She wanted him. Needed him. Hadn't had enough of him last night and never would.

She teased the crown of his cock with her wetness, then lifted her hips.

"Eden ..." His teeth clashed against her grin before he sucked her lower lip into his greedy mouth.

"Not yet," she breathed, kissing down his prickly throat as she spread her fingers over the hard planes of his chest. "I want to taste you first. All of you."

His groan reverberated through his entire body as he brushed his hands up into her hair while she licked along his collarbone. For too long Eden had been ogling the ripped, hard slabs of muscle of his body, aching to touch, to kiss, and have press her into the bed while he loved her hard, slow, and passionately. And now that he had, Eden wanted to take her time to worship the man who had saved her life.

"You know what I miss?" she breathed as she kissed his bulging abs. "Watching you on the jet ski."

"It has been a few weeks," he admitted through clenched teeth. "But I can put on a show anytime, baby."

Her toes curled as she circled her tongue over one hunk of ab. "Maybe later. The things you can do on a jet ski have always blown my mind. But now I realize you're stronger than the average man."

"Sure am. But it's not the wolf, Eden. I don't do anything humans can't do on a ski. I just do it better."

Her lips curved as she peeked up at him. "I bet you do a lot of things better."

Then she took his cock in her hand, her mouth watering at his girth, and kissed the bulging crown. Rain hissed, fisting her hair as she licked up his salty precum.

"Fuck! Eden—"

She grinned and dropped to her belly. She'd never been particularly fond of oral sex and while her thighs quivered with the need to take him inside her and unleash the orgasm building, she wanted nothing more than to see Rain come apart with nothing but her lips, tongue, and quivering fingers. Power unlike any she'd ever known shivered through her as she peered up at her man. Her mate. The man she loved with all her heart. No one had ever pulled at her so deeply or shown her such compassion. No one had his strength. His stamina. And Eden would spend her days loving him, teasing him, and forever grateful that he'd given his passionate heart to her. Because only *she* could unravel his dark, mysterious, and dangerous aura. To make him lose control and risk his soul for her. And though she believed the Goddess would forgive him, she'd never be able to show him just how much his sacrifice meant to her.

His breath gasped with anticipation as Eden parted her lips and sank her mouth over his throbbing length, moaning in delight as he growled—*actually* growled—and bucked.

"Yes! Oh, Eden—"

She ran her tongue up his pulsating vein, cupped his balls, then lowered again. Rain's thighs clenched at her shoulders, her own belly igniting as he heated, thickened, and gently guided her head as she absorbed the power rushing through her. Eden had never felt braver. Happier. Freer.

She was so fucking free. Fear? What fear?

"Eden, I fucking love what you're doing, but ... I don't want to ... get up here. Now."

His thighs released her from their prison as she sucked back up him and drew in a breath. Brushing her hair from her face, she rose onto her knees and straddled him. Rain reared, grabbing her ass with one hand and her breast with the other as he crushed his lips to hers, their tongues twining in shared groans as their hearts beat in sync. He tweaked her nipple, and she practically convulsed, gasping as she scraped her nails down his pecs and took him inside her with one smooth stroke.

Her lips parted from his with a cry. Fuck, it was intense. Tight, raw, and utterly perfect. He filled her body, heart, and soul as her spine arched and she slowly rolled her hips. Rain groaned, his hand hardening around her ass as he pulled her closer. His lips brushed hers and Eden found herself locked in the raw desire darkening his eyes. Cupping his jaw, she lifted her hips and lowered, whimpering every time he sank home. Heat built and built until their kiss was only a brush of lips and shared gasps, friction burning through them as his face chaffed hers and her nails clawed at his chest. With another deep thrust and guttural groan, her orgasm ripped through her from head to toe as she threw her head back and cried out in ecstasy.

"Rain!"

He stilled, waiting for her trembles to ease before lifting her body away, shifting onto his knees, and lowering her onto her back. Rain moved on top of her—upside down on the bed

—and planted his elbows by her head before driving back inside her. Eden clutched his straining back as every muscle bulged, his cock pulsating inside her as she met him thrust for thrust until he roared with his own release, his sharp teeth scraping over the mark burning on her shoulder and shooting yet another climax through her.

Her neck arched back as she scratched her nails down his triceps and flung her arms over her head. Rain slowed, kissed down her neck, then laid his head between her boobs, his heaving breath warming her over-stimulated nipple.

"I'm a fucking idiot going all this time without loving you."

If she had the energy, she'd smile. But all Eden could do was pat his head as she tried to catch her breath. "Yeah, but after that, I think I can forgive you."

EDEN RESTED her elbow on the door of Rain's Lexus convertible and breathed in the cool October air as they drove into Nelly Bay. Her skin still tingled from their mind-blowing sex, her belly bubbling with warmth, happiness, and their early lunch of Thai chili lime rice. With the sun shining and wind whipping through her hair, she soaked in the glorious view of Rain beside her, his hair blowing over his shoulders, beard trimmed back to his usual stubble, and dark sunglasses shielding his eyes against the stunning backdrop of the azure sky and sapphire ocean.

Her heart waltzed to the tune that her aching pelvic muscles wouldn't stop humming. After four terrifying days, the past twelve hours had been a sensational release of tension and passion. The best night of her life. And though she knew he'd enjoyed it too, he hadn't been able to hide the guilt eating away at him for biting her.

Of course, she understood his concerns. He thought she'd feel obliged to obey his every whim and while part of that might be true, she didn't feel like anything had changed in her mind, body, or soul. How could it when she'd given herself to Rain years ago? He'd stolen her heart the moment he'd arrived with Pixie in his arms, so if anything, their connection had only grown. Solidified. He might have the power to tie her to him forever, but she wanted to be tied. He wasn't one of the rebel wolves he'd told her about—evil, dominating, and would kill her without a thought—and he would never abuse his power over her. She trusted him. And she understood why her heart had refused to let him go. They were mated—bonded *and* marked—and she would love him, enjoy spending time with him, please him when she wished, and let him own her in the bedroom because she *wanted* him to. As long as she also had her fair share of taking the lead and making him come apart like she had this morning.

She just needed to help him realize that, too.

Rain slowed the car as they entered Nelly Bay. "So, how was Xena's rehab going? You know, before you wanted to eat her?"

He said it lightly enough to make her smile, though bile curdled in her stomach at the thought of her ever having wanted to hurt the koalas. "I never wanted to eat her. Just that new koala. Though Cookie did smell good."

"Yeah, she's one fucking cute koala."

"She sure is. But I don't think I'll ever use the phrase 'You're so cute I could just eat you up' ever again." Eden shuddered. Where did that phrase even come from? Probably from the people who ate lamb. "But Xena keeps improving and getting stronger in the trees. I'd been hoping to reunite her with Cookie today, so fingers crossed."

"Then they can go back to the wild?"

"I hope so. It's always my favorite part, taking them home.

Is where you found them easily accessible? For those of us who aren't wolves?"

"It'll be a hike, but you'll be fine. So, tell me, what kind of extensions do you want for the hospital?"

Exhaling, Eden sank deeper into her seat as they left Nelly Bay. "I want to do something similar to Port Macquarie, though not that extravagant." Port Macquarie Koala Hospital was the largest and most innovative in the country, having boomed after making headlines during the devastating bushfires a few years back. The dedicated vets there had saved and rehabilitated many koalas but sadly, an estimated six thousand native souls had lost their lives in the disaster and now, the hospital was leading the fight to save their national icon. "They've built a stunning center with a state-of-the-art koala clinic, scientific lab, and will conduct breeding on site in the forested yards. But they have a bunch of touristy things, too, with education, viewing decks, and a Big Koala."

Rain grinned. "We could have our own Big Koala. Use Cookie as the model."

"Don't tempt me," she sighed, glancing out the windscreen. "I just want to keep the island safe for the koalas. With the changing climate, they're struggling through summer and their numbers are dwindling. That's why I need to count them. I lost too many last year from dehydration and illness."

She'd euthanized eight adults, two more than the year before, and had cried every time.

"What would it take to build what you want?" Rain asked as they cruised through Arcadia.

"First, I need new yards and more room for the koalas in rehab. I also need to plant more trees for food. But speaking of the hospital ... there is something I want to discuss with you."

His eyebrows quirked over his sunglasses. "What's that?"

"The Cheeky Wolf." She'd almost forgotten about her more-than-generous anonymous donor until this morning in the shower. Just before said donor had dropped to his knees, lifted her leg over his shoulder, and proceeded to empty her mind of everything but his wolfish mouth.

Now, that mouth twisted with a grimace as he glanced back to the road. "Like I said, I'm not sorry."

"You lied to me."

"I *tricked* you." He lifted his finger off the steering wheel to emphasize his point. "There's a difference."

"Yes, but ... you can't give me that much money."

He shrugged. "Why not?"

"Because! We're ... well, we were friends. Now we're lovers. Mates. It's just ... it's too much."

"No, it's not."

"It is in addition to what you give me as Rain Blackwood."

"So?"

Eden clenched her hands to stop herself from reaching over and shaking him. "I can't accept that much! I told you—"

"What else am I going to do with the money?" he asked, his forearms tensing as he navigated the car through the twists and turns of the range. "I'm a fucking rich man, Eden. I have more money than I know what to do with."

"Clearly," she muttered, glancing around the interior of the flashiest car on the island. "But you can't almost solely fund my hospital."

"Sure, I can. Many billionaires are philanthropists."

Eden drove her fingers through her hair as she tried to find the words to describe the unease in her belly. "Rain, you know I appreciate it. And I love you. But I can't accept it."

"Eden." He placed his hand on her knee and squeezed as they passed the Forts and descended into Horseshoe Bay. "It's not a big deal. Honestly."

"Maybe not to you!"

"Are you *really* going to ask me to take all that money

away from the cute little koalas? What will you tell Xena and Cookie?"

"I ... I have other donors."

"Yes, but no one donates more than the Cheeky Wolf, right?"

She sighed. "No. But it makes me nervous, Rain. I feel like you own me."

"After last night, I do own you." Disgust dripped from his tone as he parked outside the hospital.

"Rain—"

"Eden, you've accepted the money all this time without questioning it. So just stop. You're wasting your breath."

Gritting her teeth, she pushed open the door and stepped out of the car. "I just worked so hard to get those sponsors, Rain. To learn that my biggest was you all along ..."

He met her in front of the car, lifting his sunglasses before taking her hands in his and squeezing softly. "Do we need to go over this again? You're my *mate*. There is nothing I won't do for you. You wouldn't let me buy you the things you needed, so I gave the money anonymously. I want to see you succeed. I want this hospital to succeed and for all your dreams to come true. You are the only person in the world who matters to me and what you care about, I care about, too."

His thumbs stroked the back of her hands, his tender touch softening the tension hardening her spine as she arched into him. "I know you care, Rain. About the koalas and about me. But it's too much."

"And if I ceased the Cheeky Wolf's support, what would happen?"

Eden's stomach plummeted. "The hospital would struggle to—"

"Exactly." He swooped down to kiss her, effectively ceasing any further objections as he whispered, "Just let me do this for you, baby. Let me help you and the koalas. You need me."

Eden moaned into the kiss as he pulled her close. Her hands fell to his chest where his heart pounded against her palm, an echo of her own as his head tilted, nose brushed hers, and tongue dove. His prickly stubble burned her skin, and Eden's knees buckled in surrender. She might not like it, but she needed him. She relied on the Cheeky Wolf's donation and if she lost it, her other generous benefactors would keep her doors open, but it would be slim pickings and a struggle to purchase her medical supplies.

Throwing her arms around Rain's neck, Eden lifted onto her toes and deepened the kiss for a moment before inching away, their new bond sizzling between them. "You're hard to say no to."

He brushed his nose against hers. "Irresistible. I like it."

"Yes, that. But ... it isn't the bond. I'll let you and the Cheeky Wolf stay because I love you. I love you both."

He grinned. "We love you, too. And if it makes you feel better, it isn't just *your* koalas I care about. I sponsor koalas all over the country and regularly give to Lone Pine and Port Macquarie."

Her eyebrows shot up. "Really?"

"I have Ned in Adelaide. Luna from the Koala Foundation, who lives in the wild near Port Macquarie. And I'm a Gold Sponsor for Tilly at Lone Pine. She was your favorite koala when you worked there. I have a plaque and everything by her enclosure to note my generosity."

If she hadn't already loved this man, she did now and he fucking knew it, if his smug grin was any indication. All the fight left her as she sank against his chest. "That does make me feel better," she mumbled into his pecs. "That you care about other koalas and that it's not just about me."

"I'm glad," he whispered, dropping a kiss to her hair. He

held her for a moment, rubbing his fingers up and down her spine. "So ... what would you like me to do about Miss Luna Black and Howling Enterprises?"

Eden gasped, her gaze jerking to his. "What? *They're* you, too?"

"You weren't getting nearly enough, Eden," he said, *almost* too innocently.

Blowing out a frustrated breath, Eden extracted herself from his grasp and stalked across the car park. "Unbelievable. This is just—"

"Baby—"

"Rain, you pay for the whole fucking hospital!" she cried, throwing her hands in the air.

The smug bastard continued to smile. "No, I don't."

Eden rubbed her temples, then dropped her hands to her side. He was right. Three local businesses also contributed to her cause in addition to any grants she received, but when it came down to percentages, Rain paid the lion's share of her funding.

He took her tingling hands in his and squeezed softly. "I shouldn't have tricked you, Eden, but I'm not sorry I did it. Please don't be mad."

She *should* be madder. Any other time, she'd have argued her point. But to what end? Rain was a stubborn, shifty man who'd just proven he would use his wealth to get his way. He wouldn't take away her funding even if she begged him to. And honestly, why would she? The koalas didn't deserve that. What was done was done. It might piss her off, but she'd never find a benefactor as generous as the man who had devoted his soul to her.

But like hell would she let him give a *cent* more than he already did.

"You're going to owe me big time for this."

"And I'll happily be indebted to you." His deep voice hit

all her soft spots, shooting shivers from her toes up into the heat taking up permanent residence in her belly. "Anything you want, Eden. It's yours. Particularly if we're naked."

The wanton woman he'd awoken would love nothing more than to be naked right now. But first, she had a job to do.

"You will owe me. Later. But right now, we have a mother and daughter to reunite."

Chapter 32

Rain had barely closed the door to the waiting room when Dee shrieked and ran over to fling her arms around Eden. The nurse had been in all states of panic these past few days and Rain had spun many talented lies to keep her from dropping in to check on her friend. But Dee seemed satisfied that Eden was recovered as she updated her on Marco and the koala who'd spiraled Eden's blood lust —recently named Scratches.

"I'm glad he was easy to patch up," Eden said as they left the newest addition and moved towards Xena's enclosure. "Wow. Look at her go."

Xena stopped mid stride in her run along the tree branch, her bum in the air as she watched Eden unlatch the gate.

"She loves her new tree," Rain said, placing his hand on Eden's shoulder. "She was having a good old climb when I checked on her yesterday."

Eden smiled and sank against him as Xena deemed them not a threat and crawled towards the bunch of red gum. "Let's add more branches so she can jump and swing," she suggested.

Dee nodded. "I'll get Caleb on it first thing tomorrow."

Rain squeezed Eden's shoulder. "I'll do it now."

"Really? Thank you, Rain."

"Always happy to help. Need to earn my keep." He flashed her a grin, and she rolled her eyes. Fuck, she was adorable. He'd always known she wouldn't be happy when she discovered how generous he'd been with his anonymous donations and while part of him had wanted to keep it a secret forever, he'd known the moment their bond had formed that he wouldn't be able to hide the truth. But Eden had reacted better than he'd thought and while she might be annoyed, she'd come around. He'd make sure of it.

Then he'd seduce her into accepting more money to make all her dreams come true.

"I'll get to it, then. Do you want a high tree and another cross-branch?"

"Let's make a V with that support." Eden pointed to the metal support on the other side of the enclosure where he could connect a branch and build another climb for Xena. "And if we could add a taller tree and more foliage in the middle, that'll give her and Cookie more room." Eden glanced at Dee. "How's she been with Cookie?"

"Excellent. We feel bad about separating them, but we didn't want to reunite them permanently without you assessing Xena first."

"Then I'll do that, and we can get on with it." Eden lifted the koala into her arms, then turned to Rain. "You know where everything is?"

"Yep. Do what you need to do, and I'll set up Xena and Cookie's new home." He swooped down for a kiss, mindful of the koala between them, then tapped her sexy butt, winked, and strolled outside towards the supply shed.

He lifted a log onto his shoulder and grabbed the tools he needed before returning to the enclosure. Marco watched suspiciously from his tree next door, munching on leaves while Rain added branches to enhance Xena's jungle gym. It didn't take long and by the time Eden returned with Xena, declaring she was in good health, the enclosure was ready for the mother and daughter to reunite.

Rain waited with Xena, the koala settling among some leaves while Eden fetched Cookie. When she returned, the little koala squeaked with glee as Eden placed her onto the branch near her mum.

"There you go, little one. Mama's strong enough to take care of you now."

Cookie's ears twitched as she raised her head to look at Xena. The bigger koala reached out, and Cookie scrambled closer onto the branch beside her.

Eden grinned and Rain pulled her into his arms, holding her close as he stood behind her, spread his legs, and lowered himself to her height. He placed a kiss on her throat, then nestled his chin on her shoulder.

"I'm so proud of you, baby. You did such a good job."

"It's like they've never been apart," she said, sinking into his hold. "It's going to be so hard to say goodbye to these two, but they have to go home eventually."

"Just tell me when and I'll take you to their home trees."

"Thank you. Do you mind if we just watch them for a while? Then I'll need to check on Marco and Archie."

"We can stay as long as you want, but the pack is coming over after watersports wrap up for the day."

Which still gave them a good five hours, so they watched mother and daughter enjoy feeding time as Cookie crawled into Xena's lap and reached up to clamp her tiny mouth around the leaf bunch Xena was happily munching on.

Once Eden was satisfied that the koalas were settled, their bellies full as they curled up to nap, they left their enclosure.

"I could probably release Marco, too," Eden said as they stopped by his tree. "Ava's worked hard on him. I wish I could keep her here all the time."

"I'm sure she'll help more now that she's living on the island."

"Yes, but she's just as eager for this war to be over and return to work as I am."

Rain tried swallowing his growl but failed miserably, and Eden's shoulders drooped with a sigh.

"Rain, don't start."

"I didn't say a word."

"Yes, but I know what you're thinking. And I just—"

"What I was going to say," he said, lying through his teeth as he brushed his lips over her shoulder, "is that you should move in. I'll kill that bastard on the mainland, then you can commute from here."

Eden turned, smiling softly as she looped her arms around his neck. "I think I already have moved in. And there's no way I could go back to Townsville like I used to. I belong with you, Rain. In your house and in your bed."

His hand hardened on her back. "Too right, you do."

"And I'll happily commute from here. That's if I still have a job."

Rain cupped her cheek, determined to be the bigger man even though it damn near killed him. "I'll talk to your boss, twist the truth, and do all that I can to make sure you keep your job, baby. I know how much it means to you."

She softened into his touch. "I do love my job."

"I know. And I want you to have it all. Although ..." The cheeky wolf inside him took control as he swooped down to kiss her. "If you want to work here full time and pay Ava to be your koala physio, I'll gladly provide the funds."

Eden stared at him, twirling the ends of his hair behind his neck. "You never give up, do you?"

"Nope."

Her chest heaved with a sigh, then she stepped out of his

grasp. "I'm letting you keep your current donations. Don't push it."

Rejection grated on him even though he hadn't expected her to say anything less. All he wanted was to make her happy. But he understood her need for independence and after taking away part of her free will, he wouldn't dare take anything else from her.

"I'm sorry," he said, meaning it as he wrapped her back into his arms. "I know you love your job and even though I want to shower you with riches and hand you your dreams on a platter, I know you need to make things happen for yourself."

She softened. "I do. And I don't need you to shower me with riches, Rain. I just want you."

His wolf spat in disgust, but Rain accepted her words as he brushed his lips over hers. "You have me, Eden. Forever. Everything I have is yours."

"And I'm yours," she whispered, pulling her body close as her arms tightened around his neck. "Forever."

Chapter 33

"Afternoon!" Kai grinned as Rain returned home to find the scouts had once again invited themselves in, lounging around in the first floor living room considering the destruction that remained on the second. "Now there's a proud, well-mated wolf if I've ever seen one."

Rain's lip curled, glad he'd given in to Eden's insistence on staying at the hospital for another hour while he met with the pack. He didn't like it, but she would be safe during daylight hours if she remained inside, and he'd rather not expose her to the smack talk of the scouts. "Mind your language, Kai. And keep your snout out of it."

"Come on, man. We all saw you claim her before high-tailing it out of here to give you two some privacy."

Chad inclined his chin from where he lounged in the armchair. "Brave of you, Rain."

"And don't you feel it?" Nate asked, stretched out beside Kai with his feet on the coffee table. "The pack bond's growing stronger."

Rain crossed his arms over his chest and glared at the scouts. He couldn't deny that the pack bond was reaping the benefits of two mated wolves. Rain hoped Tyrone was quivering in his boots. "Maybe. And if Sly rejoins us—"

"You think he will?" Hope filled Kai's eyes like a kid at Christmas, which Rain squashed with a shrug.

"Hard to say. But he's talking to me again and that's a start."

"Definitely a good sign," Kai agreed. "Now, before Boss Man Finn gets here, can I please request time off at full moon?"

Rain frowned. "We always take time off at full moon."

"Not from work, from wolfing. And the run. For when the moon goddess herself comes to serenade us."

Rain's frown deepened as Nate nodded in agreement. "Who?"

"Isla!" Kai's eyes widened as though Rain had lost his mind. "You know? Isla—"

"Yes, I get it. She's got the whole celestial moon theme going on. But I don't think she's a goddess."

"Are you kidding!" Kai's feet hit the floor as he straightened. "She's fucking gorgeous, man! I mean, we've had some fantastic artists at the Full Moon Parties, but how you managed to book Isla ... I'm forever grateful."

Rain snorted. "Actually, she's Eden's—"

"So, we can't go wolfing when we need to be in the front row at her concert."

Rain lifted his eyebrows at Chad and Nate. "You two as well?"

Chad shrugged while Nate nodded, his enthusiasm matching Kai's.

"She's a fucking star, man," Nate said. "And a stunning one at that."

Rain ran his hand down his face and sighed. They always met the artists performing at the Full Moon Party, but if he'd known the scouts were diehard fans of the pop diva who teenage girls fawned over, perhaps he'd have reconsidered booking her.

"Have you seen the video for 'Eclipse'?" Kai asked Rain.

"No."

"Oh, man. You should."

"Doesn't she just play the piano in her videos?" Chad asked.

"Ah, yeah. While living up to her reputation as an ethereal goddess of the night." Again, Kai looked at them as though they were all dickheads. "Seriously! Beach, moon, and Isla in a sheer, flimsy gown. She's fucking beautiful."

"Sounds like you'll be fangirling all weekend," Chad said. "I mean, I think she's a good singer and I love her songs, but I didn't realize you were so into her."

Nate slapped Kai on the shoulder. "Better watch this one," Nate told Rain. "Don't let him get too close."

Kai elbowed Nate away. "I'm picking her up from the airport."

"No, you are not," Rain said.

Kai's shoulders slouched. "The ferry?"

"She'll have her own entourage, and we'll arrange her transport from the ferry terminal." Rain was suddenly glad Isla had declined to stay at the hotel and chosen to rent a holiday home considering her desire to stay awhile and catch up with her friends. "But yes, you can have the night off. That's if you can resist the call of the Moon Goddess."

Kai's face deadpanned. "Isla *is* the Moon Goddess."

"No, she is not," Rain stated as he placed his hands on the armchair and threw the scouts a bone. "But don't worry, you'll all get to meet her. And not just at the concert. Isla's staying for two weeks, and we will be providing activities to keep her entertained."

Nate's eyebrows shot up. "Dibs on taking her out on the jet boat!"

"Who's taking my jet boat?"

The scouts leapt to their feet as Finn strode in through the front door.

"Just talking about when Isla arrives," Kai said. "Nate wants to take her out on the JetWolf."

"You are not taking her on the JetWolf. Take her snorkeling."

"Whoohoo!"

Finn raised his eyebrows at Rain. "They don't know, do they?"

Smirking, Rain shook his head.

"Know what?" Kai practically bounced on his toes as his head pivoted between Rain and Finn. "What's going on?"

"Yeah?" Chad frowned. "Why's she staying for two weeks?"

"Because Isla is Ava and Eden's best friend."

If possible, Kai's eyes widened even further. "We can have her over for dinner!" He clapped his hands together like an excited schoolboy. "I'll cook!"

"If you want to poison her!" Nate cried.

Calling for some sense of order, Rain cleared his throat. "You'll all get to meet Isla, but remember, you're grown men. So bloody well act like it if you want to take her on an adventure."

The scouts' spines straightened.

"We will," Kai promised.

"Good," Finn said. "Now, before any of us get to celebrate the full moon, we still have bats to kill. And we must be ready for when Lucas returns."

AN HOUR LATER, the pack had established battle plans for almost every contingency they could think of, except for one core component that remained missing. Sly's allegiance. Deep down, Rain doubted his brother would ever turn his back on him completely, but that didn't stop him from tearing off his clothes and striding into the backyard to shift. Stretching out on all fours, he wandered to the edges of the bush and released a soft howl. He had a hard time connecting with Sly as it was, but since his brother had been reaching out more, even if it was only to tell him when he was being a dick, Rain's hope remained.

"Bro. You there?" He waited a few moments, his ears straining over the silence. *"We just had a meeting. I'm sure you know what happened last night. I ... I marked her. And probably formed a Fated bond, too."* If it worked that way, and Rain wasn't sure it did. He might have felt the rush, the passion, and what felt like the Fated bond solidify when he'd slid inside her and made her body erupt in pleasure. When he'd lost himself in her and felt his heart forever meld with hers. But that didn't mean the Goddess would forgive him, nor did it shake the shame and disbelief that warred inside him, darkening what was supposed to be the most momentous occasion of his life.

Rain gritted his teeth and lowered his head, peering between the trees. *"Lucas took off. We think he's returned to Townsville and Tyrone, but he'll be back. Likely before the full moon. There's going to be a fight, and I need to know if you'll be by our side."*

The trees rustled. Birds chirped. Rain flicked his ears, and what sounded like a wallaby bounced through loose leaf litter in the distance. But no wolf.

He bared his teeth and released a low growl. *"Sly!"*

"Of course I'll fucking be there." The deep rumble of Sly's irritated baritone shuddered through Rain's head. *"And yes, I saw that fucking bat flitter back to the mainland. If he knows what's good for him, he won't come back."*

Rain turned and studied the western hills where he sensed Sly's presence. *"You don't believe that."*

"No, because the fuckers seem to have a death wish. They're the ones who started this war, but we'll fucking finish it."

Rain's hackles rose. *"Fucking oath, we will. They hurt Eden and forced my hand. She'll never be the same and I—"*

"Oh, bro, you're killing me here! You did what you had to do. Life's not perfect. Get used to it."

Rain padded down the slope to peer around the second floor of his house and across Picnic Bay. *"Don't start, Sly. You can't even deal with your own fucking pain. At least I'm trying to face mine."*

"Because you have *your mate. Remember that, bro. She's alive, healthy, and yours. Keep her that way and you'll never have a problem."*

"But I marked—"

"Yes, you marked her. It fucking sucks. But have you fallen out of favor with the Goddess? You're still pack bonded, right?"

"Yeah, because Finn—"

"Finn can't overpower the Moon, dickhead. If you were to be ousted, you would be. Just trust me that you've been forgiven."

Rain sank to his haunches and sighed. *"But our bond is tainted. She's tied to me forever."*

"So? It's what we want. The sooner you accept you can't control everything, the sooner you'll be fucking happy."

Rain's lips peeled back. *"I'll be happy when I kill that fucking bat."*

"You and me both," Sly growled. *"But don't worry. I'm keeping an eye on things."*

Rain's heart ached as he imagined his brother patrolling the west coast. Honestly, he didn't know how Sly did it. Rain loved being a wolf, but one night of hunting, running, and rolling around in the creeks was enough for him. He liked the luxuries of humanity too much, enjoyed the thrill of the jet ski and free-falling through the air.

But Sly hadn't felt the rush of a jump, cleanliness of soap, or the softness of a mattress in two years.

"*Where are you, Sly?*" His question was met with silence, but the connection didn't break. "*Are you okay?*"

"*Don't worry, little brother. I won't go far.*"

Rain swallowed the hope that bubbled inside his chest. "*So you think you might—*"

"*Don't go getting any ideas. I'm not turning back. Fate can still go to hell, but I do want to see you happy, and your mate safe. I can see how much you love her.*"

"*I do. She's the best thing to happen to me.*"

"*I understand. Which is why you should understand why I'm not leaving this bush. But I'll keep an eye on Townsville and let you know when that blood-sucking creep returns. I sense tension on the mainland. You and the pack are going to be in for a fight.*"

"*One we'll fucking win this time.*" Rain was adamant. He'd come so close and had almost sacrificed his soul to save his mate. He wouldn't risk losing anything else.

"*You and the pack have everything you need to defeat the bats, bro. Trust me on that.*"

"*And when the time comes, you'll fight alongside us?*" He knew Sly had already said as much, but he felt the need to double check.

"*Only if you do something for me.*"

Rain's ears perked. "*What is it?*"

Sly was silent for a moment, then said, "*Can you start leaving me meat again? Curlews taste like shit.*"

Rain snorted and wagged his tail, the man inside him grinning. It wasn't what he'd expected, but he'd take it. "*Sure, bro. I wouldn't want to live off the spindly legs of a curlew either. I'll get some beef to you tonight.*"

"Leave it at Cockle Falls. Don't wait for me, I'm busy and will grab it later. Besides, you have a mate to enjoy."

"I sure do."

And Sly could, too, if only he be willing to open his heart again. He might have given up, but Rain refused to do the same. His big brother was still there, still alive inside the wolf. The creature hadn't taken over.

He would get Sly back.

Chapter 34

"I'm so glad you're okay!" Ava flung her arms around Eden as they met for breakfast at Luna Views, tears springing to Eden's eyes as they rocked side to side in a crushing hug. "I've missed you these last few days, Edes. And I know you were terrified, but seriously ..." Ava pulled away, her eyes wide as she shook her head. "Watching you suffer ..."

Eden's heart clenched as her friend's voice broke. "I'm just grateful that I didn't hurt you," she whispered, remembering the way she'd eyed Ava like she was her next juicy meal. "I'm so sorry."

"Don't be sorry. You were compelled."

"I know. But I can be sorry for cutting you out like I did. Shouting at you and hiding away."

Ava smiled softly. "Don't be sorry about that, either. I understand. You were trying to protect me. And yourself. I was just so scared I'd lose you."

Ava hiccupped, and Eden drew her back into a hug, rubbing her hand up and down her back. "I know. But I'm okay."

"Yes. So, tell me!" Ava drew back, grinning as she wiped her tears away. "You and Rain completed the mating bond, right? I mean, I hated that he had to mark you, but Finn said you also forged it properly. Did you?"

"I think so. Rain said we did. And I certainly *feel* like we're bonded."

Ava's eyes sparkled as she bounced on her toes. "Isn't it just amazing? Honestly, I feel sorry for ordinary couples as this connection with our wolf shifters ... there's nothing like it. Don't you agree?"

Eden laughed. "How about we get a table, and we can talk about it."

They approached the hostess, who greeted them like royalty as she showed them to a table overlooking the gardens, promising to bring freshly brewed tea that they didn't order but wouldn't turn down.

Once they were alone again, Ava leaned forward expectantly. "So, is being with Rain everything you thought it'd be?"

Eden giggled. "Oh, it so much better. That man ... he has stamina. I've never had sex like it."

"Tell me about it. Finn's insatiable. It's totally a wolf thing."

Eden leaned close, hiding behind her menu as she whispered, "I had six orgasms last night. It was insane."

She still couldn't believe it, but Ava appeared to understand as her friend's grin only widened. "Get used to it, Eden. Our men are passionate, fiercely protective, and there's nothing more important to them than their mates. That includes our pleasure."

"Well, I can certainly get used to that. And this bond is something else. I mean, I've always loved him, but since we bonded ..." Eden drew in a breath and shivered. "There are no words."

"I know. I could never wrap my head around how I was so drawn to Finn either, but the moment our bond formed on that beach, everything was just so much brighter. We almost become one with our mates, and the sex was so much better after that. But I guess you solidified yours with the mating level."

"We did. Rain said we'd completed the emotional bond by being friends, and when I accepted that I was turning into a vampire, I accepted the paranormal."

Ava nodded. "So, you guys went emotional, paranormal, mating. Whereas I accepted the paranormal last."

"Yeah. But sensing his feelings is a little weird."

"It can be inconvenient at times," Ava admitted.

"Yes, like how I sense his shame and guilt over marking me. I hate that he feels that way."

Ava smiled sympathetically. "It was a hard thing for him to do, Eden. He just needs time to come to terms with it."

"Maybe once he kills Lucas, he'll feel better." She could only hope. "But the bond is extraordinary. Rain says we're like one. That his pulse is my pulse. That our hearts beat in sync."

Ava swooned. "It's the most beautiful thing, isn't it?"

"It sure is." Eden couldn't deny that as it was all she'd ever wanted with him, and she was glad Ava had mated a shifter, too, as at least she had someone to talk to about the rare, passionate kind of love she'd found.

A waitress arrived with two steaming pots of tea, and they placed their order for acai bowls.

"So, you said Rain's skydiving this morning?" Ava asked.

"Yep. He was super keen to get back to work, the crazy man. He won't land for another hour, but I'll go down to meet him."

Ava shook her head. "I still don't know how he does it."

"It's the wolf inside him," Eden said, pouring tea into her cup. "Makes him fearless."

"True." Settling back in her chair, Ava sipped her own tea.

"What are the chances, hey? Of both of us being Fated mates?"

"Oh, I don't know. We formed a friendship over fantasy books, remember?" Though part of her wondered if there might be more to it as Fate apparently worked in mysterious ways.

"Yes, we did. And speaking of which, Isla's landing in Sydney in the morning! She'll be here next week!"

"I know!" Isla had wrapped up her US tour as a support act and was leaving New York in only a few hours. It would take her almost a day to travel to Sydney, where she would spend a week with her mother before flying to Townsville. "I can't wait. This Full Moon Party is going to be the best one yet."

Their breakfast arrived, and the fear and darkness of the past week vanished in the bright morning as Eden laughed and reminisced with Ava, planning the many things they would do with Isla when she arrived. And what their man-obsessed, flirtatious friend would think about their sinfully sexy mates.

"She'll think we've struck gold," Ava said as they strode out of the restaurant. "Which indeed we have."

"Totally," Eden agreed, hugging Ava. "I'll see you later for dinner."

The pack would be over every night to prepare for Lucas's return, but Eden didn't want to think about that. She planned to enjoy her day while she could, so she farewelled Ava, then headed past the Moon Dive shop and down onto the beach where red warning flags marked the parachute landing zone.

Eden joined the gathering crowd, shielded her eyes, and squinted behind her sunglasses as she surveyed the cloudless sky. The plane should appear any second now and, as usual, her heart thumped madly against her ribs. But not due to fear and wonder at Rain's stupidity. Instead, the anticipation had her shifting from foot to foot, her belly clenching with warmth as she awaited the exhilaration of seeing Rain's chute open and watching him descend safely back to earth. Because while she would always think him insane for regularly jumping out of a perfectly good airplane, she couldn't deny that she found his bravery super sexy. Badass. And for the first time, Eden embraced the heat that warmed her veins because he was finally hers and she could take him home later and relish his fucking insane body. Maybe with jam.

"There it is!" someone shouted, and Eden spotted the tiny spec of a plane that must be close to fifteen thousand feet. Depending on the weather, the jump ranged between eight to fifteen thousand, and Rain had already declared that today had perfect jumping conditions.

Eden's pulse spiked as the first white drogue parachute blossomed against the blue sky, then a second and—

Heat bloomed in her chest, and she grinned. The third was Rain. She knew it. Lowering her hand, Eden fixed her eyes on the white dot. They sure were crazy, but admittingly, it was probably fun to feel the adrenaline rush through your blood and the wind whip in your hair and cheeks. It would be thrilling as hell if the warmth encasing her heart and the tingle shooting along her skin was any indication, so maybe—

Eden blinked and stumbled back in the sand. No. Those were Rain's feelings she was channeling. Not hers. And if she were mated to anyone else up there, she might feel something other than exhilaration. Her man didn't fear this. He lived for it.

Because he was fucking insane.

Chutes billowed open across the clear sky, and the solo jumpers soon flew into landing at speeds that would break legs if not executed correctly. Chad ran in second, unhooking his chute and reeling it out of the landing zone as he gazed up at the tandem masters taking their customers on a leisurely float.

Eden watched as Rain twisted, turned, then fixed the angle for a safe landing.

He ran onto the beach, and Eden bounced on her toes with excitement. Damn, any more of this and she'd need to pack dry knickers. When had watching him skydive become so erotic?

Always.

Rain unhooked his customer and straightened his shoulders, his magnificent chest puffing through his black T-shirt as he detached the chute and greeted the crew member supervising the landing zone. Eden strode towards them, mindful that he was still working as he lifted the camera and flung his arm around his client. But after the tourist shook Rain's hand and wandered back to his family with a dazed look on his face, Eden grinned and ran towards her man.

"Hey, baby!" He flashed her a smile as he gathered the strings of his chute. "I didn't die again."

"I didn't think you would." She touched her mouth to his, fighting the urge to throw her arms around him as she placed her hand on his chest and subtly gripped his T-shirt. "Did you have fun?"

"It was a fucking thrill. I have no regrets taking the past few days off, but damn, I'm glad to be jumping again."

"I sensed that."

Rain flung the chute over his shoulder and wrapped his arm around her waist. "I bet you could. Is that weird for you?"

"What? Sensing your feelings? Or feeling the rush of skydiving and thinking it would be fun?"

He chuckled. "Both?"

"I'm getting used to the feelings thing. It's kind of cool, though Ava said there will be times I find it incredibly inconvenient."

"I'm sure." He led her up the beach, the thin nylon of the chute that looked far too small to be safe brushing the back of her shoulder. "But I kind of like it because you ground me. You're always so calm, centered, and together. It helps keep my wild energy in check."

She smiled and leaned into him. "I don't think I can ever be so calm as to tame you." Not her wild, crazy, dangerous man.

"Not when it comes to jumping, you won't. I'm taking one more up, but I'm sitting out of the ten o'clock jump."

They climbed the stairs and returned to Moon Dive where the next group of thrill seekers were gearing up for their adventure. Eden shook her head as Hayden, Dave, and Johnno strode ahead of her with their chutes over their shoulders and a spring in their steps. She turned to Rain, his energy palpable as she observed his grin. His joy.

"You don't have a tandem jump?"

He shook his head. "Usually I would, but I was only put on the roster yesterday. Johnno offered to swap with me, but I need to take you to the koalas, so I said no. I'll take this eighteen-year-old birthday girl up, then we'll go."

A strange possessiveness filled Eden as her eyes darted to the young blonde awaiting in the crowd preparing for her jump. "Eighteen, hey?"

"Birthdays are always popular, age milestones even more so."

"I bet. Though if I were her, I'd be more excited about being strapped to you than jumping out of a stupid plane."

Rain chuckled as he placed his hand on her lower back and kissed her nose. "No need to be jealous, baby. I'll take you up anytime you like. Or strap you down."

"Okay." The word left Eden's mouth before she could second guess herself.

Rain froze, the joy fading from his eyes as his jaw hardened. "Fuck, I'm sorry, I didn't mean to say that. You told me you aren't open to being tied up. That's just the marking—"

Eden touched her finger to his mouth. "No. I meant take me up."

His lips parted beneath her touch. "You don't mean that."

Exhaling, Eden traced her finger down the stubble over his chin. "Rain, please. Stop worrying about controlling me. Yes, you marked me, but I believe our bond is strong enough to overpower that."

"It's not—"

"It has to be! Because I don't feel like you have any more sway over my heart or feelings than you did before you bit me. And I promised myself when I was curled up on that bed dying that if I survived that horror, then I'd stop being so scared. I have a second chance, Rain, and this"—she gestured to his get up—"can't be as terrifying as turning into an undead creature who lives off blood. So, if you want to take me—"

Rain whipped around so fast his hair spun as he shouted, "Mike! Get Eden ready to go on the ten o'clock jump! She'll be with me!"

Then his mouth was on hers, his strong arms pulling her against him until her ribs ached in protest while he parted her lips with his tongue. Eden's heart lurched, racing in harmony with his as wicked delight shuddered through their souls. Her rational mind screamed, but Eden shut that down as her hands fell to his hard pectorals and clung, her knees weakening in both fear and excitement.

Yet she smiled softly, sharing in Rain's joy as he tore away and left her dazed with pleasure.

"I won't let you talk yourself out of it now, baby. You'll fucking love it, I promise."

Then he spirited away, pumped for his second jump of the day while she stood wondering what the fuck she'd gotten herself in to.

Chapter 35

Eden engaged in some gentle ribbing with Mike as she filled out the waivers, but she didn't mind as everything he said was true. She was dating the boss and wanted to prove that she wasn't "chickenshit." Besides, she couldn't back out after sensing Rain's excitement in his wicked kiss, so she filled out the forms, then sat beside another young woman as the briefing started. Her rational mind had always known skydiving was incredibly safe as the crew would do all the work, take control, and make sure she survived while leaving her with "the experience of a lifetime." The Moon Dive team were passionate and well-trained professionals who loved the adrenaline.

Besides, she had nothing to fear when there was no safer place than in Rain's hands.

"Is everyone ready?" Patrick, the crew member leading the session, cried, and Eden threw her arms in the air and joined in the cheers. Tension eased from her shoulders as she shared a smile with the woman beside her. She might be fucking crazy, but she'd survived a vampire attack. She could handle jumping out of a plane with the man she loved.

"All right! Let's get you geared up!"

Eden pushed to her feet and headed outside where the crew began fitting them into harnesses.

Patrick approached Eden with an amused smirk. "Finally dating the boss man and letting him talk you into stupid shit."

"Yeah ..." Her breath caught as she stepped gingerly into the harness and threaded her arms through as Patrick pulled it up. "But he didn't talk me into it. I've overcome my fear."

"Good for you." He fastened the front strap. "You'll have a blast, Eden."

She was sure he was right, but she'd feel a lot better once the chute had opened as it was the actual leaping out of the plane and tumbling through the sky with no control that scared her. She'd never thought she could do it.

But she didn't have to. Rain would be the idiot who jumped out, she'd just be the insane woman attached to him risking her neck for a bloody boy.

"Look!"

Eden glanced up as chutes opened in the sky, and her heart pounded harder. Shit, he was coming back. Then he'd grab her and—

Nope. Fuck this shit. Clutching her stupid harness, she considered making a run for it. Why had she fallen in love with a skydiver? Stupid Moon Goddess and her wicked ways. Couldn't she have given Rain another passion? Like needlepoint?

Eden's hands were on the buckles, ready to unhook herself when Rain strode through the trees, leading his crew with his chute over his shoulder and determination in his stride, looking far too sexy in his black Moon Dive T-shirt, shorts, and the pack strapped to his bulging shoulders. Eden gulped, her fingers stilling as heat pooled in her thighs.

Rain pointed at her and grinned. "Proud of you!" he called, before disappearing through the crew-only doors.

Eden's heart swelled, and her fingers relaxed. Yeah, too right she could do this.

"You know him?" the girl beside her asked, and Eden grinned.

"Yeah. He's my ... boyfriend."

"Hot damn! You go girl." She extended her hand. "I'm Lizzy."

"Eden."

"You've done this before, then?"

Eden scoffed. "No. I always told Rain I wouldn't, but ..."

"I get it. I'd jump out of a plane for him, too. I think Hayden's taking me."

"Hayden's cool. He'll take care of you."

Moon Dive's doors burst open, and Rain raced towards her like an energetic puppy, scooping her up into his arms and spinning her around. *Not* how a tandem master usually greeted his customer, but Eden didn't mind as "hot damn" was right. She was one lucky girl.

"You have no idea how long I've wanted to do this," he said, his blue eyes softening as he placed her down.

"Probably never thought you would."

"I had hoped."

He kissed her again, then cleared his throat, professionalism sobering his face as he set about securing her harness. Then triple checking as he tugged the straps and clips for a second time, depressing her shoulders and squeezing her thighs.

"I don't think I'll fall out."

"I wouldn't let you. Now, what are we going to do when we're up there?"

Eden proved she'd paid attention to the safety briefing as she answered Rain's questions and demonstrated the various positions she'd assume. Then, once everyone was ready, the crew grabbed their packs, and they filed onto the bus. The crew and customers usually sat separately, but Rain pulled Eden into the seat beside him as they engaged in more cheering to hype everyone up, then pulled away from Luna Views.

Rain wrapped his arm around Eden's shoulders. "Were you honestly thinking about doing this when you were sick?"

"Not this, specifically, but like I said last night, I don't want to be afraid anymore, Rain. And watching you today ... it got me all hot."

He chuckled. "Really?"

"Yep. And I know there's nothing to fear. I'm in the safest place possible when I'm with you."

He brushed his lips over hers. "Yes, you are. I'll never let anything happen to you again, Eden. I'm going to throw you out of a plane at two hundred kilometers per hour, but you're going to love it, and I'll make sure we land safely."

She shuddered but shared his grin before pressing her forehead to his. Rain's confidence and ease helped keep her own pulse steady as she admitted, "I am scared, though."

"Of course you are. It's *normal* to be scared, baby. You're about to jump out of a plane. This is scary shit. Though not as scary as those bloody bats."

She inched away. "Do you ever get scared?"

"I'm fucking petrified today. I'm carrying precious cargo." He kissed her forehead. "But I've got you, baby. Trust me."

And she did, which was the only reason she managed to alight from the bus and stride across the tarmac into the King Air. Rain straddled the bench seat and Eden settled in front of him as he secured her to his chest and triple checked his work.

Then he wrapped his arms around her waist, dropped his chin on her shoulder, and held her close. Closer than the other instructors, hopefully, as his cock stiffened against her ass.

"I'm so fucking excited."

"I can tell ..."

"Shh." He kissed her neck as Chad sat diagonally opposite them, facing the cabin and cradling his camera helmet.

"You'll have a fucking blast, Eden. And don't worry, Rain will record every scream."

"He better." Eyeing the camera attached to Rain's wrist, Eden quit questioning her mentality and drew on his energy as they took off over Horseshoe Bay.

She glanced out the window, watching as the island grew smaller beneath her. The engines roared in her ears as people chatted with a mix of excitement and fear while the cameramen captured the memories. Chad settled his helmet on and focused on Lizzy, who was downright cheering.

"What kind of video do you want, baby?" Rain asked as he readied the camera.

"I don't know. What do you normally do?"

"Mostly boring shit. But this video we could make just for us."

"We can't talk dirty on this plane," she hissed.

"Oh, I beg to differ." Tightening his grip around her, he hit record. "How are you feeling, baby?"

She opened her mouth to reply as his hand lifted to cup her breast. "I ... this is ... stop that." She wriggled as he teased her nipple.

"That's not what you said last night," he whispered, dropping a kiss to her neck.

She giggled. "Rain!"

"Just trying to help you relax, baby. Your heart's racing."

"Because you're about to throw me out of a plane!"

She turned to meet his gaze, and he grinned. "I sure am. And am so fucking proud of you." He pressed his lips to hers. "Been dreaming of this day. Are you ready?"

She stilled. Oh shit, this was really happening. "I wouldn't do this if I wasn't with you."

"And I'd never trust any other fucker to take you up." He

kissed her, urging her mouth open with his tongue and ravishing her for a moment, before tearing away and pausing the recording.

Rain turned to the crew. "Everyone ready?"

Confirmations came from around the cabin. Eden grabbed the front of her harness as Rain readied their camera again, then slammed his fist on the button to lift the door. Wind blew into the plane, stealing Eden's breath as her pulse spiked to what she suspected was cardiac arrest levels.

"Let's go!" he shouted.

"Shit. Oh Shit." Fuck, she was mental, but she moved with him, clutching her shoulder straps as they slid towards the door and stood. Eden bent her knees, the wind deafening as it whipped her ponytail into her face and Rain grabbed the overhead handle. They hovered over the edge of the world, Magnetic Island a tiny spec beneath them as Rain shouted, "Ready? Be brave, baby."

"I hate you."

Warm lips pressed against her hair. "You love me."

Then she was falling, floating, the blue sky tumbling around her as a scream ripped from her throat. The plane appeared above her, then she was facing downwards as the drogue released and steadied their descent.

And Eden's screams ceased as she stared in wonder, wind flapping her cheeks. Rain tugged on her wrists and she shot her arms out, blinking as the world spun below her.

She'd jumped out of a plane. She'd survived a vampire attack and had jumped out of a fucking airplane.

Eden's belly swelled as a laugh burst from her chest. Holy shit!

Turning to the camera, she cheered. This was unreal. She could barely hear Rain's own cheers over the roaring wind, but felt he was having the time of his life, too, as they fell through the sky. Rain's warmth enveloped her and her heart swelled to twice its size as it tugged against his. They were one. United. And if she could be saved from turning into a vampire, survive the bite of a wolf, and fall fifteen thousand feet without dying, there was nothing that she and Rain couldn't conquer.

The ground grew closer, Magnetic Island looming as suddenly, a great gust of wind caught them and the parachute ejected, swinging her upright and halting their freefall.

Rain wrapped his arm around her waist as he kept the camera trained on their faces. "How was that, baby?"

"I can't believe I did that!"

"Loved it?"

"Yes!" She couldn't deny that or the adrenaline pumping through her as they sailed gently through the air, the canopy whipping above them. "Bloody insane, though. Oh my God."

She tried to catch her breath as Rain's lips pressed to her hair.

"So fucking proud of you, Eden. I love you so damn much."

Grinning, she rested her head against his chest but couldn't catch his gaze as she said, "I love you, too. Now give me the handles. I want to steer."

Chapter 36

Rain had completed over fifteen thousand jumps and had done all sorts of crazy shit during his sport jumping days, but none of those came close to beating this one as a high like no other flooded through his body. His wildest dream had come true, and it was more than he'd ever dared hope for.

Rain pressed his hand to Eden's belly and let her take control as he relaxed and shared in the thrill he loved most with the woman he'd die for. His timid mate was frightened no more, the tension having left her shoulders and leaving pure joy in its place as they banked right and descended towards the island.

"Maggie always looks so big from the sky!" Eden shouted over her shoulder.

"I think we forget how big the national park actually is," Rain said, placing his hand over hers to adjust their course.

"Have you explored it all? As a wolf?"

"More than I have as a man, but not all of it. Cockle Creek remains one of our favorite hangouts."

"How does Sly survive?"

"No idea. Thankfully, he's always liked roughing it, and I do keep him fed." Not only to ensure Sly had adequate nutrition, but now to also save the curlews.

"He must be lonely."

"Yep. I wouldn't be able to do what he has. Two years is a bloody long time."

"Yeah. But I think he'll come back to you, Rain."

"I hope so, Eden." He pressed his lips to her hair again. "Now, let me get us ready to land."

He took control, riding the wind and lining them up as the beach grew closer. Eden's spine tensed against his chest.

"Feet up!" Her legs shot up and he braced himself, preparing for a run-in landing. But Eden was too slow, and they slid into the soft sand.

"Oh my God, we made it!"

Rain kissed the corner of her mouth as he unattached their harnesses. "Safe and sound, baby. As promised."

He leapt to his feet, then took her hand and hauled her up into his arms. Eden flung hers around his neck and he squeezed her tight. His beautiful, fearless mate.

"I want to go again!"

Rain chuckled. He heard that from all the first timers and though her eyes sparkled with elation, Rain didn't get his hopes up as the dark voice plaguing him crept into his mind.

Had marking her done this? Had some sinister part of their bond put the crazy notion of jumping out of planes into her head? Did she possess a new level of fearlessness now that she was under his control?

Was she really?

His wolf growled and Rain lowered Eden back to her feet. "I'll certainly take you up again. One day. But right now, we need to move."

He reeled in the chute. Chad and the solo guys were

already on the ground and Hayden had landed shortly after he had, leaving only Dave and Johnno in the sky.

Eden's chest heaved as she shook her head in wonder. "I can't believe you've done that three times today."

He observed her smile, her wide eyes, and the tightness inside him unraveled. No, she wasn't under his control. The light part of their bond told him that as he sensed freedom and elation radiating through her. He didn't have a hold on her in the way the rebels did on their marks. It was just as she'd said—she'd had a near death experience and had longed for the rush. To push herself into the realm of danger and survive. Rain understood that. He'd taken many people skydiving after surviving cancer or another traumatic experience. He hadn't changed her. All Eden wanted was to feel alive.

And marked or unmarked, she'd jumped out of that plane because she'd wanted to. Because she loved him.

Their bond tugged, scorching the air between them as he tossed the chute over his shoulder and pulled her flush against his body. "Yep. I'm running on the ultimate high, Eden. Especially since I'm channeling yours, too."

"Oh, I'm high all right. That was so exhilarating. Now, I get why you do it. You're still insane—"

"Absolutely." He'd never deny that.

"—but if you died, at least you'd die having fun."

"Exactly!" Laughing, he captured her mouth and slid his tongue against hers. His cock hardened. Shit, he really needed to get them out of there. Now. Growling, he drew away and pressed his forehead to hers. "I'm so fucking happy right now, Eden. My wolf wants to burst free and claim you."

"He already has."

"That's not what I meant." He cupped her ass, pulled her hips against his, and his glorious mate giggled.

"I know. It's a bit hard for me to miss that. So how about

you close up shop, then we can go ride our high together as I don't think I'll come down for hours."

Rain secured his chutes, joked and chatted with his team, then left them to shut up shop as he spirited Eden away in his Lexus. Her heart hadn't stopped racing, and he needed to help her ride out her adrenaline in endless orgasms until she hit a wall and slept for the rest of the afternoon. The combination of fear and excitement took its toll on the body and once she came down, she'd crash and shatter.

And he'd rather shatter her himself with the erection he'd been fighting since she'd said "Take me up." No words had ever been sweeter to his ears, or more erotic.

He still couldn't stop thanking her.

"I'm fucking thrilled you came up with me," he said as he navigated the Lexus through Picnic Bay. "Fucking best jump of my life, Edes. Now all you need to do is learn to go solo."

Her desire-glazed eyes widened. "What? You mean ... jump out of a plane by myself?"

"Yeah." He grinned. "Why? Scared?"

"The only reason I could do that today was because I knew you'd jump and I'd have no choice! I *gave* you that control, Rain!"

He shivered at her use of that word but understood what she meant. She'd trusted him and despite overcoming her fear of fear, she hadn't become a complete daredevil.

"There's no way I'd have the guts to do that myself. That's why I have you." Her hand landed on his thigh and squeezed, her fingers brushing over his groin and springing his cock to life. "No skydiving school for me."

He hissed out a breath, put his foot to the floor, and

zoomed into the opening garage. "All right. We'll discuss it later because right now, I don't want to do a hell of a lot of talking."

He parked the Lexus and cut the engine.

"We will *not* be discussing it later!" she cried as he tore his leg from her grasp and leapt out of the car. "You can't make a daredevil out of me yet, Rain Blackwood. That was fun, but—"

He yanked open her door, pulled her to her feet, and crushed his mouth to hers, silencing her ridiculous protests as she stumbled against his chest. Spearing his hands into her hair, he tipped her head back and growled, his wolf salivating and groaning with need as her hands clutched the hem of his T-shirt and she released a moan of her own. Rain took her lower lip between his teeth, then dove deep. She rose onto her toes as their tongues tangled and noses squashed, heat sizzling through his vessels as his cock tented his shorts.

Fuck, he needed her. Needed to be inside her. This mating bond was out of fucking control.

"I'll go tandem with you anytime, baby," he growled against her mouth, kissing her again before releasing her lower lip with a plop. "Let's practice."

Then he spun her around, holding her back against his chest as he buried his face into her fragrant neck. Her breath escaped on a gasp as she tilted to give him better access, her hands caressing his arms as they stumbled through the garage and into the downstairs living room.

"I want you to remember how we were up there, Eden. How secure you were. The thrill. The majestic view of the world at your feet. Because I'm going to give it to you."

Her breath escaped in short, sharp pants. "Give it to me?"

"The world. Everything. Anything your heart desires. Because it is *mine*."

"Yes," she breathed, her chest heaving against his tight

embrace. "My heart is yours. I'm yours. And right now, I want you."

He smirked, his wolf bursting through his chest. "Good answer." Taking her hands, he placed them on the back of the lounge before dropping a kiss to the bumps of her spine above the top of her blue singlet. "You have me, baby. Forever and always. Now, don't move."

Rain dropped to his knee, lifted her foot, and slipped her shoe off, tossing it over his shoulder before reaching for the other and doing the same. A touch of sand sprayed in his face, but he shook it off and peeled the socks from her slender feet. Fuck, he wanted to suck her toes. How had he not sucked her toes yet? Hmm ... maybe later because right now, he needed something else.

He grabbed her thighs and ran his thumbs beneath the curve of her perfectly puckered ass cheeks clad in black lycra.

Her knees trembled. "What are you—"

Rain pressed his thumb between her legs, delighting in her gasp and the warmth seeping through her clothes. "You're already so wet for me."

"I'm always wet for you." She twisted her spine to glance down at him and lifted her hand off the lounge.

Rain bared his teeth. "I said, don't move."

She snapped back into place. "Sorry."

Exhaling, he closed his eyes and buried his forehead on the pillow of her glutes. *Fuck!* That had been an order he hadn't meant to give. An abuse of their dark bond. *Control.*

But Eden either didn't care or hadn't noticed as she curved her spine to bring his nose between her thighs. He inhaled her arousal and everything inside Rain quivered.

"Don't be sorry," he whispered, lifting his face away as he resumed his gentle massage. "That was my bad. I didn't mean for it to be an order."

"An order?" she gasped.

His gaze trailed up her spine to meet hers peeking at him from beneath her arm. "Did you not see how quick you were to obey me? That was darkness, Eden."

Her lips quirked. "Maybe, but it was also me doing as you bid so you wouldn't fucking stop. So don't you dare, Rain. You *don't* control me. Okay?"

Oh, but he did. He could tell her to do anything and she'd obey without question.

Though it *had* only been her hand gripping the couch. It's not like he'd overpowered an important personal choice. So, with a growl, he dipped his head and sucked the seam of her damp lycra pants into his mouth. She bucked.

"I get it. I don't control you." Though he could certainly flirt within the gray area as he slid his hands down the inside of her thighs. "But right now, I need to have you. To ravish you. My wolf hungers to taste you, smell you, and plunge inside your taut little body."

"Yes," she rasped. "Take me, Rain. I'm happy to oblige. To play. To submit. To you and your wolf."

He pushed to his feet and pressed his lips to her neck, nipping her skin. "Just me, Eden. My wolf can go to hell." Then he hooked his thumbs into the side of her tights and pushed them down her legs. "Kick them away."

She did, stepping out of the lycra and shaking the pants from her ankles as he ripped his T-shirt off and reached between her legs to press the heel of his palm to her hot, swollen body.

Her hips arched into his touch. "Rain!"

"Fuck, Eden." He slipped his fingers beneath the thin cotton blocking him and groaned. "You feel so good."

"All because of you."

His chest swelled. "Too fucking right."

He slid his fingers through her warm, wet folds, teasing and delighting in her whimpers as he kissed her neck and sucked at her pounding pulse. When his lips found her mark, he both kissed and grated his teeth over the cursed scar. He hated it, always would, as it was a betrayal he could never make right. Even if she did love him, would walk over hot coals for him, and respond to his touch and orders because it delighted her, the darkness would always exist between them.

But perhaps it wouldn't weigh down on him as much if rather than avoid controlling her, he focused on controlling himself. As long as he didn't abuse his power, he could remain the gentleman he'd always longed to be while keeping the animal inside him on a leash.

Except, of course, when she demanded it.

He latched his mouth over her mark, licked the puckered skin, then drew back to nip at her ear. "Tell me what you want."

"More," she gasped, her hands whitening around the lounge.

He growled. "Tell me, Eden."

"You. Inside me."

"This?" he asked, smirking as he plunged his finger inside her. She gasped, then groaned as he stroked her once. Twice. *Fuck*, she was divine.

"That'll do. But … more."

He swallowed a snigger and nipped her ear again. "Take off your shirt."

He inched back, giving her room as she lifted the hem of her singlet. Rain waited until the tight material bunched around her face, then slipped a second finger inside her.

She cried out, shuddering as she struggled to free herself. "Rain!"

He grabbed her singlet and pulled it away before freeing her breasts. Her bra hung from her shoulders as he cupped one of her gorgeous tits and pulled her bare back against his heaving chest, turning her face to claim her mouth as he wriggled his fingers. She clenched around him and cried out, clutching his neck as he stroked her through her orgasm until her knees buckled against the lounge.

He surrendered her mouth, watching as her dark eyes fluttered open. "I love watching you come undone. To feel you clench around my fingers. But now, I need to feel you around my cock."

"Yes." She speared her hand into the back of his hair. "I like your fingers. They're big and get me just right. But your cock ..."

His wolf growled, rumbling inside his chest as he nipped at her lips. "Say it, Eden."

"You're fucking huge and fill me perfectly."

His cock hardened at the praise. "Too fucking right, I do." He slipped his fingers from her and ripped her knickers down her legs. "Move."

"Where?" she asked as her body slid bonelessly against his.

"Window. It might not be like the view from the sky, but you're going to soak it all in while I plunge inside you from behind."

"Like we're diving."

"Like we're diving," he agreed, reclaiming her mouth and swallowing her gasps as he interlocked their fingers. Rain wrapped his arms around her quivering body and moved her towards the glass doors overlooking the balcony and crystal-clear water of Picnic Bay. He stroked her tongue with his, relishing in her soft moans and sweet taste as he lifted her hands and slapped her palms against the glass. He couldn't get enough of her, his wolf panting as he dropped his shorts.

"Tell me how you want me," he breathed.

"Deep. Hard. Make me scream like you did when you threw me from that plane. Make me relive the rush."

A similar kind of adrenaline coursed through him as he grabbed his pulsating cock. His perfect mate certainly knew what to say. "Baby, I'm good, but that's an experience like no other. However, I can certainly make you scream."

"Do it."

Knocking her feet apart, Rain bent his knees and drove inside her. Eden's hips bucked as she rose onto her toes and tossed her head back, a cry ripping from her throat. Rain growled and splayed his hand over her belly, crushing her to him while lifting his other hand to cup her bouncing breast as he withdrew and plunged again.

His breath escaped in short bursts, chest hair scraping her back as he held her tight and tweaked her nipple. His wolf relished in her gasps, grunting and growling as he moved in and out. But even though Rain longed to let the animal take over and seize the woman he'd marked, he remained in control. The wolf might live inside him, but he was first and foremost a man, and to uphold their mating bond—the Fated one—he needed to love his mate as such and treat her like a lady.

Though ladies could certainly be naughty while being taken against the window.

He pulled her closer and kissed her softly. "Grab hold of me, baby."

Her hand lifted to grip the back of his neck again, holding him closer while the other braced against the glass, her fingers spreading, slipping, and sliding with sweat.

"Don't stop," she breathed.

"Can't." He thrust up into her. "So close. You're just—"

She whimpered and met his gaze, pivoting on her toes to meet his movements in perfect synchronization of passion. "Touch me."

His hand plowed down her belly and into her curls, pressing and teasing her clit. Eden cried out, her head flopping against his shoulder and hand squeezing his neck. Again, her body shuddered, pelvic muscles clenching around his throbbing cock as he rode her through it, his thighs tensing until he found his own release and spilled inside her.

But they didn't stop. Friction and heat continued to build until their energy depleted and they collapsed against the glass in a sweaty mess of fulfilled desire.

Chapter 37

Rain stretched out on the daybed on the first-floor balcony, unable to let Eden out of his reach. Not that she seemed to mind as she snuggled beside him, pillowing her head on his biceps as they enjoyed the breeze blowing over the balcony and awaited the sunset. She'd come down from her high after a shower, which had been more filthy than clean, and had barely eaten half her lunch before her eyelids had drooped. Rain had tucked her into bed and she'd slept for two hours while he finished cleaning and mentally cataloguing the damage from Sunday's brawl with Lucas. He'd ordered new furniture to be shipped over from Townsville and had extracted photos from broken frames. He should have taken them down ages ago since most of them were of Sly and Shelby, but he'd been hesitant to touch his brother's things despite the bastard's blatant refusal to shift back. So, he'd slipped the pictures into a drawer, straightened the grand piano that hadn't been played since Shelby had died, then continued to tidy until Eden had woken.

But even as he lay with her content and safe in his arms, Rain couldn't shake the dread that niggled at his spine. Lucas and Tyrone would retaliate quickly, seething in their failure to execute yet another plan to break his faith. But *had* their plan gone astray? Sure, Lucas would have delighted in turning Eden and his bloodlust would drive him to hunt her until he was satisfied.

But had Tyrone wanted Eden to turn into a vampire? Had he wanted to force Rain to kill her? Or had he played into the bastard's hands by marking her? To Rain, *that* seemed the most logical as Tyrone wanted to destroy their connection to the Goddess, and what better way than to force Rain to sacrifice his values to save the woman he loved.

But Rain *hadn't* fallen out of favor with the Goddess, and that would be the ace up his sleeve when Lucas returned to find he still had the pack behind him. That they were stronger than ever with two mated wolves, three diehard scouts, and a bloodthirsty animal lurking in the bush.

Rain's arms tightened around Eden as she rubbed her toes up and down his calf. Let those bastards try to take them down, because they'd be ready.

"I could ride this adrenaline all night," Eden breathed, brushing her hand across his chest.

Rain tore his gaze from the mainland and glanced down at his beautiful mate. After her nap, they'd shared a fruit platter in the jacuzzi before indulging in even more incredible sex, then had retired to the daybed where they each wore nothing but a towel.

"You'll never come down off that high, baby. Especially once you jump a few more times."

She shivered. "Jeez, the old me would say I'm insane."

"But now you've been bitten by the adrenaline bug, and it's addictive."

"I've been bitten by a *wolf*. And you know what? I think it's done something to me."

He frowned. "What do you mean?"

"I don't feel the same anymore," she said, tilting her head

back to meet his gaze. "And not just because I survived a vampire attack. I've had a near death experience before, and it caused anxiety and fear. But now, I feel stronger than ever. I feel changed."

"You had an experience you weren't ready for," he explained. "You didn't know about our world and the existence of shifters. It's all come as a shock."

"Well, yeah. But I was bitten by a vampire and almost turned into one. Then I was bitten by a wolf and—"

"You can't turn into a wolf, Eden. And you can't explain what happened with science." He lifted her hand from his chest and kissed her knuckles. "Trust me. Wolf shifters are born and we're only male, mating with strong women who have the power to tame us and carry on the genetic line."

Her brow furrowed. "So ..."

"You have wolf blood in you, Eden. You're a female descendent of a wolf shifter." Her eyes widened. "That's the power you possess that allows you to become a Fated mate. To be brave and fearless. The fact I bit you doesn't make you that way. It's always been inside you."

Rain could almost see the cogs working inside her head to find the logic in that statement. Not that he thought it needed explaining, it made perfect sense. She was special, sure, but she harnessed no unique abilities. Only daughters of wolf shifters possessed heightened senses similar to those of a shifter and while they were powerful women, they rarely became Fated mates. But his Eden wouldn't be Eden if she didn't look for a scientific reason to validate her thoughts.

"So ... you biting me didn't make me fearless?"

He pressed his hand to her terrycloth-covered back and pulled her close. "If that were the case, women claimed by rebel wolves would fight back."

Her shoulders slouched. "True. And speaking of wolves, I haven't met yours yet."

His lips quirked. "You want me to shift for you, baby?"

"Yes. I've seen the rest of the pack in wolf form, but it's you I love. Your wolf who saved me. And if I'm to thank anyone ..."

Rain suppressed a shudder. He wanted nothing more, of course, but what if he shifted and they couldn't communicate? What if their mating bond hadn't formed as the Goddess had intended? Sure, he'd thought he'd felt their Fated bond solidify, but he wasn't sure if he could take it if he was wrong.

Yet he couldn't refuse her.

"I'll shift later," he whispered. "Just don't thank him by ruffling his ears."

She grinned. "I'll try to resist."

"Though you did see me as a wolf, Eden. When I failed to reach you the night Lucas's bat bit you."

"But I don't remember that. And I want to see you shift when you're not forced to fight for me."

His jaw hardened. "I'll never be forced. It is my choice and my honor. My deepest obligation. Because while you might think yourself fearless, it is my job to protect you. And I always will."

Smiling, she curled herself against him, her towel parting as she lifted her inner thigh over his legs. "My fierce protector, hey?"

He tightened his hands around her shoulders. "Always."

"But surely there must be something inside me ..."

When she failed to finish that sentence, he softened his hold and pressed a kiss to her forehead. "I don't know, baby. We don't know much about biting a mate, especially one we've bonded with."

"I understand that. But I'm glad I'm no longer scared. I've always tried to be strong physically, but emotionally—"

Rain rolled onto his side, resting his weight on his elbow as he brushed his fingers down her cheek. "You've always been strong. Emotionally, physically, and strong of heart. But I'm glad you feel it too because I want to have all sorts of crazy adventures with you."

"And we will," she whispered, her eyes softening beneath his hungry gaze. "I love you, Rain."

"I love you." Then he took her mouth with fierce possession, kissing her softly, warmly, and relishing her intoxicating taste as his wolf howled with pride. Damn, he was lucky to have her.

Eden clutched his shoulder and Rain moved until she was beneath him, the knot in his towel loosening as he placed his knees on either side of her hips. But while he longed to take it further and lose himself in her again, first he wanted to eat and then—

Hair prickled the back of his neck as his wolf stood to attention. Curling his hands over the cushion, Rain glanced over his shoulder.

And froze.

Fear clogged inside his chest at the sight of a black cloud rapidly approaching from Townsville.

No, not a cloud. Bats.

"Rain! They're coming!"

"Get inside!" Rain straightened and scrambled off the bed, his towel falling away as he leapt to his feet. Eden sat up, her eyes widening at the sight of the bats, but she didn't have time to comment as he tossed her over his shoulder and ran inside. Placing her back on her feet, Rain slid the doors closed, then dashed around the room to secure the rest of the first floor as he reached out to Sly.

"Fuck me. How did he find that many vampires?"

"Has me fucked."

"There must be dozens of them!"

"What?" Eden asked, and Rain realized he'd spoken aloud.

"Talking to Sly," he said, tapping his temple before grabbing her hand and pulling her towards the elevator.

"*I know! I didn't think there were that many in Townsville, but we could have been wrong.*"

"Shit." Rain and Eden stepped into the elevator.

"*Should have known he'd bring a fucking army.*"

"*Do you think they're looking to attack straight away?*"

"*We're ready if they are,*" Finn said, joining in the conversation. "*Rain? What's going on?*"

"*I'm talking to Sly.*"

Finn growled. "*I wish I could hear him. Anyway, shelter in place. I'm at Luna Views and will reach out to the scouts. Knowing that sleazy bat, he won't fly straight into battle. He'll lure us out.*"

"He'll have to as he can't come straight for Eden." Rain glanced her way as they stepped out onto the second floor. "Check the doors are locked to the bedrooms."

She nodded, clutching the towel to her chest as she raced up the hallway. Rain ran through the dining room and pulled the concertina doors closed. Flicking the lock, he whipped around as Eden returned.

"Everything's secure."

"Good." He pulled her close, wrapping his arms around her shoulders as she rested her head on his chest. Together, they watched the bats approach.

"*I don't know if he'll wait long,*" Sly growled, his breath heaving as though he was running. "*It won't be like last time. Lucas is angry he didn't get his bride, and he won't hesitate to lure her out and turn her.*"

Rain squeezed Eden tight. "He won't get her."

"*No,*" Finn agreed.

"*But this time, you have the advantage,*" Sly continued. "*Don't forget, Tyrone thinks you rebelled, brother. He and Lucas won't be counting on you having the strength of the pack.*"

"Sucks to be him, then," Rain said.

"*Exactly. So use that. We'll kill this slimy cunt, then we can kill Tyrone.*"

"Will you join us at the packhouse? Help us plan?" Rain asked, hope rising inside him as he awaited Sly's answer. But as he tugged at the bond, silence reverberated back, and his shoulders sank. "He's gone."

Eden's fingers splayed over his chest. "He'll be here, Rain. I truly believe that. But right now ..."

Rain held her tight, determination steeling his spine as her heart pounded against his. Within minutes, the bats were upon them, swooping over Picnic Bay and his house. Rain glared at the ceiling as he followed their trajectory. His jaw loosened when they made no attempt to roost, but his wolf paced and prowled, hungry for the fight.

And this time, Rain wouldn't miss. He'd sink his teeth into that bastard if it was the last thing he did.

Chapter 38

Eden dressed quickly, pulling her yoga pants up her shaking legs and slipping on a singlet while Rain shoved his arms through a tight T-shirt. Then they strode into the living room at the same time Finn and Ava stepped out of the elevator.

"The bats flew over Nelly Bay towards Arcadia," Finn said in his way of greeting, having had the advantage of the northern view from his hut, "while some settled around Hawkings Point."

"We'll search there first," Rain said, brushing his fingers up and down Eden's lower back. "The scouts should be here soon, then we'll form a plan."

"I'll make dinner," Ava said, lifting the bag of groceries she carried as she nodded towards the kitchen. "Eden, do you want to help?"

"Okay." Cooking would at least keep her distracted while the men discussed battle tactics. But while panic might have been her initial response when she'd seen the bats winging towards them like a plague of locusts, a strange sense of calmness had settled inside her as she and Rain had secured the house. She'd meant what she'd said earlier. Her mark had changed her. It'd awoken the strength inside her passed down from her wolf ancestor and she'd never felt braver. And even though the thought of falling under the spell of Lucas's compulsion again threatened to smother her newfound bravery, Eden knew she had little to worry about with Rain by her side.

Eden lifted a pot from the cupboard and studied her mate as he spoke with his Alpha. Rain's body buzzed, his biceps bulging with fierce determination as he crossed his arms over his black-clad chest and conversed softly. The elevator pinged, and the scouts strode out, their backs straight and jaws hard, all playfulness having disappeared from their eyes as they prepared to fight.

For her.

Eden gulped and set the pot beneath the faucet.

"You okay?" Ava whispered as she poured tin tomatoes into a pot for the pasta sauce.

"I will be once this is over."

Ava squeezed her hand. "Just stay strong, Eden. You're braver than you think you are."

"I know ..." Eden resisted a smile as she set the water to boil, then turned to her friend. "I went skydiving today."

"You didn't!" Ava's eyes almost popped out of her head, and Eden's grin widened. "Oh my God, tell me everything!"

Eden described the experience as they prepared dinner, enjoying the carefree moment, until the wolves gathered around the island bench and Rain placed his hand on her back, reminding her of the danger that shrouded this evening.

Not that she'd forgotten that Lucas hunted her. Craved her. And that the man she loved would risk his life to fight for hers.

"I vote we start the hunt around Hawkings Point," Rain said. "Lucas lurked in the shadows around here last time, so I doubt he's gone far."

Finn nodded. "He's going to come for her swiftly and use his army to distract us. He'll be pissed and won't hesitate to force the change himself. Or kill her."

Eden shuddered, and Rain's hand hardened on her spine. "Don't worry, baby. Whatever happens tonight, I won't let that bastard touch you."

"He'll have to get through us first," Kai said, biceps bulging as they crossed over his taut pecs. "So, what's the plan?"

"We'll take the track up to Hawkings Point. Might even go as men," Finn said, glancing at Rain. "Better to protect the ladies while the scouts prowl the bush."

Eden had known she'd be going on this hunt, too. She was the "bait", after all. But her belly still clenched at the thought.

"When Lucas appears," Finn told the scouts. "One of you will get the bite on him. Then Rain can make the final kill."

Rain's chest swelled against Eden's shoulder. "It'll be my fucking pleasure."

She stirred the napolitana sauce, then turned the pot down to simmer.

"I don't know. It all sounds too easy," Chad said, scratching his head. "It won't be a leisurely stroll to the look-out. He brought an army. He'll fight us."

Rain cocked his eyebrows. "Is it too much to ask five wolves to take down a bunch of vampires?"

"Not too much at all, Commander," Kai said. "They'll be in vamp form to fight, and once we bite them, they're pretty much fucked."

"They scream like fucking banshees." Nate chuckled, shifting from foot to foot as he peeked into the oven. "Won't be too hard to get some fatal bites. Now, do you think that garlic bread is ready? If I'm going to be killing some bats, I need to carb load."

"Yeah, we don't want to go in hungry." Rain dropped his

hand from Eden's back as she picked up the oven mitts and slid the tray from the oven. Ava drained pasta while Rain grabbed the bowls, and Eden had barely transferred the aromatic bread to a plate before the scouts were stuffing it into their mouths.

They sat around the table and ate in relative silence, but as Eden twirled pasta around her fork, she couldn't shake the tension niggling in her spine. Lucas couldn't *possibly* think he'd just swoop down and grab her. He might be deranged in his obsession and hunger, but he wasn't stupid. He'd brought an army and clearly intended to harm her wolves. The pack might have been able to take on one or two vampires, but they were clearly outnumbered. And no power inside her or mating bond would stop her from falling under Lucas's spell the moment his eyes connected with hers. She'd never been worried about Rain possibly controlling her, and finding herself unable to peel her hands from the lounge after his order earlier had been hot as fuck. But the thought of falling victim to Lucas's compulsion again shot terror through her that no wolf bite could subdue.

Unless … could that bite have—

She gasped as the thought formed. It made perfect sense! But before she could put her question to the pack, her phone rang, and Eden turned towards the island bench. Seeing Caleb's name on the screen, she stood and left the table to answer.

"Hey, what's—"

"Doctor Eden, come quick! The hospital's on fire!"

"What?" Eden cried, whirling around. Rain's chair scraped along the floorboards as he shot to his feet.

"It's on fire!" Caleb cried. "I don't know what happened! I was cutting trees and smelled smoke. I haven't seen any flames, but I called the firemen. I don't know how long they'll be."

"We need to save the koalas." The island's fire service was

on call at night, so it'd take some time for them to arrive at the station for the truck, let alone reach the hospital.

"I can go in—"

"No! Don't risk your life, Caleb. I'm on my way." Eden hung up on the young man, tears in her eyes as she looked at Rain. "The hospital's on fire."

Everyone moved, chairs tumbling as expletives were shouted, and Nate scrambled to gather the last slices of garlic bread. But it was all white noise to Eden as she struggled to draw breath. This wasn't happening. It couldn't be. Not her hospital. All her hard work. The koalas ...

Rain cupped her elbow and Eden jolted as he moved her towards the elevator. He pressed the button, and the doors slid open.

"What happened?" Nate asked around a mouthful of bread as they squeezed into the small space.

"I don't know. But the koalas—"

"We'll save them." Rain stabbed the button to close the doors. "Don't worry, baby."

"Chad, go with Rain and Eden," Finn ordered. "Nate, Kai, come with me. Everyone, keep an eye out for the bats."

Eden gasped. "Do you think Lucas did this?"

"Probably," Rain spat, his voice grating with murder. "It's the perfect way to lure us out."

"Bastard," Finn growled. "He knew we'd hunt him. Why hurt innocent animals?"

Grief speared through Eden's chest as the doors slid open and she ran on jelly legs to Rain's Jeep. She climbed into the passenger seat and had barely gotten her seatbelt fastened before Rain reversed out of the garage and shot off down the drive after Finn. Eden grabbed the dashboard and held on tight, not that she objected to the speed when her hospital, her happy place, was going up in flames. All her dreams and everything she'd worked for. The history and the memories she'd had since childhood.

Lucas had destroyed it all.

Eden pressed her fist to her mouth and choked back a sob.

"None of that, baby." Rain squeezed her knee. "Everything will be fine."

"No, it won't! The koalas can't escape the fire on their own—"

"We'll get them." Rain gunned the Jeep past the golf course.

"We don't burn," Chad said. "Much."

"But they do!" Eden focused on Finn's taillights as images of singed ears and burned claws of the Australian bushfire survivors flashed through her mind. "Shit, I'll have to take them to Townsville. They'll need oxygen and surgery and burn treatment ..."

"Don't panic, Eden. Let's just get there and see."

But they were fifteen minutes away unless Rain broke every road rule, and they still might not make it in time.

Tears blurred Finn's taillights, but Eden had no time to cry as a screech sounded over the rev of their engines. Wings stretched over the windshield, and Eden gasped as a bat swooped her, flashing his fangs. Screaming, Eden ducked and covered her head, Rain's hand forcing her down as more bats joined the attack.

"Fuck!" Rain gunned the engine past Luna Views.

"Fucking leeches." Chad slammed his hand over the rollbar.

Eden stayed down at Rain's insistence, hunching in her seat but keeping an eye out as they sped into Nelly Bay, whipped around cars, and cut off a station wagon on the roundabout, earning a much-deserved horn blast as they flew up the hill into Arcadia.

"Fuck man," Chad breathed. "There are bats everywhere."

Rain snarled. "I know."

They raced along the narrow road. It seemed like every man and his dog were taking an evening drive while people stood on the beach and gawked at the bats flying overhead, but Rain and Finn didn't slow down. Nor did Eden want them to as the koalas would be terrified. They had nowhere to go, nothing to climb, and no way to escape the fire. Xena, Cookie, and Marco were almost ready for release. All Scratches needed was antibiotic cream, and Archie had been fighting so hard to regain his energy. But now, they were going to die in a stupid fire because of a sadistic, vengeful vampire.

Eden glanced at Rain. "You better kill Lucas and kill him good."

His jaw hardened as he twisted and turned the Jeep through the hills towards the Forts. "I fucking will."

She squeezed her eyes closed as they overtook the bus on a blind corner and received another horn blast. Inhaling, she tried to find that fearless woman from earlier. Her determination. Her inner wolf.

But she couldn't stop shaking.

Then smoke filled her nostrils, and Eden's eyes flew open. Craning her neck in the direction of the hospital, a wail ripped from her throat at the sight of flames dancing through the trees.

"Fuck!" Rain spun the Jeep into the street, gravel flying when he pulled up behind Finn. The pack leapt out over the doors while Eden fumbled with her handle, shocked at the inferno raging before her. Flames licked the left side of the building, glass shattered, and the scouts shouted, but Eden heard nothing over the terrified bellows of the precious lives trapped inside.

Would the horror ever end?

She screamed and ran forward, but didn't get far before Rain snatched her around her waist.

"Don't even think about it. Finn!"

"I'll grab Xena and Cookie! Nate and Kai, go to the kindergarten. How many koalas are we looking for, Eden?"

She blinked, gasping for breath as Rain moved her towards Ava. Eden reached for her friend, and they clutched each other, crying.

"I ... I don't ..."

Smoke escaped reception as Finn pulled open the door. "Eden!"

Shaking her head, she snapped out of her shock. *Think!* "Three in the kindergarten! Four in the trees. Don't forget Archie in the ICU."

"Got it!"

The wolves ran into the burning building, leaving Eden and Ava to stare in horror. She didn't fear for Rain as he could surely heal burns like he could a broken back. But her patients—

"Doctor Eden!" Caleb raced around from the back of the hospital and flung his arms around her. "I'm so sorry! I wanted to rescue the koalas, but—"

"It's okay. Rain's gone in—"

"Shit, really?" Caleb's eyebrows lifted in a mixture of horror and awe. "Fuck, that dude is badass."

If she wasn't so terrified, Eden would smile. Rain sure was one badass man.

"Yeah ..." Ava breathed, wiping her eyes. "Oh, this smoke is getting to me."

"Let's move across the road," Caleb said, starting in that direction. "Doctor Eden, how are we going to treat the koalas?"

"I don't know ..."

"Caleb, can you please wait across the road and keep everyone at bay?" Ava asked politely. "That'll be a great help."

"No worries." Caleb raced away, shouting at the crowd

who'd gathered. "Clear this road! We're waiting for the firemen!"

Eden turned back to the hospital. Where was Rain? And what *was* she going to do with the koalas?

"We need to get the crates from the shed."

"Good idea," Ava agreed, and Eden ran, skirting the flaming end of the hospital with Ava at her heels.

"Grab whatever you can carry." Coughing, Eden unlatched the gate and dashed across the yard. Entering the open shed, she tucked one crate under her arm, transferred another to that hand, then took the third. "Grab those two and let's get out of here."

"My pleasure," a dark voice replied.

The crates tumbled to the ground as Eden spun around with a gasp. Smoke filled her lungs, and she burst into a coughing fit, tears blurring her vision as she tried to catch her breath. But there was no mistaking the tall, lean, and disturbingly naked figure of Lucas Capello standing in the entrance of the shed, not a hair out of place while fire danced in his cold, dark eyes.

Eden scrambled backwards and stumbled over a crate. "Wha-what ... Where's Ava?"

His lips quirked. "Don't worry. I have no appetite for blondes."

"Did you hurt her?"

"Your concern for your friend is stupidly misguided, but she is safe. I asked her nicely to return to the car. And now—" He moved in a blur, then stood before her, his arm snaking around her waist as he stroked his icy finger down her cheek. "You are mine."

"No!" She shoved at his pasty shoulders, but Lucas was like a boulder. Breath rasped from her throat as she struggled to wriggle free of his hold, cringing as his dick brushed her thigh and he grabbed her ass. But it was no use. The vampire's lips curled as he flashed his elongated canines. Eden's knees buckled, but she didn't stop pounding her fists against his chest.

"The wolf might have saved you once, but he can't save you now." The sick bastard's smile broadened, his nostrils flaring as he dipped his head towards her right shoulder where her mark tingled. Burned. Lucas inhaled. "I will drink you dry."

"No!" She pummeled him harder, but Lucas had her in a vise. She drew in her breath and screamed. "Let me go! Help! Rain!"

"He's not coming."

Then his mouth widened as he bent her neck sideways. With a roar, he reared back—

Except the roar hadn't come from Lucas. A black blur leapt through the smoke, teeth bared and claws outstretched. Eden gasped, her eyes widening as the wolf's jaws lunged for the vampire—

Lucas vanished in a swirl of shadow, and a paw slammed into her shoulder. Eden fell backwards into the crates, crying out as she landed on her ass. The wolf—huge by any standard—rolled onto his feet and snarled as he leapt into the air after the flapping wings.

With a deafening screech, Lucas shot off into the smoke.

Eden scrambled onto her knees. "Rain!"

The wolf turned, breath heaving and nostrils flaring as drool dripped from his teeth. With his legs spread, puffed chest, and erect tail, he was almost feral with rage. Eden didn't blame him. But when his eyes latched onto hers, Eden sank back onto her haunches. This wasn't Rain. This was—

"Eden!"

Her mate skidded to a halt in the open doorway, his gaze shifting momentarily to the wolf before he ran forth and crushed Eden to his bare chest.

Chapter 39

Rain doubted he'd ever get the fifty years he'd had scared off his life back as he buried his face into Eden's hair. Fuck, that had been close. He'd sensed her in danger upon exiting the hospital, something dark and primal taking over him as he'd palmed Archie off to Ava. When he'd asked after Eden, she'd frowned, muttered something about crates and a man in the shadows before her eyes had widened in terror. But Rain had already realized she'd been compelled and had started running seconds before Eden's scream had pierced his heart. Shedding his shirt, he'd been about to shift when the animalistic growl had cut through the smoke. Yet Rain was still surprised to see his brother, mad as all hell, standing beside his terrified mate.

Finn and Nate ran into the shed as Rain pressed kisses to Eden's dark hair. "Fuck, baby, I'm sorry. You're okay. I'm sorry. I've got you. He's gone. I'm so fucking sorry."

The bastard had almost gotten her *again*, and he hadn't been there to stop him. *Again!* Sure, he'd expected her to stay where he'd fucking left her, but he couldn't blame Eden. He was the stronger one, and she was *his* to protect.

Once he could breathe again, Rain glanced at his brother. "Sly—"

"*You fucking idiot! What the fuck are you doing?*"

Rain's spine tensed. "What am I doing? What are you doing? Why are you—?"

"*I'm protecting your mate, which isn't my fucking job!*"

Snarling, Rain switched to telepathy. "*I was saving the koalas!*"

"*You and your fucking koalas. She was almost killed!*"

"*And I can't thank you enough for saving her.*"

Sly turned, grunting in disgust as he ran out of the shed, skidded to a halt in the dirt, and lifted his nose to the sky. "*Don't thank me. The slimy cunt got away.*"

"*Can you—*"

Eden broke into a coughing fit. "I can't ... I can't breathe."

A crack sounded through the air, reminding Rain of the inferno blazing behind him, destroying his beloved's dreams and filling her lungs with smoke. Rain cursed himself once again and scooped Eden into his arms. He fucking sucked at this protector shit.

"Grab the crates," he ordered Finn and Nate before racing out of the shed. "Sly, come!"

Rain used his body to shield Eden from the heat as he ran past the burning hospital. His brother continued to growl but stalked behind him into the parking lot. He placed Eden on the lowered tailgate of his Jeep, the smoke thinning thanks to the wind blowing in the opposite direction.

"Deep breaths now, Eden. That's it."

Gripping his shoulders, she breathed in and out. In and out. "I ... I feel better."

"You still need to be seen by a doctor. Fuck!" Rain shoved his hands through his hair. There was nothing he could do about it this time. He'd recovered from the minor effects of smoke inhalation, but Eden was human and it could have catastrophic effects on her body. She'd need a hospital for sure.

Or he could hire a doctor and set her up at home. Order in oxygen. Bring over the portable X-ray from Townsville. Money talked, and he'd pay generously for the inconvenience if it meant keeping her out of Tyrone's territory.

"I'm fine. Did you"—she broke into a series of coughs— "get the koalas?"

"Ava and Caleb have them," he said, glancing at the other Jeep to confirm. "I think they're okay, though Archie might need oxygen and Scratches' tree had started to burn, but his claws look okay."

"I'll have to check on—"

Rain placed his hand on her shoulder as she tried to stand. "You can check on them later. First, I need to make sure you're okay."

"*She'll be fucking fine!*" Sly shouted, pawing at the dirt. "*Stop dicking around and go after that bastard!*"

Rain had almost forgotten Sly was there, not to mention the fact that a massive wolf stood in the middle of the parking lot where most of the rubbernecks could see him.

"Oh, I'm going to. As soon as—"

"What's going on?" Finn asked softly, handing Rain his discarded T-shirt as he glanced at the wolf.

"*What do you think's going on? You're wasting time! You saw the army he brought—*"

"I did. And unless you pack bond, Finn can't hear you." Rain glared at his brother and slipped the shirt over his head as Kai, Chad, and Nate moved into the huddle.

"Lucas almost bit me," Eden said. "Sly arrived just in time, but Lucas shifted before he could bite him."

"*I almost fucking had him! So, get to it, brother. Lure him back out and fucking destroy the bastard.*"

"We better go," Finn said, eyeing the gathering crowd as

sirens wailed in the distance. "Before we're asked too many questions or they want to examine us."

Rain turned to Ava. "Are the koalas secure?"

"Yep."

"Good. Let's go."

"Oh, but—" Caleb started to protest over at the other Jeep, but Ava placed her hand on his shoulder.

"We've got it from here."

"Yes," Eden agreed as Rain helped her off the tailgate. "Thank you for calling me, but I need you to stay and talk to the firemen. I'll look after the koalas."

Caleb's shoulders sank, but he took to his task without question. Ava and Kai hurried to secure the crates as Rain helped Eden into the passenger seat.

Then he turned to his brother. "Are you taking off, or do you want to join us?"

Sly's lips peeled back. "*I better come with you else you might fuck it up again.*" He jumped into the back of the Jeep and sat.

Rain snarled. "*Don't test me, brother. All of this I've done for you. To kill Tyrone and to save you.*"

"*And who asked you to?*"

Rain slammed the tailgate closed. "*It's what family does.*"

Sly growled as Rain rounded the Jeep, slid behind the wheel, and tore out of the parking lot just as the firefighters and police arrived. Finn was right. They didn't need to stick around to deal with the enquiries. They had a vampire to kill. And as Rain glanced into the rear vision mirror, the knot around his heart loosened. Sly might still be a bloody wolf and an ungrateful sod, hanging his head outside the Jeep with his tongue out like a fucking dog. But he'd come to Rain's aid, to Eden's aid, and was once again fighting beside them even though he was no longer technically part of the pack.

"Do you sense him?" Rain called, slowing the Jeep as they approached the intersection.

"He's heading for the bats at Hawkings Point. They've surrounded the packhouse and are ready to attack."

Rain growled, his hands tightening around the wheel.

"What's he saying?" Chad asked.

"Lucas has the packhouse surrounded."

"He wants to drink me dry," Eden said, her eyes wide as she gripped the dash for dear life. "I'm not sure if he means to kill me or turn me—"

"He'll do neither," Rain snapped, his lips twisting as he navigated the Jeep over the mountain. He shot his gaze into the rear vision mirror. "Bro, how many bats are there?"

"At least one hundred. Maybe more."

Rain swore again and swung the Jeep right.

"What did he say?" Eden asked.

"Lucas has over one hundred bats."

"Fuck!" Chad cried. "We need to take down a hundred bats?"

"Piss easy," Sly snorted, but Rain wished he had half his brother's confidence as he gunned the engine.

"We'll manage. Chad, call Finn and relay the information."

RAIN TORE down the hill into Arcadia. It took all his strength not to drive like a madman and draw attention to himself or the massive wolf in his back seat as they returned to the packhouse in silence. He could almost hear Eden's mind ticking over, her anxiety palpable, but Rain didn't dare ask for her thoughts as he zoomed up the driveway and into the opening garage. Finn pulled up in a screech of brakes beside him. But before Rain could cut his engine, Sly leapt out of the Jeep, scurried beneath the descending garage doors, and disappeared.

"Sly! Get your ass back here!" Rain shouted, but his brother was gone. "Fuck!"

"Why can't he stay and work with us?" Kai asked sadly as the garage doors closed with a thump.

But Rain wasn't surprised. Sly was being Sly, leaping ahead and taking charge like any Alpha did.

Except Sly was Alpha only to his lone self.

"He knows he can join us when he's ready," Finn said. "But let's stick to our plan. Lucas just tried to separate us from Eden, and we can't let that happen again. We'll take Eden outside and shift—"

"Fuck, I hate this." Rain's gut twisted with the memory of her screams, but he couldn't insist they leave her at the pack-house no matter how much he wanted to.

"It's the only way," Eden said, placing her hand on his corded forearm. "He won't come when I'm surrounded by wolves. In fact—"

"He will when we're distracted fighting the other vampires. It's a standard battle strategy, and one we've all trained for."

"Just like when Blair came for me," Ava said.

Rain sighed. Yes, it had worked when they'd saved Ava from the rogues, and he knew it would work this time, too. But he couldn't bear to lose Eden. *He wouldn't!*

"I know," Eden said. "But—"

"I'll be right beside you, Eden." Rain squeezed her hand. Hard. To reassure himself or her, he didn't know, but they were in this together. "There will be bats shifting in and out everywhere, but Lucas wants your blood and will only come to you as a vampire. And the moment he does, I'll bite him. And kill him."

She was his mate, and he wouldn't fail her again. He wouldn't stop hunting until he'd tasted Lucas's blood, spat his dust into the dirt, and pissed on his ashes.

He would destroy Lucas. Save Eden.

Then save his stupid brother.

Resolve hardened his spine as he studied the men who had his back. The young men he'd trained and the man who'd saved the pack from ruin. They were fighting for him and his mate just as he would fight for them and theirs because they were a pack. Together, they could do this.

"Oi, bro!"

Rain hissed between his teeth. "What, Sly?"

"Whenever you're done yacking, get your mate up to the fucking lookout."

"Why?"

"To stargaze, what the fuck do you think? Lucas is swinging from a tree, hungry and salivating as all shit, and he's not moving. So, get your hairy ass up here before I lose my patience and kill the bastard myself!"

Rain rolled his eyes. Patience wasn't Sly's virtue, but Lucas was his and his alone to kill. "We're on our way."

"Make it quick."

Sly cut the connection and Rain glanced at Finn. "We're taking Eden to the lookout." He shouldered through the pack and led the way out of the garage. "Lucas is waiting. We're going to have to fight our way through the vampires to get to him, but I'm done playing his games."

Nate cracked his knuckles. "An army of bats doesn't scare me."

"Bring it on," Kai agreed, a voracious grin spreading across his face. "We've had plenty of practice."

"Yes, but don't underestimate this battle, gentlemen. You've trained hard and we've killed four bats between us. But tonight, there's over a hundred in those trees and they'll come from every direction. This won't be like fighting the rogues, so I need you all to keep a sharp eye."

Finn nodded in agreement. "This won't be easy. I'll lead

Rain and Eden up to the lookout, and you three can cover us in the trees."

"When we reach the lookout and Lucas shifts, whoever is closest, go for the bite."

It was going to be dark, fast, and out of control, but it was the best plan he had. He'd get Eden to the lookout unscathed and kill the bastard.

Then Eden said, "I have a better idea. I should go alone, and let Lucas bite me."

Rain spun to face her. "Are you out of your bloody mind?"

"No. But listen—"

"Edes." Rain dropped his hands to her shoulders, his heart in his throat as he barely resisted the urge to shake some sense into her. "I love your newfound bravery. I really do. But I am *not* going to let Lucas bite you!"

"But—"

"No!" He dug his fingers into her shoulders. "He's a monster, Eden! Obsessed with you! Giving into him is out of the fucking question!"

He wouldn't hear another word on the subject.

"Rain's right, Eden," Finn said, and Rain's spine relaxed a fraction as his Alpha backed him up. "We need your help to lure him out, but we won't let you sacrifice yourself."

Chapter 40

"But I won't be!" Eden knew how insane she sounded. Last time Lucas had bitten her had hurt like fucking hell. When he'd had her in his clutches earlier, she'd screamed, terrified he'd kill her. Except ... "Hear me out—"

"Don't waste your breath trying to convince me." Rain's lips twisted with a growl. "I won't—"

"Rain, he couldn't compel me!" she cried, grabbing his forearms. "Before. He stared me dead in the eyes and I was in control the whole time."

The fury faded from Rain's eyes as his brow furrowed. "What?"

Eden sighed, her heart thumping. "Look, you say I can't turn into a wolf, but you bit me."

"I don't need reminding."

"And you unleashed something inside me."

"Insanity, it seems, as you let me throw you out of a fucking plane and now you want to offer yourself up as a vampire's dinner!"

"Exactly! You infected me with *your* insanity. You killed the vampire inside me. Provided me with the antidote. The bite of a wolf." He'd told her not to explain the paranormal with science, but science hadn't let her down before and Eden had never been surer of anything. "He can't compel me like he can't compel a wolf, so what if the *power* of the bite is inside me? In my blood?" She grabbed his hand, desperate for him to understand. "What if Lucas drinks from me and—"

"You infect him," Finn said.

"Yes!" Eden spun towards the Alpha. "It makes sense, right?"

He frowned. "Maybe ..."

"You can't be serious!" Rain cried. "It doesn't work like that!"

"Doesn't it?" Finn lifted his eyebrows. "We don't know *how* the bite works, Rain. Especially between bonded mates. You two are special and unlike any other Fated couple we know. Your bite *did* save her, kill the vampire, and certainly changed something inside her if she let you take her *skydiving!*"

"She went skydiving because she had a near death experience! I take that clientele up all the time."

"But think about it. You're Fated, mated, and marked. You've mixed the good with the bad. The light with the dark. You committed a crime against the Goddess, but she hasn't condemned you. And if Lucas couldn't compel Eden as I'm sure he intended to, then that makes me think she might be right."

Eden smiled while Rain ran his hands down his face with a groan.

"But what if she's wrong?" Rain turned to face her. "I can't offer you up to him like that, baby. I *won't.*"

Eden curled her hand around the back of his neck and tried to radiate calm through their bond. "I don't believe I'm wrong, Rain. But if I am, he'll have me only for a second before you get the bite on him anyway. You'll be by my side."

He growled and dropped his forehead to hers. "Damn fucking straight."

"I know you don't like it—"

"I don't. It goes against everything I believe in."

"Just like you biting me did. But you did that because you knew it was the right thing to do."

Exhaling, he drew her close. "I was supposed to protect you."

"And you did. Just like you will tonight because you know that sometimes the right choice isn't the easy one."

"Letting him bite you isn't right," he growled.

"No, but ending this is." She tilted her head and curled her fingers around his biceps as she met his pained, hollow gaze.

"But what if I don't get to you in time?"

"You will. Because even though *you* think you're too late, you always save me, Rain. This time will be no different. You'll protect me because that's what you were born to do. Like Finn said, our bond—this mark—makes us special. We can do this. Together. You threw me out of a plane, so let me face this vampire. Let me help you kill him."

Eden locked her gaze to his, her heart pounding as fear warred with hope in Rain's eyes. She knew she was right. She had to be. Because even though he'd made steps towards forgiving himself for marking her, he still hadn't freed himself of his guilt, and she had a feeling her being immune to vampires might help push him into acceptance.

"Okay." Exhaling, Rain placed a kiss on her forehead. "Let's do this before I change my mind."

Kai whooped, jolting Eden as she'd almost forgotten anyone else was there. "All right!"

"Let's kill some vamps!" Nate tore off his shirt.

Finn drew Ava to his side. "Stay inside, honey, and keep all the windows and doors locked. Invite no one in. Look after the koalas."

"Can you check them over?" Eden asked Ava. "I shouldn't be long, but—"

"I'll take care of them." Ava threw her arms around Eden and held her tight. "You're my best friend and I love you. Stay safe."

Eden smiled. "Don't worry about me. I'll be fine."

"I know," Ava said, drawing away. "These wolves ... they're fiercely protective. Rain will look after you."

"Too right, I will."

But Eden didn't doubt that for a second as they left Ava and rode the elevator to the second floor.

"We need to get to the lookout as quickly as we can," Rain said as they strode to the back door. "But it won't be easy. The bats will try to slow us down."

"That's what the scouts are for," Finn said. "I'll lead. You stay by Eden, and we'll get her there."

Rain grabbed a torch from the cupboard, flashing the light on and off before handing it to Eden and swooping down for a kiss. "I fucking love you, baby. But I need you to promise to do exactly what I say while we're out there."

Her lips quirked. "I thought you could control me."

"Don't make me."

"I won't. I promise, Rain."

He kissed her again, then straightened, protectiveness darkening his eyes. "Let's go."

Eden gripped her torch tight as Rain opened the back door, and they walked into a scene from a horror show. Bats swooped around Rain's yard, screeching and rearing for a fight. Eden swallowed as she flashed back to the night Lucas had attacked her. The scratches, the terror, the teeth.

But that was before she'd known about the paranormal world, before she'd learned about the vampires and the strong wolves who stood before her now. They'd all shifted, Kai and Nate pawing at the ground while Chad bared his teeth at the bats, their coats resembling their natural hair color with golden stripes that matched their Alpha. Finn stood tall at the head of the pack, his hackles raised, and feet spread as he readied for the fight.

But no one bristled more than her mate as he tore off his shirt and stepped onto the grass. Eden's pulsed leapt as she watched him unclasp his shorts, slide them down his legs, and kick them free. His back straightened, then his muscles shivered. Eden pressed her hand to her chest as her sexy man's legs morphed in a twist of matter, dark hair sprouting over his skin as his spine bent and he shifted into a massive black wolf.

Her breath caught. Goodness, he was beautiful, large and proud, with his midnight-black fur blowing in the breeze. He looked just like his brother, though less wild and with golden stripes glimmering along his spine.

Rain stalked forward to stand beside his Alpha and together, they lifted their snouts and released what Eden could only describe as a battle cry. The bats screeched louder, leaves rustling as some took flight.

"Eden."

She squeaked, her hand flying to her mouth as Rain's voice echoed inside her head. "Rain?"

His shoulders sank as he breathed what sounded like a sigh of relief. *"You can hear me."*

"You're in my head!" she cried, and the scouts glanced at her. Nate wagged his sandy tail while Kai's mouth fell open in what she'd ordinarily call a "happy face." "How is that possible?"

"Because we're mated, and thank the Moon, we've kept our Fated blessings." He looked over his shoulder, a flash of joy passing through his battle-ready eyes. *"But now, I need you beside me."*

Shaking off her shock, Eden ran to her mate's side. It took

all her control to rein in her natural urge to rub him between the ears. He was so beautiful.

"*And so are you*," he said, startling her once again. "*Don't shout your thoughts, Eden. You can pet me later. Are you ready?*"

Remembering what was at stake, Eden stared into the dark bush and the deafening screech of bats. Damn, that was a lot of vampires. She shuddered once, then steeled her spine. "I'm ready."

With a low growl, Finn ran up the track. Kai, Chad, and Nate leapt in various directions after him, making their own way through the bush. Eden clutched her torch tighter.

"*Good. Then go.*"

Eden ran.

Chapter 41

Rain didn't dare take his eyes off Eden as they scrambled along his private pathway to meet the Hawkings Point trail. The beam of her torch guided her as she raced up the uneven, rocky steps. Gravel and leaf litter rustled beneath her feet and his heart lurched at every slip and slide of her sneakers.

He hated this plan. No matter how confident she was, he doubted he could stand back and watch her offer herself to Lucas. He was supposed to protect her, not risk her life. How Finn had done it with Ava only mere weeks ago, he didn't know. Their mates weren't built to face their enemies, and as a pack, they'd had such little time to prepare to fight vampires at this magnitude. They were cunning, stealthy, and far more difficult to destroy than the rogue wolves.

But Rain had to admit, if Lucas couldn't compel Eden, then maybe there was more to the bite than they knew.

A bat swooped, clipping its wing past Eden's head. She ducked and screamed, stumbling to grasp a boulder. Rain snarled and leapt up beside her, ready for the bastard to shift, but the bat disappeared.

"Little fucker. It's okay, Eden. Keep going."

His mate did, brave and determined with Rain at her heels.

If it was just them wolves, they'd reach the lookout in minutes as they could all vastly outrun a human. But it'd take Eden a good fifteen, which allowed Rain to survey his surroundings, glaring at the bats above them. They screeched, swooped between trees, and scurried along branches on their tiny claws.

"Fucking hell, there are bats everywhere!" Nate cried, dashing through the scrub somewhere to Rain's right.

"And they're fucking playing with us," Kai seethed. *"They're not shifting—"*

"Got one!" Branches cracked as Chad growled and went in for a bite. Rain glanced into the darkness, his ears tilting as a scream tore through the trees. Eden froze and clutched the torch to her chest.

Rain nudged her hip with his snout. *"It's okay. The scouts have him."*

The screams died, along with the vampire.

"Fuck, they don't get any tastier," Kai spat.

"Is it dead?" Eden asked, stepping over rocks and up the steps.

"Yep."

"That's one for me!" Kai cried.

"Hey! That was my vamp!" Chad said.

"Gentlemen, concentrate," Finn growled. *"This isn't a competition."*

Kai chuckled, but Finn let it go as they approached the rockfall. Finn leapt up the steps, then drew to a halt, gravel skidding beneath his paws.

"Fuck."

"What?" Though Rain could already smell the dead flesh as he stepped up beside Eden. The glorious, ten-meter-tall granite boulder known as the rockfall stood on his left while

dense vegetation tumbled down the hill on his right. And on the narrow path between the two stood at least a dozen pasty, hungry vampires.

Eden squeaked and pressed her hands to her mouth. "Rain? What are we—?"

"*Get against the wall, Eden,*" he ordered, nodding towards the boulder. She eased back, and he stepped up beside his Alpha. "*What are you thinking?*"

"*Should have known as it's the perfect place for an ambush.*" Finn's shoulders lowered. "*Kai, Chad, Nate! We have a dozen vampires blocking us at the rockfall!*"

"*Fuck me,*" Chad breathed as another scream echoed through the trees, then ceased.

"*Make that two!*" Kai cheered.

"*Kai! Get your hairy ass to the rockfall!*" Finn shouted.

"*Coming, boss!*"

Rain narrowed his eyes and studied the vampires. Their pale, naked bodies almost glowed in the darkness, their fangs flashing as they hissed, bent their knees, and raised their arms for the fight while more bats screeched from above.

"*Get as many bites as we can,*" Finn said. "*Then go for the kill. The moment we clear the path, get Eden through.*"

"*Okay.*" Rain glanced up at his mate, who stared at the vampires in horror. "*Eden—*"

"Why do they have to be naked?"

"*Don't look, baby. Stay against the wall.*"

She tore her gaze from the vampires and rested her head against the granite, her chest heaving as she clutched the torch to her belly. "Rain—"

"*Don't panic. Stay there and when I say so, run as fast as you can past the wall and to the other side. Got it?*"

She nodded mutely. Then even though it ripped his soul in two, Rain turned his back on his mate and leapt down the rocky steps after his Alpha and into battle.

Finn slashed his claws at the first vampire, but the undead moved quickly. The vampire grabbed Finn's back leg and flung him into the rockfall with a sickening crack.

Finn yowled, crumbled to the ground, and Rain saw red. He launched at the vampire and sank his teeth into dead flesh. The vampire yelled, falling to its knees just as an auburn flash darted out of the trees and knocked the vampire onto its back.

Kai came away with the bastard's throat, and the vampire crumbled to dust. "*Three!*"

"*You get them all just because you make the second bite!*" Nate yelled as another scream ripped through the trees.

"*Hey, that one was a double whammy!*"

Rain's spine jolted as cold hands yanked his tail. Baring his teeth, he turned and spun a few circles before biting the bastard on its pale ass.

"*That's my fucking tail!*" he yelled as Kai went in for the kill.

"*Four!*"

"*Stop fucking counting!*" Finn roared, pushing to his feet. Nate ripped at a vampire's arm and the Alpha went for the bastard's throat. Another spray of dust crumbled at the base of the rockfall. "*There. One for me.*"

"*That's the spirit, boss!*" Kai yelled just as a bat darted down, shadow twisted, and brawny white arms wrapped around his neck. The vampire roared as it lifted Kai onto his hind legs, twisted his arms—

"*Let him go!*" Chad went in for the tackle, snatching the vampire by the leg and knocking it off its feet. An almighty scream echoed off the wall as Kai slipped from the vampire's clutches. Rain leapt at it and made the kill.

More dust.

Kai pushed to his feet in the scrub and jumped back onto the path. Rain turned, his chest heaving as a vampire shifted and shot up through the trees. But while it made a cowardly escape, two more descended to join the fight. Rain snapped his jaw around a white arm and flung the vampire into the rockfall. He was about to go for the kill when Finn shouted, *"Rain! Take Eden and go!"*

Dust and gravel slid beneath his paws as Rain spun around. *"Eden! Run!"*

She didn't hesitate. Clutching the torch, his fierce mate pushed off the rockfall and dashed down the steps, determination hardening her dark eyes as she ran. A vampire shifted ahead of her, and she stumbled, knocking her shoulder into the rock. But Rain grabbed it and yanked the scum out of the way, leaving it for the pack to kill as she shot past him and scrambled up the steps on the other side.

Rain ran after her just as arms wrapped around his neck. His front legs lifted off the ground and he choked, clawing at the pasty skin.

Eden spun around and gasped. "Rain!"

"Run!" But he lost eye contact with her as the vampire flung him into the granite. Eden screamed, and Rain crumbled to the ground, pain shooting up his spine. *"Go! Be right behind you."*

The vampire lunged at supernatural speed, straddling Rain before he could scramble to his feet. Cold hands wrapped around his throat and squeezed, but the ache around his heart eased as he heard Eden's footsteps fade. Rain bucked as he tried to kick himself free, digging his claws into the vampire's side and tearing away flesh. It screamed, loosening its hold, just as Finn jumped at him and sank his teeth into the vampire's shoulder.

"Thanks, man," he said, pushing to his feet. And Rain didn't look back as he bolted up the stairs after Eden.

He caught her on the second flight, her legs pumping and breath panting as she navigated her way through the darkness. They reached a flat path and Rain inched up beside her.

"Are you okay?" she asked, her hand brushing over his head. "Did the vampire hurt you?"

"I'm fine. Finn killed him."

"Good, because I can't take much more of this. I thought Finn was dead when he hit that wall."

"It'll take more than a knock into granite to kill Finn," Rain said, falling behind her as they ascended more stairs.

"Clearly. But damn, you all can fight."

Rain's chest puffed with pride. *"It's what we do, Eden. We'd rather be skydiving, jet skiing, or what not, but we were born to fight. To protect our territory and those we love, and the bats aren't welcome to either Magnetic Island or you."*

"No." Sly's voice rumbled through Rain's head as they reached the turnoff to the lookout over Rocky Bay. *"The sooner we exterminate these pests, the better. So, where the fuck are you?"*

"Coming," Rain growled, following Eden up more stairs as the path flattened and narrowed between the trees, and they gained further ground. *"Be patient, brother. We were ambushed at the rockfall."*

"I heard."

"Are you talking to Sly?" Eden asked. "Where is he?"

Good question. *"Are you still at the lookout?"*

"Eyes are on Lucas. The slimy cunt's still swinging from his tree. I can practically hear him cackling."

Rain's lips twisted. Stupid fucker. But a few more minutes, and he'd kill that cunt of a bat. Even if Eden didn't carry the power of a wolf's bite in her blood, he'd use the distraction to sink his teeth into him before spitting his carotid over the edge of his favorite lookout.

"Sly's still up at the lookout. Lucas is there. Waiting."

She shivered. "We're almost there, aren't we?"

"We have a little way to go." They took a turn in the path near the viewpoint where he and Sly used to watch the full

moon rise back when they'd just moved to the island and his brother had been a soppy sack of shit trying to woo Shelby.

Rain's heart ached. Oh, how he wished some semblance of those days would return.

THE PATH FLATTENED and Eden ran through the scrub. Bats continued to dart around them, swooping through the trees, but none of them shifted. Her toe hit a rock, and she stumbled, but she kept going, her heart pounding as she carefully navigated over the tree roots and dashed along the path.

Movement flashed across her torchlight, and she froze. Rain skidded to a halt beside her, his furry leg brushing hers.

"What is it?"

She gulped. "Cane toad!"

A fat brown toad stood in the center of the pathway. A foul, disgusting creature. Just the thought of it jumping on her—

Rain stomped his paw, growled, and the toad leapt off the path and into the scrub.

Eden's shoulders slumped as she blew out a breath. "Thank you. I can't stand toads."

Which was ridiculous considering her current predicament. She continued to run as more vampire screams cut through the air in harmony with the growl of wolves as the scouts fought. The path narrowed and Eden grabbed onto the boulders for balance, but she didn't slow, pumping her legs up and down little flights of stairs.

Then as they rounded to a descending part of the path, shadow swirled, and a great hulking vampire rose before her. Eden skidded to a halt at the top of the stairs and screamed.

The vampire moved like lightning as its cold, dead hand grabbed her forearm and yanked her forward. Eden lost her footing, and she found herself momentarily airborne before her palms collided with the gravel path at the base of the stairs. She cried out as pain shot through her hand into her shoulder, and her hip collided with the ground, dirt scraping her knees. Then a roar sounded behind her, followed by the thump of a body and snapping of bone.

Eden gasped as she looked behind her. The vampire loomed over Rain as her mate struggled to regain his feet. Then in another flash of inhuman speed, the white body swiveled behind Rain and wrapped its brawny arm around his furry black neck.

"No!" she screamed, scraping to her feet. "Rain!"

He bucked, trying to heave his back legs over his head to kick the vampire, but the monster barely flinched. A strangled snarl escaped between his bared teeth, and Eden's heart leapt. She had to help him. Spotting a rock, she snatched it off the ground.

"Let him go!" She threw the rock at the vampire and released an anguished cry when she missed. Fuck. She was useless in this fight. "Finn! Help!"

But the menacing growl that replied wasn't Finn as a black flash launched off the boulder from above her head and snapped at the vampire. The bastard screamed but didn't let go of Rain quick enough as they tumbled down the stairs. Eden scurried backwards, gasping as Rain's shoulder collided with a rock. He rolled free to crumble at her feet, and she dropped to her knees, throwing her body over his. A growl cut through the vampire's screams, then ceased them.

Rain moved beneath her, his breath heaving before he shook himself like any other dog. He lifted his head, and Eden buried her face into his soft fur.

"I hate this. I thought he was going to break your neck."

"*I'm okay, baby,*" he whispered, rubbing his snout against her shoulder.

Then he glanced up at Sly.

"*Hurry up,*" Sly snapped before Rain could even thank him. "*We're almost there.*"

More scampering sounded up the path as Finn and the scouts caught up. "*We must be close,*" Finn said, eyeing the lone wolf. "*Hey, Sly.*"

Sly bared his teeth. "*You lot sure took your time.*"

"*He can't hear you because you're not pack bonded!*" Rain yelled at his brother before glancing at Finn. "*But yes. Only a little further to go.*"

Around the boulder, up more steps, and they'd be approaching the lookout. And Lucas. Rain's heart pounded as he rubbed his snout over Eden's shoulder. "*Come on, baby. Let me up.*"

Her breath rippled through the fur at the back of his neck as she pulled away. Rain pushed to his feet, and she scrambled to hers.

"*I need you to be brave for me. Are you ready?*"

She nodded. "*Yep. I just want this to be over with before any of you get hurt. Those vampires are fucking strong.*"

"*Strong? Vampires?*" Kai sniggered. "*Rain, tell your mate to stop speaking nonsense. I've killed twenty of the fuckers.*"

"*Yeah, but I get the first bite!*" Nate cried.

"*Stop keeping score!*" Finn ordered. "*This isn't a competition. There are more bats out there and we still need to kill the one that fucking matters!*"

"*Yeah,*" Chad said, nudging Kai. "*I'd like to see you kill that one.*"

"*That will be my privilege,*" Rain said. "*Now, let's keep going.*"

"*Back in our previous formations!*" Finn ordered. "*Sly ... Rain, tell him—*"

But there was no telling Sly anything as he dashed into the scrub. Rain's shoulders sank as Finn huffed out his breath.

"*Never mind,*" the Alpha muttered. Then he scampered down the steps, past Rain, and took the lead.

"*Go, Eden.*" Rain nudged her and like the brave woman he'd always known her to be, she followed Finn's golden tail as they ran around boulders, then down more steps. Kai and Chad took off into the trees, flanking their right while Nate watched Rain's back. For the next minute or so, they didn't encounter a single bat.

"*We're almost there, baby.*" Rain could taste it, both fear and excitement coursing through him as they dashed up a narrow set of rocky stairs. "Just a little further."

But as Finn stepped out onto a large rock widening the path, bats descended from the trees in a black cloud, and Finn skidded to a halt. Rain froze beside Eden and before they knew it, the wolves were surrounded. Eden screamed, covering her head as the bats swooped and scratched her. Nate growled and leapt out from behind Rain.

Then the bats started shifting, and all hell broke loose. Kai and Chad came charging out of the scrub, snapping their jaws. But a vampire shifted behind Kai, lifted him off his feet, and threw him across the clearing. The young wolf yelped as his back hit a tree with a sickening crack, and he crumbled onto the boulders, unmoving.

Eden screamed.

"*Kai!*" Finn cried.

Nate ran down the sloping rock floor towards Kai, but another bat shifted into a hulking, blond vampire. Without hesitation, Nate ripped into the bastard's leg and Finn went in for the kill.

"*Kai!*" Finn shouted above the chaos as vampires continued to scream. "*Answer me!*"

But Kai remained silent, his head hanging off the rock at an odd angle, mouth open, and Rain's heart lurched in true fear. The bats kept coming, swarming, shifting, and attacking. Two vampires grabbed Finn, tearing him away from the auburn wolf and tossing him across the clearing.

Finn hit the granite with a thud. Nate cried out as a vampire latched onto him, but the young wolf managed to sink his teeth into its pasty arm.

Chad made the kill.

"Rain!"

He turned at Eden's shout. She'd backed down the steps, almost disappearing into the trees and though her torch beam pointed down, Rain's wolf's eyes didn't miss the fear that widened hers.

"Eden!" He pounced across the rock towards her, only for a vampire to block him. The bastard reached for his shoulders, but Rain was too quick as he ripped into the undead thigh. The vampire stumbled backwards, and Rain leapt up to make the kill himself. Dust crumbled at his feet, and Rain shot his gaze back to Eden.

She hadn't moved. Was unharmed. Of course she was, because the vampires paid her no attention. She was for their master. Their lord. The pack was the target so that Lucas could get a clean shot at Eden.

But over his dead body would he let that happen. They had less than a hundred meters to go. So, he ran, leapt over a struggling vampire as Nate tore his throat out, and—

A vise clamped around his hind leg and with a bone crunching snap, pain unlike any he'd ever felt ripped through his body. He crashed onto the rock, claws scratching the granite as the vampire dragged him down towards the scrub.

Chapter 42

Eden couldn't move, couldn't breathe, watching in horror as vampires shifted in and out of bats almost too quickly for the wolves to keep up. But Finn was taking no prisoners. He moved like a fierce predator, leaping, ripping, and clawing at the white, undead flesh. Nate and Chad had his back, coming in for the kill. But with every cloud of dust that blew off the granite, it seemed two more bats swooped down to attack the wolves while Kai lay motionless on the rocks.

Eden wanted to race to his side to check on him, but she remained rooted to the spot. The vampires didn't try to harm her, but they were fucking vile, crude creatures. One puckered his lips at her with sex in its eyes before shifting back into a bat. Another made a lewd gesture with its tiny white dick before Finn tore into its shoulder and knocked the scum off its feet. She ached to run, but the path remained blocked by the battle, and she couldn't go without Rain at her back ready to kill Lucas.

Then he called her name, and she locked eyes with her mate on the other side of the boulder. He bounded towards her, leaping over a vampire that Nate quickly turned to dust.

Just as two more shifted behind him and grabbed his back leg. A sickening rip tore through the air and Rain released a terrifying cry. His body hit the rock, and the vampires dragged him down the slope with his claws screeching over the granite.

Her torch clattered to the ground as Eden screamed and leapt up the step. Then she halted as another roar thundered and the raging, brawny black wolf returned to the battle. Sly sprang off the boulder above and launched at the vampire who'd grabbed his brother and ripped the blond's head clean off his shoulders.

Eden froze, startled as the vampire blew away in the wind.

Rain released a painful howl, and Eden dropped to her knees where her man, her wolf, tried scrambling to his feet, only to flop onto his belly when his back leg wouldn't cooperate. It hung loosely from his body, clearly broken, as though his femur had been ripped from its socket. Eden's heart pounded as Rain's breath heaved in and out, his eyes lifting to hers as he clawed desperately at the rock.

"What do I do?" she cried, blinking as tears blurred her vision. "Your hip—"

She screamed and ducked as another vampire shifted above them, but he didn't get a chance to touch Rain as Sly leapt over them with an animalistic growl.

Rain grunted and slapped his paw over Eden's knee. "*Go. You're almost there.*"

She shook her head. "I can't! Not without you!"

"*I'll be right behind you.*"

"But your leg! How can—"

His claw dug into her thigh, hard enough to hurt but not to break her skin. "*Eden, go!*"

Then a tug unlike any she'd ever felt ripped through her chest, dragging her back to her feet. Eden gasped, choking back sobs as darkness twisted through Rain's eyes.

"*I'm sorry, baby,*" he said, regret straining his voice as she stumbled backwards up the rock. Shadow continued to swish, but she didn't tear her eyes from Rain's. *"But I believe in you. The lookout is around the corner. Go!"*

And the last thing Eden saw was the utter trust in her mate's eyes before she turned and ran through the gap in the rocks.

Her breath escaped in sharp puffs as darkness swallowed her. She didn't know if the pain she felt was hers or Rain's, as her hip had taken a beating when that vampire had pushed her down the stairs. But the spike in her pulse was definitely hers as she stumbled up the rocks, hardly able to make out the pathway without her torch.

But as Rain's control slipped, her focus returned, and she powered up the rocky steps. She had no idea how much further she had to go, not that she could distinguish landmarks in the darkness, but she could do this. She believed in herself, and he trusted her. She'd use Lucas's trap to trap *him*, poison the bastard, and then Rain could make the kill.

He'd be following any minute because, despite all the heartbreak he'd caused her, he'd always been by her side.

"Good job, Eden. That's it."

She didn't know if she could reach through their bond telepathically, and didn't have the energy to try. Grabbing a tree, she veered right to avoid smacking her head against a protruding boulder and rounded another dark corner. Recognizing the narrow path leading between two curved boulders, her pulse spiked. She was almost there. Tiptoeing through the crevice, she leapt up the next few rocks, turned, and drew to a halt.

There it was. The fenced railings leading onto the boulderous headland that was Hawkings Point Lookout emerged in the darkness, trees blocking the view as she inched closer.

Had Rain healed? Was he coming? Would it be safe to step out onto the lookout?

She had no time to ponder that though as a bat dropped from the trees, spread his wings with a flash of his fangs, and flew towards the lookout. Then that smooth, Mediterranean voice beckoned.

"Come to me, *bella*. Your pack has fallen."

Rain growled inside her head. "*He's there.*"

"He's there," she whispered, unsure if Rain could hear her as she stepped forward.

"*Go, Eden. Go! I'm right behind you.*"

His voice grew stronger as Eden curled her hands over the railing. She would not run. She faced her fears now. So, steeling her spine, she stepped onto the rock, strode up the sloped pathway onto the lookout, and faced the monster who'd tried to take her life and destroy the man she loved.

The bastard who'd burned down her fucking hospital.

Lucas's eyes gleamed, his dark hair blowing in the breeze as he stood on the highest point of the lookout, his white skin almost glowing in the darkness as his lips quirked with malice.

"You came." Like lightning, he moved towards her, flashing his fangs in her face as he gripped her chin with his cold, dead fingers. Eden gasped as he breathed her in, but she was not afraid. She had this.

"You were running a fool's errand, my sweet," he whispered, brushing his nose over her temple. "An Alpha, a rebel, and a lone wolf can't defeat me. Your pack is broken, and the Alpha is hanging on by a thread if he hasn't shunned your mate for biting you. Marking your fair skin." His fingers brushed over her right shoulder where Rain's mark tingled. "But I can fix that. I can free you from his control."

Eden curled her fists as she longed to lash out, to tell him he was wrong. But she had to stick to the plan as he lifted her chin and forced her gaze to meet his, his irises darkening as he exercised his compulsion. "Tell me you want me."

Eden's breath caught. She'd only suspected on the drive

from the hospital, having been too terrified in the moment to have noticed his lack of power over her. But she'd been right. She felt nothing. No loss of control. No desire. No awe. Just pure hatred as she lifted her hands and curled her fingers around Lucas's forearms and played his game.

"I want you."

The desire in his eyes violated her skin. "We will feast together and fuck hard, my sweet. You will rule by my side. My bride. My queen."

Bile rose in her throat as she recalled that horrid dream. "Yes ..."

Then Lucas pressed his face into her neck where he'd already bitten her twice, and it took all of Eden's strength to resist cringing as she closed her eyes to the night sky and drew on her bond with Rain. She felt his heartbeat. Sensed his presence. Her hip no longer throbbed, though her pulse quickened. He was coming. There. His heartbeat grew closer and once Lucas bit her—

"I usually keep my favorite meals alive, but the Fated blood that runs through your veins will keep you tasty for years. So, I'll make this quick."

Lucas's fangs pierced her skin. Eden screamed, her fingers digging into his biceps and knees buckling as he sucked blood from her vein like a man starved. Like the monster he was. Like—

Like a vampire who'd been poisoned as he sputtered, screamed, and shoved her away. He stumbled backwards up the rock, blood dripping down his chin as he stared at her in shock. Disgust.

"What ... this is ... what is wrong with your blood?!"

Eden's mouth twisted as she rolled the pain from her shoulder and straightened, her heart racing with a pulse that was not her own as she said, "I've been bitten by a wolf."

And with a roar, Rain lunged past her and latched his

claws into Lucas's bloodstained chest. A sickening crack sounded through the air as his skull collided with the rock, and Lucas screamed, coughing and spluttering Eden's tainted blood.

But it was too late. The power Rain had unleashed within her had taken hold of the vampire, weakening him as he tried and failed to draw at the shadows and shift. Rain snarled and curled his claws into Lucas's flesh.

"You're not going anywhere."

Lucas, of course, didn't hear him as he continued to shriek. "This is impossible! Tyrone wanted you to mark her! But he never said—"

"Tyrone doesn't understand Fate," Eden said, straightening her shoulders as she stepped up beside Rain. "He doesn't understand the power of the Moon Goddess and those she's blessed."

"But he bit you! She should have shunned him! How are you still bonded?"

Eden knelt on the rock and brushed her fingers through Rain's furry shoulder as she glared death at Lucas. "Rain did not claim me. I *chose* to be with him."

Chapter 43

Rain's chest burst with pride at Eden's words, her strength and bravery reminding him exactly why he loved her as he plucked the vampire's ribs like guitar strings. The fucker wasn't going anywhere and though Rain longed to make that fatal bite, he also wanted to watch the vampire squirm as he extracted the answers he and his pack needed.

"Ask him if he lured Shelby off the island," he said, sensing Sly approach with Finn.

Eden asked, and the vampire fucking cackled. "The first Fated whore? She was so easily compelled. She'd have become my queen, except Tyrone wanted her more."

Sly's snarl ripped through the air as he lunged to Rain's side.

"You fucking cunt!" he yelled, scratching his claws down Lucas's screaming face before ripping his arm clean off.

Finn nudged Sly away, reminding him this was Rain's fight.

"Fine! But you have three seconds to kill the bastard before I do it for you!" Sly growled.

"*Patience, brother*," Rain snapped. "*Do you want to kill Tyrone or not?*"

"*I want to kill this fucker!*"

Lucas's scream turned into a snarl. "She sure tasted good, too, more to the pity. Tyrone slaughtered her, just like he'll slaughter you." He spat Eden's blood in her face, and Rain hoped his claw nipped the undead bastard's heart. "And your friend. Ava. You think you got a win over him because you killed his son? Well, his new right-hand man is crueler than that twisted pup ever was. He and Tyrone won't stop until you're all fucking dead. Especially you."

Lucas glared at Finn, who merely bared his teeth.

"*My sire couldn't kill me in the womb, he can't kill me now.*"

"Tyrone can try all he wants and recruit the meanest of wolves, but he won't kill us," Eden told Lucas. "The pack is not broken. You might have forced Rain's hand, but he did not rebel by biting me. He remains in the Goddess's grace, and we've been blessed with a bond more powerful because of it. A bond that is as dark as it is light, and that has given me strength I never knew I could possess. No one can break that. I am Fated, mated, and marked, and I have the bravery of a wolf."

She sure fucking did, which made Rain all the prouder as he peeled his lips back and unleashed a guttural growl before clamping his jaw around Lucas's neck. The vampire released one last high-pitched scream, then Rain tore the undead flesh from his body. Lucas's head rolled to the side, his mouth wide with terror, his eyes lifeless. Then he crumbled into dust and blew over the edge of Hawkings Point Lookout.

Sly stood and placed his paws on the railing as he threw his head back and released a pained howl to the waxing moon. Rain's heart broke for him as he shifted and drew Eden into his arms.

"I'm sorry, brother," he said, guilt churning in his gut as he ran his hand down Eden's soft ponytail.

Sly dropped to all fours and hung his head, but didn't reply. They might have killed two of the creatures who'd had a hand in murdering Shelby, but her killer himself remained at large among the twinkling lights of Townsville across the bay, and Sly's pain endured.

"That was intense," Eden whispered. "But he's gone."

"He is, baby." Rain lifted her chin and dropped a kiss on her lips. "We killed many vampires, and you're safe."

"And you're okay?" Her hand dropped to the thigh he'd almost lost before brushing over his hip and cupping his ass. "How's this hip?"

"All healed," he said, lowering his voice. "And I'll show you just how well when we get home."

She giggled, reaching up to kiss him again as paws thudded along the pathway.

"*You guys did it!*" Kai cried, leaping out onto the lookout. "*Fucking epic!*"

"Kai!" Eden cried, her eyes brightening with a grin that made Rain's wolf growl. "You're okay!"

"*Of course I'm okay!*" But since she couldn't hear him, he bounded across the lookout like a playful pup, his tongue lolling as he nudged her shoulder with his head. Rain growled, but Eden simply laughed as she rubbed Kai's ears with one hand, and nudged Rain in the chest.

"He's fine," Rain muttered, tightening his arms around her waist as he glared at the young wolf. "Though the bump to his head didn't seem to knock any more sense into him if he's still flirting with my mate."

"He's just happy that you won the battle," Eden said.

"*Too right, I am.*" Kai glanced around the pack. "*We fucking slaughtered those vamps. Tell me I won.*"

Rain rolled his eyes and didn't dignify that with a response.

"*You got yourself knocked out!*" Nate cried. "*How can you have won?*"

"*I killed twenty-seven of those fuckers. How many did you get?*"

"*Probably twenty-seven first bites!*"

"*Yeah, but only fifteen kills,*" Chad said.

Kai laughed. "*See? You should eat pineapple on your pizza!*"

Sly growled just as Finn stepped forward and cleared his throat.

"*Gentlemen, that's enough. You all fought bravely tonight, but this war is not over. You can celebrate your victory after we debrief. And Kai, congratulations on your twenty-seven. Solid effort. Talk to me when you kill forty-one.*"

Rain snorted as Kai's ears shot up. If he were human, his jaw would have hit the ground. "*Boss! You told us not to keep score!*"

"*You started it,*" Finn said, before turning to the pack. "*But while tonight might be a victory, we need to stay vigilant. Tyrone is not going to be happy we foiled another one of his plans. And if he discovers Rain hasn't rebelled—*"

"Which he will," Rain muttered. The rebel Alpha had spies everywhere and Rain wasn't naive enough to believe they'd killed *all* the bats.

"*He will retaliate. Hard. He didn't kill Ava, he didn't turn Eden, and he hasn't broken Rain or I.*"

"No," Rain agreed, his chest tightening as he glanced at his brother. "Sly—"

Sly's eyes flashed as he whipped towards him. "*I don't know what your Alpha's saying, but I'll tell you one thing. Tyrone is fucking angry. The rebels are stirring and Cape Pallarenda reeks of tension.*"

"Then we need your help. Come back to us and prepare to fight the bastard."

Sly snarled and turned his head away. "*When are you going to get it, Rain? I'm useless to you. That's why I gave you Finn.*"

"You didn't *give me* Finn! I called for him. To help *you!*"

"*For fuck's sake, it's like talking to a brick wall.*"

"Stop being so stubborn!" Rain shouted, unable to contain his desperation. "Please! No one wants to defeat Tyrone more than you do!"

Finn growled, but didn't disagree.

"*Maybe not,*" Sly said. "*And when the time comes, I'll help your Alpha rip his sire's throat out. But until then ...*"

Sly leapt over the railing onto the other side of the rock, then dove down into the bush. Rain pushed to his feet, dragging Eden with him as he leaned over the banister.

"Sly! For fuck's sake! I've had enough of this!"

Eden placed her hand on his back. "Oh, Rain. I'm so sorry." Her lips brushed his deltoid as he raked his fingers through his hair and glared into the dark bush after his stupid, stubborn, pain-in-the-ass brother.

Behind him, Kai and Nate released low, sad howls.

"*He's pissing me off, too,*" Kai said sadly, his jubilance gone.

"*Yeah,*" Nate agreed. "*What more can we do? We have a strong Alpha. Two Fated mates you've proven you can protect.*"

"*Yeah.*" Finn sat on his haunches and dropped his head. "*Even I thought that was a step in the right direction. But you're right.*" Finn glanced at Rain. "*Sly is stubborn.*"

"Tell me about it," Rain said, wrapping his arms around Eden's waist. "He helped me save my mate but still doesn't believe he's worthy of a second chance."

Eden sank into his hold and caressed his forearms. "That's so sad."

"It is."

But Nate was right. Their pack was stronger than ever and

the time to take on Tyrone drew near. And as a pained howl echoed from the bush below, Rain knew that Sly felt it too.

Rain turned to Finn. "Sly said he senses the rebels stirring over at Cape Pallarenda."

Finn's wolf's eyes flashed. *"They're stirring, all right. I spent yesterday cruising around Rowes Bay trying to get a read on them. Tyrone's ready for war, and I feel their strength growing. But now, I'm a bit worried about this new right-hand man of his."*

The scouts snarled while Rain tightened his arms around Eden. He might have been distracted by his hunt for the bats, but Finn—and Sly for that matter—hadn't neglected his responsibility of protecting their territory from potential threats.

"Even if he is as bad as Lucas implied, we'll devise a plan," Rain said, quite confident about that. "The bats were a challenge, but we've trained all our lives to take down the rebel wolves. Whatever they throw at us. We'll be ready."

Chapter 44

Eden longed to check on Ava and the koalas when they returned to the packhouse, but she couldn't refuse Rain's suggestion of a shower first. Blood smeared over her shoulder and chest, dirt and sweat caked her skin, and the soft powder of vampire dust clung to her hair.

Though she doubted half of the filth from her lust-filled body had washed away before Rain lifted her off her feet, pinned her to the shower wall, and slipped his proud cock inside her with surprisingly slow tenderness. Then he held her there, unmoving, as he reached for the body wash and loofah.

"Rain ..."

"I fucking hate that he did that to you," he growled, wiping the blood from her skin where Lucas's bite still throbbed. "Waiting in the shadows while he touched you, teased you ..." Rain's lips twisted as he dropped the loofah and cupped her breasts, almost squashing her with his heaving chest as he kissed her with animalistic ferocity. His tongue toyed with hers and thumbs flicked her nipples until she forgot whose oxygen she breathed. Rain slid out of her, then back in, releasing her mouth with a shared gasp. "It was the hardest thing I've ever fucking done, Eden."

"I could hardly bear it myself," she breathed, cupping his neck and twisting her fingers through his long, wet hair. "I hated telling him what he wanted to hear, and his bite fucking hurt."

Rain dropped his mouth to her shoulder and kissed the wound as though he were trying to heal her. "I'm sorry, baby. But it's over now. He's gone."

"Yes." She closed her eyes, enjoying the kisses he rained down her neck as his stubbly face sent shivers coursing through her. Though fuck, she wished he would just *move*. "It was all worth it. But I don't want anyone to bite me again but you."

His shoulders hardened as his wild blue eyes lifted back to hers. "Biting you was barbaric, Eden. It remains the worst thing I've ever done. I'll always hate that I had to do it. But after tonight ... I think it's a sin I can live with. And forgive myself for."

Eden's arms tightened around him, joy bursting from her chest as she smacked her lips to his. "I'm so glad to hear you say that, Rain. Though I thought you forgave yourself when you threw me out of your plane."

"I was pleased, yes, and I love your newfound bravery. Your fearlessness. Your need for adrenaline. But you are also powerful, Eden. The Goddess has blessed us and I fucking love that the vampires can't feed from you or compel you. They'll never be able to take you away from me."

Like they had Shelby, apparently, and though Eden's heart had broken for Sly at Lucas's confession, she was grateful for her vampire immunity, too.

"No one will ever take me away from you. Although I might leave if you don't quit talking and finish the job you fucking started and make me come."

She gripped his ass and pulled him close, trying to gain some friction herself. But she was pinned. Immobile.

"Yeah, that's killing me, too," he growled, capturing her mouth as he moved. Pleasure that Eden would never grow tired of shot through her body as he gathered speed, friction, and she lost her fucking mind.

Then again, sex with Rain always blew her mind whether he'd just saved her life, thrown her from a plane, or killed the monster who'd tried to destroy them.

She could hardly believe it had only been forty-eight hours since this had become her life. Yet she couldn't wait for every minute of her future with Rain as he palmed her breast and drove into her until she shattered. Every time, he managed to make her completely fall apart, and she him as his muscles strained, eyes softened, and he lost all sense of control. But while they might be able to break each other, no one could break them. She'd always known Rain was her soulmate. Ever since he'd brought her Pixie, he could do no wrong. He'd lied through his teeth, spun ridiculous tales, and built a mysterious aura around him that any woman would find dangerous. But she'd trusted him with every part of her being because she'd known they were destined for each other. He was her mate. Her lover. Her very best friend. Blessed, united, and fucking *strong*. He belonged to her. He owned her. And Eden wouldn't have it any other way as she came apart and clawed her nails down his chest in ecstasy.

If only she could help him bring his brother back, then her man would be complete. She'd known he missed Sly long before she'd known the truth about him. But after witnessing Sly's animalistic nature tonight, Eden wasn't sure how much man was left inside the wolf to bring back from the brink of his angry, lonely existence.

"How long do you think it'll take for Tyrone to retaliate?" she asked as they dried off and moved into Rain's bedroom.

Well, *their* bedroom, though she'd certainly need some

more clothes as she reached for a shirt that she'd worn and laundered three times this week.

"Not long," Rain said, pulling a black T-shirt over his head. "Finn and I will meet with the scouts in the morning, but I doubt he'll do anything until or after the full moon, so we have twelve days of grace."

"Well, I hope he doesn't interfere with the Full Moon Party! I can't miss Isla's concert."

Rain drew her into his arms. "You'll be at that party no matter what as it'll be the safest place for you. That's why I insisted you be at Jam's show."

"While you were fighting Blair?"

"Yep. Though I hope Tyrone doesn't interfere with the Full Moon Party either as I'd hate to tell the scouts they can't go to Isla's concert. Kai and Nate have a bit of a crush."

Eden laughed. "I think Kai has a crush on anything female."

"True. Though you and Ava have to stop encouraging him."

"Why? I like it when you get all growly."

"But I don't want to have to kill my scout."

"Oh, he's harmless. Though, I have to ask ... did you make him stop volunteering at the hospital all those years ago?"

Rain scoffed. "No. I just gave him a hell of a lot more work to do. He decided he didn't have the time all on his own."

Eden rolled her eyes. "I knew it."

Grinning, Rain pulled her close. "I couldn't risk him realizing you were my mate, baby. But he continued to do his bit, keeping an eye on the wild koalas while trekking and hiking around the island. He and Sly have helped me bring you many sick koalas."

"At least now I know how you find them in the most inaccessible places. And speaking of which, I need to go check on them. And the hospital," she said, her heart breaking. She hadn't had time to fully comprehend what the fire meant, but all her hard work, her research, her equipment was destroyed. Gone. It would take forever to rebuild and that's if her insurance would even cover it.

"Don't worry, baby." Rain ran his hand down her damp hair and pressed his lips to her forehead. "Let's check on the koalas, assess the damage, and we'll go from there."

NONE of the koalas had been seriously hurt, except for Scratches who'd suffered minor burns to his claws. Rain held the poor little guy on the table, wincing at his pained cries while Eden examined him. Ava had done her best to treat the burns with cold water, but his mate deemed the koala would still need veterinary treatment. So, she arranged for Dee to take Scratches and Archie to Townsville first thing in the morning while Rain handled the multiple missed calls from the authorities. Then, even though he tried to convince Eden to wait until tomorrow, he crumbled under the distress in her eyes and drove her across the island to assess the damage. They'd seen the hospital in flames and knew there wouldn't be much left, but it didn't lessen the ache in his heart or the pain that filled hers as they pulled up outside the police tape.

Rain rounded the Jeep, opened her door, and offered Eden his hand. She took it, trembling as she stared at her burned-out dreams. The blackened brick walls remained standing, but the roof had caved in and nothing but rubble remained of the place she'd dedicated her life to building.

Eden stepped out of the Jeep and burst into tears, her knees buckling as she pressed her hand over her mouth.

Rain crushed her to his chest. "Baby, I'm so sorry."

"It's gone!" she wailed, clutching at his shirt.

"I know it looks bad, but we'll replace everything. The

building. The equipment. No koalas were hurt, and we can rebuild. Don't panic."

"But what am I going to do until then? It'll take forever to rebuild. Marco and Xena need a few more days and—"

Heaving a deep breath, Rain drew away, clutched her shoulders, and leveled his gaze with hers. "Eden, baby. I will build you a new hospital."

She shook her head. "I can't let you—"

"Eden, I watched a vampire burn down your dreams, ran into a blazing inferno to rescue your koalas, then let that vampire bite you. Yes, I fucking killed him, but I need this." He wouldn't take no for an answer as he wiped the tears from her cheeks, though she'd stopped crying. "I've done my damnedest to keep you on this island and give you everything you need, and it wasn't enough. So, please. Let me build you the hospital of your dreams."

Rain's heart pounded as Eden blinked. Fuck, he really hoped she wouldn't fight him on this. Not now. She shouldn't be surprised by his declaration after learning the truth about the money he'd funneled her way. But as she surveyed the rubble behind him, hesitation still clouded her somber eyes.

"Rain, I ..."

He curled his fingers around her shoulders as he waited for her to continue. But she didn't. "You what, baby? Do you have any reason why I can't do this for you? Because if you do, I'll shoot it down."

"It's too much," she whispered.

"Too much to give you your heart's desire?" Rain shook his head and brushed his hands down her quivering arms. "Baby, let me do this. For you. For the koalas. I love the little guys, and no expense is too big or too small. You can have anything you want. Operating theaters, treatment rooms. X-rays. A research lab, tourist information, wild enclosures, and every drone on the planet. Name it, and it's yours. Because I love you."

He spoke every word with passion, desire and need burning inside him. He might be angry as fuck about Lucas destroying her hospital, but he couldn't deny it provided him the perfect opportunity to give Eden everything she'd ever wanted for her koalas. She fought a good fight, and he would always support her in that.

And it seemed she finally realized that, too, as her face softened and she whispered, "Okay."

Rain's eyebrows shot up. "Okay?"

She nodded, and he grinned, laughing as he lifted her off her feet and spun her around. "Yes! Oh, baby, you've made me so happy!"

He crushed his mouth to hers and Eden clutched him tight as she giggled, his glee radiating through the bond and into her. When she drew away, his heart swelled at the delight filling her sparkling eyes.

"If I don't agree, you'll do it anyway."

"Baby, you know me so well."

"I do," she breathed, as he lowered her back to her feet and caressed her cheek. "I never wanted you to have such power over me, Rain. But you do."

"You won't owe me anything, Eden."

"Nothing that I'm not already willing to give. And I'll give it all, Rain. Because we're Fated, and I love you. You can own my hospital like you own my heart."

He brushed his lips over hers. "*We* will own the hospital, Eden. What's mine is yours. Because I love you with everything that I am, and I'll build you the best damn koala hospital in the country."

"On one condition."

He quirked his eyebrows. "What's that?"

"That you build me a small vet clinic to go with it so I can stay here on the island with you."

He exhaled, relief softening his spine as he gathered her close and buried his face in her soft, mango scented hair. "Done, baby."

And as he kissed her by the ruins of her beloved hospital, Rain's wolf preened as he felt the last latch upon her heart unlock. She was his. Forever. His to spoil and cherish.

Because, finally, she would let him.

Epilogue

Tyrone paced the fort on Cape Pallarenda overlooking Magnetic Island while he and Kamar watched. Waited. But Tyrone knew the outcome of the battle the moment the lone bat arrived.

Eric, his most trusted spy, twisted out of the shadows with a sneer. "Blackwood had us fooled, boss. He didn't rebel after all."

Shock had Tyrone stumbling backwards as Kamar's low growl echoed through the fort. "What? How is that possible? Blackwood marked the bitch! Lucas saw it!"

"So did I! But I watched them tonight, boss. When my lord drank from her, it was like he drank a wolf's bite. Then Blackwood made the kill."

Tyrone kicked the historic ruin and screamed. "Fuck! It's basic lore! Mark your mate and fall out of favor with the Goddess. It's why we fucking do it! How did Blackwood find a loophole and stay in her fucking good graces?"

His plan had been solid. There was no way Blackwood was meant to come out of this on top. Tyrone had fucking *had him!*

"Wait." Kamar cleared his throat. "When did you say Blackwood marked her?"

"Sunday."

The malicious police detective snarled. "The night of the new moon."

"What of it?" Tyrone growled.

Kamar's eyes flashed. "You know as well as I do that the best time for the Fated to do dark deeds is beneath the new moon. The Goddess does not see, therefore, she cannot condemn."

Tyrone's blood ran cold. "So, you're saying ..."

"Blackwood remains Fated."

"Fuck!" Tyrone plowed his fist into the concrete wall. "So, I still have *two* Fated mates over there *and* I've lost my vampires?"

Eric had the decency to recoil, but Kamar, as twisted as he was, simply sneered. "I made the same mistake with my own mate. It took me years to figure out how she managed to escape me and take my daughter."

"But she left you with your son."

"It's the principle," Kamar spat, his eyes darkening. "I have no use for daughters, but she is *mine*. And a lot of fucking good my son did me. As you know, I couldn't turn the Fated pussy against the Goddess, so my deal still stands, Thorne. I'll fight with you. We'll take the island. And I'll kill your son if you kill mine."

Acknowledgments

This book was, without a doubt, the hardest one I've ever written. Without the support of my friends, readers, writing community, and my looming deadline, I doubt I'd have finished it anytime soon. *Island Wolf* was written with such joy, excitement, and it poured out of me with laughter and bright hope for the future. But *Island Bite* was created while my heart was breaking, my dreams were shattering, and my world was falling apart around me. I lost my muse and fell into depression due to circumstances created through no fault of my own. And I share this because I feel it's important for people to acknowledge the terrible trials they go through, that others go through, and that only by sticking together and supporting our friends can we find our way through the darkness to the light on the other side.

That is why I am incredibly grateful to everyone who supported me in 2024 and helped me keep myself together to bring *Island Bite* to life. Once again, it was my stepfather Ian and his passion for my wolf shifters that helped me piece together this story. Thank you for helping me plot scenes every day and encouraging me to get the words down, even if it was after wiping away my tears. The words might not have come so freely, but your belief in me was one of the only reasons this book ever got written.

But I'd never have had the strength to finish this book if it wasn't for my best friend Deeanna West. Thank you for providing me with a safe haven when I needed it most and for your support and encouragement. Because of your kindness, I found the strength to get back on track not only with *Island Bite* but to launch *Island Wolf* into the world. So thank you from the bottom of my heart. Thank you for being there to bounce ideas off and to ensure my paranormal lore makes sense. Thank you for loving books even more than I do. Thank you for helping me make decisions about covers and design and all those other things when I can't make a choice myself. Your support means everything to me and I hope we will be book crazy besties for a long time to come.

As always, I could never add the final sparkle to my books without my wonderful editor Nicola. Your suggestions about the relationship between my wolves and vampires in *Island Wolf's* edit helped me fix the problems I was having with *Island Bite*, allowing me to complete this manuscript and create a story that made sense. Then your suggestions with this book truly made it shine. I honestly love working with you, so thank you so much for your incredible insight and thoughts. And thank you Danielle, my wonderful cover designer, for another remarkable cover. Rain might have transformed from my original image of Aragorn to something more Henry Cavill, but that's fine! I love, love, love this cover!

Another shout out must go to the wonderful Peta from Arcane Books! Thank you for opening your store to the eager readers of Townsville and for helping me launch *Island Wolf* into the world. It means so much to authors to have a supportive local bookshop, so thank you for your encouragement, chats, and lighting the fire in me to finish the edits of *Island Bite*. We all need motivation and telling me 'no more concerts or holidays until it's finished' was just what I needed. I always leave your store inspired, and I hope Arcane Books continues to provide readers and authors wonderful opportunities to escape into fantasy realms in the future.

A quick thank you too to the super awesome tandem masters from Skydive Australia in Mission Beach! You didn't know I was lurking and taking everything in, but watching your operation helped bring the skydiving aspects of this book to life. Thank you to Jay, who *did* discover why I was watching so intently and who offered up some insight into skydiving. You have convinced me and I will take to the skies one day very soon. Also thank you to my client Scott for telling me his skydiving stories and encouraging me to give this insane thrill a go. I will do it! Because, as you say, it is *normal* to be scared.

As always, thank you to my wonderful writing community and my lovely tribe at Romance Writers of Australia for providing me a place where I can always turn to and feel safe. Thank you for helping shape me into the author I am today and for all the opportunities this organisation offers to romance writers to harness our craft. Thank you to Darksiders Down Under for bringing me over to the 'dark side' of paranormal romance. May we always be on this creative journey together.

But the biggest thank you always goes to YOU, my dear wonderful reader. Thank you for picking up this book and indulging in my paranormal twist on Townsville. Whether you've been on this journey with me for a while, whether I've brought you over from my world of contemporary romance into paranormal, or if you're a paranormal lover already, I am deeply grateful that you have picked up my story. And if you're a Townsville local, please don't be wary of the bats. You might give them all a sneaky side eye like I do now, but I promise, they're still flying foxes!

About the Author

Rachel Armstrong has always loved making up stories and is now living her dream of being an author. She writes romantic fiction about rural small towns, stirs up the suspense with terrifying villains, and places paranormal shifters in our every day world. Her novel, *The Man from Shadow Creek*, was awarded the 2024 Romantic Book of the Year Award by Romance Writers of Australia.

Rachel lives in Townsville, Queensland, with her border collie, Jacob, where she helps people live their best lives as an exercise physiologist. In her spare time, she is either reading on her treadmill or plotting out her next novel while grooving at Zumba. Rachel's a keen traveller and has enjoyed many holidays exploring historic London, flying through the Grand Canyon, and hiking volcanos in Bali.

Rachel loves to connect with readers and fellow writers through Facebook and Instagram.